Forsaken

Southern Watch, Book 7

Robert J. Crane

Forsaken
Southern Watch, Book 7
Robert J. Crane
Copyright © 2018 Ostiagard Press
All Rights Reserved.

1st Edition

This book is a work of fiction. Names, characters, places and incidents are products of the author's imagination or are used fictitiously. Any resemblance to actual events or locales or persons, living or dead, is entirely coincidental.

The scanning, uploading and distribution of this book via the internet or any other means without the permission of the publisher is illegal and punishable by law. Please purchase only authorized electronic editions, and do not participate in or encourage electronic piracy of copyrighted materials. Your support of the author's rights is appreciated.

No part of this publication may be reproduced in whole or in part without the written permission of the publisher. For information regarding permission, please email cyrusdavidon@gmail.com.

1.

"That son of a bitch." Zed Harris glared through the smoke wafting off the tip of his cigarette. If he could have circled the sight before him in gasoline and tossed the lit cig in, he would have done so.

But the fucking law would have had his ass for it. After all, burning down your neighbor's fence was still a crime, even in Midian, Tennessee, these days.

"Motherfucker." Zed stared at the high fence that stuck out like white wood fingers through the dark of falling night. "Motherfucking Barry Hostetler."

Barry Hostetler had been Zed's neighbor for thirty years. They'd always got on well enough—you didn't have to, this far out from town, with your nearest neighbor a hundred yards away instead of next door like in town—but it helped. This whole parcel had a history—Barry's dad had sold this section to Zed when he was setting out, and Zed had hauled a trailer out here. Dug a basement under it, channeling into the earth to open up more space. Painted the exterior up real nice, with whites and beiges, like cream before you poured it into coffee. Built a redwood deck that had a smell that still reached him over the smell of the cigarette burning in his hand, half-forgotten.

And then, after you do all that damned work prettying up your place, your neighbor of thirty years goes and slaps up that goddamned monstrosity of a fence along his edge of the property, making everything look like freshly spackled shit.

"Privacy fence," Zed snorted, lifting his beer and glaring at it. He could still see the top of Barry's old farmhouse—the one Barry had grown up in and inherited from his daddy, the rich son of a bitch—but everything else was eclipsed. Barry's wife, Arlene, had planted a garden just on their side of the property line. Daylilies. Morning glories. Real pretty shit, swayed in the breeze on the summer days, pleasant to look at when Zed got home from a long shift at the mill. He'd sit on the redwood deck and smoke a few, staring at the flowers. Maybe sometimes staring at Arlene; a lifelong bachelor like Zed didn't let a little thing like her being Barry's wife get in the way of a long look.

But he wasn't hurting nothing, dammit. And sometimes, after those long days, Barry'd come over and they'd have a couple beers and talk politics until the night was long in effect, black and heavy overhead, the porch light drawing in the mosquitos and flies until they buzzed thick around it in their swarms.

For Zed, that was about as social as his life got.

And now ... that goddamned fence.

Couldn't even see if Barry was out there anymore to shout, "Hey, Barry! You want to come over for a beer?" He glared at the fence like it had shot his dog and fucked his cat. He didn't have either, but ... he could imagine the ire he'd feel if either thing had happened, and it had to be close to what he felt toward that fucking fence.

"Goddamned thing," Zed muttered under his breath, taking a long drag of the cig, the tip flaring like a bright orange coal in the bottom of a grill. "Goddamned Barry Hostetler." Backstabbing son of a bitch. Good fences did not make good neighbors; they revealed rotten shitbirds for what they actually were—

A crackle in the dry brush caused Zed to sit up. There was a chill in the air, November giving a bite to it, icy teeth that sank in through Zed's sweatshirt. He stared out into the dark, beyond the reach of the little porch light. The sky hung black overhead; no stars, no moon, just an endless darkness.

"Barry, you son of a bitch, is that you?" Zed called, looking out over the edge of the deck. He'd built it himself, with a little help from Barry, so he hadn't worried about codes or deck rails. It was a one-foot step; anyone who fell off that was just a victim of natural selection, that was how Zed viewed it. "Creeping out in my kudzu, you sorry-ass motherfucker?"

There was no answer.

Zed frowned. Barry didn't come over uninvited, not even to borrow an egg or lawnmower or anything. Another sign he was a right prick of a neighbor. Zed took another drag off his cig, then sipped his Michelob Golden. "You better not be skulking out there."

Still no answer beyond another rustle in the old, fallen leaves that caused Zed to shiver as though a bitter wind had blown through. It was a pretty calm night, though, none of that.

Another crackle of leaves. "Barry, you fucking bastard." Zed put down his beer on the old, immense wooden industrial spool that he used as a table. His flimsy plastic chair strained under his hundred and fifty pounds of weight. Zed had never put on much poundage; smoking kept him thin, he told himself, arms narrow and wiry. He wore his navy work jumpsuit, smudged with grease from the machines down at the mill, which he had serviced for the last twenty-eight years. "If this is your idea of some kind of joke, you piece of shit ..."

Zed froze. He kept his head down most of the time, but ... hell, man, it was impossible to miss the shit going on in Midian these days. Talk of demons, of invasions, of ... he heard that shit at work, heard in the aisles at Rogerson's doing his grocery run ... you couldn't dodge out of it, even if you were an artful dodger of most conversations, the way Zed was.

He kept his eyes fixed on the darkness, peering out. He squinted; he couldn't see as well as he used to. Not badly enough that he needed glasses, but ... he damned sure couldn't see like in the olden days.

But ... something moved out there.

Something ... big.

It shifted some eight feet up, too low to be a branch of the pine out there, too high to be Barry ("that motherfucker!" Zed appended automatically at the thought of him).

Zed took a step back. The porch light was only a few steps behind him. The door only a step past that. He had a loaded Winchester .280 just behind the door, in case of varmints or other problems. Shotgun by the bed, twelve gauge. Good for bird hunting or home defense. He didn't tend to truck with pistols all that much, but there was an old snubbie .38 in the nightstand by the bed that his daddy had left him. He'd have picked the shotgun ten times out of ten, but it only held three shells cuz it was a bird gun, mostly.

"What the fuck are you?" Zed murmured at the moving shadow as he eased another step back toward the door. The darkness was near-complete save for his porch light. Beyond the outline of Barry's fence, he could see their porch light aglow.

It was the only other light visible from his front door.

The thing moved again, crackling leaves sounding again as it took a step forward. It made a noise like a low moan from the back of a throat. Something between a dog's growl and the gurgle of a badly clogged toilet, and Zed had a sudden hunch that toilet was going to overflow in a big way, bringing a tide of shit with it.

"Nice ... demon ..." Zed said lamely as he reached the door and felt the pressure of his hand upon the brass handle. He could feel the nicks in the surface from a lifetime of being clumsy with his keys. He'd meant to replace the damned thing at some point, but it still worked. Just fought him a little when he turned it, which he did now.

The guts of the lock slid some, making him turn it another forty-five degrees further than he'd had to when he'd first installed it. It was getting old. Zed sympathized. He was getting old, too.

The thing stepped closer to the light, and he got a look at the basic outline now.

Zed swallowed, hard. Just about took down his own tongue from the surprise.

It was ten feet tall, easy. Walking on two legs that grew black, shadowy spires out of their surface, pooling midnight running along the skin. Little spines ran like unshaven hairs an inch or two off the tawny surface of its calves, up to its massive thighs, the little spines growing in size the higher they went. Zed had a sudden image of a woman who'd not bothered to shave her legs for a week or two and almost choked on the absurd laughter that followed.

The thing widened at the waist, into a torso that looked like had been originally made for a man and then played with like clay by a kid until it was far wider and flatter than it should have been. Six arms sprouted off it, from the middle of the ribcage on up to the top of the shoulders. None of the arms was in the "right" place for a human, and none of them looked remotely human at the ends. The fingers ended in long claws.

Demons. For fucking real.

The face was maybe the worst, teeth in shadow, an angular head that looked like a dart and opened to a mouth with fangs the length of Zed's hand. He couldn't see eyes, no glare reflected in the porch light the way you might expect with a dog or a coyote, but ...

With teeth like that, Zed didn't imagine that bastard was vegan.

"Nice demon," Zed said, taking an errant step back and forgetting there was a step up into his living room. He stumbled, nearly fell, but caught himself on the frame and the door handle, cranking the lock even harder. He really would have to replace that thing soon. "Nice demon ..."

Halfway behind his door, Zed started reaching, moving slow. He found the barrel of the Winchester and pulled it up, out of sight of that ... thing ... up to his other hand. Planted his left on the frame and got his right up to the trigger, clicking the button safety and getting things ready to roll as he sighted in on that bastard thing's head.

"You ain't a nice demon at all, are you? Not with those ass-ripping teeth," Zed said, planting the iron sights right on that black horror's face. "Well, I don't need any ass ripped here, thank you very much. I can rip ass all on my own. Lemme show you—"

Zed lit off a round a little too aggressively, like he had buck fever. The Winchester roared, lit up the night. In the flash, Zed got a very clear picture of the shadowy damned thing.

And boy howdy … did he wish he hadn't.

"Fuuuuuuck," Zed murmured, trying not to hyperventilate as he brought the iron sights back down after a righteous kick. Firing offhand didn't allow for much in the way of bracing, but he was trying to use the door as a rest, which was a losing battle cuz it moved. Still, it nailed that fucking thing right in the head, and it roared under the thunder sound of the shot, the muzzle flash and its noise like a winter storm had moved in with lightning and all.

Zed fired again. And again. And again.

He ran through the rifle's magazine, six shots in quick succession.

Six hits. That thing was too big and too close to miss.

It just hung there, like it was suspended from the black sky just off the deck. Loomed in the darkness.

"Fuck," Zed breathed. He pulled the trigger again.

Click.

Empty.

Zed stared at the demon.

It moved that dart-like head around and he could swear, even without eyes, he could feel it staring at him in the darkness.

"Fuck!" Zed shouted. He slammed the door and dropped the rifle, springing away like the exit to his house was a mill machine about to throw a gear. He leapt over his couch, hurdling like he was thirty years younger and back on the track team. He felt something pull in his hip and gave zero fucks; adrenaline would keep him going now, but damn if he probably wouldn't feel that in the morning.

If he felt anything at all in the morning.

The demon tore through the door and the wall and everything in a four-foot radius on either side of the entry. Zed looked back, only for a second to see it happen, and then kept hauling ass around his BarcaLounger into the bedroom.

The shotgun … the shotgun … the shotgun …

He snatched up the old Stevens by his bed, didn't even bother to pump cuz there was no way he was going to waste time putting the round back in after jacking it out. He didn't have time; that thing was right after him and—

The demon burst through the door, dragging the BarcaLounger

with his leg like it was a fucking prize ribbon and nothing more. Plaster and wall exploded like it had been goddamned bombed, like he was living in some shithole in Afghanistan and the Air Force had decided he was a Taliban prick.

Zed unloaded on the demon—

—pumped—

—fired again—

—pumped again—

—fired his last shot—

HOLY SHIT THAT THING WAS STILL MOVING—

Zed tore open the nightstand and grabbed the .38 snubbie, hauling ass through his open closet. It led into the bathroom, and opened up into the back of the house, back into the kitchen and laundry room. There was a door there that faced into Barry Hostetler's fence ("Goddamn him!") and Zed was heading for it, on pure instinct, just getting the fuck out of there as fast as his skinny old legs would carry him.

Zed plunged through his dark closet, his shoulders brushing jumpsuits and flannel shirts and even a couple ratty old suits and dress shirts he kept for funerals and the like. The demon roared in the bedroom behind him, apparently over its dinner of buckshot, and he heard it start moving again, claws ripping up his floorboards like a dog from hell.

Shit, now he was glad his beagle had died six months ago of old age and he hadn't replaced it yet. Otherwise, he'd have been scrambling to save ol' Jimmy, too, and he was pretty sure, blind and lame as Jimmy had been at the end, he'd have ended up underfoot by now—

Zed burst out into the bathroom, rounded the tub at high speed. He didn't usually navigate his house at a flat sprint, but he'd lived here long enough that he could do it, especially with the blood pumping like it was now. He snapped up the .38 and fired a shot blind. The bathroom lit up like day for a flash and he was on, into the back of the laundry room as that thing came smashing through the tub and busted it into about a billion shards—

A couple of 'em caught Zed in the ass like shrapnel, and he gasped as they got him. Felt like a snake had jumped up and bit him in the right cheek. The sting was followed by the feeling of warm blood running down his backside and leg.

Zed didn't give a fuck. Zed had to get the rest of his ass out of here before he got bit a lot worse.

Throwing his gun hand over his shoulder, Zed fired again as he staggered a step. Blew out his fucking eardrum, as if the rifle shots and shotgun blasts and hammering of his fucking heart in his ears hadn't already.

There was an outside door in the laundry room, RIGHT THERE, and he fumbled for it with his left hand, fired again with his right. He was jerking the trigger pull on the .38, probably didn't have a hope in hell of actually hitting anything, but he didn't give a shit about that. He wasn't exactly running on all cylinders, but Zed had put together that that demon thing had eaten six .280 rounds and three doses of buckshot without doing much other than slowing down.

.38 rounds, even these +P's he had loaded … that thing'd smile its way through them.

Ripping the door open, Zed scrambled with the screen beyond, head over his shoulder looking for *it*. He could hear it moving, pieces of the bathtub still in its way, a low gurgling noise coming from less than ten feet behind him.

Zed reached for the screen door, muscle memory leading his hand right to it through long practice. Just rush through and—

He spun around. The outside screen door was already open, and there, with his face shining in that porch light—

Was Barry Hostetler, an AR-15 clutched in hand.

"You motherfucker!" Zed shouted, but there was a delirious tinge of joy in it.

Barry said something, but hell if Zed could have heard it. There was a ringing in his ears, and he jerked his head toward the bathroom. Barry took a step back and Zed burst out into the chill night air.

The demon followed, ripping through the exterior bathroom wall a second later.

Barry was swearing and Barry was firing, and Zed couldn't really tell which was which cuz he was aiming over the sights of his .38 at the same time Barry was completely unloading with the AR. It was a thunderstorm of bullets, and in the flashes, Zed could see the flying brass discharging out of Barry's rifle, all over the redwood deck.

Any other time, he might have been pissed as hell about it.

But now …

"Goddamn, it's good to see your motherfucking ass on this side of the fence, Barry!" Zed said as his .38 ran dry. He clicked the trigger three more times, the cylinder turning but no flash nor bang nor jump of the barrel in evidence. He didn't even notice until the fourth time it happened.

"I heard you shooting at something!" Barry shouted over the roar of the AR and the ringing in Zed's ears. "Wasn't going to let you eat shit if I could help!"

The damned demon was out now, roaring and ripping and tearing up his trailer house. Zed was falling back, Barry just letting loose at it, calmer than he had any right to be given what was coming at them.

Then Barry tripped on the edge of the deck and tumbled, AR slipping out of his hand.

"Barry!" Zed shouted and halted his retreat. He paused, broke forward and headed for his downed neighbor as the damned demon came slithering (!) across the deck toward them, now on all fours like a panther or cheetah or—

Some rough beast, straight outta hell.

Zed got down next to Barry just as the thing came at them, and Zed managed to get a hand on the pistol grip of the AR, slinging it up and letting 'er rip in the face of that thing. It took a few shots right to that dart-like head and hissed, drawing away for a second.

But only a second. And not very far; a foot or two at most.

"We shoulda put a rail on the deck, Zed," Barry grunted.

"You'da just stumbled ass-backwards over it," Zed said, firing off the last few rounds and hearing the dry clicks as the thunder of the gunfire faded. He was surprised he could hear anything after having enough rounds fired off all about him to have constituted a minor war. There was damned sure a thunderous roar in his left ear. "Can you get up?"

Barry was ghostly pale. He shook his head slowly. "Nope. Broke something. Something important. Back maybe."

"Shit." Zed cast the rifle aside. It wasn't any good without bullets, after all. Didn't seem to be of much use with them, if he was being honest, but it had kept the damned thing off them for a short bit, hadn't it?

"You should go," Barry said, pale face all grimaced. "Get outta here."

"Ain't leaving you," Zed said. The thing was moving around, coming about, swinging its head toward 'em. "Couldn't make it over that goddamned fence in time, anyway."

Barry let out a grunted laugh that turned into a whimper of pain. "Figures."

"What's that?"

Barry looked right at him and smiled through the pain. "We're about to get *et* by some demon thing ... and you've still got a cork up your ass about that fence."

The demon came around, teeth bared in the dark, catching the porch light, which hung loose from the wrecked wall, still shining its light. Zed stared at death, saw it coming.

"We were neighbors, Barry," Zed said, quiet, surprisingly earnest. The ringing in his ears was picking up now, like a steady thrum, as though someone were turning up the volume on it gradually.

"Still are," Barry said, smiling weakly. Damn, he looked washed out in this light. Was it the thing coming after them doing it to him, or just the pain from whatever he'd broken? Zed didn't reckon he'd ever find out. "I'm about to die for your dumb, grudge-carrying ass, after all."

Zed actually smiled. "Yeah. I reckon there's tha—"

The demon came at them before he had a chance to finish.

*

Morning light shone in through the sheriff's office window, but Erin Harris could feel the chill permeating through. The heater in the sheriff's station didn't quite keep up with the cold outside; the temp had dropped precipitously after midnight and was now lingering just above freezing, as evidenced by the hints of misted frost on the edges of the window.

That was damned sure not the only thing chilling Erin, though. Hell, the weather probably wasn't even in the top five, if she was being real honest.

"... so we found what was left of Barry and Zed after ... whatever got 'em had its fill," Casey Meacham's high voice droned on. "You can probably imagine that Arlene is just about inconsolable—"

"I bet you tried to console her, though, didn't you?" Amanda Guthrie's voice cut through the pinkish light that was Erin's whole world, her eyes closed as though she could make all her problems—including this conversation—just disappear if she didn't open them. "With your dick."

"I think the dick thing was implied just by you asking Casey if he tried to console her," Duncan said, in his composed way. She could imagine him as he'd looked before she'd closed her eyes, leaning against the wall next to Guthrie, arms folded in front of him, not showing any of the amusement that Guthrie wore like a second skin. Third skin, maybe? Demons didn't have actual skin, though, did they? Second shell, she supposed, momentarily distracted by that pedantic bit of wondering. "It's not like he would console her with empathy or a friendly hug."

"I don't know what lies y'all have heard about me," Casey said, sounding just a little charged up by that accusation, "but I'm not so crass and tasteless I'm gonna get up on a mourning widow—not even a real silver fox, which I am not saying Arlene Hostetler is—without giving her some mourning time. I mean there's low and then there's snake belly low, and then there's that shit right there. Besides," he sniffed, "in my experience, if a woman's looking for a quick roll after a deep mourning time like that, she don't take much prodding." A pause. "Well, I mean, she takes a good prodding with the—"

"Jesus, Casey." Erin opened her eyes to find the taxidermist leering at the OOCs from across the sheriff's office, which ... was now her office, at least temporarily. "You couldn't just let it pass, could you?"

"Of course he couldn't," Dr. Lauren Darlington said from her seat across the desk from Erin. "Letting an opportunity for a lewd comment go by without swinging at it until it's dead in the dirt—well, that's just not Casey."

"I've dealt with a few real pigs in my time," Addison Rutherford Longholt said, her silver mane of hair ragged around her shoulders. Wife to Bill, mother to Alison and to Brian—only one of the three still alive at this point—she seemed to be holding up surprisingly well, though her hair didn't show it, "but you, Casey ... you do indeed take the pig cake. A real mudder of a cake, too."

"He's very charming once you get to know him," Ms. Cherry said from her place leaned against the wall next to Casey. "All this sex talk—it's bravado."

"I ... don't really care," Erin said, her mind already charging in other directions. "I've got way more things to deal with than trying to get Casey to not act like a total dickweed." She shifted her gaze to him. "But Casey, seriously ... knock it the fuck off. We got a lot of people coming through here now, trying to save this town. The last thing we need is you driving someone decent away by being a disgusting prick."

Casey drew up like he'd had his foot stepped on. "Now, come on, Erin. You can't possibly think that someone living under threat of death is going to seriously give a fuck about me being me? Right now? I mean, there's Maslow's hierarchy of needs, and I'm pretty sure that getting offended by me being a randy sex machine is somewhere above survival, y'know?"

"That's an interesting perspective," Dr. Darlington said. "People are already traumatized by having to fight a war against demons, so what's a little sexual harassment compared to all that, huh?"

"That is *not* sexual harassment," Casey said, voice rising. "I have zero power over any of them people." His voice lowered, becoming a little too casual. "I think the demons kinda do a better job of creating a hostile environment around here than me."

"Why does it not surprise me that you'd be very clear on that distinction?" Addie asked, rhetorically, of the ceiling.

"I am what I am," Casey said, very zen about it. "No point in denying the urges that I have bound into my very self. I embrace—"

"I don't fucking care," Erin said, losing the last thread of give-a-damn she had for this conversation. "Keep from tripping over your dick while you're on duty with the watch, or I'm going to send your sorry ass packing. Or, worse, lock you up in the jail, horndog. I don't care what you do or say in the privacy of—well, in privacy, off-duty—but so help me God, Casey," and here she sat forward, feeling a fire behind her eyes, "if I find out you're preying on some pretty teenage thing that's just lost her parents or some such sexual predator shit—you're going to learn what southern justice is, because you will be hung—and I don't mean it the way you are probably thinking, guttermouth. Stay off the girls of this town. They're going through enough right now without you taking advantage of their sorrow to slip your tip in."

Casey flushed red. "I don't know what you've heard, but Ms. Cherry is taking plenty good care of me."

"Fine, whatever," Erin said, all the fight gone out of her. It had been so easy to get riled enough to take it to Casey over—hell, him being a jackass over the years.

Once it was said, though, it was like poison leaving her soul. A little residue lingered, making her wonder if she'd gone a little too gung-ho at him. She wasn't exactly sick over it, though. More like ready to move on.

"Human on human action is fun to watch," Amanda Guthrie announced, and the unmistakable pleasure in her voice made Erin feel sick again. "However it happens."

"I took you for more of the disillusioned Hamlet type," Addie Longholt said. "'No man does not interest me—'"

"'—Nor woman either, though by your smiling you seem to say so,'" Duncan said.

Addie smiled at him. "Wouldn't have figured demons for fans of the Bard."

The corners of Duncan's mouth moved ever so slightly upward. "I read his works when I first got here. They've stuck with me ever since."

"Yeah," Guthrie said with dry annoyance, "like a plague upon you, the dust of humanity. Also—*Hamlet*? What a shitshow. Accurately captures humanity, though, I suppose, in its key elements. Glorious, foolhardy, stupid revenge—"

"We've gone from discussing Casey's sex perversions to Shakespeare in one conversational turn," Erin said to Dr. Darlington, as though they were alone in the room. "How does that happen?"

"The Bard made a lot of sex jokes," Guthrie said. "Most people don't know that nowadays. Kinda sad how stupid you meatbags are about your own literary history. Bawdy humor is now your most celebrated literary classics. I mean, have you even read *The Canterbury Tales*? There's one in there that literally involves farting in someone else's face. Your most celebrated literature is that of the lowest common denominator. I mean, why we let you bottom-dwelling freaks have this rock of a world—and how you invented cell phones and microwaves—well, it's all a giant fucking mystery to me."

"Speaking of giant fucking mysteries," Erin said, opening her eyes again. When had she even closed them? God, that was becoming a defense mechanism if ever she'd had one. "Can someone finish the morning report? Pretty please? With a donut on top?" She looked at Casey.

The heat in Casey's cheeks was fading, turning from cherry red down to a mere light crimson. "That thing out at Zed Harris's—" He looked up at her. "Any relation?"

Erin shrugged. "If so, it's way back. My parents never said anything about us being kin." She thought about it for a second. "Course, Zed's such an ornery bastard, I doubt we'd have claimed him even if he was a cousin or something."

"That's a good point," Casey said, and he lifted his little clipboard. "Arlene is taking shelter with Father Nguyen for now. I had Ms. Cherry take her over there," he nodded at the olive-skinned woman to his left. "You get her settled?"

"As best I could for the poor dear," Ms. Cherry said with a shrug. "It took some talking. She knew she couldn't stay at home after what happened to Barry and Zed, but ... to leave after such a traumatic event ..." She shook her head. "She's with the Father now. Hopefully, he'll work through it with her."

"Shame we don't have any counselors around to help," Erin said, just expressing the thought that came immediately to mind. "I mean—you know. After disasters, they usually send people in to do that with FEMA, don't they?"

"If anything qualifies as a FEMA disaster area, I'd think Midian would," Casey said. "The trailers would be a step down from anything we got around here—even Zed's," he chortled under his breath, "but ... we sure could use some aid." He looked at Erin somewhat earnestly, then away, quickly, like he didn't want to be caught doing something as foolish as hoping. "You, uh ... ain't heard from anyone in Nashville or DC about ... all this, have you?"

"Like Reeve before me, the FBI and TBI and anyone else I could call at the state or federal level all seem to be real adept at ignoring me," Erin said with a shrug of her own.

"Welcome to the bureaucracy, sweetcheeks," Guthrie said with a healthy leavening of scorn, prompting Erin to roll her eyes.

"Bureaucracy, bullshit," Ms. Cherry said. "This has to be intentional, ignoring of us in our hour of need."

Guthrie chuckled. "What's that old quote—'Never ascribe to malice that which can be adequately explained by stupidity.'" She snorted. "Hanlon's Razor."

"That's not bad," Dr. Darlington said with her characteristic dryness. "But I'm with Ms. Cherry. This shit here is way too much for Nashville or DC to ignore just out of simple bureaucratic laziness. Someone's actively put us on the ignore list, like an ex whose calls you don't want to take."

"Who do you imagine is conspiring against you?" Guthrie asked, not bothering to hide her amusement. "Some corps of demons deep within the government, whose mission is to stop news of evil rising from leaking out?" She shook her head slowly. "It's not malice driving this lack of response—mostly. It's indifference. I mean ... have you seen the stats on opioid deaths in some of your rural hamlets in this state? If they can ignore that, a few unexplained demon deaths are easy peasy."

"But ... even the press ain't paying an ounce of attention," Casey said. "Come on. 'If it bleeds it, leads,' and we're bleeding gallons out here. Where's the cameras?"

"Wrong place, kiddo," Guthrie said. "Seriously. You think the people behind the cameras give a shit about some nowhere village in the middle of Tennessee? I mean, if the president nuked you—yeah, they'd be here with full cameras. Someone shot up your school with an AR? Pffft, they'd camp twenty-four seven on all your lawns, looking for a comment from some bastard with two teeth. AMTRAK derails around here? Every motel room in town is going to be occupied.

"Demons invade from below and kill all your asses?" Guthrie faked a yawn. "That ain't gonna trip a single trigger in New York or DC or LA. They don't give a fuck about you under normal circumstances, and if a few thousand small-town hicks are killed by demons without a single news camera to watch ... did they really die? Cuz you might as well have not existed in their universe to begin with, for all they care."

"That's eloquent," Erin said, stirring. "And horrifyingly indifferent. But ..." She shrugged, feeling a little indifference of her own. "It sounds about right. Anything else from last night?"

"The usual calls," Casey said. "No other bodies that we found. Though ... I mean, we still have a couple groups out on calls."

Erin blinked. "Well, all right, then." She looked up and frowned. "Is that ..." She hadn't even realized someone was missing until Casey mentioned the bit about others still being out on calls. "Where's Arch?"

That provoked a quick shuffle of looks around the room. Dr. Darlington stared at her feet, clearly trying not to say anything. Addie Longholt got strangely—or maybe not so strangely, given Arch was her son-in-law until just a few weeks ago—pale.

Duncan was the one that finally answered. "Where do you think?" he asked, his voice as level as ever.

Erin just rolled her eyes. "In the thick of it, surely." Because that's where he always was.

*

"I'm gonna need y'all ... to clear on out of here," Archibald "Arch" Stan announced through the megaphone, voice crackling through the static the device made. He was feeling a little tentative about it, no lie, but he did his job and said what needed to be said, staring over the curve of the megaphone, which was blocking only a small part of his view of what were perhaps the largest ... things ... he'd ever seen.

Giants.

Demon giants.

Arch's feet were firmly planted on browned grass, a patch that looked out over a hollow that spread like a small valley before him. It wasn't particularly wide, more like a runnel between two hills, sandwiched between copses of trees. Locals called it "Hanley's Fold," and it was a nice little place for picnics, public land maintained by the parks department.

Well, up until now, anyway, when it had become a squatting ground for ...

Demon giants.

Arch had the megaphone in one hand and his sword in the other, looking over the mess of litter, cow bones, uprooted trees and all manner of other mess that giants had apparently made.

"I don't think they're paying you much heed, Arch," Chauncey

Watson said, peering over thick-rimmed glasses at the dozen or so giants spread out over Hanley's Fold. Some were scratching themselves, some were sleeping. A few were eating. A couple were engaged in some sort of slapping contest that produced noises so loud that Arch cringed with every hit, even though they were a good hundred yards away.

"I might be fine with that trend continuing," Barney Jones said. The old pastor looked like he was about as daunted as he'd ever been, his eyebrows drawn together in anxiety over the nest of hornets Arch was presently poking.

"Y'all get on back over there," Arch nodded behind him. The sun hadn't made its way over the hills in Hanley's Fold, so the air had a little more bite here than it probably did at the station. His coat was zipped up against the chill of the early morning, and frost glistened on the grass, even without the benefit of direct sunlight to really make it sparkle. "I'm going to wrap this up and warn 'em to move on one last time before we start up with them."

"Feels like it would have been smarter to just ambush 'em," Keith Drumlin said, frowning, his thin face dogged by bags under the eyes. He looked haggard to Arch's eyes, but then, the man had lost every family member he had about a month or so ago, a feeling Arch could well identify with. Arch supposed he didn't spare much thought for his looks at this point, so it probably made sense Keith wasn't worrying about it, either. "You sure you're not too busy thinking like a sheriff's deputy to act like a demon hunter, Arch?"

"Just get on back to the truck, will you?" Arch asked, shaking his head and gripping up that megaphone one more time. He'd had a little talk with Duncan over the phone just a short while ago after he'd figured out what he was dealing with. The OOC had been pretty clear about the path he should take with these particular demons—once he'd more or less narrowed down what they were. "And get ready."

A little murmur or two of dissent emerged from the few of them that had bothered to leave their vehicles and stand with him here at the top of the rise while he tried to address the giants. Much as he might have preferred to just stab these danged demons every chance he got, Arch wasn't so blinkered he didn't realize that some of them might prefer not to get down and dirty with demon hunters with holy blades.

Apparently these giants, though, in spite of what Duncan had said … might just need a good stabbing to get them to move along.

Their faces were like compact boulders of darkness, some cross between stone and insect carapace, with a greenish-brown tinge. If they'd been a few feet high, they might have almost been cute. With heads that stuck up to near twenty feet in height, though ...

Well, cute was not a descriptor available. Not at that size.

"All right, y'all," Arch said, lifting the megaphone up and turning the volume switch even louder. "Listen up, if you don't want to end up a cloud of brimstone and particulate matter, demons—"

That got one of them to stick its head up. It stared at him with beady black eyes from beneath that rounded head that lacked any sort of neck. It spoke in clear, slightly accented English of the sort that Arch might have expected from the Queen of England. "I say, my good man," the giant chittered, "why would you go and assume that any of us are—what was it again? Demons?" It made a clicking noise. "Terribly insulting."

"Yes, I'm terribly insulted," said a giant at the first one's shoulder. It bore a long scrape across its massive chest, which was shaped almost like three mammoth orbs stacked into an upside-down triangle. They came to a triangular waist and then thickset legs, trunk-like, with only a small joint discernible as a knee. "I feel as though I should consult with my lawyer. This reeks of defamation."

"We've been impugned by the local law enforcement," another of the giants said in yet another proper British accent, sticking his head up from the slapping contest. "This is actionable for certain." It fixed its eyes on Arch, and dark lids blinked over eyes the size of basketballs. "You'll be hearing from my attorney immediately about this."

"Uh huh," Arch said, doing his best not to roll his eyes. "What's that you're going to sue me for, exactly? And how are you going to fit into the courthouse?"

A ripple of excitement ran through the giants, making Arch cringe from the noise. Big creatures, big sound, he figured. "How dare you!" the first one said. "Are you trying to fat shame me? Because my size is entirely related to medical concerns, and for you to single me out for it ..." Its eyes glistened black as it stared down at him. "Well, I just—I never!"

"I'm sure your excess height's just a pituitary issue, too," Arch said dryly. Did these things really think their baloney was going to work on him? He thought about it for a second; if they were human shaped rather than absurdly giant ... it just might, for other cops. Threats of lawsuits did tend to make almost anybody, especially a police officer, think at least once more before stepping into that particular bear trap foot-first.

"So brazen," one of them said, affecting a slightly more Cockney accent than the others. "He's insultin' us through and through!"

"No respect or empathy for our conditions," another said, voice straining almost piteously.

"Assuming we're some sort of scum because of our medical issues," still another said. "I see how it is in this town. Bigots all the way through."

A horn sounded behind Arch, and he waved them off. He wasn't quite done with trying to negotiate—yet. It was definitely drawing to a close, though. "I'm going to give you thirty seconds to gather your things and start filing out of town—"

"You hear that?" the frontmost giant asked. "Things haven't changed down here at all. He's a modern-day Bull Connor, hating on us because we're black."

Arch stared in dull disbelief at the black-carapaced creature. "You … must be joking." He didn't trigger the megaphone, but he said it loudly enough that the demons heard.

The front giant tipped its head sideways, a very peculiar gesture from a creature like this, almost human looking. "Why would I be joking? Are you impugning me further?"

"Because I'm black … and you just called me Bull Connor," Arch said, staring at it.

The beady eyes blinked. "You … are black?" Its head turned, peering down at him. It looked to its fellows. "Does he look—I didn't even realize—" It turned back to him, and let out a sigh. "All right, well—sorry about that. I can't really see your kind all that well, if I'm being honest and—since I'm being honest—I don't really care what shade you are." The giant's shoulders rose up above its dome-like head, like it was becoming slightly more hulking. "You all taste the same to me anyway."

It swept at him.

Arch led with the sword point, swinging it up in time to catch the palm of the creature as it came at him. It drove its palm into the tip of the blade and he felt the shudder of impact even as the giant dissolved into a smoking, stinking cloud of brimstone.

Coughing, Arch tried to hold his breath against the reek of the creature as it puffed. His own blood pressure spiked as the sulfur stung his eyes. He'd smoked a few demons in his time, and they all lit off in a stink like this. But none had been quite this big, even that giant fire sloth he'd wiped out last week.

Arch stumbled out the other side of the demon's cloud as it dissipated, megaphone still in one hand, sword in the other. He shook off the smell and looked over the giants beyond, still spread over

Hanley's Fold, watching him with shocked, black beady eyes.

"You went and killed him," the next nearest giant said. "That's a wrongful death suit for sure."

"Habeas corpus," Arch said between watery coughs, keeping a wary eye on the things in case another broke toward him.

"Actually," that same giant said, tone changing to something approximating a lecture, "the standard of proof in a wrongful death suit is considerably lower than a criminal case, and producing a body is not necessarily required, because the burden of evidence is set to 'A Preponderance of Evidence' rather than the more rigorous, 'Beyond a reasonable doubt'—"

"I've had about enough of the litigious giants," Arch said into the megaphone, calling over his shoulder to his waiting crew. "Let's get this show rolling." The roar of engines behind him filled the air.

"I think he means to murder us!" one of the giants squealed down in the fold. "Police brutality! Police brutality!"

The cry was taken up by others, and once again, Arch found himself rolling his eyes and sighing. "I gave you a chance to clear off," he said into the megaphone, announcing it down into the quaking, shaking giants that were pulsating with paroxysms of anguish. "But no, you wanted to play lawyer—"

They all stopped, and their heads swiveled at him as one. He guessed about ten pairs of black eyes were on him, every giant utterly still. They didn't stay that way for long, though; not a word was exchanged, but they all burst into motion at the same time, charging up the hill—right at him.

*

Gary Wrightson had had about enough of this shit.

He wheeled his wheelchair through the hallway of his office, having completed his morning bowel movement with some element of success. He couldn't feel anything below the waist, so merely managing to complete something as basic as this? Well, it was the mark of a good day if your standard was, say, not getting shit in your undies.

Gary Wrightson had never been satisfied with the goddamned minimums, though. That was Commie loser bullshit, as far as he was concerned. Pussies worried about achieving the least possible. Gary wasn't a pussy. He could have afforded an electric wheelchair, by God. But he stuck with the old-fashioned one and wheeled his own ass everywhere, dismounting and crawling if necessary, because he had the upper body strength of a damned Olympian. It came in handy, too, when he needed to kick ass.

And he felt that need coming on.

"I have had about e-goddamned-nough of this shit," he said, bursting out into the garage area of his plumbing company's warehouse headquarters. Two company vans waited before him, his kingdom's own chariots. "And I've serviced toilets for the last fifteen years, so me saying enough of *this* shit—that oughta to *by God* tell you something about the level of shit I have reached my limit with!"

His two employees staring back at him blankly. Ulysses Borden was an old, decrepit, and nearly useless bastard, but he got places on time and worked at about 20% of what Gary considered to be efficient—high marks, sadly, in this day and age.

Then there was Marina Garetsky, who had come from Eastern Europe somewhere and taken to the plumbing trade like a teenage boy to fucking. Enthusiastic to the point of carelessness sometimes, but she probably worked at 40% efficiency, which was godlike compared to most of the people Gary had hired.

And in fairness ... Gary only gave himself a 60% efficiency assessment. Goddamned wheelchair slowed him down, but hell if he'd let it stop up his efforts. Hell no. He'd plunge his way through. Pipe snake it if necessary.

Gary Wrightson, by God, got the job done. It said so on the side of his company vans.

"Vhich shit are ve talking about, boss?" Marina asked in that thick accent of hers. She wore her jumpsuit in perfect regulation, always clean. 50% marks just for the area of uniform cleanliness. Ulysses just stared at him. Fucking useless.

"This demon shit!" Gary slammed the local fishwrapper, the Midian *Times-Gazette*, down on the table where they had their planning meetings. "Do you know how many calls we've gotten this week?" He held up a single hand. "Five. Five calls. You know how many calls we get in a normal week?"

Ulysses just stared blankly. Goddamned fucking useless.

"By this time in the veek ... twenty-five," Marina said.

Gary let his eyebrows rise a millimeter or two. She was probably close, but it wouldn't do to admit it flat out. Marina's efficiency rating was rising by the moment, goddammit. She was becoming more useful all the time. "You're wrong, but in the right direction," Gary said, not really caring if he was clear. Better if he wasn't. Wouldn't want her thinking he was complimenting her. She might get complacent, and laziness could seep in. The proper ingredients to continued upward achievement were a harsh diet of criticism, fed like broken glass through bleeding lips until you were motivated to smash the face of the person feeding it to you into pieces. "The point is—by God, business is turning to shit. And not in the good way, where we fix toilets and sink emergencies and all else, guaranteeing enough revenue to make payroll. This has been the other kind of week, the kind of week that taps into my savings, eating up my very important fund for my next 'fuck hookers in Reno' trip." Sure, Gary couldn't feel his dick or get hard on his own, really, but he could still feel the goddamned strange, vestigial urge to scratch that itch every now and again, so he by God scratched it, however he had to.

"Why don't you just go to Ms. Cherry's?" Ulysses asked, staring at him with those vacant, empty eyes. Ulysses was probably a couple years from full social security, and Gary could smell the weakness and complacency that this had produced in the old bastard. He moved like he had lead in his hands and complained of arthritic knuckles. "Well, by God, get out of the plumbing business if you've lost your fire!" was Gary's common response. Because he had no time for that kind of negative, lazy thinking. That kind of thinking would lead you right to second place in the ultra-competitive Midian plumbing game. And like Vince Lombardi, there was no place in Gary's game for second.

"Because I follow the appropriate laws of my home state, by God, Ulysses!" Gary roared at him. "Which is why I refuse to partake in any illicit substances save for alcohol here in the great state of Tennessee, but I will get high as fuck next time I'm in Reno." That was true. Gary had a lot of respect for the law. Well, most of the time. He had some issues with some of the Commie bullshit that had seeped into labor laws, but he still followed them. Mostly to keep from getting his ass sued off and having his 'hookers in Reno' fund absorbed by some goddamned hack lawyer prick.

Marina just stared at him and eventually shrugged. "My brother is prostitute. Thinks he got better deal between us. Hah!" Marina slapped the table in jubilation. "His attitude change first time he have to deal with client with scat fetish. Then, his high horse suddenly not so high." There was a sparkle in the woman's eye at that. "Like quarter horse. Or baby pony."

"Hah!" Gary slapped the table as well. There were few things he enjoyed, as a plumber and working man, more than hearing tell of someone on a high horse getting brought low. He was fully aware of the sneering disdain and borderline disgust most people treated those in his trade with—all the way up until they needed their toilet unclogged. Something about their indoor plumbing going right to hell awakened the egalitarian in every sneering elitist. They still weren't willing to plunge shit with him, though.

Gary recomposed himself and cleared his throat. "Anyway, like I was saying before we were distracted with Marina's excellent story of her brother's sneering whoring face getting brought low into shame, where it properly belongs, and Ulysses's dumbass comment that bordered on racketeering in trying to convince me to partake in wanton criminality—I was making a point about how shitty things are around here, again, not in the good, revenue-producing way." He slammed his fist into the table again, and by God, his upper body strength made the whole thing shake. "This town is going right down the tubes. Well, I tell you what—I won't stand for it. I mean to drag this place back out using the plumbing snake of my own strength and virtue to pull it along."

"That's awfully dramatic, Gary," Ulysses said, looking at him through tired, jaded eyes. That old sonofabitch—just an old dog that was better off on the damned porch with the puppies. Couldn't run with the big men, the ones of vision, and ambition.

"You know what else is dramatic?" Gary stared him down. It wasn't the first time Gary Wrightson had, by God, taken a stand for something important. "Watching your revenues take a shit when you should be taking the shit and ..." Gary paused. It had felt like there was a plumbing metaphor there, but ... by God, he'd reached the end of the words he had and no rhetorically powerful analogy had presented itself. "It doesn't matter! The money matters. People dying—that matters. These people are potential customers, and if you want to keep collecting a paycheck, you time-marking, parasitic son-of-a-bitch, we will solve this problem now, or else I'm laying your ass off!"

Ulysses didn't even raise an eyebrow. "Go ahead. I could use time on unemployment. Catch up on a few things around the house, I reckon."

Gary felt a twitch in his eye. He paid that unemployment insurance out of his own pocket, goddammit.

"Boss, your blood pressure," Marina said. She must have seen his face go red.

"You're right," Gary said, taking a deep breath, getting a handle on himself before he lost it. He had a whole rant lined up on the labor movement and its excesses, which were currently bleeding him dry. "Thank you, Marina." His face was probably as red as a cherry tomato. Ulysses seemed unfazed—of course—useless old horse needed to be put out to pasture, preferably with a shotgun, and then sent straight to the glue factory. What was the human equivalent of that? Florida, Gary decided. "I hope you get gang-raped by a bunch of pissed-off, hopped-up Cubans, you goddamned lazy-ass Commie," he said to Ulysses, who took it with a shrug. Probably hoping to get laid off.

They sat in silence around the table for a few minutes as Gary tried to get his breathing under control. He had practiced a meditation from an app on his smartphone just for this. Once he had his breathing down, he looked up. "All right, so here's what we're going to do—"

"Go home for the day?" Ulysses asked. Lazyass.

"You can go home for the rest of your goddamned short-ass life, Ulysses, if you want," Gary said. "You know how men of your age die within two years of retirement? It's because removed from the arena of contributing to society in a useful way, you realize what a worthless turd you are. So go die of painful realization, if you want. I give no damn whether you do or not, I just wish the government would send me a refund for all the money I paid into your unemployment and social security if you check out early, because it seems mighty damned unfair that I foot the bill for all that when you're probably gonna drop the first time you try and do something around your house and realize, 'Holy shit, I'm a giant fucking lazy ass who's been a drain on Gary all these years.'"

"Boss," Marina said, looking at him with those goddamned canny eyes of hers. She was slick, like a Russian spy. Sure, not a classical beauty, but her efficiency and cleverness gave her an aura of danger. Gary shifted in his wheelchair, feeling the sawed-off shotgun, like a metal lump, poking him in the back. Damned thing always poked him in the back, and after a long day, it fucking hurt. The price one paid for security. "How much of this new … anti-demon fervor is driven by your mother camping in your guest room?"

Canny goddamned Eastern Europeans. They'd thrown off the shackles of the fucking Commies and developed a lean, hungry desire to kick ass and take names. Gary could respect that. "If I had to assign it a number," he said, hedging just a little bit, "I'd say … eighty-five percent." He felt the bloom of redness on his face, but it dissipated quickly. No shame. Not for this. Shit needed to be taken care of, after all.

Marina just nodded. "Okay." Fighting clogs, taking on demons. Gary felt like she'd be up for anything. Ulysses, though … wasn't that just America for you? Native-born gets lazy; hard-working immigrant comes in and takes everything through sheer effort and pluck. Ulysses

just stared at him dully. Sorry-ass. But Marina ...
  Goddamn, wasn't this country grand?
  "Well, all right, then," Gary said. "We're going to fight us some demons and get this shit settled." He felt a glow of pride in him, and he wished he could stand up and salute the American flag that hung in the corner of the room. He didn't, though, because his legs were fucked. But he wished he could.

*

The sound of engines blasted through Hanley's Fold all around Arch as the watch sprang into motion. The stink of diesel exhaust was particularly heavy as Keith Drumlin nearly sideswiped Arch as he skidded past down the hill toward the giants, his consecrated, spiked grill just about making Arch hole-y rather than holy, as he would have preferred.
  "Watch yourself!" Arch shouted over the roar of engines, though what he really meant was, "Watch out for me!" Seemed less polite to call it out that way, though. Unlikely Keith heard him, in any case.
  "Assault! Battery!" one of the giants shouted as Chauncey Watson collided with its shin, producing a scream that terminated in a POP! and a blast of brimstone as the giant was sucked right on back to Hades, where it dang sure belonged.
  Arch let the cars get out in front of him and watched Hanley's Fold turn into its own version of a demolition derby. He'd heard about Erin's little adventure with those doggone shadowcats in the quarry over by Shade's Hollow last week, and they'd used the same strategy a couple times since to cut through herds of demons that seemed to be heading toward Midian.
  As yet, though ... it didn't seem to be making much of a dent in the numbers of dead bodies turning up around here.
  Well, there was a good fight that needed to be fought, and a race that had to be won. And keeping the faith was something Arch was reasonably decent at.
  Braeden Tarley ran his pickup truck into a giant who was screaming about civil rights violations, and the mechanic went and violated him into a cloud of sulfur, which was a relief to Arch's tortured ears. It didn't help with the unmuffled noise of some of the watch's vehicles, but ... every demon scream that ended brought the decibel level down a notch or two. Couldn't complain about that.
  Drops in the bucket. That was how Arch was looking at this. Draining the ocean one bit at a time. "Faith of a mustard seed, gotta

move mountains."

Oh. Here came a mountain now.

One of the giants had slipped through the messy line of cars that were tearing up Hanley's Fold, spinning their wheels and whipping into their opposition. It was getting pretty close to closing time by Arch's reckoning. Maybe a half dozen giants remained, and they seemed to be well hemmed in—

Except for this one.

"I'm going to squash you, little man!" the one with the Cockney accent thundered as it raced up the hill toward him, beetle eyes locked on him. "And then I'm going to crush your friends in their little play cars—" He raised up a fist and came at Arch, a good twenty yards off.

Arch just stared at him. He considered taking a knee; the prayerful man in him would find that somewhat righteous, to bow and pray.

But the football player in him couldn't countenance that. It wasn't as though he needed to get down on his knees to pray, after all.

"Oh, Lord," Arch said, keeping his eyes open as the giant churned the earth coming toward him, "With but a sling in my hand, I face Goliath."

"What?" the giant started to slow, peering down at him. "Whatchoo talkin' 'bout—"

Arch whipped the blessed dagger he'd gotten from Father Nguyen in a hard throw, end over end, at the giant, who stood there, less than ten yards away, but slowing. Its eyes took in the sight of sailing, silvery metal hurled toward its flesh, but all it could do was just about trip over its giant feet trying to dodge.

There was no dodging this, though; Arch had kept it up his sleeve until the last, and his aim was true. He'd been practicing. Ten times out of ten, ninety-nine out of a hundred, he could land a blade in his target now with a good throw.

And landing the blade ... was all it took with these things.

"AIIIEEEEEE—" the giant demon screeched, tripping over its own feet. It started to fall—toward him—but Arch remained steadfast. Throwing himself in one direction or another wouldn't do a blessed thing, after all, not at this point. The giant loomed over him, skidding and tripping like a dog over its own legs as it tried, tried to keep from getting pricked by that little knife hurtling toward it—

It failed.

The blade caught it flush in the right-hand orb of its chest; the giant had tried to turn sideways, but there was no turning enough to dodge that knife. It made a subtle hiss that was drowned by the shout, the scream, and blackness seeped out in the shadow of its figure, like dark tendrils reaching out from the point of impact.

Arch watched it happen, the motion so fast his brain couldn't quite keep up with it. He got the gist, though.

The demon was sucked back to wherever it had come from, leaving only a sulfurous stink behind to make Arch nearly gag, even holding his breath as he was.

"That was bold," Barney Jones's voice boomed in Arch's ear, the crack and hiss of the slight static in the earpiece augmented by the roar of the engine in the background of the pastor's (borrowed) vehicle, a monster truck he'd gotten from Father Nguyen. "If I didn't know better, I'd worry about you and your state of mind."

"Didn't seem much point in panicking by the time he was on me," Arch said, triggering his mike. "It was all settled by then, anyhow."

"I suppose," Jones said. He didn't sound skeptical. More ... amused, maybe. "Still and all ... man just coming back from a death wish might want to be a little more careful about the situations he puts himself in."

"I agree with that," Arch said, and mopped his brow. It was a cool day and he hadn't exactly exerted himself, but he was still plenty sweaty. "Let's pack it on in," he said, hitting the button on his mike again. "Looks we've settled this one." No more giants were in sight.

Thankfully. Arch mopped his brow again. Still sweating.

Next time—if there was a next time with giants—he was most certainly staying in the car. "Thank you, my Lord, for delivering me from evil ..." he began to pray as he walked, on stiff, adrenaline-hobbled legs, back toward the Explorer that waited to bear him back to the station.

*

Darla Pike sat alone at the kitchen table, staring off into space. The wall in front of her was white, stark, free of any child's doodles, surprisingly—the hall was not so fortunate, nor were several other surfaces in the house. It was like a game; see how long she could lose herself in the work of researching dark rituals before coming up and finding some possession defaced with crayon, two shamefaced little devils caught in the act with messy hands and guilty looks.

She had no mental space for worrying about that now, though.

Who gave a shit about crayons on the wall when your husband—your lover, your partner, your provider—had died?

No, she thought, mind tightening as she corrected herself, he was *murdered*.

"Mommy?" came a soft, curious voice from the other room. She heard it but said nothing. The TV was on, *Bubble Guppies* playing in the background. Forever, *Bubble Guppies* was playing, as near as she could tell. That and *PAW Patrol*. Let the kids rot their little brains watching that shit.

It wasn't like they needed their brains for anything important, at least not right now.

Darla stared at her long fingers, against the white pine finish of their kitchen table. It was marginally paler than she was. She'd gotten darker since moving down here, to the south. It wouldn't have been her first choice—or in the top fifty, top one hundred—fuck, she wouldn't have picked rural Tennessee if she'd been on fire and it was the last place on the planet where she could get a cup of water—but here she was, brought by fate and by Jason, her husband ...

And Jason had gone and gotten his ass killed. Gutted, really, just about. Oh, they'd tried to hide it when she had to identify the body, but the sheet was so damned crimson there was no disguising what had happened to him. It had bled through in patches, no mere droplets; the whole sheet was red like a bullfighter's cape, from under his armpits all the way to his groin.

She hadn't bothered to examine him any further once the body was released to her, because why bother? The circumstances all told the tale to her satisfaction.

He'd been found, alone and carved up, in an abandoned warehouse. They might not have wanted to say more, but she could read the chicken entrails—literal ones, in this case—well enough. The slimy gizzards told all, if you knew what to look for.

Murder. Betrayal by a demon he'd summoned to invoke aid ... or something else? Well, that wasn't quite so clear.

But murder. That much was sure.

"Mommy?" That little, beseeching voice came slightly closer. It intruded on her thoughts, impaired her concentration, and she ignored it once again.

She had an idea of how it might have gone down. She hadn't been to the factory where it happened to confirm it for herself—there'd be signs only she would recognize—but she had a pretty clear picture in her head. Jason had tried to summon a demon for power. Because that was what he did. Schemed. That he hadn't told her about this one? There wasn't enough charity in Darla Pike to give him the benefit of the doubt. He'd done it not to surprise her, as one with a sweeter disposition might have assumed, but to curry favor separate from their joint plans.

That was galling. But probably fair play, in a turnabout sort of way, because she'd been gathering demon favor absent his knowledge for almost two decades now.

"Sleeping your way to the top," was such a disgusting thing in the corporate world. Darla couldn't countenance it—understand it, sure, but not countenance it—because there was just no way in hell that degrading yourself like that would ever truly pay off.

Darla Pike was a fucking Rhodes scholar. Using her body simply to earn money offended the shit out of her. It bothered her that anyone would allow themselves to get stuck at the mercy of some unenforceable contract of understanding between a woman in need of a few bucks and some asshole with more sperm than restraint.

How many women had thrust themselves (she almost gagged at the irony of the phrase) into compromising positions in an effort to climb, only to find themselves—literally and figuratively—on their backs at the end of it? Promises unkept, the verbal contract unexecuted, both prospects and self-respect burned, like bridges, to ash.

If Darla Pike was going to suck a dick in exchange for advantage, it was going to be a demon dick under demon law, where the enforceability of the contract was absolute, where the payoff was fucking guaranteed under pain of agony, of soulburn, of time in the fucking pits thinking about how you should hold to your contractual obligations. The hell version of debtor's prison: these were the sort of exchanges Darla could get behind.

Power for power. Sex for the ability to casually fuck over anyone she chose.

She'd done nothing that bothered her, nothing that she deemed "too far"—because there was nothing too far out of bounds for her to earn the guarantees that when the shit came rolling down—and, oh, was it warming up—she was going to escape the pile of refuse that was called humanity and ascend her sweet, demon-fucked ass out of the huddled masses yearning to breathe anything but sulfur.

Power? She had it. Markers upon markers from the most hellish creatures imaginable. A veritable panoply of unholy armor at her disposal. Almost twenty years she'd been making deals and trading things that she didn't honestly give a shit about—and some of which she actually enjoyed—building up a cache of favors.

And Jason? That Johnny-Come-Lately?

Pfft.

He'd been useful for a while, but if he'd gotten wise to the game and started doing his own deals without her, then he was a liability.

She hadn't seen it, either, which bothered her like an itch on the taint from an ingrown hair. She'd thought he was just doing his best, trying to provide for their family, both monetarily and in preparation for the literal hell that was to come.

"Mommy." A little head nuzzled its way against her side, up against Darla's breast, soft pressure that gave her a flashback to breastfeeding. That tired, exhausting worst of times, when she was so sore it felt like she'd rubbed her nipples in broken glass. Which was a thing she had done, once, to please a Moroch'tai. She'd been young and the deal was decent. That was a marker she'd probably call in soon. "Mommy?"

Darla bent her head. A little blond moptop had snuck in under her arm and was looking up at her with the most stunning grey-blue eyes, like a stormy sky. Big and watery, Jay's eyes were, always on the verge of tears. "Crybaby," Darla muttered, looking down at him.

"Mommy, I'm hungry," Jay whined. He set his lower lip to full extension, and his tone carried a whine seeking appeasement.

Darla's blood boiled—just for a second—before she caught herself. "What would you like to eat?" she asked, dead of tone.

"Peanut butter and jelly."

Big fucking surprise there. Darla stirred. They had the frozen kind she could just pull out of the fridge; it'd only take two seconds. Jay was about at the age he could have done it himself, but he was looking for attention, too, so clearly he needed to ask Darla to be his slave today, to ensure he knew he was loved. "All right," she said, not letting any of her other thoughts out, and got up to get his sandwich.

It only took a few seconds to retrieve a plate from the cupboards and slap a circular PB & J sandwich right out of the fridge onto it. Emeril Lagasse she was not, nor was it required here. Jay set to work munching at it, and she'd almost sat down to think again—believing she might just get away with it—when the next question came.

"Mommy?" Jay asked, smacking his lips together, peanut butter probably gluing the soft palate to the bottom of his mouth. He'd need a glass of milk, and she started to get up to answer that call before he even asked, but his next question came as a surprise. "When is Daddy coming home?"

Darla might have felt her heart plummet within her chest, her soul drop into her feet—

If she hadn't sold them both a fucking long time ago in exchange for power.

"Never," she said bluntly as she opened the fridge and got out the milk. "He's never coming home."

She didn't look at him as she poured the milk.

*

Helen Farrell sighed, the sheets sodden and sweaty, arrayed around her in tangled bliss. The room stank of sex, of perspiration, and it hadn't bothered her until just now. *Shut up shut up shut up*, she told her brain as it engaged, little stirrings of guilt crawling around in her belly like rats at the bottom of a mine shaft.

"Oh, man," Jake Klewe said, stirring next to her. He had pecs, he had abs, he had the sort of body that would have put Helen's late husband—fire captain Marty Ferrell—to shame. Marty had a pony keg where his abs had been when they'd first met, and she hadn't said a damned thing about it in the almost thirty years they'd been together, as he slowly crawled toward the two hundred and fifty-pound mark over their years of marriage.

But Marty had died two weeks ago. Jake was his best friend. And the guilt—

Fuck the guilt, Helen told herself. This was just Helen doing what she needed to do to get by. It was mourning—but done her way. To hell with the black dress and the mourning—

Black panties and a matching bra stripped off in the heat of passion in a way she hadn't felt in two decades, sweated out under the tender pressure of Jake's solid body ...

No guilt no guilt no guilllllllt, Helen told herself again.

It wasn't working.

But GOOOOOD. It had been so good in the middle of it.

"I think I need a drink," Helen said, gulping down a breath. She hadn't felt as pinched under Jake and his more muscled, compact frame than she had with Marty toward the end. His belly would push down on hers and make it tough to get a full breath while he was laboring atop her. She almost felt like he was on her now, pushing down, making it tough to get a lungful of air.

Fuuuuuuucking guilt!

"I'll get you one," Jake said, springing up, his naked—and toned—ass retreating toward the door as Helen was left in the sweaty, tangled sheets of her marriage bed. Shit, was it hot in here? Or was it just Jake's glutes?

She heard him make his way to the bar in the living room, open the liquor cabinet. Gin, neat, that was Helen's drink, and Jake knew that, of course. How many times had she and Marty entertained him over the years? How many parties, how many get-togethers, how many times had she stared across the table, sitting next to Marty but looking at Jake's firm chin, his tight shirt …

Gyahhhh. That fucking guilt. It was like a weight in the belly, alleviated only slightly by that pulsing feeling in her vagina. Guilt, or lack of satisfaction? She'd done the lack of satisfaction thing for twenty years.

Fuck the guilt. And just let Jake fuck her. That was her decision, but it didn't lighten the black pit in her stomach one iota.

A knock came at the door, and Helen sat bolt upright. "Who is it?" she called—to Jake, not whoever was at the door.

"Dunno," Jake said, and he appeared in view, over the edge of the bed, frowning, gin in hand for her, caught in the straight line between the edge of the bed and the front door. His naked ass was just holding there, his elephant trunk of a dick retracted now. It had been huge ten, fifteen minutes ago. She'd felt every inch of it, and God had there been a lot of inches.

Now it looked puny, and he turned away, showing her his ass. Oh, that ass.

"Don't answer it," she called. "Anybody who knows me would have called."

"What if it's some mourner come to express their best wishes?" Jake's voice had a kind of songlike quality to it, distant and drifting.

"I don't want them to see me—us—like this," Helen said, scrambling for the covers. "Just let it be. If it's important they'll call, or they'll come back later." *When we're dressed,* she didn't say.

Jake took another step toward the door. "I have to answer it," he said, almost raptured, dreamlike. His ass flexed with every step as he moved to the door.

"No, no, no—" Helen cast aside the sheets, scrambling for clothing. She was dripping, God, that was disgusting, but she shoved her panties on with her pants, ripping them up to her hips in record time, like she was twenty again, like she'd been caught in her room with her first boyfriend. Didn't even worry about the bra, either, she plunged into her blouse and let everything hang where it may, sprinting out the bedroom door on bare feet toward Jake and the door—

He opened it.

The tight-assed, cut-abbed, square-chinned fucker.

She made it halfway into the living room when he got it all the way open, naked as a damned jaybird, showing the world and whoever was outside the door his flaccid dick and matted pubic hair and slightly flushed cheeks (which Helen had thought was cute until he'd gone and opened the goddamned door naked). She almost got her mouth open to deliver a hellstorm of a rebuke, but …

When she saw who was waiting out there … she just shut right up. Couldn't even help herself.

"Thank you," came a soft, almost raspy voice, as a man of medium height, of medium build, hidden beneath robes, slipped in through the front door. He had peering eyes of deepest black and wore a brown cowl over his head like a Gregorian monk or some shit. He was wearing robes, too, that covered him from top to bottom, but tight enough she could see his figure clearly. Not as clearly as Jake's but … it was all there, under the hem.

"Who in the hell are you?" Helen asked, staring at the man who'd just entered her house without so much as an invitation. She was more poleaxed than worried, although, she realized a tad late, maybe she oughta be both. Especially given that her husband had been murdered not two weeks before.

The man seemed to seep across the room, as though he were floating, not walking. He reached back and beckoned to Jake, who followed him toward the couch and loveseat. The man paused, sniffing. "And here as well." He looked down at the couch, angling over to the loveseat, where he brushed his robes out of the way and sat.

"Here … what?" Helen asked, still dumbstruck.

The man cast his dark eyes toward the couch he'd just avoided. "The stink of your sin is upon it." He sniffed, his pointed nose moving slightly beneath the cowl. "Faded, though; not as obvious or recent as comes from there." He waved a hand toward the bedroom.

"Excuse me?" Helen asked, her jaw dropping a couple inches.

"You feel it, don't you?" he asked, level, that rasp like the scratch of a needle on a record. "Your sin. It wrestles in your guts, like snakes crawling one over the other. I would say it would kill you but … it won't. Sin corrupts, you see. It eats us within, hollows us out. Accumulates and rots all it touches. It built within him," he gestured to Jake, who stood there, staring dumbly, the door wide open and his naked ass visible to anyone who walked by, "until he could restrain it no more … and then he released it into you."

Helen frowned, those butterflies of guilt flapping inside in spite of the fact that this man was filling the air with crazy talk. "Get the hell out of my house," she said.

"I want to 'get the hell' out of your house, indeed," the man said. "I want to get all the hell, all the sin … out of here. I want to destroy it, but you see … sin can't simply be destroyed. Not with the snap of fingers, not with the flip of a hand, not with a wish. It is … persistent.

It is … ever rising." He gestured to Jake, who moved across the room toward the man as though following a command.

"Who are you?" Helen asked, the anger fading as she watched Jake move stiffly toward the man.

"I am a humble worrier," the man said, "fearing for the hearts and souls of men, you see." He reached into his robes and came out with a knife, which made Helen take a step back. "No, no," he said, waving a hand at her, as though to assuage her worry. "This isn't for you." He brought the blade to his lips and breathed deep.

Orange flame flickered, his pale lips suddenly aglow as though he'd swallowed fire. The man kissed the knife, and the heat set the silver tip to blazing, as though it were freshly forged. The man turned as Jake came up to him, his member growing turgid, and Jake shaking his head slightly, as though drunk. "He comes back to sin, you see." The man reached up, taking Jake's penis in hand, just like Helen had not that long ago. She watched, horrorstruck, as he grasped it, from the shaft all the way down to the balls, like he was going to do something like what she'd done just minutes before—

The knife moved cleanly, swiftly, and the sizzle of burning hot blade against flesh and meat and bone made Helen vomit right there. She turned her head before it was even done, couldn't stand to watch, and the smell of stinking meat that filled the air made her think she'd never be able to have a hamburger again without thinking of Jake getting his dick and balls cut off in her goddamned living room—

Jake said nothing. Drifts of smoke wafted up passed his unblinking eyes and blank face as the man with the blade cast Jake's manhood aside as though it were nothing. "His sin," he announced with complete calmness, "has been purged. Forever. It will rise no more."

"What the fuck did you do?" Helen cried, though she knew goddamned well what he'd done on an intellectual level. Her eyes saw; her mind couldn't get a fucking grip on what had just happened, though.

"I elevated him," the man said, so steady, no trace of emotion. "Man is a slave to his beast-like lust, a prisoner to sin, easily led astray by his weakest parts." The man stood, putting the blade away under his robes, with no apparent concern for the heat of the knife. "Now, he will sin no more." He tapped Jake on the forehead, and Jake's head moved only slightly under the force of the push. "His mind is clear—"

"He looks like a goddamned zombie! And he didn't say a word as you—" Helen moved her hand, gesturing from the man to the end of the couch, where he'd … discarded Jake's penis and balls with a careless toss, "—you gelded him like a horse!"

"Sacrifice is a necessary part of purging one of sin," the man said, rising. "Now ... earlier, you asked my name. But I will not give it to you, for you—you are the vessel of sin." He made a hand motion at Helen, at her belly. "You have received it unto yourself, you carry it within you. It cannot be excised, it does not rise, it is never expelled. You carry the traces with you, always. Such is your fate, to be a ... scapegoat."

He did not smile, did not emote, only stared at her, coldly.

"What are you saying?" Helen backed up a step.

The man turned to Jake. "Cleanse the world of your sin," he said.

Jake stood, still, for a moment—

Then his head turned to look right at—

Helen.

Helen screamed, tried to run, but Jake was on her in a hot second before she even made it to the hall. He tackled her, rocked her across the back of the head with a blow, and she could only struggle, dazedly, as he pummeled her. She lashed out, weakly, at him—aimed for the crotch with a knee but—

Oh, right.

Helen Farrell only had time to remember—vaguely—why that didn't work, as Jake Klewe beat her to death with his fists, her world swirling in darkness, her last vision of his handsome face and square chin utterly merciless and covered in her blood.

2.

Darla Pike was a mother on the brink. It wasn't because of her husband being dead, either. She could feel the strain, indeed, and it had zero to do with Jason being cold and carved into like a dressed turkey carcass on a coroner's table across town. Hell, she was at peace with that almost before it even happened.

No, the thing that was driving her nuts now ...

"Why isn't Daddy coming back?" Jay asked.

... Was the endless fucking questions. The same endless fucking question, really, over and over.

Darla was standing at the sink, looking out the window beyond into the backyard. They had a view of trees, which, honestly, Darla would have traded for the Chicago skyline in a hot second, if that was where the hot spot had been. She wished that it was in Chicago, or New York, or Los Angeles. But no, it couldn't be in a civilized city; it had to be in Midian, Tennessee, where high culture looked like a tractor pull and a monster truck rally that came once a year.

But here she was, staring at the trees, dead husband, two kids, and trying to figure out how to explain to Jay for the thousandth time this hour that the reason Daddy wasn't coming back was because he'd been a cold-blooded, stupid-ass cock and betrayed Mommy by summoning a demon he shouldn't have in the mad scramble for power.

That probably wouldn't translate for a three-year-old, though.

"Because he's not," was all she said.

That didn't stop the questions, of course. "But why?"

Because Daddy got fucked in the guts by a demon-bladed dick, probably, Darla fought real hard to keep inside. She didn't know that for a fact, but it was the most pleasant of her assumptions for how he went out. Demons were notoriously vicious when you pissed them off—at least the kind they were trying to gather to their cause were. Which was a key reason why Darla had about a million markers from demons she could call in and hadn't used any of them yet to come and babysit the kids for an hour.

Oh, you want your kids babysat? Some of them would put on agreeable faces, but even if she managed to word things so perfectly that a lawyer with infinite time and funds couldn't find a loophole in her request, she'd come back and find them having been taking to the pits for the interval she was gone, probably shown unimaginable things. Safe as houses, just mentally traumatized forever, catatonic, a nice project for Child Protective Services and fifty psychologists to try and unwind for the next few years.

So Darla stood at the sink, stared out at the trees—why couldn't it have been Chicago?—and tried not to lose it when she heard, "But why, Mommy?" again.

"But Mommy ..." came the little voice again and Darla heard a little crack in her jaw. This was it. She was going to—

Ding dong.

"Saved by the bell," she muttered, turning around and breezing past Jay as he jumped up from the table. It was the doorbell, which of course meant everyone had to run for the front door, even though the two kids weren't allowed to open the damned thing, ever. That was a Mommy and Daddy thing. Mostly Mommy, since Daddy was absent so much up to now.

Now it'd be a Mommy thing forevermore. Or as long as her sanity lasted, whichever.

"Who is it? Who is it?" Mera was squeeing as she jumped up and down in front of the door.

"If you'd get out of the way, I could tell you," Darla said, that thin thread of motherly patience clearing her daughter aside more effectively than a hearty shove. Mera was two, and she already knew better than Jay when her mommy was about to explode. Girls were just better that way. She stepped back, shamefaced at being on the receiving end of even so gentle an admonishment.

Darla reached the door and looked out through the peephole, knocking her forehead against it as she drew closer to it than intended. It was like the door had a gravity well that sucked her in, such was her surprise at what she saw.

But no. It didn't have a gravity well. Just a particularly heinous sight waiting on the other side of the peephole.

"Well, aren't you going to let me in?" Marischa Pike asked through the door. "I can hear you talking and breathing in there."

It was her mother-in-law.

"Fuck," Darla breathed.

"Fuck!" Jay said happily. "Mommy, what does 'fuck' mean?"

Darla thumped her head against the door again. This was not her week.

*

Erin rolled the police cruiser up to the curb in front of Helen Farrell's house and shifted it into park, taking a long breath. The street was all lined with cold, empty tree branches bereft of any leaves, skeletal limbs reaching up to the sky like supplicants praying. She threw open the door after checking the side view mirror to make sure it wouldn't get sheared off by a passing car, then got out, slammed it behind her, and zipped up her big, heavy-duty windbreaker. It read SHERIFF on the back and was something every deputy had.

But in her case, the title was mostly true, now.

Oh, sure, if County Administrator Pike had still been alive, she'd probably have been dragged into court by now for just taking up Reeve's mantle and doing the work without anybody so much as mentioning another special election. But Pike was dead, deader than a doornail; she'd seen the body herself. She truly believed he'd bit the big one at the end of Lafayette Hendricks—that goddamned cowboy's—sword.

And the fact was … no matter what she said to Hendricks, she didn't know how to feel about that. If ever there was a fly in the ointment, a stickler that seemed to be trying to make life hell for the watch … it had been Pike, at least until recently. She wasn't totally convinced he'd pulled a 180 on that, either, but … killing the man was awfully extreme.

Which was why she was glad she hadn't been involved but wasn't too sorry that it had been done. "Damned shame," she muttered, like she was trying to convince herself of it standing there on the street, cold wind blowing past. It didn't take hold any better this time than the other times she'd said it.

Erin started her slow walk around the car and grabbed the spiked baseball bat from the passenger side before she started up the sidewalk. The front door to Helen Farrell's house was thrown wide open, a nice view of part of the living room all the way clear into the bedroom hallway available from here. The closer she got to the front door, the easier it was to see why a couple of the neighbors had called 911.

She wasn't a hundred percent sure until she actually made it to the threshold, but once she did, it confirmed it for her easy enough. There was no way in hell that identifying this body was going to be an easy task. It was splayed out in the hallway, and the head had been destroyed like a piñata, pounded into the carpet until all that was left was wet chunks.

"Uhhhh," Erin let out a low grunt, glad she'd skipped breakfast, not so glad she'd been drinking coffee like it was life itself she was sucking in. She looked away from the human wreckage for a moment, steeling herself, then stepped over the threshold into the house.

The place had a certain stink to it. She raised the bat in a ready swing, looking to either side, clearing her corners as she came in. Others from the watch were already on the way, so she felt no particular need to be extra brave and clear the whole house herself just now. A cursory examination would do just fine until backup got here.

The wind whipped hard outside, jarring the front door with a squeak, and rattling the windows. "Jesus," Erin muttered, halfway between a prayer and a plea. She'd caught sight of something on an end table in the living room that threatened to make her stomach turn aflip again.

It was some guy's bait and tackle, sitting there like a conversation piece or a coaster on the glass surface. God, it looked puny like this, lying like it was the table's own genitals. Stroke the lamp, watch it rise, Erin thought grimly. That thing wasn't going to do any more rising, though. If it was real, it was fully Bobbited, and its rising days were done.

A car pulled up outside and Erin heard footsteps follow slamming doors. Dr. Lauren Darlington came in a moment later, followed by Ms. Cherry. They'd all left the station at the same time, but Erin's bat out of hell driving style had gotten her here fully two minutes or more early. "Shouldn't have waited for that light, ladies," she said.

"Get me one of those lovely gumball machines, I think they are called? And a siren?" Ms. Cherry asked. "For my dashboard? And I will hang with you through every red light next time."

Erin snorted. "What are you afraid of? The cops pulling you over?"

The madam of the local brothel raised a perfectly shaped eyebrow. "No. I'm afraid of being hit by someone who does not hear me running through an intersection until their bumper is through my windows and taking my fucking head off."

"Traffic accidents are the worst," Dr. Darlington said. "One time, in the ER, we had this couple brought in. She'd been blowing him while he was driving—" Darlington paused and looked at Ms. Cherry, suddenly abashed.

"Go on," Ms. Cherry said. "And don't look at me like this; you know I am very well aware what blowing someone is like. In a car, while they are driving. It's called road head."

"I, uh—" Dr. Darlington started to say.

"Maybe save that story for later," Erin said, "once we've cleared the house. But I have a feeling I know how it ends—like that." And she pointed at the severed dick on the living room end table.

Both the women turned to look. Only Darlington did a double take. "Is that ... a novelty prank penis?"

Ms. Cherry answered. "I think it's real."

"There's no blood," Erin said. She didn't move to check it.

"And trust me, those things bleed like crazy when damaged or severed," Dr. Darlington said. She didn't move toward it either.

Ms. Cherry sighed, and walked over to it, lowering her own holy blade, a short sword; there was not much chance of a demon jumping out from behind the couch, after all, and the living room was a confined space with no entries or exits to other rooms save via that hallway where the corpse was. The madam picked the penis up by the tip and dangled it before her, sniffing. "Removed and cauterized at the same time," she pronounced after peering at the part where it normally would have been attached to a human body. "It's real ... but it's not magnificent."

Dr. Darlington blinked a few times, then turned to look at Erin. "Did she just ... make a Seinfeld reference?"

Erin shrugged. She'd been a toddler when that show went off the air. "We should check the rest of the house before we, uh ... get too caught up examining the minutiae." She cringed. "Not that it was 'minute,' magnificent or not." Now she was unwittingly insulting the genitals of the dead.

Was the person who those ... uh, things ... belonged to ... dead?

They fanned out, moving through the five other rooms of the house quickly. The kitchen was mostly open to the living room, and it was empty of life ... or death. No bodies, no demons. Two other bedrooms were silent as well. A laundry room proved empty of everything but piles of clothing, washed but not folded.

"Looks like mine at home," Dr. Darlington said. Erin just nodded. Who had time to fold laundry in a demon apocalypse? Part of her hoped she'd die just so she wouldn't have to do it. Extreme? Maybe. But she really fucking hated folding laundry.

"House looks clear," Erin said, slinging the baseball bat over her shoulder, careful to avoid letting any of the nails rip her jacket. Doubtful there was money in the budget to replace it if she did. But it wouldn't have to be folded after its next washing. Not that she washed her windbreaker very often.

"Yeah, it's totally clear except for that woman's corpse over there and the severed dick," Dr. Darlington said dryly. "Any idea who the dead lady is?"

Erin worked her way slowly over to the carcass. That was all it was now, a carcass, ooze of blood running in a wide puddle along the yellowed, aged oak floorboards. "I know you shouldn't assume, but … based on the height and weight and body type … it looks like Helen Farrell to me." Erin just shook her head. She'd talked to Helen Farrell not two weeks ago.

Erin had been the one sent to break it to her that Marty was dead, that they'd found his body at the side of the road.

"This is a little far outside Midian for normal demon stuff, ain't it?" Dr. Darlington asked, prompting Erin to frown. The doc was the least likely to lapse into improper English, but here she was, drawling as she stood staring over the body. Not like there was much else for her to do, Erin realized. It wasn't like there was even a face to blow into for CPR, and it'd be hard to revive a body without a head.

Erin looked down at the body, avoiding the puddled blood, which was oozing to one side to follow the slightly warped plane of the wood floor. There were chunks of skull everywhere, though; someone had flat-out pulped this woman's head, and she couldn't imagine much more ire being directed toward her than this. The hair was soaked, what was left of it, all smeared with the back of the skull against the ground in a mash of gore. "The address is Culver, yeah," Erin said. "But we've been getting calls out this way some. More and more as time goes on." She wanted to shake her head. First Marty, now Helen …

Another family wiped out completely. God.

"Like the trouble is widening," Ms. Cherry said, looking down at the body casually. More casually even than the doc. Strong stomach on the madam, Erin thought. Really strong. This sort of thing would have nearly sent Erin running, once upon a time.

"Big surprise there," Erin said. The body seemed … normal below the neck. Excessively so. Clothes hung loosely on her slightly plump form, jeans snugged at the waist, a little roll of muffin top hanging over the waistband, not too much. Her green blouse rode up just a little from the position of the body, and her feet were bare and pale, the bottoms calloused, like she walked everywhere barefoot.

"She had sex recently," Ms. Cherry said.

Prompting Doctor Darlington to let out a, "How in the fuck could you know that?"

"Side of the neck," Ms. Cherry said, pointing at where the blood-drenched remainder of the jaw met the throat. "Beneath the gore you can see—"

"Slight bruising, consistent with a hickey," Dr. Darlington muttered, sounding very clinical, like she was reading it out loud for the benefit of a tape recording during an autopsy. She was peering at the corpse. Erin couldn't see any hickeys. There was just a shit ton of blood in the way, the neck was drenched in it, and the shirt was covered down to the shoulders, Helen Farrell's breasts visible through the wetted slick like she'd been in hell's own version of a wet t-shirt contest. That made Erin feel a retching reflex for some reason. She kept it down, though, not wanting to look fucking stupid in front of the other ladies.

Looking at a headless corpse didn't get to her, but thinking about a blood-based wet t-shirt contest in hell? Yeah, that did it. Brains were weird things. Especially Helen's, what she could see of it, distributed all over the goddamned place. Yuck.

"Still, making the leap from hickeys to sex," Dr. Darlington said, shaking her head. "I don't see it."

"Look closer," Ms. Cherry said. "Her clothes—they're disarrayed. She hurried to dress—"

"She could have been sleeping," Darlington said.

Ms. Cherry pursed her full lips, making wrinkles around them like smokers got after many years of the practice. "I don't think so. But you could confirm my guess with one simple exam, couldn't you?"

Darlington blinked at her, cool eyes staring at the madam. "I'm not performing a pelvic exam on a corpse here in her hallway. Or at all. That's more a job for the coroner than me."

Ms. Cherry shrugged. "It's hardly any skin off my nose, dear. It's not as though you lack for corpses to examine if you got the yearning to do so. Just pointing out what I see." She nodded toward the bedroom down the hall. "Sheets ... very much askew. Could be normal toss and turn, but ..."

Erin turned her head to look. The sheets were tossed, like Ms. Cherry said. "She was a new widow," Erin said, feeling the need to defend Helen Farrell. She'd watched this woman go through shock, through tears, the last time they'd spoken. It didn't seem proper to stand here in her home, over her body, and talk about how she might have been fucking somebody two weeks after her husband died and minutes before she herself went.

"Ms. Cherry shrugged again. "We all cope with grief in our own ways."

Dr. Darlington had a frown that bordered on a sneer. "And you think her coping mechanism was—" she gestured toward the bed, "... that?"

Ms. Cherry looked at the severed member on the end table with great significance and then turned back to Darlington and Erin. "I only know what I see, and what I conclude from it is ... yes, that was how she was coping."

"I don't ... see that it matters if she was," Erin said, trying to shake the thoughts of a new widow doing some fresh fucking out of her head. Whatever—or whoever—Helen Farrell was doing, it wasn't her business.

"It matters if it got her killed, doesn't it?" Ms. Cherry asked, and the entire place seemed to chill around them.

"We don't know that sex—if that was even what she was doing—was what got her killed," Erin said, and now the hesitancy she'd felt at smearing Helen's reputation, even in this most private of settings, seemed to compound on itself. "People are dropping like flies around here, and not because of some secret rendezvous. I mean, think about what we ran into last week out at the Jackson farm. That whole family was ripped apart like tissue paper and strung up around their house." If she hadn't already had a coarsened stomach, that would have done it. In a town filled to the brimming with horrific scenes, that one had been particularly noteworthy.

"We know that whoever she was having sex with sure did have a bad day," Dr. Darlington said, eyeing the dick on the table. "I hope he had a good time since it would appear it was his last."

"You can't, uh ... reattach it?" Erin asked, cringing slightly. The thing just looked deflated, sad, like they always did when they weren't up and at ... well, her, in the cases where she'd seen 'em.

Darlington shook her head slowly. "The cauterization plus it being detached this long? The best vascular surgeon in the country couldn't reattach that thing. Maybe not even if they'd been standing there right when it happened and got straight to work."

Erin stroked her forehead. "So ... we've got a dickless man somewhere ... no body on that—"

"Bet he wishes he were dead," Ms. Cherry muttered, and when she drew looks from Erin and Darlington, she just shrugged. "In my experience, a man without a working penis has a very sad life. Much angst."

"In my experience, men who have a working penis and use it too much end up having a very dramatic life," Dr. Darlington said dryly. "Which is only a step or two above sad, in my opinion."

That made Erin chuckle in spite of herself. "Okay, so—dead body. Dickless man wandering around somewhere? Or dead nearby, maybe?" She looked to the doctor for an opinion.

"Sad life or not," Darlington said, looking up from Helen's body, "the cauterization means he's not bleeding to death—probably. No trail of blood. He'll live—again, probably. Walking, though?" She shook her head. "That's a major surgery. He shouldn't be walking. Physically, it is possible to afterward, but ..." She shuddered. "Just so I get this straight in my head—are you suggesting he had sex with the widow Farrell, then dismembered ... his member? Tossed it on the table and walked out?"

Erin let out a slow breath. "Hell if I know. I've got a dead body, a severed penis, and nothing else. I'm just trying to assemble a story here, a theory for what happened."

"The sex was so terrible he cut off his own twig and berries afterward," Ms. Cherry said softly. "He should have come to my establishment."

Erin and the doctor exchanged a look and both burst out into a case of the giggles. It didn't last long. "So ... I think we need more than what the crime scene alone tells us," Erin said, mopping at her eye. That laugh had wrung out a single tear. Or so she told herself.

"If only you had forensic pathologists for this sort of thing," Dr. Darlington said.

"I've got you," Erin said.

"I'm not a forensic pathologist."

"No, but you're what I've got," Erin said, taking another look around the place. "Can you do an autopsy or not?"

"I can, but I'm useless on hair and fiber work, and many of the countless other things pathologists do," Darlington said. "And you want an autopsy report? Here it is: she died of having her head crushed."

"Heh," Ms. Cherry said, and when the two of them looked at her, "They both lost a head here." And she pointed at the severed dick.

Erin didn't laugh at that one. Her phone buzzed, and she saw the station's number. "Harris," she said, accepting the call.

"You might want to get down here, Erin," came the slightly high voice of Casey Meacham. "We got a little thing going on ..."

"Get down where?" Erin asked, a chill running through her blood.

"The station," Casey said tautly. "And ... you should hurry. Like ... now."

"Ross," the man in the black suit said, flashing one of those plastic and leather wallet IDs at Arch. He looked like a serious fellow, big nose and high cheekbones, thinning hair, probably in his thirties. Arch could see his eyes, and they were dark, brows arched low in a permanent state of suspicion, and focused entirely on him from where Ross stood just on the other side of the sheriff's station counter. Sure enough, his ID read GARRETT ROSS. Arch looked at it with a little suspicion of his own.

"Martinson." His partner thrust her ID out. She was blond, heavyset, in her twenties. Looked like she'd be hell to go up against on a football field, in Arch's opinion, way worse than Ross. Her ID read EVELYN MARTINSON. She still had her sunglasses on and stood a head shorter than Ross.

Arch tilted around to look at Guthrie and Duncan, who were standing by the coffee pot. "FBI IDs. You see that?"

"I'm not blind," Guthrie shot back immediately. "Yeah, I saw it."

"Just making sure it wasn't my tired eyes reading more into them than was there," Arch said, catching the amused burn from Guthrie's gaze. What he'd really been asking was if these FBI IDs were secretly like the OOC IDs, complete with some sort of mind control spell. He turned back around to Martinson and Ross, trying to remember which was which. Ross was the guy. "What can I do for you fine folks from Washington?"

If Ross heard an unwelcoming note in Arch's voice, he didn't let on. "We're here to investigate the sudden rise in crime in this area."

Arch just looked at the man. "Oh, are you?" He wasn't a very sarcastic person by nature, but this he couldn't help. "Well ... good."

"Could we speak with your sheriff?" Martinson asked. She didn't look like she was very patient. Not a smile from either of them yet.

"You could ... if he hadn't been murdered a couple weeks ago," Arch said. He cast a look over his shoulder again. Just about everyone that was here was watching this exchange—the OOCs, Casey, sitting at the dispatch desk, even Benny Binion, who had just gotten off shift to be replaced by Casey.

Martinson and Ross exchanged a look. Which was which again? *Ross was the guy, Ross was the guy*, Arch tried to burn that into his memory. It'd be awfully embarrassing if he called Martinson by her partner's name.

"We having an acting sheriff," Arch said. "She's out at a crime scene right now." He looked over his shoulder at Casey, who nodded. "Be back shortly, I expect."

"She's on her way now," Casey said.

"Maybe you can answer a couple questions for us in the meantime, Deputy Stan," Martinson said, leaning her heavy frame onto the counter, elbows first. "How many murders have you had in this area in the last few months?"

Arch didn't even try and tally that one up. "More than I can count."

"That seem a little funny to you?" Ross got in on the leaning act. "Having that many people die?"

Arch kept his cool. "Well, I've known a lot of these folks my whole life, so ... no, I don't find it particularly funny. What I do find funny is that after we've been screaming about it for months, y'all finally decided to show up now. Better late than never, I suppose."

The agents exchanged another look. Then Martinson took up the questioning again. "To what do you attribute this rise in violence?" she asked.

How best to answer that one? "To persons doing evil things," Arch said, "in increased numbers."

Another exchanged look. Ross picked up the baton. "Do you have any idea who the culprits are?"

"For every single murder? No." Arch crossed his arms.

"We've looked at your booking records," Martinson said. Her blouse was undone one button too far, and Arch had to look away. With the leaning and the crossing of her arms in front of her, she was showing him more than he cared to see. He didn't know if she was oblivious to this fact, or just wanted to make him uncomfortable, but either way, he didn't want to look right at her, and he didn't. "You haven't made a single arrest, haven't pressed charges against a single criminal for any of these killings."

It was awfully hard to prosecute a demon, Arch didn't dare say. He sat there in silence instead; what else could he do? Lie? "We're probably in a little over our heads," he finally admitted in lieu of telling falsehood.

Martinson and Ross traded another look. This time they both smiled. "Who's in charge now?" Ross asked.

"Deputy Erin Harris," Arch said, trying to stifle the burning feeling that was stuck in his craw. "She's on her way back right now. Shouldn't be too long, because she drives like a bat out of Hades."

"Who are your friends back there?" Martinson asked, nodding at Guthrie, Duncan and Casey.

"Casey's on dispatch," Arch said, "and as for those two ..."

"We're with the Bureau of Alcohol, Tobacco and Firearms,"

Guthrie said, taking a few steps forward and flashing her ID. "Guthrie and Duncan."

Martinson and Ross both stared at the badge. Neither evinced much reaction to it, though Ross finally said, "Okay." And that was that.

"Your dispatcher is a civilian?" Martinson asked, eyes on Arch again.

"Times are tough," Arch said. "We've got a lot of civilians pitching in right now."

"Where are the rest of your deputies?" Ross asked.

"Well, one got murdered," Arch said, "one quit the force ... and that's about it for this end of the county. All we got left is auxiliary deputies."

Another look traded. Arch wasn't ridiculously impatient, but these two were slowly making him crazy him with the looks. It reminded him of how he and Alison used to do that, talk without talking.

Ouch. That one still drew a pang.

Through the plexiglass doors, past the agents, Arch saw motion as the Ford Explorer he'd been using for months now came squealing by on Jackson Highway, turning into the parking lot, lights flashing. They flipped off and it came to a stop as the SUV rolled up just outside. Erin was out in a hot second, slamming the door and galloping up to the entry. He watched her smooth at her mussed hair, the blond locks tangled because she really hadn't seemed to care much about her looks with a war on. She came in a hustlin', hurrying to get that door open and into the lobby, the heating unit above it whirring to life and belching out a blast of hot air as she came in, messing her hair up even further.

"Erin Harris," she said, coming up to the agents at the counter with a spring in her step. She extended her hand to the guy, first, who shook it, then the woman, who looked at it like she was being handed a dead fish.

"What, are you twelve?" Martinson asked, ignoring the proffered hand.

"Yeah, I'm twelve," Erin said, taking the gibe in stride. She was young. Nineteen? Maybe twenty now, Arch thought, trying to remember if he'd missed her birthday somewhere in all this demon mess of the last few months. "Twelve, and running the household in the absence of strong parental figures." Her jaw ended up clenched. "So ... would you care to step into my office and discuss the, uh ... shitstorm going on around here?"

Martinson and Ross looked across the counter at him, a kind of *Seriously?* duo of looks. "She's the lady in charge," Arch said, "you'll be wanting to talk with her, I expect?"

"I'm starting to see the genesis of some of your problems," Ross said, the older man almost leering at Erin, then Arch, in turn.

"I doubt it," Arch said. He looked right at Erin, trying to trade the kind of look with her that Martinson and Ross had so effectively used to communicate.

All he saw was anger, and she wasn't looking at him. "Right this way," she said, heading for Reeve's old office, the two FBI agents following after. Arch debated with himself and finally landed on an answer—

Yeah. He wasn't sitting this out. These people had come loaded with confrontational attitudes, and they seemed like they'd have no problem tag teaming Erin.

"Keep an eye on the desk, will you?" he asked Guthrie as he passed.

"What do I look like to you, a secretary?" Guthrie shot back. There might have been some good-natured sarcasm in there somewhere, but Arch had no time for it.

"You look a little like my mother, actually," Arch said. "Mind doing my laundry while you're at it?"

"Best watch out, big boy," Guthrie said with a savage grin, "I might mess up and put some itching powder in your jock strap. You'll end up scratching at it so much you might accidentally pleasure yourself."

"Hell of a professional environment you're running here," Martinson observed as she cast a look over her shoulder at Arch and Guthrie.

"Well, it's just like with the feds," Erin said, eyes burning but a smooth smile cracking her lips. "You can't tell them shit." She closed the door behind Arch as he came in, and from the way Martinson's eyes lit up, Arch had a feeling this meeting was going to be … interesting.

*

"Mom," Gary Wrightson said as he wheeled himself in the door, the squeak of the mechanicals pushing down the garage door outside. "Ma!" He raised his voice when she didn't answer.

"I'm in the shitter, what do you want?" Mary Wrightson shouted, muffled, coming from the door to his left.

Gary paused, giving his weary arms a rest as he parked the wheelchair outside the bathroom door. It was just in the entry, and he pulled off his work boots and cast them aside. The nice thing about being in a wheelchair was his shoes didn't get too dirty and didn't need replacing as often as they had before he'd been paralyzed. It did matter whether he left them on or not, though, cuz damn if having his feet covered didn't still overheat the shit out of his ass. Still smelled, too. "I wanna talk, duh."

"So talk," his mother's voice came through the door. "If you can't hold your damned water long enough for me to wipe and come out."

Gary did not define himself as a patient man. Patient men were losers who waited for the fruits of victory to fall in their little bitch mouths. That wasn't Gary. Gary went out and seized life and victory by the goddamned plums. Waiting for wins to come your way was like expecting a nipple to just drop between your lips. Getting out there and finding a woman to sit on your lap would make it happen a lot quicker. "Talked to my employees today about this whole demon thing and how it's fucking my business in its tender ass."

"Oh yeah?" Mary Wrightson raised her voice to make herself heard, but she sounded like she was yelling at him.

Gary felt a pang of rumbling hunger in his belly. "Yeah," he said, wheeling on past the bathroom door into the kitchen to satiate himself. Food didn't drop into one's mouth by itself any more readily than a fine breast did. So off he went to seek it. "Marina was pretty on board. That girl's efficiency is coming right up, by God. Ulysses is still as goddamned useless as tits on a boarhound."

"He's old," Mary shouted. "What do you expect? Old people get fucking useless, and old men are the worst. Women that age at least still got a drive to get shit done. Old boys, I swear—unless they're taking them some Viagra, it's like all their momentum just vanishes along with their sex drive."

Gary nodded. It didn't surprise him that men's utility was tied up in the potency of their block and tackle. He'd read the Napoleon Hill masterwork *Think and Grow Rich* about a billion times, and Hill made it a central thesis that having a highly sexed nature was integral to a man's success. That was just as logical to Gary as night following day. After all, if you weren't motivated to go get laid, which was man's first, most urgent desire, how likely was it you'd be motivated to do any other of the damned things further down the list? "Still disappointing," Gary shouted, wheeling himself through the extra wide door into the pantry. "Motherfucker wouldn't lift a hand to save his useless ass if I was wheeling him up a ramp to throw him in a chipper shredder, which—fucker ever ends up leeching that unemployment insurance I have to pay—I might just do it. If I thought I could get away with it. Useless motherfucker."

"You can't get mad at useless people. I mean, you can, but it don't help." The flush of the toilet sounded, the smooth rush of water moving in perfect rhythm into the reserve tank as the bowl drained. Gary didn't truck with these new, bullshit, low-flow toilets. It may have been a moneymaker for him, having to constantly unclog those suckers, which were clearly designed for the micro rabbit turds of beta-male soyboy vegan cuck bitches, but he'd tracked down some pre-owned, high-flow classics for his house. Toilets designed to dispose of the massive, meat-filled dumps of an apex predator and carnivore confident in his place at the top of the food chain.

"I can and I will, useless or not," Gary muttered, pulling a box of precooked bacon off the shelf. Twenty seconds in the microwave and he'd be eating a little slice of porcine heaven. Or eight. He wheeled backward out of the pantry and spun, heading for the microwave and pulling a paper plate as he did so. Bedding the bottom of the plate with a paper towel, he ripped open the box, then the plastic and layered the bacon on the plate, then slapped another paper towel on top and put it in the microwave for twenty.

The toilet flushed again, and his mother emerged a moment later, drying her hands on a towel and then tossing it over her shoulder blind. His mom was many things, but a great housekeeper was not among them. "Some men are born great, some men have greatness thrust upon them, but most don't ever even achieve the middling level of being able to so much as tie their own shoes without faceplanting like the fuckups they are. That don't make 'em bad people—it just makes 'em people you have to deal with sometimes."

"Don't I know it." Gary watched the plate spin in the microwave, lit by the orange glow of the bulb within. "That's my customer base, after all. Good people, fine people, within their own little parameters. I admire them better from a distance, where I can't see the cracks in the facade. Ulysses, though—I see that motherfucker up close, and it's all cracks and no facade these days. He has suctioned himself to my ass and is plunging my wallet for all it's worth. I keep running the numbers, and he's a middling asset at best. Maybe even a liability, because he keeps getting worse and worse. If I'm going into this demon-fighting thing, though—at your behest, I might add—I don't think he's the kind of person I want to rely on."

"Well, you ain't got to," his mother said. "There's a whole bunch of people already fighting this fight. You just get in your van and roll it on over to the sheriff's station on Old Jackson Highway, and—"

"I am a general of men, Momma," Gary said as the microwave beeped and he popped it open. The smell of sweet bacon filled the air. "I go rolling up there now, without anyone on my team, and—

they're going to laugh me out of the place. 'Oh, a guy in a wheelchair. Why don't you just sit back here at headquarters and do a desk job, making make some calls for us.'" He tore savagely into the first slice of bacon, ire rising. "Trust me on this. I've been dealing with this ableist bullshit since I was eighteen." He waved the half-bitten piece of bacon in front of her. "But if I go in there with my own squad already started ... nobody puts this badass Baby in a corner, you know what I'm saying?"

His mother's eyes fluttered as she rolled them. "Son, people might take you a hair more seriously if—"

"IF I WASN'T IN A WHEELCHAIR?!"

"If you didn't quote *Dirty Dancing*," his mother finished, undeterred by his outburst.

"Well, fuck that," Gary said. "That's just a damned good movie. Fuck the haters. I'm my own man, I go my own way, by God, I blaze my own trail with these two wheels." He ate the other half of the piece of bacon and rolled himself over to the plate to grab another.

His mother let out a long sigh. "I know you ain't likely to listen to me on this, but I'm a gonna say it anyway. You—you, my son—my boy—"

"Oh, fer fuck's sake, Momma, get to it. Sugarcoating it ain't going to make the shit medicine taste any sweeter."

"Well, actually, by definition, sugar would make any medicine taste sweeter, shit or otherwise—"

"Fucking get to it, Momma."

"You got a chip on your shoulder, boy," she said. "It predates the wheelchair, but most people didn't know you well enough as a child to realize that. I do. Your brothers do. But most people? Not a clue. So they look at this scrappy man on wheels, taking no shit from nobody—you know, save for when you gotta drain a poop-clogged toilet—and they think it's got something to do with your injury. When really, it's just you are an ornery son of a bitch. And I mean that in the most literal way possible, because your momma—"

"You are hell on no wheels," Gary said, cradling the plate of bacon.

"Damned skippy, and the whole county knows it," Mary said. "But, son ... I ain't never been a mover and shaker around here. Your daddy made the money, had the bosses, dealt with the people. I never did. Never had to, which was good because anyone who tried to boss me around, paycheck or not, was going to end up with a smack upside the head that—if he was lucky—wouldn't include something metal and heavy being in my hand at the time. But you—you're your own boss. You answer to the customer, and you're real good at putting a sweet face on things when you gotta. That said—"

"Aw, this oughta be a devastating attack on my character after all that nice buildup."

"—you are a grade A fucking prick sometimes, son. You could be a mover and a shaker if you applied that sweetness of dealing with customers to these people trying to save our town and our county." She nodded at him. "You got a gift, boy. You ought not squander it by being as goddamned ornery as your mother. If you gotta rally your employees so you can go in there with a squad—well, you do that if it helps make you feel like a big man, and helps you make the contribution to this effort you think best fits. Fucking do it. Go big."

Gary squeezed the wheelchair arm. "Well ... I do generally go around feeling like I could use a height advantage every now and again."

"If you're worried that they're going to take you in and just make you some desk jockey cog in the machine—well, I'd say that's fair. Cuz they ain't seen you roll the 400 meter dash in your chair. Turn that motherfucker into a holy instrument and put some spikes on the wheels—"

"That's really how they kill demons? I gotta get me some holy weapons."

"—you'd flat up show them all. But my point is, Gary—you need to get in on this. Saving our town, our home? It's more important than what role you end up with. Though I'm sure you'll do great things regardless of where in there you get placed."

"Ain't no lead dog like me going to be content watching the asses of the other dogs after running his own destiny for so long," Gary said. "That no-scenery bullshit? Ain't going to fly. I know you say that maybe it don't matter if I get desk jockeyed, but dammit, Momma—that ain't me. I'll go to them, you watch—but I'll do it my way." He nodded once, swiftly.

She stared at him, inscrutable. "Well, all right then. But do me a favor?"

Gary's eyes narrowed. "What?"

"Take your brothers with you?"

"Fuck, no, Momma—those peckerwoods—"

"Gary ... take your brothers with you." She put a hand on his arm, and for a second he thought she might wrestle with him over the bacon plate. But she didn't, which was good because that might just be the death of her. "If you need a posse, they'll hang with you long after your cheesedick employees leave you behind. Especially that impotent Ulysses bitch. A demon gets so much as one nip of his wrinkly ass, he's going to start offering toothless blowjobs to any hellspawn that'll let him loose. That useless motherfucker would collaborate with the goddamned Commies, I know it in my heart."

Gary nodded slowly. "He is a union man, I'd say." Still ... his brothers. Ugh. But ... blood was thicker than water and all that shit. "All right ... I'll call 'em." And he pulled his cell phone out of his pocket and found the first contact on the list he'd need. When it answered, he launched right in, because who had time to waste? "Terry? It's Gary, your brother. We need to talk."

*

"The sin of these fallen creatures oozes and reeks, the stench defiling what was once a pure earth," Brackessh said, staring out the window of the car as it rattled along, his new servant beside him at the wheel. He was a faithful servant, too, would be more faithful than any corrupt and fallen creature could be, now that all the instruments of his sin had been removed from his body.

The servant nodded. There was little he could add, after all.

"At the beginning of days, I was there," Brackessh said, "when your race was new and free and ... innocent. But, oh you fell, as did my own brethren. Sin. That corrupting knowledge, of all the things you did that went against the will of ... well ..."

The twist of emotion rolled through Brackessh, his shell quivering as he stared out the car window, sun beaming down on a cold tableau of dead, skeletal trees stretched over a winding road. Brown fields lay beyond, sun-dappled and dead, winter settling upon them like twilight upon a day.

It was a cycle, was it not? Death and life? But unlike in the fields, when death came, life did not follow again—no, no. It was all death, from then on. The pits, perhaps. Other fates. Brackessh had tasted those places, been cast to those places, once, before receiving a shell and clawing out to here. There was a darkness to it, a chill. Death beyond death, but no life beyond death, not for anyone so afflicted by ... sin.

Sin.

"We will purge it, you and I," Brackessh said, touching his servant on the shoulder. He could, barely, feel the howling thoughts within, the ones from before, when sin had been on this creature's mind. Sin and nothing but. Such flimsy things, these humans, man. Slaves to their impulses—to one impulse above all.

Desire. What a fickle thing.

"This is simpler, is it not?" he asked his new servant. A nod was his reward. "Of course. Freed from the fleshly desires ... now your thoughts harmonize with my own. Now ... you can be a solution to the problem rather than caught endlessly in it yourself ..."

"... How?" came the strangled voice from his servant, surprising Brackessh. He stared into the dark eyes of the man—though he was hardly a man now, no will of his own. Sin ... sin had darkened these creatures. Purge the sin into a scapegoat, slaughter it, remove the temptation to sin again ... a simple cycle, but one that would free mankind ...

"By making every one of your brethren as great as you," Brackessh said, simply. "Turn here." And the servant did, steering the car down the dirt side road. "We will become ... more ... together ... and we will make great things happen."

And perhaps, if Brackessh and his servants did enough good here, perhaps, just perhaps, he might ... finally ... be allowed to go home.

3.

The bank of the Caledonia River wound through the park, the water low against the shore, a cold biting chill coming off the water and sending Bonnie Tiller's skin into what felt like full-body nippling. Not to mention her actual nipples, which could do a boffo job of cutting glass right now. She shivered and thrust her hands deeper in her jacket pockets, trying to turn her face away from the wind.

It didn't help much.

These midday walks along the banks of the Caledonia were the only thing that let Bonnie cope. It was the last remnant of her old routine that she clung to, a last bit of grace from the good times in Midian, before …

Well, before everything went to hell.

Before Halloween on the town square turned into a massacre, before giant demon cats started tear-assing through country homes, before some immense lump of demon flesh ten feet tall ripped through the flanks of town, leaving a tornado-like trail of devastation in its wake …

Yeah. Before all that.

Bonnie liked to remember those days. Back when she'd just been a carefree twentysomething trying to find a job that could keep her busy and maybe put a little money in her pocket. She'd been unemployed for nearing a year now, enjoying the free time that came with that and a steady unemployment check. It didn't exactly make ends meet, but with it plus her credit cards—gosh, the balances were getting high on those—she made it. Always telling herself that when she got back to work, she'd shrink those balances in no time.

But she'd passed on a couple of jobs she didn't really care for. Bartender? The hours sucked. Waitress, same, plus you got to deal with people being assholes or pinching your ass. Bonnie wasn't that much of a people person. Bonnie was more a cat person.

It'd all work out, though. She was sure of that. And the daily walks along the bank of the Caledonia around noon, an hour after she woke up, helped cement that in her head.

The breeze blew through, pleasant, if chilly, and she shivered again. She listened to the whipping sound of the wind, the chop of the waters as they lapped the stones at the shore.

Listened to the ... meowing?

Bonnie looked around. She could have sworn she heard meowing, but ... maybe it was her imagination. She had cats at home, she was probably just mentally dragging them into her walk. Kitreena and Felucius were the names of her cats. They were waiting at home, lazing their days away. She could sympathize.

But she could swear she heard ...

There it was again. The sound of a meow.

Bonnie looked down the bank. Had it come from this direction? She furrowed her brow, squinting into the distance. There was a thick line of trees obscuring part of her view, but it sounded like it was coming from up—

There! She saw the cat, high up on a tree branch, extended over the river and dangling. It meowed again, a beautiful black and white long-haired tabby, legs curled up beneath it as it sat there, eyes almost beseechingly on a man who was standing beneath it.

"Here, kitty," he said quietly, holding out his hands. He looked like he was trying to beckon it away from the edge.

The wind came through again, sending that chill through Bonnie, templing the bumps across her skin. A subtle cracking noise issued from the tree branch with the cat upon it, and Bonnie hurried forward as the man jumped up and grabbed the tree and started to climb. He seemed to be trying to get to the cat before the branch finished cracking under its weight.

Bonnie's heart thumped heavily. "Ohmigod," she whispered, and ran off the path, down to the bank, threading between the other trees that lay between her and the unfolding drama.

The man climbed up the tree trunk with relative ease. He had strong, bulging muscles, dark hair. "It's okay, kitty," he said in a soothing voice that Bonnie heard so clearly as she reached the base of the tree. "It's okay," he said again as he got to a fork in the trunk and paused, bracing himself. "Here, kitty. Come on. Come on in before that branch breaks and you end up drowning in the river. Come on." He rubbed his forefinger and middle finger together the way Bonnie did at home, trying to entice the cat in.

The tabby kept its legs carefully underneath itself but did not ease any closer to him. How could it not feel the danger of the branch? Bonnie wondered. The wind picked up again, rustling the trees, and swaying the one the cat was on.

Another crack issued.

Bonnie's heart nearly stopped. Her hand flew to her chest, her mouth open.

She couldn't even find anything to say.

"Come on, kitty," the man said, and she could hear the desperation in his voice. He could see where this was going—the cat was going to end up in the water soon, so soon—

The man reached out and climbed up another few feet, putting himself at face level with the branch. He was getting close, now, the cat only twenty or so feet in front of him. But he'd never be able to climb all the way out to the cat—

The wind picked up again, and the branch cracked once more, bowing even more dramatically now. The cat let out a hiss and a cry as it dug claws into the tree bark in a mad bid to hold on.

"No, no, no!" the man shouted, grabbing at the bough and holding it, as though he could keep it and the cat from plunging into the icy waters of the Caledonia below. "It's okay," he repeated, once he had his hands on the branches.

Bonnie, standing twenty feet below and feeling miles away, helpless to help, doubted it was anything approaching okay.

There was no way this man could hold the branch and keep the cat from falling into the river. And it was so cold! The poor kitty ... it would ...

A strangled little noise issued from Bonnie's throat. She could scarcely imagine watching this, but she was rooted to the spot, a spectator without any ability to affect the scene as it played out before her.

The branch cracked once more—one last time—and the man let out a little shout as it started to dip even further—

"No!" Bonnie shouted.

The branch began to fall, dropping slowly toward the river, taking up a forty-five-degree angle toward the water. This was it; the cat was going to plunge into the icy waters, to drift its beautiful black and white fur beneath the current and—

The bough ... stopped moving.

The man had it, gripped tightly in both hands. It had definitely broken loose from the tree, but somehow ...

He'd caught it.

He'd saved the cat.

"It's okay," the man said, bringing the branch in toward him, slowly, trying not to jar the kitty loose. "It's okay, little darlin', I've got you ..." He brought it in, slowly, slowly, until the cat was now safely over the bank. Then, shifting the branch to one hand, the tip wobbling slightly, he brought it in closer, bringing the tip subtly up in order to balance the kitty the closer it got to him.

Bonnie let out a breath of relief. "Oh, thank God," she said, staring up at the man. He really was handsome. Maybe a little more so because of what he'd just done.

He brought the branch in with tender, loving care. The kitty was still holding on tight, claws probably dug in. "It's okay," the man said again. The branch was tilted up at a forty-five-degree angle now, and the man was carefully bringing it in through a nice little gap where there were no branches on either side to get in the way. The cat, for its part, was angled, just trying to hold on, as the man raised the branch up even more slightly, and kept pulling in the branch, one hand over the other, as though dragging in a rope length by length.

"Just like that," the man said softly. "Just like that. It's okay, kitty. It's all okay."

It really was okay, Bonnie thought. She felt like she could breathe again.

"It's okay," the man said, the tip of the branch with the cat on it rising again. Now that he had leverage, he was raising the branch up. The cat was angled above him at ninety degrees, then one-twenty. Bonnie peered up; that was a little strange. Was he trying to keep the cat from jumping to another branch, or—?

"Nice kitty," the man said, and his mouth started to twist. "Nice kitty."

His jaw seemed to unhook from its normal position, opening wide, chin touching his throat as it dropped open. The man lifted his head up, maw gaping like a character from the old cartoons. His chin separated into two, lips blowing out like a puffer fish and expanding so that his mouth was—God, it was huge, two feet, three feet in diameter—and he kept raising the tree branch with the cat on it—

The kitty jumped and slid, claws finally losing purchase as the angle got too steep. Bonnie's heart leapt as the cat fell. It could make it, it could dodge, it could—

The man's neck seemed to dip sideways alarmingly fast, reminding her of a lizard shooting its tongue out and snagging a fly. But in this case, his whole head zipped two feet to the side and the cat disappeared into his open lips, wide eyes vanishing as the mouth snapped shut like a Venus flytrap—

"NOOOO!" Bonnie screamed the last hissing scream of the cat cut off midway replaced with the sound of crunching flesh and bone. The man's jaws worked powerfully, then his head snapped around black eyes following to her, locking on Bonnie as she stood there under the tree.

"How ... how could you ...?" Her mouth drifted open, as though she could unhook her own jaw to gape.

The man just stared at her for a moment, his jaw still working.

Then he swallowed. And his lips came open again.

Nothing was there ... but blackness.

"Nice girl," he rasped, and his jaw started to unhook again. This time Bonnie saw it head-on, blinking at what had once been such a handsome face ...

His neck moved, swiftly, like the jumping of a snake at prey, and Bonnie didn't even have time to run before the jaws reached her and clamped on, the wash of the river, the chill of the breeze, and the sunlit day disappearing, forever, into darkness, as she followed the cat.

*

Erin took her seat and stared at the feds. Ross and Martinson. Unremarkable man, heavyset woman. Other than that, Erin had a hard time distinguishing them. "Get you a Coke?" she asked.

Ross and Martinson traded a look. Martinson answered. "You mean an actual Coke? Because I prefer Pepsi."

Erin looked at the woman. The FBI agent didn't have an inch of yield in her flinty eyes. "We can probably swing that," she said. "And you?" she looked at Ross. "Coffee? Tea? Anything?" *An enema to dislodge that stick from your ass?* She kept that one to herself. For now.

"No thanks," Ross said. Erin watched his eyes, he watched hers; maybe he didn't trust that the coffee in a small-town sheriff's station would be to his liking. Maybe he thought they'd try and poison him.

Didn't matter either way. "Casey," Erin said, hitting the call button on her phone, "see if you can track down a Pepsi for Agent Martinson." Erin smiled at the lady agent. She did not get one in return.

"You're awfully young to be in charge of a sheriff's department in the middle of a crisis, aren't you?" Ross asked. Erin shifted her gaze to him; so he was going to be the bad cop here. Probably figured she was too young to know how this worked.

"Well, the shit hit the fan and I was the one who raised her hand to do it," Erin said, trying to smile sweetly as she said it. "If somebody else had ... their lucky ass'd be sitting in this chair." Wouldn't be lucky, though.

Martinson turned her head to look at Arch, who was standing quietly behind the door. Both agents were standing perpendicular to him, and their hands were damned close to their holsters, which rested obviously on their hips. Neither one seemed very comfortable, which made a certain amount of sense. If Erin had been the outsider coming in, nothing about the situation in Midian would have seemed reasonable to her—but police corruption would be right at the top of her explanation list. How else did you explain hundreds of murders and not one single collar? "You didn't want the job?" Martinson asked Arch.

"I was grieving at the time," Arch said, even more stiffly than usual. "My wife was killed last month, see. Erin's doing a fine job."

"Mmhm," Martinson said, looking again at Ross. Erin could almost read what passed between them this time—deputy loses wife, still no arrests. Is that because the deputy killed his wife? It was a game of connect the dots, and Erin doubted any of the dots led to "The demons did it." Which was a shame, since it was the truth. "Any suspects?" Martinson asked instead.

Subtle she wasn't; Arch's face tensed at the implication. "I reckon—"

Arch didn't do lying, and that was a problem. "We have a suspect," Erin cut in. "He's in the holding cell right now." True enough; the *body* responsible for Alison's death was still in the holding cell. Gradually getting around to talking more, too, though he was hardly a chatty Cathy, even now. Mostly nonsensical, and what sense he did make ... didn't sound real good.

"That's not in any of the reported data," Martinson said.

"We've been busy," Erin said, smiling sweetly. "Too busy to report to TBI or to y'all." *Nor are we fucking required to*, she didn't bother to add. Being sheriff wasn't her job, but that much she did know. Lots of departments didn't report shit to the feds. They weren't the boss of anyone, and murder wasn't even a federal crime. The Tennessee Bureau of Investigation had jurisdiction here if they wanted to snatch it, and she hadn't heard shit out of Nashville since that time a demon had created a wreck so nasty it shut down the entire interstate. Hell, that had even been a local response, from the nearest Tennessee Highway Patrol post.

Another traded look between the feds. That was getting old. "It's hard to understand what's going on out here," Ross said, looking back at Erin. "You've got a murder rate that makes Baltimore or New

Orleans look like a sunny day at Rockaway Beach. That maybe makes the Old West look idyllic. You might even be safer walking through the streets of Baghdad naked, with a sandwich board saying, 'Infidel' on one side and 'Muhammed was a pedophile' on the other. While burning a Koran."

"Nice touch," Erin said. "You think that'd get you stoned? Or jailed?"

"Dead either way," Arch said. That man was taut, arms folded in front of him, hanging out behind the door.

"At least in Baghdad, I have the option to cover my head and not wear a stupid sign. Here ... what do you do to keep from getting slaughtered? What are the risk factors?" Martinson asked. Her voice was thick, like her, but it seemed like a genuine inquiry, in spite of the brusqueness of her bearing.

"Well ..." Erin started to say, then a thought occurred and she pushed the button on her phone just as it beeped. "Casey—" she started to say, then realized he must have been calling in to her while she was calling out to him.

"We got a call about some shit in progress out on Warner Pike," Casey said. "Fred Mickelson ... he was sounding pretty tore up about it."

Erin frowned. Fred Mickelson was a dour old man who didn't emote in public, other than to scowl and crab. If he was 'tore up' about something ...

"Your dispatcher doesn't sound very professional," Ross said.

"That's because he's an amateur," Erin said, springing to her feet. "Unpaid." Sort of. Not paid much, at least. It was nearly a labor of love, being in the watch. "Y'all want to see what's going on around here?" Erin caught the slight nod from Martinson and Ross. "Well, come on then. We'll show you." And she beat feet out the door, which Arch held open for her, waiting for the two feds to follow.

*

"What the hell are you doing here?" Darla asked as Marischa Pike, her mother-in-law, strolled in, leaving her suitcase on the doorstep like she expected some servant to come along and collect it. Darla gave it a quick eyeballing, then pretended she didn't see it and closed the door behind her. Hell if she was going to bring the cunt's suitcase in.

"What does 'hell' mean, Mommy?" Jay asked as grandma strolled in, patting him on the head and that was all. "Hi, Grandma." Kids were adaptable. Jay had long ago realized grandma wasn't a hugger.

"Gramma!" Mera's articulation left something to be desired, but Darla cared fuck-all about correcting her right now. Seeing her mother-in-law was quite enough for her to deal with. Mera came streaking across the floor and caught Marischa at the knee.

"Oh, you're getting so big," Marischa said, patting Mera on the head as well, and then withdrawing to her full height while looking subtly displeased at the touch and the weight added around her limb. Mera held on.

"Mera, let your grandma go," Darla said, just keeping herself from adding, *You know she doesn't like it when you love on her, the dry old bitch.* "What are you doing here, Marischa?"

Marischa spun on her. "How can you even ask me that?" Her Botoxed face was as inflexible as always, and her bobbed hair was perfectly coiffed. "My son is dead. He died here, in these hinterlands. So I am here, in this ... place," her distaste dripped like acid off her tongue, "because ..." She stared right at Darla, "... I'm needed. For the children." And she brushed against little Mera's hair, but only for a second before withdrawing her hand as though it had been tainted somehow.

Darla just stared at her. What did you say to that? Which part to even begin with? The unconvincing bit about her son, or the strangely misplaced desire to "help?" Which Darla didn't believe. Marischa was about as useful as a second anus. You really only needed the one. "You're going to help?" she asked.

"I am," Marischa sniffed. "And ... I just couldn't imagine staying in Chicago and going through all this ... grief ... alone."

Grief. Sure. She was just draped in it, along with Chanel No. 5.

Quick thinking was Darla's greatest advantage. She diagnosed what was going on here, or at least reasonably supposed. Marischa and her son hadn't exactly been close. She'd never been here to visit them before. They didn't get to Chicago to visit her very often—maybe once every two years? There was little to no phone contact. Hell, when Darla had called to inform her about Jason's death, it had been a two-minute conversation.

"Marischa? Jason ... he's dead."

Silence. Some muttered pleasantries. A dial tone less than ninety seconds later.

Grief? Sure, okay. Darla could see that, maybe. Maybe Marischa was just the worst person in the world at expressing grief.

Or, more likely, her husband had gotten his sociopathic disregard for humanity from his mother. Which meant her being here was ... posturing.

Darla sighed. Like she needed this shit right now.

But what was she going to do? Toss the woman out the door? In the scale of things, it might not matter, but it'd damned sure raise a red flag or two. With whom? Hell if Darla even knew anymore. But she needed eyes on her actions like she needed a good fucking in the ass—not at all, at least right now.

"Thanks for coming," she said, pasting on a smile right out of the book of one of these stupid cunt southern belles that were so ubiquitous around here, hating herself even as she did so. She did keep the "bless your heart," to herself, though. Even someone as oblivious as Marischa might catch the sarcasm.

But she could carry her own fucking luggage in.

*

"I want to thank y'all for coming out here today," Gary said, addressing the little assemblage in front of him. He was behind his desk in his office, his three brothers and momma all sitting or standing before him. Momma sitting, Paul sitting, Terry and Larry on their feet. Larry looked bored as hell, already checking his watch. Dark hair, dark beard, he looked he was going to bolt and join the Taliban any second.

"Hell, it wasn't like we had anything else to do," Terry said, thin, utterly insincere smile pasted on his chubby-cheeked baby face. Terry was a salesman, a go-getter. Gary respected that—up to a point.

Gary nodded along at that. Business was tough around here for everybody right now, except maybe the funeral home directors. He made a mental note to look into that business, see what the entry costs were. Demand had to be pretty good, especially now, but probably even at its baseline it was a steady business, he imagined.

"Yeah, thanks for including me in this," Paul said resentfully. He was the other middle child, just a couple years older than Terry. He was resentful about every fucking thing. "Not like I didn't have other shit to be doing today."

"I knew you wouldn't," Gary said, ignoring the sarcasm and purposefully rubbing it on in just to grind Paul's gears.

Larry looked at his watch again. He was the baby of the family, using to being accommodated. "Can we, uh … get on with this shit? Whatever it is?"

Terry perked up a little. "Is this about Momma's estate? Are we going to pick out the stuff we want with Post-It notes or something? You know, to keep from fighting after she's gone?"

"My house got wrecked by demons weeks ago, dipshit," Mary said, turning around and looking at him. "Ain't a damned thing left to put a Post-It note on, 'less you want some salvage to haul away." Like an afterthought, she reached out swatted him across the back, right around the kidney. Never even saw it coming.

"Ow, Momma!" Terry said, flinching, holding his side. Momma didn't pull her slaps, Gary knew from hard experience. It wasn't as easy to dodge them in a wheelchair, either, which had taught him to control his smartass mouth, at least when it was pointed at her.

"This ain't about estate planning," Gary said, "or business. This is about this town, about this county, and about the shit that cost us our inheritance, cuz I think we all know by the way she hits us up for cash in turn, Momma ain't got much of a pot to piss in—and now no window to throw it out of."

"You ingrate shitbirds!" Mary shouted. She tensed as though she were going to rise out of the chair, come over the desk, and deliver a much-deserved swatting. Gary prepared himself to wheel backward, but, as he had suspected, she unknotted herself a moment later. If she didn't come at you fast, and she wasn't in range, she'd blow off the steam and give up on getting you. Probably. He might get blindsided later.

"Well, we have taken care of you, Momma," Paul said, shifting back and forth between butt cheeks in his chair. "'Cept for Larry."

"I'm between jobs at the moment," Larry grunted, chewing on a fingernail. "Thanks for pointing it out, big bro."

"Larry's still finding himself," Mary said, "all right?"

"Funny how he never seems to 'find himself' working," Terry said under his breath. Catching a death glare from his mother, he subtly took a step back from her, elbow blocking her from slapping him in the side again.

"He's the baby," Paul said. "She babies him."

"I have about enough of your ungrateful ass," Mary said, snapping her fingers at Paul. "You are treading on dangerous ground, mister."

Paul rolled his eyes and subtly inched his chair away from her, just outside arm's reach. "You gonna send me to my room, Momma? I got my own house, my own job—you know, the things Larry struggles with—"

"You little turd!" She launched out of the chair at him and the whole office snapped into chaos. Paul was on his feet and up against the wall holding out his hands, keeping the chair between the two of them. Terry was trying to mediate, thrusting himself in the middle of it until he got another smack upside the head for his troubles, then he withdrew.

"Well, this just got interesting," Larry said, one eyebrow cocked, still chewing his nail, working it free slowly a millimeter at a time, with patience as he watched the spectacle unfold.

"Goddammit!" Gary banged the desk. "This ain't about who's the baby, or who has a job, or who has the most success in this family—" that was him, no doubt, "—it's about the shit going down around here that's dragging this county down the tubes. We are *Wrightsons*, dammit! We are not sideline sitters, by God—"

"'Cept Larry," Paul muttered, drawing a venomous look from his mother, still separated from him by the chair that he kept between them like a lion tamer keeping his charge off him.

"I got some prospects coming up," Larry said. He always said that.

"—we are the water carriers around here, okay?" Gary was on a roll, and crosstalk wasn't going to derail him. "We make shit happen in Midian and in Calhoun County. Movers and shakers and, by God, earth-quakers. That's the Wrightsons. Pillars of the goddamned community. And our community needs us." He dropped his voice an octave for sincerity's sake. "Our *family* needs us."

"You're tired of Momma squatting in your guest bedroom, ain'tcha?" Paul asked, cracking a smile.

"You are the bitterest damned fruit of my loins, boy!" Mary erupted again. "I should have aborted your ass! With a clothes hanger! And tossed the scraped-ass bits of you into a dumpster!"

"Jesus," Terry said, paling.

"Seems to me," Paul said, looking a little peaked himself, "that going to a proper clinic would have been a bigger favor for you than me, since I'da been dead anyhow." He swallowed like he was trying to keep down breakfast.

"For fuck's sake," Gary breathed. "Look at us. At each other's throats. Daddy'd be pissed if he could see us now."

"She brained him upside the head in a bar fight," Paul said, looking right at Gary with a *Dumbass!* sort of glance. "I doubt he'd fall over with shock at her saying she wished she aborted me. Besides," and here he turned his eyes to his mother. "I've always known she hated me."

"Maybe we should just forget this and get on with the—" Terry said.

"What in the hell have I ever done up to now to convince you I hate your ass?" Mary asked. She was still piping hot.

Other than that abortion shit? Gary thought. Because that was quite enough. "Hey, this ain't productive," he said.

"It's all there in our names, Momma," Paul said with a fake smile. "You're Mary. He's Gary. Terry. Larry. And ... Paul." He pointed at himself, then hummed a few bars of something that sounded to Gary like *One of These Things is Not Like the Other.* "If you'da loved me ... you'd have named me 'Perry.' To fit the rhyme scheme."

"Jesus Christ, boy!" Mary said. "'Perry' is a name for goddamned Frenchmen, all right? You want to be a fucking frog eater? Might as well have just named you 'Pussy.' 'Pussy Wrightson.' Cuz that's what the kids at school would have called you with a goddamned French name on you, boy. And you gave 'em enough reason to call you pussy as it was, and not good ones."

"Fuck's sake, Ma," Gary said, putting a hand up to his face like he could block out this shit show.

"Besides," Mary said, "I didn't know we were going with a rhyming scheme until after Terry came along. I was so fucking hopped up in the hospital from having you—nine pounds, eight ounces, like passing a goddamned rolltop desk out my cooch—I let your dad name you. So don't blame me for that shit. But hell if I'd name you Perry and make you a pussy. Not with my genetics attached." She spat on the floor of Gary's office.

Gary let it pass. Trying to civilize his mother was a task beyond his considerable skills. And motivation. "Okay. We get all that shit out of our systems now?" He looked at Paul, who looked about as happy as a man whose balls had been caught in a Cuisinart set on high.

"No," Paul said.

"She took thirty-plus years to fuck us up—" Terry said.

"Speak for yourself, I ain't thirty yet," Larry said, stopping chewing his fingernail long enough to smile. He was twenty-nine.

"—don't reckon we're going to fix that shit in thirty minutes or less, like a Domino's pizza delivery," Terry said.

"Y'all seem all right to me," Mary grunted, finally backing off the chair between her and Paul, "'cept for being borderline pussies in some cases. But I blame society for that; ain't no stemming the tide of feelings being injected directly up your asses like a gravel enema. This world is getting weak as hell."

Gary puckered his asshole tighter at the thought of a gravel enema. They all did, judging by the way everyone stiffened. "Well, I can't do nothing about the weakness of the world," he said, not disagreeing with her because ... how could you? People these days were weak. They had no guts. They whined about the least little shit. Here he was in a wheelchair, and he'd sooner have that enema than whine like a regular person about the microscopic, first-world problems that defined their existence. *Ermagerd, someone said something mean to me! Ermagerd! Feel sorry for me! My feeeeeeelings!* Not him, by God. He was busy achieving shit. Like excellence in plumbing.

"Well, can't do nothing about that," Gary said, trying to break the spell. He sensed everyone in the room thinking along the same track. "But this shit in this county—we can take action here. Momma's talked to y'all about it—people are doing something about these ... demons." The word still felt curious in his mouth, an air of unreality around it every time he spoke it aloud.

Demon ... Demons ...

Nope, still weird.

"What are we going to do?" Terry asked, his babyface cheeks like a squirrel's, filled with nuts.

"We band together," Gary said, slamming his fist on the desk. For emphasis, by God, because this moment needed emphasis. "We join up with this watch. We—"

"Hey, boss," Ulysses said, opening the door to his office and slipping his head and one shoulder in, tilted precariously at a diagonal angle. "Went out on that job you asked me to."

Gary just stared at him. "Can this wait?" He raised his hands to indicate his family—*I'm kind of in the middle of something.*

"I couldn't get enough water to flush the toilets out there," Ulysses plodded on, the ignorant fuck. "This was out on Rudner Road, hooked up to city water so it wasn't a well problem—"

"Goddamit, can't you see I'm in the middle of something, you useless old shit!" Gary just about threw his stapler but caught a look from his momma warning him against it. "Trying to put together a team to address the problems of this town and you are talking my goddamned ear off because you are so fucking incompetent you can't figure out how to check water—never fucking mind! I'll send Marina and she'll figure it out, you efficiency-less fuckstick—"

"No need," Ulysses said, the old man's ire rising in time with Gary's own. "I talked to the client, and they said they were going with Noonan's Plumbing—"

"You fucking useless-ass old bird!" Gary threw the stapler. Ulysses ducked out and it splintered the door frame. Even Larry took a step back, though he didn't stop chewing his fingernail. "It ain't enough that you're worthless—you gotta go costing me customers because you're too goddamned lazy to bother to learn your fucking trade! You Communist sympathizer undermining motherfucker! Take the rest of the goddamned day off and fuck up shit around your own house, you diarrhea turdwagon shitass—" He tossed a paperweight for good measure.

"Get ahold of yourself, Gary!" Mary shouted. "You're acting a fool."

"Big bro needs an HR department," Terry said with a guffaw, but Gary, by God, had no time to deal with his smartass right now.

"You see this shit?" Ulysses's car door slammed in the distance. "It ain't enough we got our business problems to deal with. We got demon infestations going on in this town, eating our customers, ripping up houses with perfectly sound plumbing that might need to be tuned every now and again—this has gone far enough. I want this big problem solved so I can go back to being happy, making money, and going to out Reno for a fun trip every now and again."

"You need to lay off them whores, big bro," Terry said seriously. "They'll get you right in the pecker with that chlamydia."

"Sex workers in the state of Nevada must be tested every single week for STIs and STDs," Gary said, without a blush of shame even as his mother looked at him through slitted eyes. "Larry's going to pick up another five infections at a bar before I get even one, by God—"

"Hey," Larry said with a drip of annoyance, "ain't nobody sleeps with Hannah Finch and don't get a little something for their troubles, you know what I'm saying." Nods all around. "I learned my lesson." He self-consciously scratched his groin. "After ... you know ... a half dozen times." Catching the looks, he threw up his hands. "What? I can't help it if she's really good. She's had lots of practice. The juice is definitely worth the squeeze is all I'm saying."

"Boss," Marina stuck her head in, was momentarily distracted by the dent where he'd thrown the stapler, then was right back on track a second later. "You know how you wanted me to listen to the police scanner?"

Gary felt his annoyance at the interruption fade. "Yeah. And?"

"I got something," Marina said. "Big ruckus on Warner Pike. Calling all hands."

"Fuck yeah!" Gary would have stood and saluted if he could. Instead, he pushed back from the desk and rolled for the door, making Larry jump out of the way or risk losing a toe. "Come on, boys—let's go see what this shit is all about." And he didn't wait to see if they were going to follow. He knew they would, by God.

4.

Fred Mickelson had lived alone for years and years, ever since his wife Dottie died. That had been June of 1986.

Not a day went by that he didn't still feel like she was lingering around in the house somehow. In the doilies on the tables, the velvet and cross-stitched pictures on the wall. The old TV cabinet as big as a table with an itty bitty black and white screen built into it. The tuner had only ten channel possibilities. And it hadn't worked since the nineties.

But it was all there, all the same as when Dottie left, and all Fred did was make sure it was lovingly maintained ...

And watch sports. Ballgames. Races. Hell, he'd even caught a cricket match one time when nothing else was on.

He had a garden in the spring and summer. He had a bunch of old books that he'd delve into in the winter. Ludlum, Mitchum, Clancy—they were all right there, on the shelf. He kept himself busy. And that was all he needed.

Fred was sure busy now, though. He'd had a damned stomach virus the last few days, and he was shitting like a goose.

Making his twentieth trip to the bathroom since he'd gotten up, he passed his face in the old, medicine cabinet mirror just inside the bathroom. His toilet was an old porcelain model from decades past. Still worked like a charm. Same cool ivory as the bathtub, though that was new because he'd had to install one of those safety rails for when he got in. As he dropped trow and carefully lowered himself onto the seat, Fred reflected—not for the first time today, as his hemorrhoids were constantly reminding him—that getting old sure did suck.

Dottie might even have been a little lucky she hadn't had to deal with this.

"Ungh," Fred grunted, a little because he was sorry he'd had that unkind thought. And he also grunted because the hemorrhoids were like a hot poker thrust right up his ass. Like someone was trying to turn him into a smuggler for razor blades. Right up the keister.

He shifted from cheek to cheek. It didn't help. "Jesus," he muttered. "Please, Jesus."

That didn't help, either. The sting was biting, just fierce. Felt like someone was grabbing him by the asshole and dethreading his colon a few inches at a time. He wanted to pucker it tight, refuse to let any out, but dammit, he hadn't a good shit in what felt like a week—

The fire just kept growing, though. Someone had lit one right under him. There was a soft plop in the water, and Fred almost hollered, "Touchdown!" out loud in relief because he must have passed something to make a splash like that—

Less than a second later the pain in his anus flared harder than anything he'd ever felt. Right on the tuchus, right in the middle of the hole, it felt worse than hemorrhoids, worse than pushing his own anal sphincter back into himself—which he'd probably have to when this was over—it was like some world-ending agony, like his guts had fallen out his back end, pain beyond pain, agony beyond agony, and Fred let out a scream—

Something had bitten him right on the hemorrhoids.

"They got my ass!" Fred screamed and shot off the toilet faster than he had in decades. He damned near crashed into the wall, pants around his ankles. He hit hard, still screaming, trying to turn and see what could have produced such acute pain—

It was a snake. Rising out of the toilet, black-skinned like tar, inflating as it rose, like one of those Indian cobras out of a damned basket, getting bigger and bigger. It was four feet tall—now five—now six, Jesus!

"What the hell?" Fred stumbled back, through the bathroom door as the snaked wobbled. The bottom of its body split, like it was creating its own legs down there. One of them stepped out of the toilet, dripping water on his tile.

Fred shuffled away, pants still around his ankles, belt rattling on the floor. He blinked, blinked again, and thumped against the door, the mammoth, world-ending pain in the middle of his keister momentarily forgotten. Fred's mouth worked up and down as the snake stepped free of the toilet and balanced on those two legs, its black, scaly hood popping out on either side of its neck.

And then, as the snake gained its balance ... another one followed, started to rise from the toilet.

Fred didn't have words; didn't even try and form any. He was out the bathroom door faster than he'd done anything since he was all-track back in high school. He slammed the bathroom door and locked it from the outside, then ran down the hall, pants around his ankles damned near tripping him, and plunged for the side of the bed where he kept two things—a phone, right on the nightstand, and a pistol, underneath the mattress.

He didn't know which to go for first. He ended up coming up with the pistol, an old Mauser with an extended barrel and pointed at the door to the bedroom while he dialed the 9, the 1 and then the other 1 with fingers more dextrous than they'd been since the first time he'd sunk them in a pussy.

"9-1-1, what is your emer—"

"A goddamned demon snake just bit me on my asshole!" Fred said. It was all he could think of. The bathroom started to creak, then something started to bang against it. And it didn't sound like it was going to take no for an answer.

*

Erin turned onto Warner Pike, and Arch had to hang on for dear life because she drove like a lunatic fresh out of the asylum. It wasn't healthy to take an SUV up on two wheels on a corner, but Erin didn't seem to be bothered by it. It bothered Arch plenty, though, especially when he considered that one of his last memorable experiences with Erin involving driving included her going off a dad-gummed cliff down the side of Mount Horeb, dang near killing her, if not for the grace of God ... and maybe a little demon magic juice remedy taken intravenously.

"Arch, you look like you're about to shit," Erin said, not doing a very good job of concealing her amusement at his discomfort.

"If I hadn't already this morning, I believe this would prompt it," Arch replied.

Erin took another corner, this one a natural S bend in the road, about twenty miles an hour over what the yellow sign they'd just passed suggested.

"Those feds are still behind us," she said, glancing at her rearview for a second before gluing her eyes back onto the road ahead. In Arch's estimation, that did not help. The sirens were wailing, adding a soundtrack to his desperation.

"So's Casey, Father Nguyen, Duncan and Guthrie, Drumlin and McMinn ... I'm guessing Pastor Jones is following with Tarley shortly if he's not almost there already."

"Barney Jones drives that Buick like an old woman," Erin said, taking another corner and bringing Arch nearer to the Lord by inspiring a sudden desire to pray. "We'll beat him by five minutes, easy. I think Dr. Darlington and Ms. Cherry might make it before us, though."

"You sure this is the right moment for an 'all hands'?" Arch asked. She'd called for it, and he hadn't wanted to question in front of anyone in the watch, let alone the feds.

Erin's face went steely, her jaw set. "We have a chance to get some real help for this town, outside of this ad hoc, spaghetti-against-the-wall thing we've been throwing together. These feds, if they see the shit we've got going on—they could push a real alarm button, get agents swarming into this town." She shot him a grin. "We might finally be done being outmanned and outgunned. Hell, maybe they'll even convince the governor to call in the National Guard to help us out." She turned back to the road, and her jaw unlocked, showing the first sign of a smile. "We might finally see some daylight on the end of this, Arch. Get our town back instead of fighting this endless, hopeless battle."

That one set Arch's eyebrows back just about over his head. "You haven't been acting like you see it as hopeless. The way you talk in front of the others, we're two steps from winning this thing."

Erin was back to taut. "I'm rallying the troops, Arch," she said. "We've got no room in our game for thoughts of losing. The stakes are just too high for that. We have to lay in, and we have to fight like it's going to be a forever game. Us against them. Us alone against them. We need solidarity. That sense of community that Southern towns are known for." She cocked her head slightly, taking another S curve at what felt like ninety but was probably just north of fifty. "At least we have, until now. We get some help ... maybe we can back it off some."

"I don't mean to burst your bubble," Arch said, "but I'm not so sure those feds are going to bring in anything like what you're hoping for."

She looked at him sidelong, out of the corner of her eyes. She was mostly still paying attention to the road, but it wasn't much comfort. "What do you mean?"

"Let's say this Martinson and Ross see what's going on here," Arch said. "Let's say they become true believers, and press the panic button. What do you think their superiors are going to say, they start hollering about demons from—well, you know where—showing up in the streets of a small Southern town?" Erin didn't answer, so he went on. "They're going to be thought of as crazy. And their bosses might not be far off, because what's happening here—it's crazy, Erin."

"I got possessed by a demon not that long ago, Arch," Erin said. "You think I don't know it's crazy here?" She whipped the car around one last curve, and Warner Pike straightened out, a mailbox with the name Mickelson emblazoned on it. She pulled the emergency brake and damned near drifted into a fence to make the turn, but she made it, and they came pulling up to a farmhouse with a single dusty old pickup truck parked in front of it.

Arch was out of the car a second after Erin stopped it, mostly relieved that he'd survived the trip and vowing that even if he had to ride back to the station with Casey and listen to the man's stories of grotesquery the whole way, it'd sure beat to pieces having to go through that again. He kept from dropping to his knees and kissing the dirt. Barely.

"Whoo-eee," Casey said as he popped out of his truck a second after doing his own drift into the drive. "You know how to drive it like you stole it, Erin!"

She smiled tightly at him, checking her pistol to see if a round was chambered before she hefted her nail-encrusted baseball bat over her shoulder. The feds were pulling up behind them just then, and Arch could see Martinson's round face squinch up into a scowl at the sight of the bat. She didn't look much happier when she caught sight of Arch's sword, which he'd already drawn.

Another car came cruising up a moment later, a small, four-door sedan, and Father Nguyen threw it into park, his black outfit accented by the white collar, and a cross with sharp edges, shining bronze in the sunlight, held in his hand. The feds saw that, too, and exchanged another look. Ross seemed like he might break his silence first, from what Arch saw, but he didn't get a chance.

The windows of Fred Mickelson's two-story, white frame house, built into the side of the hill—blew out as black-shrouded, snake-like creatures came flooding out in a wave, and all Arch's thoughts about dying in a car wreck or the how the feds were handling their first sight of demons—all that went out the window with the snakes, in favor of surviving the next few minutes.

*

"Thirty seconds!" Gary shouted in the confined space of the van. He was in the driver's seat, keeping one hand on the wheel, Paul in the passenger seat. Everybody else was in the back, sitting their asses on the ground, because it was a plumbing van, by God, and he didn't need seating so much as he needed storage space for all the shit he used in his trade.

"We coulda taken a few different cars, you know," Larry whined. He was still chewing his fucking nails.

"Take the wheel, Paul," Gary said.

Paul blinked at him, looking across from the passenger side. "… What?"

"Take the goddamned wheel, Paul!" Gary shouted, and his brother reached over and did it. "When I slide out of the seat, you slide in." He waited until he got stunned nod from Paul, then set the cruise control and put his hands down on the armrest, bracing for a second before heaving himself into the rear of the van with one good shove. His legs followed, thumping and probably banging something, but hell if he cared because he couldn't feel it.

"What the fuck, Gary?" Terry asked as Gary just about landed on his lap, face down.

"Don't get all excited, peckerwood," Gary said, righting himself and dragging his wheelchair out of the straps where he secured it while driving. "I just need to be ready when we deploy." He pulled himself up into it, feeling alive again as his lower back made full contact with that double-barreled shotty he sat on all the damned time. "Now, Larry, the reason we didn't take separate cars is because—do Navy SEALS take five helicopters to a job when one will do?"

Larry thought about it a second. "I don't know, man. That Pentagon is pretty fat. They probably do sometimes, you know—"

"No, they fucking don't!" Gary shouted, slamming a palm against the wheelchair's armrest. The thump reverberated throughout the van. "This is our goddamned Black Hawk, okay? We ride to battle together on the wings of vengeful fury, as a family and a team!"

"Hear hear!" Marina said. Gary hadn't even realized it, but she'd squeezed herself in the back with his momma. Hell, he hadn't even realized his momma had come along. That drew a frown; women were supposed to be protected, not fight, but hell if he was going to say jack shit to his momma. She'd slap him right out of his chair.

"I think we're coming up on it!" Paul shouted from the front seat as the van bumped sideways a little. "I see cop lights flashing in the driveway. Looks like some shit's going down already. Stuff's crawling out the windows of the house."

"All right, let's get ready," Gary said, reaching down for a duffel bag he'd put behind the driver's seat. It was just out of reach. "Terry, be a useful person for five seconds and hand me that army duffel, will you?" Terry gave him an acid look but complied, and the heavy duffel landed remorselessly on Gary's lap a second later. "Thanks, you pointless sack of fuck." He unzipped it, and with a nod to Larry to move back, dumped the contents on the floor of the van. Swords and pipes and aluminum baseball bats all came falling out, along with a butcher knife and a short shovel and an old electric Stratocaster guitar.

"The fuck is this?" Terry asked, gawking.

"Everybody take one," Gary said. "You got to arm yourselves against evil." He tossed a look over his shoulder out the windshield. "Paul, the driveway is packed, you goddamned idiot. Take us through the fence, it looks like it was constructed by the goddamned Chinese in a factory with QA engineers that were too hopped up on opium pipes to give a shit about their jobs." The van could take it, he was sure.

Paul blinked at him, disbelieving, for about a second, and Gary gave him the older-brother look he'd been giving him all his life. For just a second, Paul looked like he was thinking about arguing, then he swerved the van into the fence like a good lemming. Probably just wanted to avoid the argument he knew was coming, that would roll over his pussy-ass ability to argue back. He lacked persistence. Not as bad as that wet powder baby Larry, but still ... it interfered with his ability to really become someone.

The van crashed through the fence and onto Fred Mickelson's lawn, where a fuck ton of demon snake things were slithering and walking(!) their way across toward the convoy of vehicles parked on the drive. "Yeehaw!" Gary shouted, clutching his wheelchair armrests tight and counting on the securing straps binding his wheelchair to the van to keep him from tipping over before he could deploy for battle. That'd be fucking embarrassing.

"Jesus Christ!" Larry screamed as everyone in the back except for Gary got tossed around like they were on a spin cycle. Good thing everyone got a grip on a weapon before Paul had off-roaded this bitch. Especially that Stratocaster. That motherfucker was heavy. Looked like Marina had claimed that one. He was mildly envious. The guitar was going to be a good weapon, he could tell. Probably kill fifty demons today with just that.

The van rattled to a stop and Gary unstrapped the wheelchair before Paul had finished shifting it into park. "What the fuck is—" Paul was saying.

Gary didn't have time for his bullshit. He wheeled over Larry's foot

("Goddammit, bro, that's my foot!") and threw open the door. With no time for the slow-ass wheelchair ramp to get its shit together, Gary yelled, "Hooo-ahh, motherfuckers!" rolled the wheelchair back, lifting the front two maneuvering wheels off the ground, and lunged it forward over the edge. It hit the ground a moment later and thudded, landing near perfectly. Gary accepted the jarring sensation in stride and rolled toward the nearest demon thing in front of him, pulling out the machete he'd strapped to the side of his wheelchair as he did so.

"Wait!" a shout reached his ears. He didn't dare look away from his foe, but out of the corner of his eye, he could see a small Asian man dressed in a priest's garb. He was holding up a bronze cross, which he'd just delivered unto one of the snake things with a firm smash. It had turned into a black cloud that dissipated in a hot second, and now the little man was looking at Gary as he wheeled furiously toward his first target.

The snake-demon hissed at him, its forked black tongue whipping like it was going to toss his salad. Gary was racing the wheelchair up a small rise and he didn't give a fuck. The machete was ready on his lap, and he was using both hands to wheel furiously as the snake broke for him. It was coming for him, he was coming for it, there was going to be a clash and Gary already knew the victor was going to be him.

"... *Because I want it more*," he whispered as the thing leapt at him.

Gary seized the machete and whipped it across the snake's flight path as it came at him. It met the thing's long neck as the fangs were an inch from his face. Gary was looking it in the eye, it was looking him in the eye; staring contest from hell joined—

The snake puffed in a cloud of black, the stink of sulfur just about making Gary heave. Smelled like the rankest cabbage fart he'd ever caught wind of, like his momma had gotten into the kimchi again and was letting loose with no remorse.

"Motherfucker!" Gary said, wheeling around to rejoin the battle. "Damned right. Best man won."

The priest had stopped a few steps away from him, gape-mouthed. "Where ... where did you get that machete?"

Gary hoisted it up. He could see his family members flooding out of the van. Marina had beat them all out, and she was, indeed, doing a great deal of killing with the Stratocaster. He felt a little swell of pride and mentally increased her efficiency rating by ten percent. "Paid a Unitarian preacher from Craigslist to say some prayers over them in Chattanooga a couple nights ago. Fifty bucks and two hours later ... we got a bag full of badassery."

"Two hours?" the priest asked. "He spent two hours blessing your weapons?"

"Nah, the two hours was driving," Gary said, wheeling forward again. There were snakes to kill, didn't the priest see that? "The prayer took thirty seconds!" he shouted, not looking over his shoulder to see the man's reaction.

He heard it, though. "… Thirty … *seconds*?" The man asked. "I spend fourteen hours … chanting … burning incense … not sleeping … and the … the Protestants … *thirty seconds?*" A pause. "GOD – DAMMIT!" the priest screamed to the heavens.

Gary would have laughed, but he was too busy killing demons. The machete rose and fell, and Gary laughed and laughed. So this was what battle felt like. Fuck, yeah.

*

Erin was in the thick of it, snake demons slithering and standing and running and throwing themselves out of the house, out of every goddamned window and crevice and—shit, was that one slithering out of a fan pipe on the roof?

"Holy fucking balls, man!" Casey screamed, actually hitting the highest end of the register, making Erin do a double take to confirm it was him and not some little girl standing where he'd stood a moment before. He was high stepping, knees about his chest, and occasional shrieks tearing out after he finished his exclamation about one of his favorite body parts. Huge snakes were slither-racing around his feet.

Erin's, too. She brought the bat down and sulfurated one, then another. They were hissing and flooding, and she didn't hold her ground long, jumping up on the tire of the Explorer as Arch did the same on his side of the car. It was a damned reptilian army, and it had definitely claimed the low ground.

"Jesus!" Nate McMinn screamed as one of them devoured him whole like a fucking anaconda or python or something. Her last sight of him was his body being crushed in the unhinged jaw of one of those things, its rippling black flesh moving as it took the man in.

"NATE!" Keith Drumlin screamed, plunging a blade into its side. The snake puffed into sulfur, a black cloud—

And there was Nate again, upright at a forty-five-degree angle where the snake had eaten him, cramming him down its now-vanished gullet. He maintained that position for a brief moment, and Erin studied him. Blood ran down his nose, his cheeks; his body was malformed where it had crushed him while eating him—

Then Nate fell over, and as he landed on the ground, Erin knew the man was dead. Nothing Keith had done in that bright moment in which he'd reappeared had changed the outcome one damned whit—he'd been dead the moment the snake had breathed him in.

"Don't let 'em get you!" Erin shouted, redoubling her efforts at stabbing down. The snakes were writhing and filling the channels between cars now, flooding like they'd been let loose in a living river of black, scaled demon skin. She was fully on top of the hood of the Explorer now, swinging the bat down in lazy arcs like she was golfing.

A crash drew her attention. A van with the words WRIGHTSON'S SPEE-DEE PLUMBING emblazoned on the side came racing across the lawn, running over upright snakes as it came. It thumped to a stop a short distance from them, where the snakes were not nearly so thick, and the doors flew open. A man in a wheelchair shouted, "Hoo-ah, motherfuckers!" and plopped out the side, racing along like he was in the Paralympics. Father Nguyen was shouting at him, and a flood of others came out of the van after, raising weapons high and charging into the slithering mess of a fray. Somewhere in the midst of it, Erin thought she saw Mary Wrightson, that angry old cow, but she didn't have a chance to confirm.

Something thumped on the back of the Explorer, rocking the whole vehicle on its shocks. Erin cast a look at Arch, who was draped over the hood next to her, swinging his own blade down, trying to make a dent in the snake flood that had them engulfed. He looked at her questioningly, she looked right back, and they both turned toward the back of the vehicle as one—

It was Martinson, climbing her fat ass up onto the roof of the Explorer. She had a pretty fierce look in her eyes, and her gaze found Erin's. "You could have warned us," she said, sounding pretty put out, "that it was demons." And she reached under her jacket and brought out her standard-issue pistol, slamming a magazine home in it before reaching it over the side.

"That's not going to do—" Erin started to say.

But Martinson opened up, her first shot hitting a snake crawling right under Erin and—

The snake disintegrated, an aura of brimstone almost forcing Erin's head back from the edge of the car. The next shot killed another, and another, and another.

"Demons," Martinson muttered. "Fucking demons."

Erin looked at Arch. Holy bullets? The FBI agent was carrying holy bullets?

"Huh," Arch said.

Erin didn't need to say anything. She just smiled and kept golfing for snakes. She didn't need to drive it home to Arch; the FBI wasn't useless in this after all.

*

Gary was right in the middle of his element. This was the shit that got you to Valhalla, damned right it was. The shit Gary had craved—the conflict he'd sought every day of his life, it felt like. He raced the wheelchair forward, blocking the escape of the snakes on this flank. They were knee-deep over by the cars, but Gary couldn't do anything about that. Here they were thinner on the ground, a manageable amount, and also walking on their own two damned legs(!), thin little stalks that shouldn't have supported a baby fern, let alone fifty- or a hundred-pound snakes.

But they walked, and they ran, and they charged at him, and Gary By God Wrightson sent them motherfuckers back to hell, where they fucking belonged.

And loved every minute of it.

"Oh, my God, the battle," Gary breathed, swinging the machete as he spun his wheelchair around. The snakes were coming at him, smelling weakness.

It was their own goddamned upper lips they were smelling as far as Gary was concerned. There was no fucking weakness here. He swung and swung and bested all comers.

He wanted it more than they did. He knew it. And he felt like before they puffed in those black clouds, they by God knew it, too.

"HAAAAAAAH!" Gary screamed as he rolled down a hill at a thick knot of snakes. He ran two over with his wheels—which he'd had the preacher bless, too, of course—turning them into clouds, and then sliced down the third. "I love the smell of brimstone in the morning!" he shouted to the heavens. "Smells like fucking victory. Let's grab life by the scrote, by God!" And he tore into those motherfuckers.

*

Barney Jones came crashing through the fence on the left side of the driveway, drawing Arch's attention from where he was swinging, futilely, at the endless flood of the creatures still swarming out of the Mickelson house. "Someone needs to shut off the spigot from Hades," Arch muttered as Barney jumped out of his car with Braeden

Tarley and they both started wading in. The snakes thinned on that side, just as they had on the flank where that plumbing van had come bursting into the fight. The vast majority were right up the middle, where Arch and the convoy had parked, and they'd established a pretty effective moat to keep anyone from getting into their cars or even getting on the ground and fighting. Nate McMinn had taught 'em that lesson pretty well. His corpse was being slithered over near constantly by the things. Arch just counted himself lucky that they hadn't gotten up on their feet and started leaping over the cars like they'd shown they could do on the edges of the fight, where they had more room to maneuver.

Then one leapt over him like a jumping fish, and Arch didn't have more than a second to regret jinxing himself by thinking the danged thought.

"FUUUUUUUUCK!" Casey screamed. The man was definitely hitting the high notes right now. Arch expected the taxidermist was wishing he'd stayed at the dispatch desk instead of passing it on to Benny Binion. Fear of snakes. Had to be.

Well, Arch couldn't much fault him for that, especially with these particular snakes. Nasty critters.

Felt like they were all leaping now, and Arch switched his swinging to skyward as the blue above started to turn with shadow and scale. "Get 'em!" he shouted, not realizing until a few seconds after he blurted it that it was about the most useless directive he could have given. Oh, well.

"Swing for the skies!" Erin shouted. Arch couldn't see if her command was followed because the skies were suddenly filled with jumping snakes. One of them smashed into the Explorer with enough force to rock it. Arch dang near fell off, but caught himself with a sweaty hand on the smooth hood, producing just enough friction to right himself after experiencing a sharp second of that weightless feeling like he was about to take a tumble through empty air. His gut threatened to leap through his throat, and it didn't quite settle even after he'd secured himself, waving his sword up and popping two more leaping snakes.

This was not making it any better, Arch realized, but what else was there to do? He swung, trying to keep his own little corner of the sky clear of black demon snakes, and hoped that the sun would come shining through soon, though it didn't look so great from here.

*

Erin didn't like snakes, but she didn't have it in her to scream like Casey was doing. He was swinging his tomahawk wildly even before the damned things had started leaping over them in swarms like flies. They even made a kind of buzzing sound as they jumped, slithering bellies writhing as they hurled themselves like high jumpers, or like salmon up a stream.

Martinson let out a short bark of a shout and her gun went off again, then again. She seemed to be aiming up now, but Erin couldn't tell for sure, because she was too busy minding her own black-cloud mess of snakes heaving themselves every damned where.

"No bag limit, boys!" came the shout of that damned plumber again, wheeling himself around wherever. Gary Wrightson, she thought, though she didn't really know him by anything other than reputation. "Get some!" She couldn't tell exactly where he was because of the sheer volume of leaping snakes, but he sounded closer than he'd been a few minutes earlier. He might even have been herding them toward the Explorer for all she knew. He certainly didn't seem deterred by the sheer volume of snakes, almost like they were running from him and into her crew.

"I think we're in the middle of the press," Arch said, voice elevated. "Barney and Braeden are on one side, those Wrightsons are coming in on the other. The snakes are funneling right through us."

"Lucky us," Erin said, swinging her bat. The thick of the fray wasn't her idea of a choice place, but this was probably where she needed to be as a leader. Martinson had stopped firing, but Erin could see her swinging her gun atop the Explorer's cab, whacking a snake as it flew past.

Things seemed to be thinning, didn't they? Or maybe that was that Erin's imagination. She didn't stop swinging, but pretty soon she could count the number of snakes leaping overhead at any given time. Five, then three, then one—then none.

Turning on the hood, she found herself looking over the side of the car. She could see dirt driveway again, a snake slithering pitifully past all by its lonesome. She reached down and whacked it all the same, turning it to sulfur stink, then cast a wary eye in the direction it had been heading.

There was a goodly number of the damned things streaming across the road, disappearing into the long grass of an unmowed field across Warner Pike from the Mickelson house. The grass was swaying, too, looking like it had absorbed an uncountable number of the black-scaled creatures. The last of them were vanishing now, and Erin let out a ragged breath as she watched them go. Decisions swirled around her head—pursue? Try and chase them into the tall grass, knowing that—hell, they'd have a bitch of a time seeing those things coming in that. It'd be as bad as chasing those shadowcats into the woods.

"We need a holy blessed bush-hogger," Erin muttered to herself. Or what did the county use to clean out those nasty areas where snakes dwelled in the tall grass of drainage ponds? Ditch Witch? Something like that.

"You better run, you limp dick reptiles! Fuck yeah, we win!" Gary Wrightson shouted, wheeling himself down the slope onto the driveway and running over a fleeing snake straggling its way toward the road. The black-skinned thing popped under his wheelchair tires, and Wrightson pumped his hands into the air, a machete clenched tight in one. "That shit—was *the* shit!"

Whatever that meant. Erin just took a breath and settled her head back on the hood for a hot second. It was still warm. They'd only been here a few short minutes and look what all had happened.

Martinson stuck her round face over Erin's from atop the cab of the Explorer. "So ... you got a demon infestation?"

Erin blinked, looking up at the FBI agent. "Yeah. And it's a doozy. Got some experience with that?"

The woman just stared at her for a second, then broke into a crooked smile. "Hell yeah, we've got experience with that. We're the fucking FBI. You think we haven't run across a demon or two in our time?"

Erin's sigh was almost to the heavens. Relief at last.

*

"The flood of sin hangs deep within this place," Brackessh said, sniffing the air outside the white, corrugated metal trailer home. It was up on blocks, with thick grass covering the spaces between them rather than a metal skirt. The entire structure squeaked and Brackessh nearly cringed to feel it radiating out from within the structure, the sin so heavy in the air as to be stifling.

He drew a breath into his shell, held it—counted. He touched his head; it ached to be this proximal to sin while the deed was still happening. He brushed his hands against his face, waiting. Waiting.

Waiting.

A fierce cry let loose from within the windows at the far end of the trailer, joined by another voice in a cacophony of pleasure. Of course there was joy in sin, else why would anyone partake of it? "You do not drink deeply of bile," Brackessh whispered, "but of sweet drink and wine you will take more than your fill ..."

The sin subsided, the deed done, the horror of the soul purged into the willing vessel, and Brackessh could breathe again. It was as though a tightness in his shell had vanished, and he led his follower up to the door and knocked. "Wait," he said, though the command was hardly necessary.

"Where you going?" came a female voice from within. "I wanted to cuddle."

No answer save for the opening of the door, and a naked man with blank eyes staring out at him.

Ah, fulfillment. Brackessh lifted his knife out of its place by his side and kissed it deeply, loosing the flames with his licking tongue. It hissed and sizzled, silvery blade glowing white with heat.

"This will cure you," he whispered to the man before him, staring at him, blank eyes filled with what Brackessh regarded as trust—but it was really just his hold.

Time to make it permanent.

"This is the instrument of your sin," Brackessh said, putting the hot knife to flesh and searing it as he removed the offending piece of the man's anatomy. It was fine and firm in his grasp, and Brackessh held onto it a moment longer than was perhaps necessary before discarding it into the high grass by the side of the trailer. "Better to lose the offending flesh than lose your soul." He looked into those blank eyes, saw trust. "Now go—purge your sin from this earth." And he looked at his other follower. "Help him."

Brackessh waited outside through the screaming. He listened, though it gave him no pleasure. Sin was sin, and the vessel that carried that sin needed to be destroyed so that it could corrupt no others. The cries, in a voice that had been ... so pleased only moments earlier ... they brought Brackessh no joy.

But they did bring satisfaction, to think that perhaps soon he would wipe out the sin entirely, even in so small a corner of the world.

And then, maybe ... go home at last.

5.

Gloria Tyler knew a mark when she saw one. Overweight, belly hanging over his belt, she could have spotted this guy from ten miles away, let alone two tables. He had the partial combover to cover his thinning black mat of hair, had the chubby face that was fixed on the stage, watching Ida Bell do her dance, bare legs, bare ass, bare cooch and titties, all whirling around that magical pole.

This was Moody's Roadhouse. Low light, a girl on stage, drinks flowing like water from a tap.

And Gloria Tyler had found her a mark. Hot damn.

"Hey sexy," she purred, slipping in behind him and resting a hand on the back of his neck. He shivered under her touch, his fat neck producing a little handful of chub at the scruff as he leaned his head back to look at her. She imagined grabbing him by it, leading him anywhere she wanted him to go.

Hell, that was what she was going to do to him. Just a little less literally.

"H—hi," he said, looking up at her with big, watery brown eyes. He was clean-shaven, and his cheeks looked like he'd secreted away a whole bag of peanuts in there. When he got old, his jowls were going to hang halfway to his pecker, Gloria thought while burying a cold laugh. Verbalizing that wouldn't get her any points.

"You want a private dance, darlin'?" Gloria leaned down, breathing into his ear. She'd just taken a swig of mint mouthwash backstage to kill the cig breath she knew by experience turned a certain class of customer off. He looked the type. Weak little bitch. She ran a finger down his shirt's buttons one by one, letting the touch linger just between his man boobs.

"Y-yes," he said, and she beckoned him up, and he damned near fell over himself standing up. She balled up her fist on the front of his shirt, taking hold of him as he gasped slightly. That was good. This boy was soft, and she knew what soft boys liked.

A woman to get hard with them—so they could get hard.

And Gloria was going to get him hard, all right.

"Come on, sugar," she said, and led him through the twisty, close-pushed tables, through the shouting men making their pleasure known at Ida Bell's dance. They howled the loudest when she did a flip on the pole, used it to neatly divide her body in two, just the smallest strip out of view, right up the middle of her. Funny how the men hooted and hollered at that, just a momentary hide, when they knew in a few seconds she'd give 'em the full glory shot.

Gloria dragged him through the arched door in back, though she didn't have work too hard at it. He took a last look at Ida Bell on stage as she gave 'em the money shot—flat on her back, cooch toward the audience, and man, did the dollar bills rain down.

Gloria was up in thirty minutes herself, and she had it in mind to get a rain of her own before she even got up there.

"In here," she said, pushing his tubby ass into one of the private booths. He was breathing hard and she could hear it, like little gasps in the night. Shit. And she hadn't even really started riling him up yet. "You asthmatic?"

"Yep," he said, and fumbled in his pocket, producing an inhaler. He took a snort, which was good because Gloria wasn't in the mood to deal with him collapsing in the middle of her fleecing him.

He put it away, and she started the show.

Gloria let the music be her guide. She lived in the rhythm, her body moving in time. She kept off him for a minute, then two, letting the anticipation build.

He was breathing hard, little piggy snorts coming out.

Gloria slipped in close for the first time and undid her top. Her titties slid out, just a foot or so from his face.

She thought he was going to lose it right there.

Gloria dialed it back, pulled herself away, to the extreme end of the little booth. Entice, withdraw—it was just like sex in that regard. In, out. Sitting still didn't move anybody the way they needed to be moved.

Slipping in close again, Gloria put a hand on his shoulder. Ran her acrylic nail tips across his collarbone, up his neck to his ear. Stroked him.

Building up.

Then she pulled away again, caressing her own breasts. She was following a routine, an easy thing she'd ingrained into her memory long ago. It was the same two or three dances, really, just sped up or slowed down according to the rhythm of the music.

She turned away, showing him her luscious ass, hidden only by a g-string, then slapped it.

He jumped at the crack. Or maybe the noise.

Gloria backed it up on him and heard the piggy squeal of anticipation. She stopped it a few inches away, then slipped off the g-string.

It was dark in the booth. Doubtful he could see much of her cooch, but a little was all she was aiming for—yet. Another buildup. He made a squeaking noise, nonetheless.

Gloria came back around, showed him that thin line of bush she had left. Ran her finger along it. It was less of a hedgerow and more a shrubbery these days. Every third Tuesday she got everything around it ripped out by the damned roots at a wax parlor in Chattanooga, then used the trimmer to do the rest herself. It set her apart from the other girls, who had a lot of nothing going on there, bare lips flapping in the damned breeze.

She didn't truck with that, Gloria didn't. Who wanted a pussy with no bush? Pedophiles, that was who. Not her clientele. She was after real men, not perverts—though they were hard to come by in a place like Moody's. Still, real men after real women. That was her game.

Because Gloria was at least fifty percent real. Just not her tits, because they were fake. Or her lips, cuz they had collagen shots in 'em. Or her eyes, cuz they'd been lifted to help hide her age. Or …

"Come on, baby," she said and dropped a hand gently on his crotch. Ooh, he had some game in there. A stiff one greeted her, straining at his khaki Dockers. She smiled to find the effect she was having on him already. "How you doing?"

He took a gasping breath. "Good," he finally decided.

"Oh, yeah?" She brought her fingers together at the point of his bulge, giving him a little rub. "You doing good?" Fed back his own words. Men ate that shit up. Tell 'em the same thing they just told you and they thought you were agreeing with them. She'd read about it in a book on manipulation.

"I'm doing real good," he breathed, that little asthmatic rasp making its way out again.

"You want to be doing even better?" she breathed, right into his ear.

He nodded. Couldn't even form words.

"We can go out back and get this one rubbed out for you, one way or another," Gloria whispered. She ran her fingers gently along that seam of his pants again, feeling the erection bulging beneath.

"Oh—okay," he said.

Gloria Tyler knew a mark when she saw one.

"Come on," she said, standing him up. "Twenty for the dance, first." She held out a hand.

He froze. This was always the dicey part, but she needed him to pay for the dance before she could have him leave the booth. John, the owner, would have a shit fit otherwise. She was glad this fellow hadn't questioned why they couldn't stay in the booth—because that was another thing John would have a shit fit about. Hooking in his booths would be a real problem for him, especially since he didn't get a cut of it.

Finally, the chubby little bitch went for his wallet and pulled out a twenty. She saw a fat roll inside, and not the kind he was keeping in his pants, neither. "Come on," she whispered and pulled him out of the booth, down the hall toward the EXIT sign lit in the neon gloom.

Pushing through, Gloria felt the kick of cold air hit her bare flesh. This was so much easier in the summertime, even when it got hot and humid. There were cars parked out here, the building a U, wings of the structure encircling them before the parking lot gave way to woods. It made a nice little cover for illicit activity; only the dancers coming out the back would see anything, and they knew to turn their heads. Even the goody-two-shoes ones that never did this sort of shit. Losers. Leaving money on the table.

"Over here," Gloria said, keeping her teeth from chattering. The midday sun was high overhead, but she led him over to a corner of the building where an old wooden fence was supposed to keep people from messing with the building's electrical. The gate in front of it was always unlocked, though, and Gloria opened it now, leading him inside, then letting it shut behind her.

It was a small space, a little bigger than the booth but not much, an electrical box at one end, a bare wall next to it, and two panels of fence making up the rest of the walls. "Now, we ain't got a lot of room to work here," she said, turning on him, leaning into his ear, trying to make this private, just for him, special between the two of them. "If you want, we can do it facing each other, and you lift me up. I don't weigh that much, and I'll either look you in the eye the whole time, make you really feel it—or not. Whatever you want, darlin'. But if you don't want to strain, or have me lookin' at you, I can turn around, and you do whatever you want. $100 for straight up, only $50 if you want a blow—$125 total if you want that as a warm-up first. Anything in the back door is $200, unless it's just a finger during the act—that's $25." She pulled back from his ear. "So ... what'll it be?"

"Uhm," he said, his gears a spinnin'. That was the danger, giving him the full load before he'd given her a load. She ran fingers over his crotch, coaxing him as he thought it through, pushing him subtly—or not—back to thinking about what he wanted and how it was right here for him to get. "Um—um," he let out a low moan as she turned up the intensity slightly on the rub, then found his zipper and gently worked it down. She smiled as she pulled it out, and boy howdy, was he ready. "Straight up, you face the wall," he said, words cascading out in a rush.

"$100, baby," she said, and he almost tore his wallet in two pulling out the bills. Gloria balled them up in her fist and put her knuckles against the bumpy, painted concrete block wall. Her hands could take it.

"Oh, yeah," he moaned, and she heard him unfasten his belt. This was going to take about two seconds. Because Gloria knew a mark, and an easy one at that. She'd spend five to ten minutes total with him, and make $120 bucks between the dance and the quickie.

Fancy lawyers in their offices didn't make money that quick or easy. People working their jobs? They might turn their noses up at her, but she left a trail of satisfied customers who parted with big bucks, easy. Her little prick-ass classmates from high school? They fucked their husbands, did housework, raised kids, all that shit. Nannies made $20k a year, professional cooks made $25-30k. Housecleaners, same. Plus they worked their jobs, lots of 'em, in addition to all that—and made $20 or $30k a year, period. They did all that other work for free.

Gloria Tyler thought they were all marks. She danced for money, she fucked for money, and she got paid at an hourly rate that made high-priced lawyers look cheap by comparison. It was the easiest, most fun job—most of the time—that she could have imagined.

And all those dumbasses that looked down on her? They fucked for free, cleaned for free, raised kids for free, and worked for pennies compared to her.

Who was the dumbass? Gloria almost laughed as her chubby man of the minute took a gasping breath and keeled over behind her. Way before she would have thought he'd be done.

"What the fuck—?" Gloria spun, bare ass catching something as she did so. Whatever it was stung, cutting her, a little drip of blood running down her butt cheek.

Holy shit.

Something was there, tall and black and hairy as hell, ripping its way into her mark, tearing into his back with teeth the size of a wooly mammoth's tusks. Her fat boy's mouth was open, jaw hanging low, poised to scream but nothing coming out.

"What the shit?" Gloria didn't stare for more than a second. She'd been in this business for a long time, and had learned that when things went sideways, you could go one of two ways—

Let it happen, usually getting your ass hurt or worse in the process. Girls who did her job were at a much higher risk of violence working without the benefit of the law behind them.

Which was why Gloria fought back.

She was no fucking mark.

This wasn't even the first time she'd been attacked out here, but it was the first time she'd been attacked that it wasn't an aggressive john doing it, thinking he might recoup his hundred bucks. Well, Gloria had a remedy for that.

To her left was a length of pipe that rested in a small pile of refuse, and she lifted it up and swung it, hard, at the black creature—it really looked like a black tar version of Swamp Thing—that had her John up and dangling in its mouth.

"Ah—AHHHHHHHHHHHH!" her John finally screamed, getting his breath. Blood was soaking his shirt around the neck, and his pants were down, hanging loose around his ankles, his erection already flagging as his dick hung just about chest level for Gloria.

"Put him the fuck down!" she shouted, swinging past him and whacking the damned thing on the arm. It made a solid, sickeningly mushy noise as she gave the bastard a hearty thump. It had black eyes, too, that had been focused on her. Big claws, too, one of which must have just about slit her ass cheek when she first spun.

The critter writhed in surprise and pain at her hit, pulling the screaming John back to cover where she'd whacked it. Well, that just left its other side exposed, and she came at him hard, giving it to him in the side.

"Put his ass down!" Gloria screamed as the thing fell back through the fence gate, ripping a couple boards off as it did. She pursued, going at the sumbitch and whacking it on its tar flesh every time it gave an opening. "Put—" Whack! "—Him—" Whack! "—Down—" Whack! "—Goddamn—" WHACK! "—YOU!"

The last hit got the thing to drop ol' John, and he hit the pavement screaming. Crimson poured out of the back of him as he landed on his knees.

"Get the fuck outta here!" Gloria didn't let up. She gave that Swamp Thing motherfucker all manner of hell and it squealed at her, pile of shit that it was. It spit out a little blood and black bile, and she could just about sense it getting madder at her. Its surprise at her fighting back had gotten her this far, but it wasn't taking much damage she could see, and was likely to turn on her here in a second once it got over the surprise and realized that. She wound up and gave it a golf swing to the midsection that bowled it over, and decided this was about as good as the getting was going to get. "Move it, tubby!" And she grabbed her John by the back of his shirt and started dragging him back to the door.

Gasping, moaning, crying, he still went along, scrabbling on his hands and knees until he got upright, then waddling with his pants still around his ankles. She pushed him ahead, toward the door, and he fumbled to open it but failed. His whole back was soaked dark, his shirt ruined for good and hanging with a good slit diagonal across it.

A roar behind them. A look back told Gloria that Swamp Thing wasn't happy, and it was coming for them.

"Lemme!" Gloria shoved him just to the side, pushed down on the handle, and swung it wide. "In!" she hip checked him inside and followed, kicking his legs in so she could shut the door without breaking his ankle and jamming shit up for herself. He was in a squealing pile on the ground, but Gloria kept her fucking wits about her, trying to keep one step ahead.

She slammed the door and flipped the interior lock; as long as no moron came along and pushed the bar to activate the emergency exit function, it wasn't going to be able to be opened from the outside.

"The fuck was that?" Gloria asked herself. No time for that question, though. Other concerns pressed in. "GIRLS!" Gloria shouted over the throbbing music. "We got shit going down here!"

The dressing room door was a curtain, not a door, and it was just to her left. A bouncer waited within to keep some overambitious patron from accosting the girls. Today that was Toby, and he stuck his head out the curtain and looked at her as the first THUMP rattled the door.

"Not you, fuckhead!" Gloria screamed, pipe in hand, blood from her ass cheek staining the door. "GIRLS! Get your guns!"

Gloria didn't know what girls in places like New York did in the trade. Counted on bouncers to walk them to their cars, maybe. This wasn't New York, though.

This was Tennessee. And not Nashville, neither, with its polite society that looked down at someone wanting to heft a Colt rather than rely on a police department whose average response time was measured in minutes.

The door thumped again, rocking on its hinges. A line appeared in the metal surface as Swamp Thing gave it hell.

They didn't have minutes, and that was probably how far away the cops were.

"What's going on?" Samantha popped her head out of the curtain, and when she saw Gloria all fucked, blood running down her leg, she popped the rest of herself out a second later.

She'd listened. She had a Ruger in hand.

Because these girls weren't no city flowers; they were rednecks, some of them, trailer park girls, others. Not one wilting goddamned violet in the bunch.

Here they came now: Yvette with a Colt. Myrna with a Beretta. Stella with an old Cimarron revolver, like she was some cowgirl out riding the range. It fit with her dancer outfit, actually.

Last came Ida Bell, fresh off the stage, not wearing anything but her high heeled glass shoes and concerned expression. But she had her own Sig in hand and Gloria's HK VP9 for good measure.

"Get your bitch ass out of the way, Toby!" Gloria said, shouldering the big man aside to take her gun from Ida Bell. "Unless you've got something stronger than your ham fists to stop the shit coming through that door in ten seconds, maybe you should just sally back and dial 911 while the big girls handle this, hm?" Toby looked at her for just a moment, then disappeared through the curtains, hopefully to go do just that.

Gloria joined a tight line with the other girls, aiming carefully over Yvette's shoulder, cuz the hallway was tighter than virgin snatch and her fucking John was still lying on the floor, sobbing and crying and partially blocking the door. If the thing made it through, it'd trip on him while they filled it full of lead.

"What's this shit?" Yvette asked. "Pissed-off ex-husband? Angry John's wife?"

"Demon, I think," Gloria said, ignoring the pain in her ass cheek. That was going to leave a mark. She might even have to have that shit touched up by her plastic surgeon later, keep it from scarring. Who wanted to see a scarred ass whirled around on a pole in front of them?

"Ooh, they been talking about those 'round here lately," Ida Bell said. She was aiming between Myrna and Stella. It was fixing to get loud in this hallway.

The hammering was getting worse, the door folding. A needle scratched behind them, the DJ killing the music and probably fleeing out the front.

"It took a few hits from a pipe and just got madder," Gloria said. "Y'all be careful. It comes through—open up on it." She blinked, turning 'round. Yvette was the only one fully dressed among them; everyone else back here was just on break. She looked like she was ready to get off shift, had her clothes on, cross hanging loose 'round her neck. Not the sort of thing she'd have worn on stage.

The door thumped again, rattling on its hinges. It was coming in.

Now that the music was gone, Gloria could hear every sound. The whimper of the John on the floor, clutching at himself. He was bleeding a fair amount, crying, pants still around his ankles and ass hanging out in the breeze. They had that in common, Gloria reckoned. The chill of the outside air ran up against her skin, flushed from the heat of the action—near-fucking, then fighting, then running. She took a breath to steady herself and her aim.

"This shit for real?" Myrna asked. "Or am I tripping balls right now?"

"It's for real," Gloria said, thinking of that black-ass Swamp Thing. "Though I can hardly believe it my own self."

Maybe she should have run, Gloria thought in the moments before the door came crashing in. Left the whining John behind and booked it for her own hide. Stole someone's keys, took their car, run for it. She might have made it out the front before this thing got into the back, started doing its damage.

But ... nah. That wasn't Gloria Tyler.

She knew a mark when she saw one, and she'd see one every time she looked in the mirror from now on. That poor bastard whining on the ground? He damned sure didn't deserve to die, not to that thing. He just wanted to get his cock rubbed, get his rocks off, and go on living his life.

Gloria wanted to go on living her own life too, but she wasn't going to do it while throwing some poor bastard to the wolves. The door rattled one last time on its hinges, then ripped off, and the girls all opened fire as one, flashes lighting the dark of the hallway as they lit into that motherfucking black Swamp Thing together.

*

"Well, this has been a hell of a way to start a day," Gary said with a puff of pride. His chest felt like it was inflated, ten feet wide, but in a good way, not a I-been-eating-eight-thousand-calories-a-day-for-ten-years-and-never-done-a-lick-of-cardio kind of way.

The battlefield—and that's what this was—was nice and cleared off, save for one poor bastard's carcass that had been smushed in the gullet of one of those fucking snake things. The face was absolutely wrecked, looked like a smushed child's toy he'd once pulled out of a toilet.

Erin Harris stared back at him evenly. She didn't seem to know what to make of Gary, which was just fine with Gary. He'd seen Erin around, before all this started, and hadn't thought much of her then. He didn't think much more of her now, though apparently she'd usurped the position of sheriff for her own. How that worked, giving a fresh-faced teenager a job like that during a demon invasion, he didn't know. "It's the way we start every day around here, lately," she just said, even as you can be.

"Well, hot damn," Gary said. That was awesome news.

"Erin," Mary Wrightson said, walking past, hand on Larry's shoulder. "It's all right, son," she whispered low. Larry was sniffling.

"Ms. Wrightson," Erin said, watching her go past, then filtering her gaze back to Gary. "So ... you in charge of this, uh ... band?" Here she looked at Marina, who was brandishing the Stratocaster.

"Haha, good one," Gary said without actual mirth. Marina had done a damned fine job with that guitar. "Yeah. I'm their leader. We heard y'all were needing some help on the radio, figured we'd drop by." He thrust his chin out, defiant, half expecting her to throw a verbal jab at it. Daring her, really. Cuz he had his battle-proven "band" now, and hell if they hadn't just saved the day.

"Well, we sure do appreciate your help," Erin said. She was the stoic type, not what he expected from a teenager or whatever she was. Couldn't much older than a teen. Hadn't she just graduated high school a minute ago? She was definitely behind Larry in school. She flicked her gaze toward Fred Mickelson's house, which was just a wreck at this point. Gary would not have wanted to be the contractor in charge of restoring it—though he knew enough subs he could have managed at this point. "Mind lending some aid in making sure the house is clear?"

"Damned skippy," Gary said, wheeling himself around to take the lead. Her eyebrows shot up as he went past her, rolling toward the front door and fighting his way up the incline of the hill. The door was lying on the front lawn, blown off its hinges like some SWAT team had done it in on the way out of the place. There was a nice step in the way here, and Gary sighed. "Fucking assholes," he muttered to himself as he rolled right up to the stoop that raised six inches and fucked up his ability to take a wheelchair through.

"It's okay, I'll—" Erin started to say. She was gesturing over her shoulder, flagging for some help to come with 'em. The skinny Asian priest started this way. Casey Meacham, too, looking a little pale even for him, that taxidermist sex fiend sonofabitch.

"I got this," Gary said. He locked the wheelchair brakes before hurling his machete inside and leaping right out like a fish jumping out of water. He hurled himself over the threshold, bracing for impact. The trick was to take the hit to the parts of his body he couldn't feel, by God, he did, a hard hit rumbling through his legs. Less of a landing on the palms, cushioning the shock to his upper body. He didn't wait more than a quarter second after landing before he grabbed the machete, put it in his teeth, and started crawling his way through the house.

"What the fuck?" Erin was still standing outside.

"Mmrmmahrhmmm!" Gary said. By God, he'd show her that he was a leader of men.

"Holy hell, Gary," Casey said, popping in behind him as Gary elbow-crawled his way through. "I think you busted your knee. It looks like it's on the back of your leg."

Who fucking cared? Gary didn't even deign to acknowledge it. These were extraordinary circumstances, and by God, they required extraordinary efforts. He checked to make sure he wasn't bleeding out—he wasn't even bleeding—and kept going.

Through the living room, then Gary glanced into a kitchen. A snaked hissed and came at him. He spit out the machete and snagged it, swinging as the thing lunged. He turned it to stink as someone gasped behind him.

"Merciful God," the priest whispered.

"Maybe he is," Gary said, clutching the machete, "but I ain't." And he moved on, dragging himself down the hall.

A sound came from down there, and Gary picked up the pace, cruising along, imagining himself in a war, crawling under barbed wire. He booked it down the hall, keeping the machete in hand and careful not to nick himself in his haste. He made it in front of a door before he found the origin of the noise.

It was another snake. A fat one, with a distended belly full of something. Something big.

"By God, I bet that's Fred Mickelson in there," Gary said as Erin and Casey stepped up behind him, taking more care with his legs than he himself did. "Let's get him out!" And he launched himself off his elbows into the bathroom.

The snake came at him, but it was slow and lethargic and lazy and pathetic, like one of those soft fucking college kids who'd never encountered an actual adversity in their lives and thus had to whine about being "triggered" and "micro-aggressed" because they'd never experienced aggression of the macro kind.

Gary had felt the bite of macro-aggression. He felt it every goddamned day, mostly in his palms where they wore into the wheelchair, and in his back and spine, at least north of where he could feel it, from riding hard on days when he had a lot of calls.

"Smile, motherfucker! This is my fucking kingdom in here!" Gary shouted, hurling himself off his elbows into battle as the snake lunged at him. He caught it in the mouth and it burst, sulfur smell puffing out hard enough to gag a buzzard off a gut wagon. But not enough to put Gary BY GOD Wrightson off, fuck no. He'd plumbed his whole adult life, and this wasn't anything to him. He'd smelled shit that'd put more hair on a fucking Navy SEAL's chest. And no goddamned snake demon was going to beat him in the bathroom. This was his house. Metaphorically.

Fred Mickelson's partially digested corpse hit Gary head-on, some sort of stomach bile splashing him as Fred's head bounced off his shoulder. They collided, and the corpse lost. Gary just gritted his teeth and made sure the machete didn't land in anything important to him. Fred caught it in the arm, but he was well past giving a fuck.

"Fucking shit, Gary!" Casey's voice came from the threshold of the bathroom. "You all right?"

Gary spat, a little of that snake's stomach bile that had been thick on Fred coating his face. "Might need an eyewash. See if you can find a cup, if you ain't too busy jacking off right now, Casey."

The priest snickered. Someone stepped into the bathroom and a towel tickled Gary's shoulder. He wiped his face with it, then heard the sound of the pipes rattling, a little water trickling, then stopping. The towel made its way down to him again, wet this time, and he brushed its cool surface across his eyes like he was in high school chemistry again and had one of those accidents where something blew up in your face. "Thank you," he said, then wiped his face with the dry side. Nothing was burning, and he'd gotten the goop out of his eyes. He opened them experimentally and looked up.

Erin Harris was standing there, not looking anything but a little furrowed in the brow. "You all right?"

"I'm fucking fantabulous," Gary said. "While I was dealing with that, I don't suppose any of the rest of y'all got ambitious and checked out the bedrooms or anything?"

"The rest of the house is clear," the priest said. "I checked. A little bit of a disturbance in the bedroom. Some blood. I think he might have gotten eaten in there."

"By God, a useful person," Gary said to Erin. "You must feel so blessed to have him in your squad. Useful people are such a goddamned rarity these days."

She just raised an eyebrow. "If the house is clear, that means—"

"No," Gary said, just shutting that shit down right there. "We ain't done. Tell me something—where did these things come from?"

Erin stared at him. He thought she might have been starting to get it, a light of awareness dawning in her eyes. "From here, in the house."

"But they don't come out of thin air, right?" Gary asked. He was pretty sure, but not totally sure.

"No."

Gary turned to look at the toilet. The bowl was broken, pieces of the porcelain shattered and lying all around where the snake had made its bed and lay down to digest Fred. "That's what I thought. I bet they came out of here."

"Out of the commode?" Casey asked, looking like he might do a double, triple, even quad take at the busted toilet.

Gary tossed a look at Fred's corpse. "Look at his ass."

"I already did," Casey said. "A little wrinkled for my taste, even before he got ate, but you know, sometimes a little smoke on the roof means there's a fire in the chimney—"

"What the fuck is wrong with you?" Gary asked. "His ass has bite marks on it, you dumb, dick-led, hillbilly motherfucker. He's bleeding from it." He pointed; Fred's pants weren't even on right, though he still wore a shirt, stained yellow. His pants were all bunched up and twisted 'round his ankles. "I think he got attacked right here, on the john, ass-first—because these things came out of the toilet."

"They were pretty big," Erin said. "Those pipes aren't exactly huge, are they?"

Gary shook his head. "No. But a snake can squeeze tight. This ain't the first time I've seen a big one come up through a toilet, neither. Something funky's going on here, though. Fred ain't on city sewer, not this far out. Which means they'd have come up from the septic, and—I just don't like any part of this."

"So they came up from the septic, who gives a shit?" Casey asked. "I mean, other than Fred when these things got 'im. Hell of a way to go, in the middle of your morning dump—"

"You goddamned hormonal goon," Gary said, "a septic is a closed system. How the hell did these things get in the tank? That's my question. Marina!"

"Yeah, boss?" She peeked in. She must have been lingering just outside the door, listening. He mentally tacked another five points onto her efficiency rating. She was getting good, the little minx. Due for a raise. At least a cost of living adjustment.

"Get the snake from the van," Gary said. "The fiber optic one. With the camera." He turned back to the shattered toilet. "I want to see what's going on Fred Mickelson's septic system."

*

Erin stepped outside the Mickelson house, taking a breath of wintery air and purging the stink of both rotting flesh and demon stomach pile from her nostrils with one intense gasp. It was rank in there, and no one but Gary Wrightson—and apparently his Eastern European assistant—seemed prepared to deal with it for very long. Father Nguyen stepped out behind her, taking a cleansing breath of his own, and Casey was out right after that, almost gagging.

Gary had been right about one thing—this was a hell of a way to start the day.

Martinson was all over her a second after she hit the cold, outside air. "Got a minute?" the fed asked, pudgy face all wound up tight.

"For you, I've got a lot of minutes," Erin said, "especially if you can bring us some help." Now it was Erin's turn to be wound up tight.

"How long has this been going on?" Martinson asked. Erin didn't bother to wonder too hard where her partner was.

"Since summer," Erin said. This was a fact she dwelt on often; it had been really late summer when Lafayette Hendricks's sorry ass had come blowing into town, and demons had seemed to follow after. Arch swore up and down that Hendricks hadn't started the problem, but Erin couldn't quite shake the idea that he was the cause, and she didn't necessarily want to change her mind. It was a whole lot easier to hate him.

"Hm," Martinson said, pulling out a small notepad and writing SINCE SUMMER in big letters in the middle of the sheet. "This might be what they call a 'hotspot'—"

"It is," Erin said. She'd heard enough of that word starting out on this demon hunting path.

Martinson made another small grunt. "We usually only see one of these at a time. However, of late—"

"Yeah, there were like twenty or something for a while," Erin said. When Martinson raised her eyebrow, Erin couldn't help but take a small swipe. "We hear about things like that even out in the backwoods, you know."

Martinson bared her teeth in wry amusement. "Interesting. Most places we've visited in the past that experience this sort of activity—it's not necessarily distinguishable from tuned-up, high-level criminal activity, at least not in the statistics."

"Yeah, the 35,000-foot view just looks like a lot of people being dead," Erin said. "No drive-bys, no guns ... it's swords and knives and serial killer shit every day but in a thousand different ways. Hannibal Lecter would be grossed out by the stuff we've seen come through here lately."

Martinson nodded along. "That's not atypical. We've had hotspots hit in New Orleans, Detroit, Chicago, DC, Baltimore—places where you might expect higher-than-usual murder rates anyway. We were able to disguise the increase among the regular numbers, but ..." She shook her head in a very, tsk-tsk-tsk sort of way, like she was trying to puzzle things through. "I don't see how we could do that here."

Erin was stuck a couple stops back. "So ... you hide these incidents?" It wasn't exactly a mind-blowing revelation, since DC had been ignoring their cries for help from the beginning, but to hear someone with some authority verbalize it ...

Martinson gave her a look that was half condescension, half knowing smile. "How would you explain to the public that there are demons? Ancient creatures that we read about in our myths and stories. That this modern world we've built isn't ours alone; that demons never left?"

Erin had given it lots of thought over the last few months. "Just about like that, I reckon."

Martinson smiled a little wider. "If it were my decision ... oh, hell, who am I kidding? I wouldn't tell the people. No chance. They're not ready to handle it. Not even close."

Erin raised an eyebrow. "We've had to tell them around here," she said dryly. "It's been our most effective defense, trusting people to want to—you know, preserve their own lives."

Now Martinson's smile got patronizing. "Here, things are maybe a little different. You can't expect that everywhere. This is the Bible Belt. People are probably more willing to accept a weird supernatural explanation for things that don't fit the framework of everyday life. You try an explanation like that in New York City, it's going to cause a panic."

"Well, I'd hate to see a run on organic kale," Erin said, "and all the arugula go flying off the shelves along with the Fiji Water as people prepared for the demon apocalypse, but here's a thought—just maybe people deserve to know about potential threats to their lives?"

Martinson shook her head. "We protect the people from these threats. They can sleep safely in bed at night knowing that we have a response ready for these types of situations."

Erin felt a dull throb in her temple, and she summoned up all her southern charm to try and find a way to say what was on her mind without being an utter douche nozzle about it. "Well, begging your pardon, ma'am, but we've been swimming with the fucking sharks out here for months, and your folks haven't showed up even once—after all our calls, begging for help—so I guess I kinda question whether you actually protect people from these situations, since a fuck ton of my people have not been protected by anyone, including myself, unfortunately."

That ... probably wasn't it, Erin reflected a moment later.

Martinson seemed to take it in stride. "Look, it's a fact of life that not everyone gets saved. Police response times are longer out here, right? Than in the city?"

"Sure."

"Well, think of our ability to respond in a similar manner. In bigger cities, we have field offices. Agents close at hand to assess the situation. Out here? We have nothing. And there's been a hell of a lot going on in the more densely populated areas lately. Like you said, tons of hotspots have been going off, and some of them in some fairly major population centers. Chicago just got hit with a wave of demon activity that's higher than almost anything we've ever measured. It's tapering off now, but we had to go deal with that. Now that it's subsiding ..." She waved a hand in Erin's direction.

Now you've got time for the little people, Erin didn't say. Instead, "You've got the ability to follow up on non-critical leads." And she just about kicked herself for softballing it.

"Exactly," Martinson said with that same smile that Erin was starting to think was a little patronizing. With a nod, the FBI agent walked off to do who knew what, leaving Erin standing by herself. But not for long.

"Seems like the FBI knows a thing or two about demons," Arch said as he sauntered up.

"A thing or twelve, yeah," Erin said, watching Martinson go. She found her way over to Ross, and they started talking. Too quiet to hear, too subdued in terms of body language to pick up much emotion.

"That was a surprise," Arch said. "I figured the FBI wouldn't know diddly-squat about demons."

"Seems our betters at the bureau have been participating in a demon cover-up all these years," Erin said. The bitterness seeped out. "We normal folks can't handle these sorts of high-fallutin' secrets, you see. We might panic and injure ourselves while cleaning out the local grocery."

"Having seen a run or two on Rogerson's when snow's expected ... I'm not sure I fully disagree with that approach," Arch said. "But it seems to me folks ought to have a chance to defend themselves."

"Exactly what I said." Erin looked at Arch. "We've pulled together as a town because we knew what we were up against and could fight back. That only happens because we were aware of what it took to fight demons." A little pang of annoyance seemed to rattle in her soul—that was thanks to Hendricks, damn his eyes. And the rest of him.

Arch just grunted agreement. "Speaking of our troops ... Nate McMinn."

Erin closed her eyes. It didn't blot out the brightness of the day. "I know. I saw him."

"Someone's going to have to inform his family."

That felt like a gut punch right to Erin's midsection. "I guess that's on me."

Arch didn't argue. "Lucky thing that Gary Wrightson showed up with his crew."

Now it was Erin's turn to grunt. "I guess."

Arch studied her with his usual inscrutability, maybe turned up a notch or two. "You don't approve?"

Erin looked over her shoulder to make sure Gary wasn't rolling up behind her even now. Or one of his relations wasn't sneaking by behind her as she trashed him. "I don't like any of 'em. The Wrightsons are assholes, down to the last. You ever deal with Larry? Arrest him, I mean?"

Arch thought about it. "No. But I think Fries might have had a tale or two involving him. Bar stuff. Drunk and disorderly charges."

"Right. I was there at Fast Freddie's for a couple of them. He's a lazyass, bickering, good-for-nothing piece of shit. His older brothers never looked much better in my estimation, and his momma is a fucking white trash nightmare. If you never heard Reeve's story about her—"

"Oh, I've heard it."

"—don't get on her bad side when she's got a heavy object at hand 'less you want your skull creased." Erin let some of the tension out in a sigh. "Her wheelchair-bound sonnyboy? He seems like a nut with a hard-on to prove himself able, not just willing."

Arch raised an eyebrow at that. "That's ... harsh."

"It's a bitch of a world," Erin said, looking over her shoulder at where Dr. Darlington stood, a sheet pulled over the crushed body of Nate McMinn, "and I guess my job right now is to be even bitchier, fight back hard enough to make a dent in it."

Arch took a moment, maybe trying to analyze what she was saying. "I'm not sure that's—"

"Erin," Casey said, trotting up while keeping a wide stance, like he was trying to keep his legs from rubbing together. She cursed herself for noticing that. "We got a call—incident at Moody's Roadhouse."

Erin rolled her eyes. Moody's Roadhouse. That fucking strip club. The only thing older and uglier than the building was the strippers-slash-prostitutes who worked there. "Arch, you want to handle this?"

She knew the moment she saw his reaction: Nope. He did not want to handle this. "I *can* go," he said, rather guardedly, "but—"

"Just handle it," she said, turning away. "I gotta deal with these feds—and Nate's family." Which was probably still better than dealing with those aging trollops out at the Roadhouse, but she didn't feel the need to say so to Arch, whose lips were puckered like he'd just drunk the juice of a whole lemon.

*

Darla was trying to concentrate on the pages of her book. Dusty, worn, written on parchment with a quill and an inkwell— just turning these pages, stroking them, gave her a feeling akin to brushing against a lover. They didn't make books like this anymore; now it was all cheap paper, covers bound and slapped on so some conglomerate could get it on a shelf for twenty-five cents and sell it for twenty-five dollars. There was no beauty to them, no elegance. Cheap pages, cheap binding, produced cut-rate by a bunch of sweaty men in a factory press.

But this—this book was written by hand, by a monk, over the course of months or years. Illuminated from the original text, countless hours of care put into it—

"That's not even legible," Marischa said, sniffing, as she looked over Darla's shoulder. The kids were watching *PAW Patrol*—again—on the floor in front of her. Marischa strutted by, wearing short shorts that revealed veiny legs, the purple bulges still visible after countless laserings.

Darla controlled her eye roll. "It's in Latin." It was not. But

Marischa wouldn't know that.

"I don't know how you read those things," Marischa said. It was her normal tone—perfectly dismissive of anything she didn't understand. "So dry."

Darla glanced at the demon language scrawled onto the pages. This one had been quite the find. Twenty bucks at an estate sale. If they'd known its actual worth, she'd have paid thousands. "This one's quite gripping, actually." Five hundred sacrificial rituals. The monks had skipped the illustrations—probably out of propriety, since they surely knew what they were reading—but kept the text whole and unchanged.

Marischa made a dismissive noise. "Kids … who's hungry?" she asked.

Jay and Mera stirred out of their television-induced torpor. "Me," Jay said. Mera just nodded.

"Where can we go to get a quality beef short rib?" Marischa asked. "Something very intensely personal to the chef. Revelatory. Expressive."

It was all Darla could do not to snort. "Chattanooga. Maybe Knoxville." She made it sound like a fucking painting.

"Well, how far away is that?" Marischa asked.

"Forty-five minutes to Chattanooga. An hour or more to Knoxville." With the kids pent up in the car the whole time. Darla wasn't doing that, but she wouldn't mind sending Marischa all by her lonesome.

"Well, let's go. Dinner's my treat."

"I don't think that's really gonna suit the kids' palates," Darla said, rubbing her finger along the inside of the book for comfort. It felt good against her fingertip. Reassuring somehow. "They're more into mac and cheese."

"Mac and cheese, mac and cheeeeeese!" Mera shouted.

Darla just smiled. "Why don't you go without us?"

Marischa looked like she'd eaten a pine cone and tried to shit it out whole. "I've come all this way." So prim. "And you won't even let me take you out to dinner? Besides, artisanal mac and cheese sounds good to me as well."

Darla snorted. Figured that mac and cheese would be haute cuisine in these days of infantilization. She wasn't keen on driving an hour so Marischa could try to squeeze them into one of her pretentious restaurants. "I don't have a problem with you paying," she said instead, rather coolly, "but you might want to pick somewhere the kids will like. And closer." That would be less likely to end in complete disaster."

"Nonsense, they'll love it," Marischa stood. "Let's go."

"You know … I'm just not hungry right now," Darla said, still stroking the book. "I find my appetite is just … gone … since Jason …" she tried to stare off into the distance, pull off that imitation of grief that she'd learned to do in childhood to throw people off the trail of her not giving a fuck about things that only tangentially involved her. She fake-mopped a tear at her eye. "Go on without me. You can take my car."

Marischa blinked at her. "Why would I take your car?"

"Car seats," Darla said, letting her voice crack. It was mostly from glee at thinking of her mother-in-law suffering the ride with her two hellions. *Suck on that, you old bat. I bet it goes great with artisanal goat cheese.*

"Oh." If this deflated Marischa's enthusiasm for her plan, she didn't show it other than a slight wrinkle on each of her jowl lines. "I suppose. But, we can't have a family dinner without you." Now it was her turn to activate the waterworks, and these came off real. "I just … to lose my son so recently … I feel the need to hold tightly to what I have left …"

She wasn't looking exactly at Darla, but Darla knew what she was doing. Marischa employed emotional manipulation like one of her plastic surgeons used a scalpel or a laser. Expertly.

The problem with guilt, of course, was that it relied on empathy.

"I hope you're not trying to guilt me," Darla said, seeing the ten-thousand-ton weight heading her way and taking an able step to the side. "Because I have my own feelings about what's happened, about the tragedy—and I'm working through it in my own way, and that doesn't involve subjecting myself to a happy, uncaring public who doesn't give a shit about what I'm going through." Boom. She served that guilt ball right back at Marischa like a spike in a game of volleyball. Which was something Darla was expert at.

Marischa took it in the teeth, huffing. "Well—I—I wasn't trying to make you feel guilty, I was trying to pull our little family together after—"

"We can pull together just fine here in town," Darla said. "The kids love pizza. There's a pizza place in Culver. It's simple, no pretensions, which they'd hate, by the way, and you don't need to put them and yourself through a two-hour hell of car tripping in order to have a family meal." She stared evenly at Marischa, trying to put in an appeal to sanity. The truth was, Darla herself might have appreciated haute cuisine, but she'd hate life by the time the ride was done, and restraining the kids in a restaurant setting sounded less enjoyable to her than visiting actual hell. At least in hell, she'd have people she could ask for help. Marischa would be less than useless keeping her kids from holy terroring in a fancy restaurant. They were too young and too wild to restrain themselves in such a place.

"Fine," Marischa said at last. "Pizza." She made it sound so vulgar. Probably because she knew it wouldn't have artisanal crust or mozzarella di bufala.

Darla didn't smile at her small victory. She just brushed her fingers against the interior pages of her book. She was still planning for the largest one.

*

Arch pulled into the parking lot of Moody's Roadhouse with a welling tension in his shoulders. They felt ropey and taut, and when he put the Explorer in park, he did it with a little more gusto than was perhaps called for.

"Well, well," Guthrie said, grinning at Arch as he got out of the car, "look who got sent to deal with the strippers and whores."

Arch looked at the stately older woman standing under the big sign that declared this place the roadhouse, and nodded at Duncan, who stood beside her, unspeaking. "Wondered where you two got off to while we were fighting snakes."

"Just trying to stay out of your way while you were dealing with the lawful authorities," Duncan said. "Of the human variety."

"Yeah, we don't mix so well with the human sort of law enforcement," Guthrie said, still grinning. "Your laws are way too arbitrary and random for us to understand. 'These drugs, which will not kill you, are illegal; these other drugs, which will definitely kill you, are totally fine and regularly prescribed.' I don't know how you people sort it out."

"Somehow we muddle through," Arch said, passing her and stepping into the darkness of the roadhouse. His eyes adjusted quickly, and he found himself in a dimly lit bar, a half-dozen barely or not-at-all clad women sitting on the stage while some big fella in a black t-shirt and pants gibbered and cried uncontrollably.

"Shut up, Toby, you little bitch," said one of the dancers, a woman who didn't have a stitch on. "You didn't even face the damned thing." She turned her head and caught sight of Arch. Throwing her brownish hair back over a bare shoulder, she stood, and Arch tried real hard not to look any lower than her collarbone. She had to be in her forties, maybe younger if she did a lot of drugs, but nothing above the belt moved when she walked. Not that she had a belt. "Officer, I'm Gloria Tyler. I'm the one that first encountered the demon."

Keep your eyes above her collarbones. That was Arch's advice to himself. She made it easier—marginally—by stepping to within a couple feet of him and acting like nothing was out of the ordinary. They were just two people having a conversation. And one of them had a huge, heaving fake chest and no clothes on. Blood dripping down a leg, too, though he couldn't see where she might have been wounded. "What, uh ... happened here?" Arch asked. His voice was only a little strangled.

"A demon busted down the metal door to the parking lot out back," Gloria said. "I managed to rally the girls before it came in, and we got armed and shot it up."

Arch blinked. Shot it up? "How ... how'd that go?" he asked, feeling way off his game.

"It ran off," she said, pointing at the back. Arch followed her acrylic nail, chipped to a rough edge, and sure enough, there was a busted-down door in the back, a metal one that looked like it had been folded off its hinges. A few bullet holes dotted the wall around the frame, but only a few. "That way. Out back."

"What did it look like?" Guthrie sidled in.

"Like Swamp Thing, but made out of tar," Gloria said. "I don't know that the bullets did much other than scare it. Seemed to just disappear under its skin. Yvette swung her cross necklace at it once we ran dry; maybe that's why it took off, I couldn't say for sure."

"Demons don't like holy objects," Arch said, still feeling a bit strangled. He looked past Gloria—if that was her real name—and toward the other women on the stage, all of whom were—blessedly—dressed. He scanned 'em, then stopped midway at Yvette. "Hey, Yvette," he said, feeling even more strangled now, somehow.

"Hey, Arch," she said back, very neutrally.

Arch nodded his head, once, in acknowledgment of her greeting, then averted his eyes as though she, too, were nude. "Well, I reckon we'll do what we can about this, unless there's anything else, Miss ... Gloria?" He looked at the lady.

"If I think of anything else, I'll tell you." She gave Arch a once over, smiled slightly, and meandered off.

Guthrie, never missing an opportunity to be a pain in the duff, leaned in and whispered, "What's the matter? You know that chick over at the stage?" He nodded his head toward Yvette.

"She, uh ..." Arch said, taking a nice, long look at the floor, which was covered with shattered glass, probably from when the patrons of this establishment made their exodus, "she goes to my church."

Guthrie let out a low cackle. "This is a moment of delicious irony. Displeased by the appearance of a sinner in your midst."

Arch didn't roll his eyes often, but he couldn't resist the urge now. "We're all sinners."

Guthrie was undeterred. "It bothers you that a woman who bares her body and feeds the salacious lust of man for silver comes to your church, doesn't it? Rubs off on your holiness?"

Arch just sighed. "You never heard about what Mary Magdalene did before she followed Jesus?" He chucked a thumb over his shoulder. "Yvette's a nice lady, and while I may not approve of her choice of professions," it caused a little tension in him to say it this mildly, because he was roiling a little inside for a couple reasons he didn't care to put a finger on, "I love the sinner and hate the sin, not vice versa."

Guthrie just stared at him with smoky eyes as her lips quirked at the corner. "Ugh. You people." And she stalked off.

"Your partner is a real piece of work," Arch said as Duncan sidled a little closer, a little trace of a smile evidencing itself on his extremely plain face. A rare thing, that.

"She reads the passages about the temptation of Christ as a helpful instruction manual," Duncan said. His gaze flicked over the dancers. "You might want to start taking your dog for a walk every now and again."

Arch tried to suss out that one and failed. "I don't ... have a dog."

Duncan cleared his throat and pointed down. Arch followed his finger and realized he was pointing at the front of Arch's pants. "Dog," the demon said. "Walk it."

"What? No," Arch said. "That's not ... appropriate." Though there was some tenting going on that didn't reflect the best on him. Arch shifted in his khakis to reduce the effect. Addressing the underlying cause was right out.

Duncan's forehead wrinkled. Another rare display. "Seriously?"

Arch looked around to make sure Guthrie wasn't lingering in earshot. "Seriously."

"Look, I lived with you for a while," Duncan said, "and hearing you and Alison go at it like wild ferrets every night gives some idea about your capability and vigor as a man. You can't go from sixty to zero without applying the brakes. You need some sort of outlet."

"Or what, I'll die?" Arch just stared him down. "My wife dying applied the brakes, thank you very much."

"Looks to me like you're revving up again," Duncan said, sparing one last glance for the front of Arch's pants.

"What's that?" Guthrie chose this moment, of course, to reappear.

"Demons," Arch said, trying to draw attention back where it belonged. "You know what this black tar swamp thing is?"

"Clearly," Guthrie said in a dry voice, "it's the manifestation of all the racial unrest and unsettled rage in this place, given life and taking the form of a most powerful totem and local symbol of unresolved oppression—a tar baby. A giant one."

That ... caused Arch to raise an eyebrow. "Really?"

Guthrie looked serious ... for about a second. "Nah, I'm just fucking with you. It's probably a ... what?" She looked at Duncan. "Graanz-ahz-zeez?"

Duncan nodded. "Slime demon. Pre-dates that story by millions of years. It's a predator, likes the taste of meat and flesh, and is drawn by human activity of all kinds." He glanced around the roadhouse. "Though it does seem to tend toward the loud and rowdy for some reason. It doesn't often go attacking quiet country churches."

"Such a disappointment," Guthrie said, "like so many of our brethren."

"Why do you think it was drawn here?" Arch asked.

"It probably smelled the sex ten miles off," Guthrie said. "Demons can sense high urge or emotion—some of them anyway. Strong appetite—gluttony, lust, whatever—it's more potent than someone just living everyday life. Kind of a residual psychic sense we have, but it's not a very conscious thing. Like a low-functioning version of what Duncan can do."

"Except mine's impaired," Duncan said.

"You need a spiritual enema, my friend," Guthrie said.

"I don't trust you to administer anything of that sort," Duncan said.

"I don't blame you," Arch said, drawing guffaws from both of the demons. "Did y'all pick up any of the chatter about the snakes? At the last call?"

"Snakes are all that's left at last call," Guthrie said. "All the good men go home early, and even the decent ones leave well before closing time."

"No," Duncan said, ignoring Guthrie. "Snakes?"

"Big ones," Arch said. "Came through a toilet, blew out the windows of a house and came crawling out of every crack. Ate Nate McMinn—"

"Was he the one with the big, thick glasses?" Guthrie asked.

"No," Arch said. "I think that's Chauncey Watson you're talking about."

"I can't keep you people straight," Guthrie said. "Was he the pastor?"

"No," Arch said. "That's Barney Jones. Who's black. Nate McMinn is—was—white."

"I told you before, I don't pay attention to race," Guthrie said. "Flay you, you people all look the same to me."

"Well ... okay, then," Arch said, "I'm not striving for equality under your banner, that's for sure, especially if it involves me losing all my skin."

"How big were these snakes?" Duncan asked, still frowning at Arch.

"Well, one of them opened its jaw wide and ate Nate whole. So ... pretty big. Started splitting their tails into legs and walking, some of them. And leaping and—"

Duncan's frown deepened, and he looked at Guthrie. "Unvanore?"

Guthrie frowned back. "Sounded like maybe Harvacronga to me."

Duncan shook his head. "Harvacronga don't split their tails or walk."

"Unvanore don't have a jaw that can move wide enough to eat a human, even a scrawny one, in one good gulp," Guthrie said.

"So y'all ain't heard of something like this before?" Arch asked.

"Lots of snakes in the world, my friend," Guthrie said. "We don't know every species of the demon variety any more than you could name one of the ordinary, garden variety."

"Coral snake," Arch said.

Guthrie just stared at him. "I was looking more for Kingdom, Phylum, Class, Order ..."

"You keep looking, then."

"What do you want to do about this racist totem swamp thing?" Duncan asked.

"Go after it, I reckon," Arch said. "Now that the woods are clear of those shadowcats, we oughta be able to hike after it a spell, right?"

"Ugh, hiking," Guthrie said, lifting a foot to show that she'd worn heels. "In these shoes?"

"Come on," Arch said, and started for the back door. He would have tipped his hat to the dancers, still huddled around the stage, but he didn't have a hat. He just sort of nodded instead, uncomfortably, and stalked toward the rear of the club, where fresh air and some element of freedom enticed him onward, and out of the perfumed, uncomfortable environs within.

*

There had already been two milk spills by the time the appetizers showed up, which in this case was garlic cheesy bread of the sort that Darla couldn't resist even though it made her yoga pants stretch even tighter at the seams. Only one tantrum, though, and that was Jay, because of one of the milk spills.

"See," Darla said, eating cheesy bread and pausing between bites to address Marischa, "isn't it better that this is happening here, rather than in a place with quiet conversation, kale, arugula, and gastrique?"

Marischa's nose was wrinkled. She was nibbling the cheesy bread as though it might be poisoned, apparently hesitant to show even the slightest sign of enjoyment. "What is this?" she asked, wrinkling her nose further.

"It's bread with cheese on it," Darla said. "Probably a gallon of butter, too. Taste the carb-y goodness."

Marischa put it down on the little bread plate, which was plastic and made an unsatisfying noise as she did so, prompting a further frown. Probably upset because it wasn't served on crystal or something. Darla had liked the fact that her in-laws were affluent when she married Jason, definitely a few rungs higher than her own family, but sometimes ... well, you could take the rich bitch out of the Gold Coast, but you couldn't get her to take the silver spoon out of her ass.

Darla could smell an uncomfortable question coming a mile off, brewing on Marischa's face like a storm off the coast, gathering strength. She pre-empted it. "What are you doing to fill your time these days, Marischa?"

Marischa adjusted the napkin in her lap. Darla had lost hers to the first milk spill. "I spend quite a bit of time on fundraisers for charity ... certain clubs that have my membership ..." Her voice drifted off and she stared into the distance. "It has become more difficult to concentrate lately. I think of Jason, and ..." She faded off again.

Darla was a couple steps ahead. "I have the same problem. But the kids keep me busy most of the time." And she really only missed him every now and again, when she wanted to stick a hand up his ass like a puppet and watch him squirm. That was fun. For everything else, up to and including the business of getting off herself, she had plenty of others she could call if she felt the urge. And Jason, for all his ambition, hadn't been of much use at home for a long time. In fact, if he'd been looking to betray her, he couldn't have died at a better time, because his source of professional power—the office of County Administrator—was diminishing by the day as things crumbled around them.

Tears were for losers, or people who'd actually lost something.

Darla hadn't, not really. If the life insurance money came through, she'd actually be in a better position without him. Probably wouldn't do to say that out loud, though. Instead, she went for, "It's tough."

Mera started crying right then, apropos of absolutely nothing Darla could discern. When she asked, all Mera said was, "I dropped it." It took a minute to work out that "it" was a crayon. Once returned, things settled down, the children focused on coloring comically exaggerated pictures. "Beats the hell out of a Peter Max," Darla said.

Marischa looked scandalized but let it pass. "I don't know how you're going to do it. Going forward without him, I mean."

Darla kept what she was feeling well tucked away. "I don't know, either." *With enough money, I can hire a fucking nanny to do the work your son wasn't, that's how. And get to the real job of sealing up the last of the alliances I need to move this fucker over the finish line. And with a big fucking dildo that operates as long as I want it to, and knows where the clitoris is because it's made that way.*

"I'll help you as much as I can," Marischa said, watery eyes boring into Darla's. "You can move back to Chicago; no need to stay here now that Jason's gone, and his terrible job is …" She shook her head. "I don't know what he was thinking. He could have been anything. Becoming a county employee in this … this …"

"Hell?" Darla offered, then realized her misstep.

"Yes. Hell," Marischa said, catching a funny look from a waiter as he went past holding a pizza high. "This place is hell. You need to move back to civilization, post haste. Remedy that error of my son's judgment and get these kids in good schools. I bet they don't even source anything organic around here."

Darla shrugged. She hadn't figured on living long enough for any potential consequences of inorganic living to catch up to her, but you couldn't say that shit in mom's groups, so she nodded, feigning sincerity. "I'll think about it. Suze Orman says you're not supposed to make any dramatic moves for a year after a big event like this. Give time for the emotions to settle down, you know."

Marischa made a near-choking noise deep in her throat. "Spend another year in Tennessee? Are you out of your fucking mind?"

"Fuck," Jay repeated. "What does that mean, Momma?"

"Literally, to strike," Darla said. Marischa did indeed look stricken. "It's an old Germanic word." She stared at her mother-in-law, then smiled sweetly. "Etymology."

"Oh," Marischa said, looking abashed for only a beat before moving back to her own hobbyhorse. "I just think that … given all that's happened, it'd be better to get the kids moving forward, adjusted—

you know, deal with the big changes all in a sequence."

"I don't know that that's wise," Darla said with perfect reserve, "but I'll think about it."

"Sweetheart, they're going to bounce back from this quicker than you are," Marischa said.

Darla kept her expression blank. *I doubt it.* "I'll think about it," she said again. She only needed to put this old bird off for so long. The end was coming; she just had to be ready for it when it arrived. And though it felt like it was getting close ... she was nowhere near ready, and having her mother-in-law around wasn't going to make it any easier ... unless she could get away and start striking some deals while Marischa babysat the kids ...

*

"Help's coming," Ross said, coming back up to Erin with Martinson at his side. The two feds showed no excitement at this prospect, but Erin's emotions had been on mute for months, so she barely cared that they didn't seem enthused by this.

"Hell yes," Erin said, which was about as excited as she got these days. "What kind of help?"

"Lots of agents," Martinson said. "Trained to deal with demons. You won't have to do this citizen army thing anymore."

Erin raised an eyebrow at that. Disband the watch? Surely not. "How many people are you bringing to the party?"

"Enough," Ross said. "We've managed crises of this size before. Don't worry. We're pros."

"Good to know," Erin said, not sure where she should file that information. Probably right next to the sensation of relief she'd felt for all of five seconds before it drained away at the thought of demobilizing the watch.

*

"The problem with your kind ..." Guthrie droned as they hiked through the woods, Arch's windbreaker zipped up all the way to his neck like his momma had done it for him before letting him outside, "... is that you've got no real perspective on what you've got faith in."

"And you do, I suppose?" Arch asked, tired of discussing ... well, anything ... with Guthrie.

"I know more than you, fleshbag," Guthrie said. "Secrets of the universe are at the disposal of any demon. We possess ancient knowledge—because most of us have been around in one form or another since the beginning. We saw how things went down in the early days of man."

"Duncan said that the chapters of the Bible with the temptation of Christ were like an instruction manual to you," Arch said, stepping over a wilted fern. "Since I know that, can we just skip this part where you sow seeds of doubt and try to rend my faith?"

"Fuck you, Duncan, for ruining my good times," Guthrie said. Duncan just shrugged. Guthrie turned back to Arch and doubled down. "Why would you believe in a God that let your wife die, huh? How can you believe in the goodness of a God that would do that? I ask you."

Yep, that prompted an eye roll. Arch couldn't hold it back anymore. They'd walked a couple miles over hilly terrain, and he was a little tired, a little annoyed, and a little … something else from being in that strip club in the presence of naked flesh, even as … unappealing as it might have been under ordinary conditions. "I didn't realize that a condition of my faith was that I had to explain the genesis of the belief in my heart to a demon, but … sure, it's been a wild month or two, why not?"

He turned, drawing in a slightly ragged breath. The incline of the hike had been steep. "What do you think God is?" Arch asked, looking Guthrie in the eye.

Guthrie stepped under the shadow of a big bough, shade running over her features and hiding her eyes. "Nuh uh. Whatever I know, I know. No faith involved. You can't see, feel, touch, taste—what's the fifth sense?" She looked to Duncan. "Oh, hear. Yeah. You can't do any of that to prove yourself right. So you rely on … what? A book written in the fifth century? The song of your heart?"

"I rely on a book passed down through the ages, sure," Arch said. "And you can argue its provenance all you want, I don't care."

"A convenient demurral," Guthrie leaned in. "Some interesting stuff included … like wrathful vengeance … some other, equally interesting omissions. But that you'd go and choose to dedicate your life to this book, this hodgepodge of collected stories—"

"I don't dedicate my life to a book," Arch said. "I dedicate myself to the Being I think authored it—through others."

"Still, if I did that, say, with the works of L. Ron Hubbard," Guthrie said, "you'd think I was a nut. And lawyers would be crawling out of the woodwork to sue the shit out of me just for saying that."

"If an antagonistic statement is made in the forest, and no one hears, do you still get disconnected?" Duncan quipped.

"Fucking lawyers will make it so," Guthrie said. "And sue your ass blue. But my point still stands—you're taking divine inspiration from a book you don't know is divine."

"See, and this is where we inevitably butt heads—" Arch said.

"Oh, one of us is a butt head, all right," Guthrie said.

"—because you're asking me to quantify that which cannot be quantified," Arch said. "You're asking me to define something that exists beyond—"

"Who wrote your Bible?" Guthrie asked. "Literally, who wrote your—"

"There were a few sources," Arch said. "For one, the Priestly source—"

"Bullshit," Guthrie said. "Who wrote it? You said 'divine author.' You think God put his finger on the hand of men and scrawled it out on the parchment—"

"Sure."

"And he did those miracles in the pages?" Guthrie asked. "Saved those men from the fire in Babylon—" She stopped and cringed slightly. Too late, though.

Arch just laughed. "You walked into that one. It'd be hard to doubt a miracle I'd seen performed on my own flesh, wouldn't it?"

Guthrie's face tightened. "Yeah, congrats, you walked through demon fire. That doesn't mean anything. What I want to know is—"

"No, no," Arch said, "you ask me if I believe in miracles? When I've seen at least one with my own eyes? Twice, technically, since that Gideon demon bellowed fire at me, too, and I survived unburnt."

"So God saved you ... but he didn't deign to save your wife," Guthrie said. "Care to explain that?"

"You're asking me, as a child, to explain the action of a parent," Arch said. "I can't do that; I don't know. I don't *see*. There are things my momma did I still can't figure out. And don't even get me started on the things my daddy did—"

"That's the cheap way out," Guthrie said. "The child's way out. 'I don't know, because I'm a baby and can't walk and talk yet.' Pffft! You're a grown man."

"I'm a human being bound to this form," Arch said. "If you think this is the last stop, the sum of our journey in the universe ... then yeah, I guess we should be able to evolve or something and explain, eventually, how there's not anything else. But I don't believe that. And I'm not sufficiently evolved to 'see' it—if that's the case. And I don't believe it is."

"'Believe,'" Guthrie said. "I like it when I hear that word. You know why? Because it's simultaneously an admission that you humans know nothing for certain ... but it also galls me a little. Because 'believe' is a statement about how you see the universe. There's hubris in it. You're bugs here. Specks, at best—"

"And what are you?" Arch asked.

"Slightly more aware specks," Guthrie said. "But every time I hear a human say, 'I believe,' in that breathy, eager way of theirs ... I laugh a little inside. 'These fleshy lumps have delusions of meaning in their lives,' I think. That an ant could understand the anthill, let alone believe that the human looming above it, casting you all in shadow, has some benevolent interest in you, you little ant—you? Ha! What makes you think your God—if he exists—didn't just stumble along and find you here and think, 'Wouldn't it be nice—wife at home cheating on me with the plumber deity, kids hate me for being a dick—wouldn't it be nice if these tiny little beings thought I was awesome? So he wrecks some of your mounds, sides with certain of your people over others, tosses down a favor every now and again, like a benevolent dictator trying to inspire a case of Stockholm Syndrome in the ants—"

"When we started this conversation," Arch said, reaching the crest of a small rise, "you wouldn't even stipulate to admitting there was a God. Now you're making the argument that he's there, just indifferent or manipulative."

Guthrie's eyes narrowed into tight slits. "And?"

"Nothing," Arch said. "Just interested to see how far you'll move the goalposts in the next ten minutes."

Guthrie forced a pained smirk. "Well—"

A roar caused Arch to turn, as a beast some eight feet tall shredded through a small tree and lurched at him. It was huge, hulking, seemed to be dripping black tar, as so many of these demons did. Dripping with evil, he wondered? Of course, the oiliest of them were the ones like Guthrie, who didn't so much attack with claws as with tongues—

Arch thrust out his sword and greeted the creature with the point. It caught the demon right in the center of the chest during its charge, and it paused, looking at him with black eyes for a second in surprise before—

It burst into a sulphuric cloud, disappearing as the wind picked up, thankfully carrying the stink away.

"Well," Guthrie said, "that was ... pathetic."

Arch scoured the landscape around them. The demon had seemingly come out of nowhere; he wanted to make sure no others were sneaking around just out of sight.

"I mean, really," Guthrie said, "that thing was so big ... and it went down like a little bitch. Another disappointment. I'm so ashamed for our kind today."

"Because it popped like a stink balloon on the point of a sword?" Arch asked, brushing past Guthrie and clapping her on the shoulder as he did so. A heavy pad greeted his hand, which was no surprise. Guthrie did look a little like a linebacker today. "Or because you're doing a poor job of knocking my faith from beneath me right now?"

A short, seething noise slipped out through Guthrie's gritted teeth. "Your God killed your wife. Or let her die. Yet you still worship him? How do you explain that shit other than indifference or malice?"

"I explain it by free will," Arch said, looking Guthrie right in the eye. "God doesn't *make* me do anything."

"Then he lets bad things happen to you."

"And if He didn't?" Arch asked. "What kind of free will would I have? Would anyone have? What do you think my God is? Some genie? Some Get-Out-of-Consequences-Free card? What would any of our choices, our lives here *matter* if He just ... swooped in and made everything right? I mean ... then maybe this would be our last stop. We'd have heaven on earth, because ... what more would there be?"

"You've got some fucked-up ideas about the way things work," Guthrie said.

"I didn't choose for Alison to die," Arch said. "At best, you could argue she chose it, by putting herself in front of that demon and fighting him. Her death meant something—to her. She fought for this town, she fought against evil—she fought for her fellow man, like I do. And it ...kills me that this was the sacrifice demanded. But this ... is not the end." Arch took a step and brought his face inches from Guthrie's. The demon almost recoiled. "You ask me how I believe—I don't have an answer for how. The why is more important anyway—because I do. Because I feel it. There is meaning here, in this world, but it is not the end, it is not the be-all, end-all—earthly matters are not the sum of my life in this universe. It's bigger than that, bigger than you and me, sitting here on a hilltop as you try and get me to fall into your nihilistic trap. So I can ... what? Believe nothing? Stare despairingly into a black abyss, thinking no consequence matters because it happens in a vacuum? That's better?"

"Then you'd at least be free," Guthrie said.

"No, then I'd be a real slave," Arch said. "To my earthly body and fleshly desires. To whatever I wanted in the moment, or here." He tapped his chest. "I don't need your despair, thank you. I don't need your offer of ... nothing. Of my bodily cravings satisfied and my soul emptied." He glanced at Duncan. "I'm not just a man, and not just flesh to be sated here, now."

"Yes you are," Guthrie said. "You are just that and nothing more."

"So you 'believe,'" Arch said, and almost smiled. Then he turned, catching the slightest hint of a smile from Duncan, who was trying to hide his face, and started back down the hill.

"I don't believe, kid," Guthrie called after him. "I know."

"So do I," Arch said, not turning back. "It's just that what I know ... is different from what you do."

"You're wrong," Guthrie called after him. "And when you get to the end and figure out there's nothing else ... what then?"

"I think I'll look back and realize I spent my life helping people as best I could and doing all the good I can," Arch said. The green surrounding him felt unusually vibrant and alive, insects chirping even in the chill of the wintery woods. "And I'll be just fine with that."

*

Gary was staring at the little screen on the end of the pipe snake. This was a fancy model, not dissimilar to what SWAT teams used to look under doors before they busted 'em down. He adopted a similar policy—identify the clog, then smash it to pieces, thus restoring the proper flow of water from a toilet or sink or drain.

This, though ... this shit was something else.

"Is wet on way down," Marina said, looking over his shoulder in the stinking, confined bathroom in Fred Mickelson's house. By God, Erin had had the grace to have ol' Fred's corpse removed from the room, otherwise this would be a whole lot shittier. "But the septic is ..."

He knew what she meant. It was damned sure murky, as one might expect of a chamber filled with piss and shit. "Look at the tank level down there."

She nodded. The septic wasn't anywhere near filled, which was ... strange. "Maybe he had it serviced recently?"

"Maybe," Gary said. "Shame we can't ask him. Either way, a snake could make it from the bottom of the tank to the top, easy, the size they were. My question is—where the hell did they come from? Things that size? This septic ain't that big, so there's gotta be an external entry somewhere, unless they just ... spawned in there, like yoga-pants moms at a city park." They did seem to spring out of nowhere.

"Must be crack in system," Marina said in that broken English.

"Explains water level drain down there. Is leaking out."

"That seems logical, but ..." Something about that bothered Gary. He rotated the fiber optic snake, looking around. It had night vision and showed a clear picture of septic tank walls that looked ... well, about like you'd expect something buried in the earth, exposed to shit and piss and all other manner of bodily fluids for untold decades might look.

"Something tickling your spider sense?" Marina asked. Gary looked at her funny. His legs were folded up beneath him so he could maneuver the snake over the hole down into the bottom of the toilet's busted remainder. "Is movie thing," she said. "From *Spiderman*. Big in America. Less so in Poland."

"I don't reckon I have a spider sense," Gary said, turning back to the screen. "But something's tickling my plumber sense." He glanced at the reserve tank, which was slightly cracked. He'd shut off the water before they'd started, but ... he felt around, ran a hand down his legs. Frowned again. It was certainly damp; the toilet bowl had drained, but it wasn't ... outrageously wet. "You didn't drain the reserve tank on the toilet, did you?"

She stood and lifted the porcelain lid off, peering down into it. "No. But it is empty."

"Hmmm," Gary said, putting the snake's screen and control interface down on his lap. Now that he was assured there were no more snakes down there waiting for him—and their path to him was plugged if there were some hiding in the murk—he didn't mind focusing on some of the ancillary details. "Lemme check this ..." He pushed his legs out of the way and leaned over to the valve and turned the water back on to the toilet.

He waited to hear the familiar rush of it filling the reserve tank, then draining out the cracks, probably drenching him below the knee. "Gary pissed his pants!" one of his brothers would say, and he'd shoot them the bird. He actually had occasionally pissed his pants when he'd first been paralyzed, because it took him a while to get a grasp on peeing when he couldn't feel his dick. He was long over such stupid and childish insults and didn't give a fuck now.

But ... no water came draining out of the reserve tank. Not a drop.

"Check the sink," Gary said. Marina did; nothing came out. "Kitchen?"

She left the bathroom, and Gary sat in the silence, waiting for her. "Nothing," she called from somewhere down the hall. Her soft footsteps went somewhere else. "And not in the other bathroom, either," she said a few moments later.

Gary's frown deepened. "Check and see if some enterprising soul turned off water to the whole house, willya?" He waited, listening for Marina to leave.

She did, and a few moments later came back, appearing in the doorway. "I found the valve. No pressure either way it turns. No water to hose bibs, either." She shook her head. "None at all."

"Huh," Gary said, thinking it through. "This is well water. Maybe old Fred's pump is shot, but … timing on that's a little funny …"

"Worse than timing of demon snakes climbing up and eating his whole ass while he was taking a dump?" Marina asked. She was almost smiling; her goddamned Eastern European sense of humor was black as night itself.

"Ain't much could beat the timing of that," Gary agreed, but even this joke didn't erase his frown. He was worrying over something as stupid as the water being off in the house of a man who'd been attacked and devoured by demon snakes.

What the hell was wrong with him?

6.

"Hey, Terry," Gary said as he crawled back up in his wheelchair. Marina knew better than to try and give him an assist; he'd chew her ass off for showing him pity. It was a struggle, but by God, like all struggles, it was one that produced bigger muscles and a greater resistance to bullshit adversities that would come along as surely as stupid ideas to some college egghead. "You mind running next door and asking the neighbors if they got running water?"

"You think they're still using outhouses out here?" Paul inserted himself into the conversation. "You an anti-rural bigot, you slick city motherfucker?"

"Don't be such a prick, Paul," Gary said, heaving himself back on top of the double-barreled shotgun. "You know goddamned well I'm not asking because I think they're shitting in an outhouse or anything." Though Gary had a lot of respect for outhouses. If success was making the best of what you had on hand, digging a giant hole in the earth and boxing it in to control the smell and disease seemed like a great big winner to him. Beat the hell out of digging an open latrine and just leaving it there to squat over like a goddamned savage. Which was also not exactly wheelchair accessible.

"I can go," Larry said. Apparently, he was done chewing his nails. Probably figured this would be the easiest thing asked of him today, and he'd be able to bank it. "But I asked the neighbors about whether they had water," he'd whine when Gary asked him to chop up a demon later.

"No, Paul should go," Gary said, "I might have some lazy, dickless assignment come up later that requires your special skills. I don't want you to expend all your finite energies and have you blow your impotent load right now."

"Gary," his momma said, bespeaking of the deep disappointment in his language that only a mother could convey with a name alone.

"What the hell am I doing this for?" Paul asked.

"Because I'm secretly hoping that the neighbors are going to treat like you Ned Beatty in *Deliverance*, you little whiny bitch," Gary said.

"Living in town has changed you," Paul said. "For the worse. You anti-rural pickle dick sumbitch."

Gary threw up a bird at him, then another for good measure. "Ain't no water in the Mickelson house. I want to know if the neighbors, who are probably drawing from a similar-depth well, are having the same issue. Now, did I sufficiently explain my thinking so that you feel comfortable moving your velvety smooth pussy next door and asking a couple questions of the neighbors? Or do I have to get some crayons and paper and explain it slower?"

"Goddamn, you're a prick," Paul said, turning away and heading for the van. "I'm taking your car. Who knows how far away the next mailbox is?"

"Take Fred's," Gary said and tossed him a set of keys he'd had Marina pull off the rack inside, anticipating this. He didn't want to lose his mobile armory. Or give Paul a chance to drive off with one set of his wheels.

Paul fumbled the catch and picked them up out of the grass. It didn't take a rocket scientist to work out that the car pulled farthest into the driveway, the big long sedan from the eighties that looked like a fucking old-man car, was probably the one he was seeking.

But Paul was not only not a rocket scientist, he wasn't even qualified to assist a rocket scientist in picking out an all-purpose hammer. He squinted at the keys like they were a foreign object. "Which one is his, you reckon?"

Gary just pointed to the front of the line of cars in the driveway. Buick? Caddy? Hell if he knew, but he recognized an old man car when he saw one, and he knew which car had been parked here—neatly—while the rest of them had slewed in at just about any angle. The old man car was parked straight as an arrow. He pointed. "There, you shit-brained cockknocker."

Paul made another face, resentment just bubbling, but he didn't answer back save with a thrown middle finger. Then he headed over and started her up.

Once he was in for a minute, he rolled down the window. "I'm blocked in."

"Go off the goddamned road, you idiot." Gary gestured toward the end of the driveway. Most everyone had left, and it was pretty flat ground around the driveway on the left side. This was common fucking sense, by God. It took about a twenty-point turn, but Paul eventually managed it, getting onto Warner Pike and on his fucking mission, the old-man car disappearing behind the trees that grew heavy at the edge of the property.

That settled, Gary was on to the next thing—wheeling himself over to Erin Harris, who watched him come with one eyebrow higher than the other. She'd caught his exchange with Paul, he guessed, and was eyeing him skeptically. "What's up?" she called as he wheeled over to her.

"Weird shit," Gary said. "The septic's near dry, and we can't get any water to the house."

Casey Meacham came wandering up, a flicker of amusement lighting his face. "What do you need water for? You wanna boil some eggs?"

"Well, I need to sterilize the instruments so I don't give you an infection when I help deliver Gus Terkel's next baby out of your ass," Gary fired away. Casey blushed; Gary wondered if it was the first time the little shit had ever done so. He turned his attention back to what mattered. "Fred's house here was on well water. A dry septic and lack of water are ... damned weird."

Erin shrugged. "You're telling me that when those snakes came rising up out of ... wherever ... they didn't hit the pump? Or crack the septic?"

Gary didn't have much of an argument for that; just a feeling. "Maybe. But it doesn't ... something's not right." He couldn't put his finger quite on it, though. Probably cuz she made a damned logical point.

She just stared at him. "Well, okay. What the hell do you want to do about it?"

"I'm having my second-least useless brother ask the neighbor if they're having the same problem," Gary said. He chewed at his lower lip. "You recall when last we got rain?"

A curtain fell over her features, clouding her response like her emotions were shutting down. "Back around when the water was flooding over the top of Tallakeet Dam, as I recall. Been in a drought of sorts ever since."

Gary nodded. "Yeah. Summer's what I thought, too. But ... far as I know, water's been plentiful. Nobody's been complaining about turning on the tap and nothing coming out." Something about that itched him, too.

"Well, we've got a lot of other problems," Erin said. "Seems to me a drought—even if it's starting to hit some of these outlying parcels of land—is kinda low on the list."

"Not for everyone," Casey said, apparently regaining his goddamned confidence at a useless time. "You remember the last meeting? Ronnie Richards was bitching about his lawn dying cuz his sprinklers weren't pumping right."

"I must have blocked that out of my mind on account of it being trivially stupid," Erin said. "But yeah. I recall that now." She shrugged again. "Okay. We're in a drought. Water table's down. We've been there before. If we have to institute a water rationing—I mean, Ronnie aside, lawns dying seems like a pretty minor concern at the moment. And we're in winter anyway, so grass is dormant, right?"

"Should be," Gary said. "I don't know ... Something about this whole thing is bothering me."

"As a plumber?" Casey asked, goddamn his smiling eyes again, "or as a newly minted demon killer?"

"Well, as the sumbitch currently on the receiving end of your stupidity, what's concerning me right now is getting you a tall glass of shut the hell up, which is gonna be straight up because I ain't got any water to dilute it."

Casey seemed to think for a moment. "I don't think that metaphor works."

Gary grabbed his wheels and scooted forward, bumping Casey in the shin with one of his footrests. "How's that work, you dumb, oversexed sonofabitch?"

"Owwwww!" Bent double, the taxidermist reached for his shin.

"Hey!" Erin objected. "Leave him be. He doesn't mean anything by what he said."

"If your words have no intended meaning," Gary said, scooting back outside arm's reach to avoid reprisal from the dumbass, "you should shut your gob and leave the speaking to people who got shit to say."

He caught a little flicker of anger in the back of Erin's eyes, but she covered it up pretty well. "Look ... you're new—"

"Older than you," Gary said.

She gritted her teeth and went on like he hadn't interrupted her, "—new to this, anyway. So lemme say this—we could sure use your crew's help. And I don't know about this water thing you're on, but ... it kinda seems unimportant compared to people dying."

"Yeah," Casey mumbled.

"It's going to seem a lot more important," Gary said pointedly to Casey, "when you can't get the lube off because your shower ain't working, and you keep sliding off the toilet—which won't flush."

"Come on," Erin said. "We've basically got a societal breakdown going on here."

"No, you don't," Gary said. "You've got mass casualties. You got a lot of death. But society ain't broken down yet. Food's still on the shelves at Rogerson's. Clean water's still running through your pipes. People are driving to work, especially those that work out of town. Some are leaving cuz they've had enough of this demon shit. Getting in their cars, driving out of town, hitting the interstate and boom, they're gone. Society *is* functioning. Ain't mass looting happening. Ain't a total upheaval taking place of the sort you'd see in an SHTF incident. We've got an external threat ripping at our nuts, but our nuts are still intact."

"Thank God for that," Casey muttered.

"You think this *isn't* the shit hitting the fan?" Erin asked. So she did know what SHTF meant. Bully for her.

"I think there's a mighty big pile of shit still sitting in reserve, yet to blow against the blades," Gary said. "I ain't trivializing what we're going through, because it's hell—I'm just saying hell's got some depths, man. We're not at the lowest level—yet. If hell's got nine circles, we're maybe at the third."

She just stared past his shoulder for a minute. "Well that's a ... compelling vision of the future." She focused in on him. "Still ... if we're trying to keep things from getting worse, it seems to me that the fight is what's important. The demons rising and destroying and killing—"

Gary shook his head so hard he thought it might have flown off his shoulders if it hadn't been weighted down with the biggest brain in this conversation. "No, no—yeah, that's important, but you're neglecting the long-term strategy—"

"Look, jackass," Erin said, finally letting the heat go, "I'm fighting a war here. As best I can. You show up, and five minutes after arrival you seem like you're wanting to run shit. That's great. Where were you when we needed a leader to step up—weeks ago?"

"Minding my business," Gary said. "Trying to live my life, until things got so cocked up I couldn't do so anymore. I'm a citizen soldier, lady, and that means I don't come off the bench until you professionals in charge of maintaining civil order have screwed the pooch so hard that I gotta do so."

"Can you even get up off the bench?" Casey asked, snorting.

Gary rolled right into him again, without warning, and this time the little shit hit his knees. "Say that again, you ableist, sexpot piece of shit. I'll roll this wheelchair up on you and bury it and myself up to the waist in your ass—'cept you'd probably enjoy that, and my only consolation would be I wouldn't have to feel it."

"Jesus Christ, I get rid of one cocksure prick and another rolls into my life," Erin said, putting a hand over her eyes.

"Well, I ain't one of your troubled, felonious boyfriends, lady, so listen up—I'm only doing this cuz it needs to be done," Gary said. "Because you and everybody in your group didn't get it done. I don't want to be here any more than you want me here, but the way I see it, you need every hand you can get manning a gun—or whatever. Holy swords. Knives. Baseball bat with nails through it? Really?" He shook his head. "You professional types have failed in your profession. So I'm here because I've succeeded in mine, now I gotta show you how to do your job by doing it better than you do."

He stuck two fingers in his mouth and let out a loud whistle. "Wrightson crew! Head for the van. We're getting on out of here. Got shit to do."

"What about your brother Paul?" Marina asked. She'd been lingering behind him a few steps, watching and listening and staying the fuck out of it, which marked her as smarter than anyone else in his group.

"He'll catch up," Gary said, wheeling around. He didn't have anything more to say to these people that would be productive anyway.

"Thanks for all your help," Erin fired after him. "Dickwad."

Gary threw up a bird. "I'd thank you for your service to our county, but it'd be like thanking the fire department for showing up and having a circle jerk while your house burns," he called over his shoulder, not bothering to look back. "Way to suck at life, girl."

"Prick," she muttered behind him.

"Infant," Gary tossed back. He wasn't going to let some tweener, barely-out-of-high-school bitch get the last word on him. "Go sip your bottle and sit on your momma's lap while you fill your goddamned diapers—"

"If one of us is wearing diapers, it ain't me," she called back.

"I've got full fucking control of my bowels *and* my life, thank you very much!" Gary shouted. If she said anything else to him, it was lost as he rolled up to the van and activated the wheelchair lift, the whine of its machinery blotting out the surrounding noise.

"You sure that was the wisest course?" his mother asked, coming up beside him while he waited for the lift to reach bottom.

"You were the one who taught me most people are useless," Gary said, feeling rather than seeing Marina lurking behind him, listening. Smart. "You ain't getting soft in your old age, are you?"

"I'm more getting worried my town is going to go down if we don't figure out a way to work things out," Mary said softly.

"Leave it to me," Gary said, rolling onto the lift and hitting the button to start pulling it up. "We're going to sort this shit out. With or without the elite professional failures that have led us down this path."

And in his mind, that was that.

*

Arch saw Erin coming before she reached the sheriff's station door. Cheeks red like the cold wind had been whipping at her, she was flushed as she threw open the outer door with an excess of violence. She was a little gentler on the inner door, but not much, and then she was storming behind the counter, walking with a purpose.

"Anything happening?" she asked curtly as she threaded through the desks toward her office.

"It's quiet for the moment," Benny said from his place at the dispatch desk. "I'm sure shit'll break loose again any time, though. You know how it is. We never get a break for long before the phone starts ringing off the hook."

She just nodded at that and passed through into her office without another word, slamming the door behind her.

Father Nguyen had been sitting in a chair by the wall, eyes closed, waiting. He opened them at that. "What's going on with her?"

"Probably just the usual," Benny said. "Lot on her shoulders."

Maybe. Arch wasn't so sure. "Lemme go see," he said, pushing off the counter, where he'd been waiting, and making his way to her door. He opened it without a knock.

"What the hell, Arch?" Erin asked, standing by the window, behind the desk. She had her back to him, but she'd turned when she heard the door open and close. "Knock."

"Thought maybe you were in distress of some stripe," Arch said. *And didn't realize we were formal to the point of knocking*, he didn't say.

"We got the feds working to bring more people in," Erin said, turning to look at him. "Ross said they're sending agents. Talked about … standing down the watch because they could handle it from here."

Arch raised an eyebrow. "The pros from Dover, huh?"

"So they say." She didn't seem convinced.

"We supposed to just pack up and go home, then?" Arch asked. "Call it a day. A week? A year?"

"Well, seeing how it's almost December, callin' it a year doesn't seem too premature. You know how most folks seem to go on mental vacation about the second week of December and check back in somewhere in January."

"Not in our job," Arch said. It was true; cops tended to do lots of traffic stops toward the end of the month and the year. Lots of drunk drivers to pull in, lots of family strife at the holidays.

"What if we could go back to just being cops again, Arch?" Erin asked. Her voice had a far-off quality to it, like she was daydreaming. "No more demons, cuz ... someone else is on it. Back to writing tickets and—" She shook her head. "I mean ... you always did that while I was riding the desk before, but ... we could go back to that, maybe, once the feds take care of ... all this."

"You think they're going to swoop in and just solve this problem we've failed to solve?" Arch folded his arms in front of him.

"If they're professional demon hunting agents ... yeah, maybe." She turned around. "Think about it. We only ever had Hendricks and that little British prick that were pros. Hendricks is gone, and that—what was that Cockney's name? Caused us more trouble than—"

"Lonsdale," Arch said. He wouldn't forget that name, not ever. Lonsdale had set into motion the events that had cost him Alison.

"The FBI turns loose ... fifty, a hundred people who know what they're doing, who work as a team, who are equipped to do the job ... shit, did you see what that dickhead Gary Wrightson did today with his inbred family and one of his employees? It was like the cavalry riding in while we were huddled on our cars." She looked down at the desk. "We lost Nate ... because we're having to fight this fight. Nate was an ordinary Joe, Arch. He had a family. And he died because—"

"Because he believed in fighting for his home," Arch said. "What are these feds fighting for? Doing their jobs? Well, whoop-de-doo. They got no stake in Midian. Maybe they're good, and maybe they can help us clean up this infestation, but—come on, Erin. We've been in this from the beginning, or as near to it as not to matter."

"And we've been failing, Arch," she said softly.

That rubbed him wrong. "Speak for yourself," he said. "I've been doing my part. As much as I can."

Now her cheeks flared red again. "I didn't say you haven't been. You saying I'm not?"

"I didn't say anything of the sort," Arch said.

"You're thinking it, though, aren't you?" Erin stared him down. "I heard the same shit from that Gary Wrightson, questioning whether I got it in me to lead this fight. Because I'm a woman, probably—"

"Or maybe because you're twenty," Arch said.

"I didn't see you raise your hand when the time came to spearhead the fight, Arch."

"I'd just lost my wife." His face burned. "I wasn't ready yet."

"Oh, and you're ready now?" She flicked the sheriff's badge on her chest. "You sure? I guess we could wait a little longer if you're not, nothing serious going on here right now, after all—"

"I never once ducked out of the fight, Erin. I was there all along, even when I maybe had other things on my mind—"

"Fighting is not the same as leading—"

"Leading ain't the same as winning—"

"This is not about my age," Erin said.

"Maybe it's not *just* about your age—"

"You don't like being led by a girl."

"I don't like being led by someone who lets some jackwagon Johnny-come-lately plumber throw her into a tizzy. I don't like being led by someone who thinks that the feds are going to come in and somehow miraculously solve all the problems we've bled ourselves dry trying solve ourselves. I don't like—"

"Me," Erin said. "You don't like … me."

"Get your head out of your duff," Arch said. "It ain't about you. It's about what you're doing right now, how you're thinking. If people are clashing with you, it ain't because you're not a fine person. We got along just swell back before all this blew up—"

"Did we?" Erin asked. "Or did you agree with Reeve when he kept me sidelined all that time? Out of the field."

"You were nineteen," Arch said. "Lowest person on the totem pole. Maybe it had something to do with Reeve not wanting to put a girl in harm's way, but he got over that once this shit broke loose, because he damned sure put you in the middle of it. And you took up the cause. Credit to you: I never saw you flinch away, Erin, not even after falling down a mountain, not even after Reeve died. But this—this moment—if you're feeling the weight—"

"I'm feeling the doubt," she said, looking at him with a fire in her eyes. "From you. From Gary. From everybody."

"I think you're feeling it from yourself more than anyone, then."

"Get the hell out," she said and pointed to the door. "I don't need this right now."

He just nodded. What else was there to say? One thing: "I took care of that demon out at Moody's."

And that was it. He opened the door and closed it, more softly than she had, and left her to her thoughts, which he suspected ran only to self-pity. He cursed himself for adding to it. But he didn't go back to apologize.

*

Lunch was such a resounding success that Marischa went right to bed as soon as they got back from the pizza place, pleading exhaustion from her travels. That did not bother Darla, for what felt like very obvious reasons to her. Getting her mother-in-law out of her hair felt like sweet glory, almost as wonderful as putting her kids down for their afternoon naps. Sure, Jay was still making noise in his room, but Mera was out, and neither were all up in her hair, which gave her time to settle back down with her book.

Ritual of Unending Sorrows ... no. Ritual of Forcible Glories ... not really up her alley, since it spoke of men with a ceaseless appetite of lust. Her appetite for lust was somewhat limited at this point, constrained by her exhaustion from raising two kids, now alone.

Ritual of ... Infinite Power?

Now that held promise.

She scanned through, reading quietly, the only noise in the house the muttering of little Jay, his occasional chirp as he talked to himself rather than slept. She'd read through this book a dozen times before, how had she not seen this ...?

Oh. She'd seen it. It was just ...

Every time, she'd dismissed it. The pact was with a demon named Beelzahar. "Sounds like a German sex act," she muttered to herself. If it was, it wasn't one she'd ever knowingly performed or partaken in. And she'd done a lot.

This ritual ... "Yikes," she muttered, reading it over again, translating the demonic script slowly, to make sure she didn't make a severe error. She'd need to go through it line by line, with a copy of the Devil's Dictionary—not the Ambrose Bierce version—handy, to make sure she was on point with what she thought was being asked.

Now she remembered why she'd dismissed this one before. She'd first picked up this book in her early twenties. It didn't apply then, seemed ... far off compared to other rituals, ones where she'd just surrender her body for a short spell in exchange for power that was real, tangible, now. Or involved an easy sacrifice, one that didn't bother her—she'd killed a hobo one night in an alley in Chicago with a knife right across his throat, and it hadn't bothered her any more than any of the countless goats or chickens or any other animal she'd slaughtered to pay homage to demons in order to stockpile favor for a better afterlife.

This one, though ... whew. It was heady. The cost was more than a bum the world wouldn't miss and that she didn't give a shit about.

Still ...

She had to be sure. She'd gotten on the wrong side of these pacts before and had them go wrong. One time she'd been abused in all ways by a demon for eight hours because she'd slightly misinterpreted a word. The contract was ironclad; she had a favor from him now that he'd have to pay up on when she called, but she'd also been in agony for weeks afterward, cursing herself for her carelessness. That had happened early on, and nearly put the end to her demon-summoning days.

But no. There was no price she wouldn't pay. She'd seen this coming early—the end of the world. Things couldn't go like they were going now, not forever. A reckoning would arrive, a final one, in which all this opulence and stupidity and greed and cowardice would be held to account. It was in the wind, she could smell it like the nearby dairy farm on a windy day.

Darla Pike was going to be ready, too. She'd spent most of her life preparing. This ritual, though ...

It was a great leap forward. Power beyond power. Favor beyond favor.

But it was also asking more of her than she'd been willing to give. At least up until now.

"Omelet, eggs," she muttered to herself, curled up on the sofa, her feet beneath her, "some breakage required." That made her feel better as she read the ritual again, trying to see if there was something she'd missed.

*

Erin didn't need any more shit right now, she was full up to her eyebrows. "Assholes, assholes everywhere," she muttered to herself. It had the virtue of being so very true.

Seriously, Arch was on her now, too? She could see it coming from Gary Wrightson. That guy was a full-blown, testosterone-spewing penis avatar, so sure of his own dick and its primacy in the universe that he'd be whipping it around everywhere he went.

But Arch? Arch Stan? Stepping on her toes like a bad dancer?

Fuck.

She wouldn't have called that. Not from him.

"Goddammit," Erin said, leaning her face against the office

window. It was cool against her forehead. She took a moment to take her hair out of her ponytail, some stray strands having escaped at some point between the start of the day and the snakes leaping over the car and her, and Nate dying, and Gary Wrightson and Archibald Stan both taking a turn gang-banging her confidence.

Fuck. Why couldn't things just work out?

Well, maybe they would. Maybe these feds would bring some help, would bring some actual assistance into town, start rolling back the darkness. Shit, couldn't they use some good news around here? The best news Erin had gotten in the last few weeks was when she'd sent Casey out to the Sinbad motel to find that Hendricks had cleared the fuck out, removing one loose cannon from her deck.

But depriving her of a decent source of info at the same time. Silver linings, clouds ... didn't get one without the other.

They hadn't seen hide nor hair of his red-headed girlfriend since Hendricks had blown town, either. Erin made a mental note to ask Ms. Cherry if Lucia was still hanging around the brothel. It wouldn't have surprised her if that was the case; she didn't seem to venture out much that Erin could recall. Ever. Had that hangdog look about her on the few occasions when they'd had dealings, and that was enough to convince Erin that whatever was broken in Lucia was the shit that probably allowed Starling to come flying in anytime she wanted.

Erin probably wouldn't have had much of an issue working with Starling, even in spite of their mutual lousy choice in men. Maybe because of it. Maybe because Erin was feeling the bite of pragmatism, of staring down a demon apocalypse and finding her side of the board pretty spare.

Yeah. Maybe the feds would bring actual help. But if so ...

Why the hell wasn't she more excited about it? Hell, she oughta be jumping for joy at the thought of real pros, people who knew what the hell they're doing, leaping into the fray here. She might have an army of gifted amateurs, but every time she lost one—like Nate—she'd feel this sick feeling, the one that was in full residence in her belly just now. Not helped by Arch and Gary Wrightson and their bullshit doubt throwing.

Time. That was what she needed. Time to pass, things to get better, hopefully. She stared out at the horizon, wondering if there was a brighter day ahead. Then frowned, cuz this one had got cloudy, all the way to where the earth met the sky. Hopefully, that wasn't a sign.

*

Now there were three.

"Destroy the vessel of sin," Brackessh said, "and you purge it from your life forever." He looked at the three faces before him, blank, intense, staring. "Remove the instrument of sin that corrupts your flesh, and you break its power over you."

His hand was a little bloody, but nothing compared to the faces of his servants, which were slicked and coated, as though they were covered in war paint from chin to forehead. Their chests were bare; they were ready for the war against sin.

Small nods were all the acknowledgment he needed. They'd destroyed another scapegoat, another carrier of the seed of wickedness. It was necessary, of course, and Brackessh knew it, looking into their bloodied faces. All of it necessary.

"Why?" one of them asked, surprising him. There was a flicker of uncertainty across that servant's face—the first that he'd brought into his service when he'd arrived here.

"Why what?" Brackessh asked, burying his surprise. "Why do you sin? Or why must you purge it?"

No answer. His hold had, perhaps, faltered, just for a second. The face that had changed, just a moment, to ask the question, was now as slack as the other two, eagerly awaiting his words.

"You sin because it is part of you," Brackessh said, touching the servant who'd spoken, leaving a finger mark in the trail of blood dripping down his face. "A vestigial evil, a kiss of darkness upon your flesh. But you don't need it. You must move beyond it." He reached down, touched the bare place where sin's hold had once been upon the man—before Brackessh had removed it. "You served this organ and its desires. Not decency. Not goodness. How many times did your flesh lead you astray?"

That produced a questioning look—again, just for a moment.

Brackessh smiled. It was a pleasure to teach. This was fortunate indeed. "You didn't think of it leading you astray, do you? You never considered that? How much time you spent in its service? In pursuit of lust? Why, half a man's life he spends chasing, impressing, trying to capture beauty—fleeting and transitory—and why? For brief moments of sin. To blacken his soul with a stranger or a partner? To slice off little pieces of your life, your desire, your wishes, your time—the unit measure of life—and give it to ... whomever? A transitory beast, rutting with you for a night? What a waste. To what? Satiate these temporary whims? Do you not see how shallow that is? How it distracts you from the important work you could be doing in life? The worship you could be ..."

Brackessh shook his head. "No. To dwell in sin is the height of waste. It leads you to disease. To despair. Emotional turmoil. A waste of life. It is … a sin to waste so. Think of all you could accomplish without slaving yourself to … that. To … *lust*." He pronounced it the most despicable thing he could.

Blank eyes met his. They understood, he thought. Of course. Their minds were with him, with his, now.

"Come," Brackessh said, leading them back to the car, leaving behind another blood-soaked scene, this one messier than the last for the presence of those squalling cast-offs that had started crying after the scapegoat was killed. He'd had them killed, too—no servants among them, after all. "We have much to do," he said, into the lovely silence. "So very much more to accomplish."

7.

Audrey Sheehan had basically had enough of waiting for her husband to get his shit together five years ago. She'd waited since high school, when she and Rocky started dating. Endured their engagement. Suffered through a wedding night where he—still—couldn't seem to find her clitoris with both hands and a flashlight, not that he bothered with either nor any other helpful marital aids. Then she'd gone through ten years of marriage, two kids, and had finally hit FUCK IT when Lee Brice had moved in next door.

Oh, Lee.

He worked out; Rocky didn't. Lee had muscles on top of muscles, veins standing out on his forearms.

Rocky had a beer gut.

Lee worked from home, had time to do stuff during the day.

Rocky vanished for ten hours at a stretch, and maybe came home on a "good" night if he didn't get lost at the bar and blow through more money than they could afford to lose in beer, shots and pull tabs. "Get off my ass, bitch," was Rocky's response to Audrey's simple request: *Don't spend money we don't have, cuz our credit cards are maxed and they ain't giving us any more.* "I work hard for my money."

But he didn't have any money, she said, when it was all said and done and all the bills were paid.

Whose fault is that? he fired right back.

Apparently, hers. Score another one against Rocky, because Lee had loaned her two hundred bucks to make sure the lights and gas didn't get shut off. "No big," he'd said with an easy grin.

Lee listened to her. And boy did she have a lot to say.

Rocky? Fuck if she could even find his ass these days to say something to, short of walking into Fast Freddie's after his shift was done. If it had been cheaper, she'd just as soon leave him there.

Which was why, after six months of just talking with Lee, sharing with him, hanging out with him, having his actual fucking help with her kids ...

It had just happened that she fell into bed with him, one night when Rocky was late at the bar.

And Lee? Found the clit without even having to look for it. Audrey had come three times that night, something she'd never even done by herself. Jesus, praise the heavens.

"You should leave his ass," Lee said as she snuggled in close by his side. A horn honked in the distance; the sound of Midian at night. "Move in with me. Bring the kids. I'm more of a dad to them than he is."

These were the moments when Audrey actually felt the guilt. "He's an all right dad ... when he's here," she said. Lee's chest was so firm. Like his cock. Last time she and Rocky had tried, he'd gone soft halfway through. Drunk, again. And blamed it on her putting on weight.

Lee didn't seem to have a problem with her weight, which was maybe—*maybe*—ten pounds over where she'd been in high school. After pushing out two kids. That was a fucking miracle. And a lot of goddamned yoga.

But Lee, he fucked her with his eyes open and intense. God, it was exciting in a way it had never been with Rocky.

"But he's never here," Lee said, running his fingers down her ribs. God, he knew how to make her wet in all the simplest ways.

Audrey shivered. "Yeah. You're right."

"So why not leave him?" Lee asked. "Move in with me. I've got plenty of space."

Audrey felt a little chill, like someone had moved the sheets off of her, even though she was up against Lee's warm side. "I don't know." Something was holding her back. What the hell was it?

Shit, her marriage had been over for a while, hadn't it?

What the hell was keeping her here?

"You hear something?" Lee asked, lifting his head off the pillow.

"That horn honking off in the distance," Audrey said, sitting up. The sheet did fall off her body now, causing her nips to nip out. They'd already been on the way to that—again—thanks to Lee. "Other than that—"

"Shhh," Lee said, and put a finger over her lips. She recoiled away; she knew where it had been and didn't care for him sticking it on her like that. "You don't hear that?"

"Hear wh—" she started to ask.

Then a floorboard squeaked down the hall.

"Probably just one of the kids out of bed," Audrey said, getting up and reaching for her nightgown. Maybe Raymond. He was the oldest, tended to wake up sometimes needing a drink of water.

"That didn't sound like a kid," Lee said, sitting sideways on the edge of the bed. She caught a glimpse of the crack of his ass against the sheets, and boy did it look good. Beat the hell out of Rocky's fat ass, his beer gut hanging over his belly. "It sounded like—"

The door squeaked open, light flooding into the room. A tall silhouette stood framed in the light from down the hall, in the kitchen, where Audrey always left it on as a night light for the kids. She could see the belly hanging over the pants, see the long hair, thinning up top, but not the face ... though she knew it well enough to guess what it looked like right now.

Pained. Because she knew he saw ...

"Well, well," Rocky said, a little choked. "What do we have here?"

"Shit," Lee said, on his feet in an instant, still naked as a jaybird.

"Rocky," Audrey said, getting up herself. "What are you doing here?"

"This is my home," Rocky said, slurring his words. Fuck. He was drunk. "Why wouldn't I be here?"

Because you're usually twice as drunk at the bar right now, she didn't say. Instead, "Look, I don't know what you're thinking—"

"I'm thinking y'all are fucking," Rocky said, with a surprising amount of levity. "Like rabbits or something. And have been for a while, I'm guessing."

"It ain't what you think," Lee said.

"It's ... pretty much exactly what he thinks," Audrey said. She shrugged when Lee tossed a look over his bare shoulder at her. What the hell was the point of denying it now? Rocky was an asshole, and dumb, but not dumb enough to ignore his lying eyes when he saw his wife and neighbor in bed naked together late at night.

"Well, uh, I—uh—" Lee said.

"I see how it is," Rocky said, staring down Lee. "You come into my house, had some of my supper—and you thought, hey, this is pretty good. Used my toilet. Sat in my chair. Thought—it's pretty good to be Rocky—"

"Your chair sucks, man," Lee said. "It's got springs sticking up out of it. I sat in it once, and then I realized why you spend so much time at the bar."

"You tried my wife, too," Rocky went on. "Decided she was pretty good, huh? Huh?"

133

Lee shrugged. "Yeah. She's fair." Audrey shot him a scathing look, feeling the heat on her cheeks of betrayal. "Uh ... very good?"

"I wouldn't know," Rocky said, stepping a little further into the room. "See, I don't remember, it's been so long."

"Whose fault is that?" Audrey asked. "You'd have to be here to—"

"It's my fault, I guess," Rocky said, hint of a smile in his voice. "I ain't got a three-mile dick like your new boy toy here, so ... yeah. But I'm here every night, eventually. And you always say no—"

"Because you come in stinking drunk at three in the morning," Audrey said. "What do you expect me to say? You expect me to be excited, getting woken out of a dead sleep? You expect me to—"

"You guys hear something?" Lee asked, looking around.

"I hear a dumbass who's been fucking my wife on the sly opening his goddamned gape-hole when he ought to be shutting it!" Rocky exploded.

"No, I hear something, too," Audrey said. It was a dull sound, growing in intensity, a little like a train in the distance but closer. Something was rattling, then a crash, like a car smashing into the fence out back, and then—

The wall exploded behind Lee and something plunged into the room. It was taller than a dining room table and cylindrical, she realized after her eyes had caught up to it. It moved in a slinking pattern, like a worm—a giant worm.

The worm ran through Lee, who barely had time to throw out a, "What the f—?" before it was on him, then over him, her lover disappearing beneath its engorged body as it swept through the room.

Rocky dove to the left and the worm skimmed the doorframe, splintering it, leaving a round space of a couple inches busted on either side. It cruised down the hall and smashed into the wall at the far end of the house, disappearing into the night. She heard it smash into the neighbor's car, setting off their alarm, and then heard nothing else until it smashed into another house in the distance.

"What ... the hell was that?" Audrey asked. Drywall dust was landing on her tongue because her mouth was hanging open. Cold night air had rushed into the bedroom, chilling her through the robe.

"I ... I think that was a demon worm," Rocky said, getting to his feet. He stood, blinked, and then straightened. "The kids."

He plunged back through the hallway and through Eva's door. He was only in there a second and then was across the hall, into Raymond's room. He stopped at the doorframe there, leaning back, a rush of relief visible on his face from the light shining from the living room.

"Are they …?" Audrey asked, making it to the shattered door of the bedroom.

"They're fine," Rocky whispered, audible over the car alarm in the distance. "Still sleeping, both of them."

Audrey's hand found her forehead. Kids could sleep through anything. Even a giant worm smashing through their house.

She turned, looking back at where the worm had entered the bedroom. Lee lay there … or what was left of him did.

"So, uhm …" Rocky said, coming up next to her, holding his body in a very stiff way, angled away from her. "… Your boyfriend kinda looks like he bit the dust there."

Audrey brushed some stray, mussed hairs out of her face. She sniffled. Lee was dead, no doubt, crushed under the weight of that … thing.

"I think that's one of those demons everyone's been talking about around here," Rocky said. "Came right through the wall … man." He shook his head.

Audrey said nothing. What the hell was there to say?

"I don't know what you want to do," Rocky said, "but I think … I want to take the kids and get the fuck out of town. Tonight. Right now. I've seen enough shit, I don't need to see no more." He looked right at her, and she looked back. "Let's leave. Us. Together, as a family. We can drive through the night. My aunt's got a place in Maine, she's got extra space—keeps asking why we don't come visit. I'll get a job up there. I'll quit drinking. You and me … we could start over." He smacked his lips together. "What do you say?"

What the hell was she supposed to say? She looked down at Lee, what remained of him, then back up at her husband. His deadly earnestness was there in his eyes, even though they were a little dulled.

"I'll pack the kids, you pack the car," Audrey said, and she was in motion. Hell if she was going to wait around this hellhole for another slug demon to come busting through and kill someone else she cared about. "I'll drive."

"All right, then," Rocky said, and then he, too, was moving. "I really mean it about quitting drinking."

"Sure," she said. She couldn't really think about that right now. A demon had just come busting through the wall, had killed Lee. Standing around seemed stupid. This was the shit going on in Midian right now, and Audrey … just wanted out. In this, she and Rocky were on the same page, maybe for the first time in years.

Compared to that, why would she care, right now, if he quit

drinking for good or not? If he quit for a day, it'd be better than anything he'd done in years.

And because really ... what else was there to do?

*

"Did we lose Paul?" Mary Wrightson's voice pierced the quiet as they drove toward town, Gary back at the wheel, shoulders so stiff he could have stacked a board on them levelly. "Where's Paul?"

"He fell, bravely, in battle," Terry said, deadpan. "We didn't want to tell you because we were afraid it'd take the heart out of you."

"Oh, Paul," Mary said after a moment's silence, the thump of the van wheels against the rough highway the only soundtrack. "Well ... at least he didn't go out like a pussy." She waited a second. "No, really ... where is he? I saw him after the fight." She reached out and whacked Terry. It was a rich *SMACK!* that did Gary's heart some good, being as it didn't hit him. "And shame on your sorry ass, trying to fool your mother like that."

"Goddamn, Mom!" Terry said, through his hand, which was—Gary assumed—pressed against his face where she'd hauled off and hit him.

"Watch your goddamned mouth, profaning the Lord's name!" Mary hollered. When she got to this volume, it was hard to tell if she was being ironic.

"Your family is ... quite the group," Marina said from the passenger seat. She was bolt upright, like she expected trouble to come sweeping in at any time. The mid-afternoon sun was sinking low in the sky, days shorter here at this end of the year.

"Yeah, they're a real band of blunders, aren't they?" Gary asked, taking a second to look back. Larry was staring at the racks of plumbing equipment, looking bored. Terry was holding his face, looking resentfully at his mother. And Mary was scowling at him, looking like she might deliver another hit just for the sake of making the point.

"Where's Paul?" his mother asked again, looking at Terry with added menace.

"I sent him to check on the neighbor's water supply back at that house," Gary said. "Surprised he ain't called me yet."

"You left him behind?" Mary was winding up.

"I gave him the keys to Fred's car and he drove off in it. So it wasn't like he's without wheels," Gary said, girding himself in case she found his answer unsatisfactory. "I had to make good my escape after throwing down verbally with that Erin Harris cow. Couldn't just sit around and sulk—I had to make a dramatic exit, you know."

She looked at him with furious eyes, but the storm subsided after a moment. "That rings true. Pride demanded you leave as you did. And if you covered your brother's exit by making sure he had a car … I can't hardly fault you. Still …" She rummaged around in her bag until she pulled out a cell phone and dialed. "Paul?" she asked after a few seconds. "You all right?" Gary didn't watch her face, but he could gauge what was being said and how she was reacting just by tone. "Calm your ass down, boy. No, I didn't forget you. You got a car, don't you? Well, then … hey, if you keep whining, I'ma hang up on you. Talk like a bitch, get slapped like a—yeah, exactly. Just come on back to town. We're going to—Gary, where we going?"

"Grantham Reservoir," Gary said. They were on the outskirts of Midian right now, and he was heading for the hilly country just down the road past town. "Did the neighbors have water?"

"You hear that?" Mary asked. "He says you're a prick for sending him then leaving him, Gary."

"I don't fucking care what Paul thinks," Gary said. "The wolf don't give a goddam what its meal thinks of it while it's eating the motherfucker. Did the neighbors have water?"

"He says you should go on up to Billy Brand's house," Mary said, "and give him a blow job—for four to six hours. Just suck him off, good—"

"Fuck you, Paul," Gary said. "Billy Brand is a damned decent fellow, at least twice the man you are before he even takes his pants off." Billy had always been fair to Gary. It didn't bother Gary that Billy was into dudes any more than it presumably bothered Billy that Gary wasn't. "Probably gets laid five thousand times as much, too, you permanent dry-spell motherfucker."

"He ain't fucking me," Mary said.

"I didn't say he was fucking our mother," Gary said. "I said he was fucking no one."

"You called him a motherfucker, okay?" Mary sounded pretty heated. "It's implied that if you're a motherfucker, you're so goddamned low you'd fuck your own mother. Except his own mother has standards, all right, and—oh, take your own dick out of your mouth before speaking, Paul. No one feels as sorry for you as you do, boy." She pitched her voice high. "'My momma don't love me, nobody loves me. I think I'll just have some ribs removed and fellate myself forever.' I didn't raise you to be Marilyn Manson."

"That rib thing'd explain why he don't leave the house much,"

Terry said and got another almighty smack on the cheek for it. "The fuck, Momma?"

"He didn't say shit to you, you stay the hell out of it," Mary said.

"I'm getting real tired of this runaround," Gary said, "did the neighbors have water or not? Answer me, Paul, or I'm turning this van around, finding your ass, and we're going to play chicken. I'm guessing I'll win, because you're probably on a back road, bent over to suck yourself off, which means when I slam into your car head-on, you're going to bite that little dangle off, probably swallow it on down, and you'll never see it again."

"Should I put him on speaker?" Mary asked. "I'm putting him on speaker." She sat there for a second, fiddling. "How the fuck do you turn on the speaker?"

"Like this," Larry said, doing it for her.

"—you're all a bunch of goddamned assholes, and I don't know how I'm even kin to you fucking pricks, but goddammit I wish I wasn't—"

"Well, you can put your bellyaching aside," Mary said, "cuz I squeezed your numbnuts ass out at four o'clock one morning, so you're definitely related to the rest of these cheese dicks, at least on one side of the genetic tree. Unless you were switched by those nurses with the bowling ball-size sticks up their asses—'Do I want to breastfeed'? Fuck, no, I want to sleep while you bitches feed this whining, yappy little ass. Do you think my tits are covered in leather? Or that I'm getting too much sleep to begin with, with a kid already at home? Sorry-ass bitches, I wouldn't be surprised if they took one look at my kid and said, 'No, no, this one's going to be too easy for her to raise. Let's find some bitch's kid and swap 'em to make her life a hell.' And here we are, thirty-odd years on, and you're a fucking little turd if ever there was one, Paul—"

"Jesus, Momma," Terry said. She raised her hand to him and he shut right up.

"Paul," Gary said, feeling the heat rising to his face, "I need to know about the damned—"

"They didn't have fucking water, okay?" Paul said, crackling over the line. "No agua. Said it went off last night, hadn't come back on. They thought maybe it was the pump went out on them. It's an old well, and they'd called someone for service but you can imagine how many well-drillers are happily servicing Midian right now."

"Damn," Gary muttered. "All right. We'll see you at the reservoir." He nodded at his mother.

"What?" she asked.

"I'm done talking to him," Gary said, looking into her blank expression. "You can hang up now."

"Well, maybe I wasn't done talking to him, did you ever think about that?" Mary asked.

"Well, you gotta hang up now," Gary said. "I signed off—dramatically. Ain't you ever seen a TV show?"

"They never say 'bye,'" Larry piped up from the back. "Everybody on TV's got a terminal case of being a dick. Talk about rude."

"What the fuck, people?" Paul asked. "I'm still here, you know. I can hear this whole stupid-ass conversation."

"Dammit," Mary said, staring at the phone. "He's right, boy. He called the ball on this conversation end—I'm required to hang up. Talk to you later."

"What?" Paul asked. "Fuck all you. Especially you, Gary, you—" He was cut off as Mary hit the end button.

"So the neighbors were without water, too," Marina said. "Beyond coincidence now."

"Probably," Gary agreed. "But we need to see the state of the reservoir to know for sure." He was biting the inside of his lip a little now. This ... did not sound great.

*

Erin was staring out the window, back at the sheriff's office. It was getting too late in the day, hours after she'd had her little blow up with Gary Wrightson. The sun was real low, and out her window she could see Old Jackson Highway rolling quietly beyond the uncut high grass, snaking its way north toward the interstate and south toward Midian.

It'd be pretty chilly out there right now. Heavy jacket weather. The deep of winter, even though it was only just before Thanksgiving. Weird weather, she'd call it, but then she wasn't a weatherman. That was all to the good, though, because she had the sense to be able to at least tell it was raining when it was raining. Sometimes those bastards couldn't even seem to manage that.

"How you doing, Erin?" Casey asked, knocking on the open door. His voice held a note of concern.

"... Fine," Erin said, wheeling back from the window to look at Casey, briefly, before turning back in time to see a pair of taillights go by on the highway. "Fine as a frog's hair."

"That's mighty fine," Casey said, apparently taking that as an invitation to come in and sit down. He stopped short of putting his feet up on the desk, at least. "But you don't sound it."

"Well, I'm squarely in the midst of a demon war, Casey," Erin said. "I expect my version of 'fine' under current conditions more includes 'we're not currently bombarded by 911 calls from people presently dying.' Whereas before, my definition of 'fine' might have extended to … oh, I dunno … a couple cold beers in front of me, a date with a nice man—"

"With a big dick."

She ignored that and kept on. "—a whole weekend off ahead of me … that kind of thing."

"And … a man with a big dick, amirite?"

"Stop projecting your fantasies on me, Casey," Erin said, rolling her eyes to the ceiling. "No, I do not need a man with a big dick right now."

"But … minus the demon war … then, yeah?"

"Jesus Christ," Erin muttered, looking back at the window. "This is check-in time, right? Where's everybody at?"

"Arch was dispatched to a call up on Mt. Horeb," Casey said. "Chauncey went with him, seeing as he was heading home anyway. Tarley and Jones are following behind. Ms. Cherry and Dr. Darlington went with the OOCs to a call off the square, something about dogs going nuts around there." Casey shrugged. "Not sure what that's about, but I got everything lined up. Benny's at the phones—"

"You've been hanging out a lot when you're off duty," Erin said, looking at him with curiosity. "Why is that?"

"Not a lot of taxidermy going on this season for some reason," Casey said. "I finished up one of my last jobs—Sheriff Reeve's fish—and realized … ain't nobody to pick it up nor pay for it." He shook his head. "I've had five of those lately. And not a lot else coming in, y'know? Man starts to get discouraged. Like there's no appreciation for my work these days."

"I guess I hadn't thought about how a demon invasion would affect the local taxidermy industry," Erin said. She hadn't meant to be sarcastic when she spoke, but goddamn if it didn't come out that way.

"Our local economy is a very tightly interconnected web," Casey said. "Like the food chain in an ecosystem. Predators have come and disrupted things, you know? I'm about ready to start making blankets of animal skins and stockpiling 'em for warmth in case the shit hitting the fan cranks up a couple notches."

"I think plastic ponchos would be of more immediate use if shit was hitting the fan. Literally, I mean."

"You got a point there, but seeing as I lack the capability and skill to turn soybeans into plastics, or however factories do that ... I gotta do what I can with what I have. Can't even plant a garden this time of year. Though I heard the growing season was shit from the people who did."

"All that rain we got early on, I expect," Erin said.

Casey shook his head. "All the dryness we got at the end, actually. Scorched the fuck out of everything, even the hay."

"That sucks," Erin said, looking back out the window as a panoply of lights streamed past her window. A big eighteen wheeler, a tanker of some kind, silvery in the twilight and aglow red with its running lights going, went by a little above the speed limit. "At least we still have Rogerson's and ..." She blinked. Another tractor-trailer went by.

Then another.

And another.

And ...

She stopped counting after ten, all in a row. More kept coming, though.

"What the fuck?" Erin got to her feet.

"What's that?" Casey asked.

"Like a damned convoy," Erin said. "We never see that much truck traffic this way. Ever." Thoughts of feds, and aid, and disbanding the watch gave way pretty quickly to a general suspicion, and Erin started for the door, grabbing her coat as she went.

"Where you going?" Casey asked, following after.

"One of those tractor-trailers had a taillight out," Erin said, putting on her coat as she went. "I need to go find out what that's all about."

Casey was squinting at her as she put her back against the Plexiglas door and shoved out backward. "... A broken taillight? You need to know what that's about?"

"No," she said, as cool night air hit her in the face, and she called back her answer as she broke into a run. "The convoy! I need to know what *that's* about!" Because what the hell were a load of tractor-trailer tankers doing coming through Midian right now?

*

Arch stepped into the trailer to find another sort of scene that he'd hoped he'd never encounter in his policing career. That had been a modest expectation just a few months ago. Now, it was a hopeless one.

"Good God," Chauncey Watson said, a step behind him.

The trailer house's door was hanging off the hinges. What was inside was a sight to behold; blood smearing the walls, what had been a human body beaten to death with a strength and persistence no normal person possessed.

Arch kept his sword in hand. "Yes, He is, but this is hardly a reflection of His good works."

"Huh? Oh," Chauncey said. "I don't know about that, Arch. How do you figure—"

"Not today, Chauncey," Arch said, "I already argued this point with two demons."

"We're living in some strange times, Arch. Interesting ones, as the Chinese would say."

That was one way to put it. Blood lay thick on the carpet; the skull of the victim was completely shattered, the head nearly removed from the sheer blunt force trauma of someone—or someones—laying into it. Brains, blood, fragments of skull, they were all spread out along the shag carpet in a splatter pattern.

And to think—before demons had come to Midian, Arch really only saw horrific stuff like this at the scene of car accidents on the interstate. Now he just stared, trying to decide how it had all gone down.

"You reckon anyone else is still here?" Chauncey asked, clicking on a flashlight and shining it around the room.

"Don't know," Arch said, stepping past the body, not worried overmuch about fouling the crime scene. It'd been a good long while since any CSI crew had made the trek to Midian. "We should probably find out since they know we're here after all this jawing."

"Should we wait for Barney and Braeden?"

"They'll be here when they get here," Arch said. "You just back me up and we'll get it done before they do." He eyed Chauncey's blade. "Don't stick me with that and everything'll be just fine."

Chauncey nodded.

Arch stepped past the body and through the main room, then the little kitchen. A couple bedrooms waited beyond, the double wide's spacious interior cast in shadow. Some of the overhead lights had either not been changed or had been broken in whatever fracas had gone down here. Arch pulled the flashlight off his belt and clicked it on, sending the beam out ahead of him.

There wasn't a lot to see. It was a pretty typical home, some nice touches—a quilt on the wall, a lever-action rifle on proud display above an electric fireplace. "Who lives here?" Arch asked.

"I think it was Brent and Maybelle Jenner. You know, the couple that—"

"Right," Arch said. They both worked at the library in town. Tireless, those two. He brought the beam back around to the body, trying to see if he could pick out that it was Maybelle Jenner under all that blood and with the head reduced to nearly nothing, but—no. He didn't know her well enough, couldn't picture her, even when he concentrated.

That was happening a lot lately. He reckoned it was because too many people were dying that he only knew in passing.

The trailer stank of death. That deep-soaked smell of gore, that coppery tang of blood seemed to hang in Arch's nose. He was getting used to it now, but Chauncey was making one of those glottal stop gagging noises in the back of his throat as he walked past the body. "Is it the smell or the sight that's getting to you?" Arch asked.

"Little of column A, little of column B," Chauncey said, then gagged.

"I'm sorry," Arch said, shining his light into the short hallway leading to the trailer's two bedrooms.

No noise but Chauncey's gagging, and a quick look with the flashlight revealed a whole lot of nothing. Disturbed sheets, kicked off the end of the bed in the master. The pillows were half off the bed, too. Arch caught a whiff of something as he came into the room. He looked at Chauncey. "Does that smell to you like …?"

Chauncey just stared back, blankly, through his Coke-bottle glasses. "It's a little funky in here, yeah. Whaddya reckon it is?"

Arch just blinked at the man. "You don't know?"

"No. What is it?"

Arch turned his face away. "Never mind, then." He played the flashlight over the sheets. Yeah. The one that covered the bed looked like it had been sunk into, an impression of butt prints rode into it real good. Arch felt a little heat in his face. "Nothing in here," he said, now anxious to leave.

"What happened in there, Arch?" Chauncey said, giving way as Arch hurried to the other end of the trailer. There was a laundry and utility room there, empty of anything but the stuff you'd expect in such a room.

"No demons in here," Arch said, walking past him and the corpse to the door.

"What happened?"

"Nothing that seems pertinent to matters at hand," Arch said, opening the door and stepping out into the yard. It was a couple steps down, and he found himself with wet grass whispering against his shoes. The moon was getting high overhead, and man, was there a kick in the air. A real chill, winter's hard touch finding its way across the top of his scalp, which tingled from it.

"Well, I want to know," Chauncey said. A car engine purred in the distance, just beyond the trees that enclosed the gravel driveway.

"If you ain't old enough to know," Arch said, "I ain't gonna tell you." Chauncey was probably fifty and had never been married, to Arch's knowledge. He regretted his glibness the moment he said it.

Barney Jones's car pulled up next to the police Crown Vic Arch had taken for this call. He'd left the Explorer for Erin. Felt a little resentful about it, but he'd done it, unasked, nonetheless.

"What do we have here?" Barney asked as soon as he got out of the car.

"Go take a look for yourself," Arch said. "Trailer's clear, no demons. Let me know what you think."

Pastor Jones nodded, mellow and mild, like he was about to do something no more unusual than greet his parishioners on Sunday morning. "Come on, Braeden. Let's make a visit."

Tarley nodded at Arch as he passed, and they were up the steps a few seconds later. "Wheweee," Tarley said, in his low, gravelly voice. "That ... is damned gross."

"Language, Braeden," Barney said.

"Sorry, pastor."

"You fellas come on in here in the bedroom," Chauncey said, disappearing up the steps behind them. "Tell me what you think happened in here. Arch and I have our suspicions, but—I wanna see what you fellas think."

Arch couldn't help but smile. That was a cleverer approach to finding out what he wanted to know than he would have credited Chauncey for.

"Dang," Tarley's muffled voice came from somewhere in the bedroom. "Somebody was having some fun in here before everything went tits-up—err, I mean, sideways. Sorry, pastor."

"I don't think 'tits-up' is that bad," Jones said in his low, comforting baritone.

"So ... you fellas, uh ... you sense it, too, huh?" Chauncey asked. "Tell me what you're getting here. Don't leave out any details, no matter how insignificant you may think they are. They could literally help us solve the case."

Barney Jones cleared his throat. Arch could hear it through the trailer walls. "Seems like someone was having relations in here to me."

A pause. "Arch?" Chauncey asked. "That's what—are you kidding me? That's what you wouldn't tell me?"

Arch chuckled. "If you didn't know, I wasn't going to say." He raised his voice to be heard inside.

Barney and Tarley let out chuckles of their own, and Arch could hear the trio clomping their way back to the door through the trailer's thin floor. They paused near the body, and he heard Braeden say, "That's Maybelle Jenner—I think." They came out a moment later.

"What kind of demon did this?" Tarley asked, his cheeks looking a little hollow. Man had lost some weight after his daughter's death. Even Olivia Jones's cooking hadn't been able to put that meat back on his bones. Probably kept him from looking like an absolute skeleton, though.

"I don't rightly know," Arch said. "Some questions I have, though—where's her husband? Seems he was here recently."

Barney just nodded, but Tarley chuckled. "Real recently," the mechanic said. "Pretty strong in there, if you know what I mean."

Chauncey just looked at him blankly. "You mean the smell? In the bedroom?"

"Yeah," Tarley said, almost laughing, "it just reeks of—" He caught a cockeyed look from Barney Jones and cut it off. "It, uh ... is fragrant."

"I just thought that was bad housekeeping," Chauncey said. "You fellas are saying that's ...?"

Jones answered him. "Yes."

"Damn," Chauncey said, and shuffled his feet from side to side, hands on his hips. "That's ..." He looked down. "What the hellfire and brimstone ...?" He stooped and picked something up. Squinting in the darkness, he brought it up.

It glistened just a little in the light of the trailer's front porch. Cylindrical, with a mushroom shape to one side, it came to an end in a bulbous sack on the other. It took Arch a second to get it, and Braeden Tarley must have figured it out next, because he let out a visceral, "Ooh!" and cringed.

"Good Lord," was Barney Jones's only response.

"What? What is it?" Chauncey asked, staring at it through his thick glasses.

"Good grief, Chauncey," Tarley said. He looked paler than usual. "You don't know?"

"What?" Chauncey turned it this way and that. "No, I don't—OH SHIT!"

He dropped the severed member and jumped back from it like it was a bomb about to explode."

"Well," Barney said, "I reckon we found the missing husband. Or at least a part of him."

"That's a pretty important part, pastor," Tarley said, and he was just about crossing his legs. "Personally, I don't think I'd like to go anywhere without it."

"Why couldn't any of y'all have just told me what it was?" Chauncey asked, shaking his head, letting out a deeper gag every few seconds. "You could have—blecch—said something—"

"Man, you've got one of your own, presumably," Tarley said. "How could you not recognize it?"

"It didn't look like one—gagggg—being all … disconnected like that—blechhhh—it looked … weird and different and out of place not connected to a—oh, Lord—"

Chauncey's guts let loose and he heaved up his dinner into the high grass by the side of the trailer. Arch didn't envy the man.

"This is quite the scene," Barney said. "We got a dead wife, a mostly missing husband … and no sign of demons."

"Yeah," Arch said, listening to Chauncey dry heave, all the good stuff already come up. "It's quite something, all right." He wondered if anyone else had seen anything like it.

*

The tractor-trailer pulled off to the side, last in the long line, as Erin pulled off behind it, angling the police Explorer slightly so that if anyone crashed into it from behind, it'd slew off to one side. Many a cop had been killed by some dumbass smashing their own cruiser into them; this was a hedge against that. Standard procedure these days.

Old Jackson Highway wasn't exactly alive with traffic this evening. Still, better safe than sorry. When she pulled this one over, though, ahead she could see the brake lights of the other tankers as they all pulled off, too. Simple observation of their caboose truck's sudden stop to flashing lights, or were they talking on a CB to each other? Erin would have bet on the latter.

She took the slow approach as she got out, planning to circle to the passenger side of the truck so as not to be standing, exposed, on the shoulder, between a big truck, which stuck out onto the highway some ten feet, and traffic. Slow night on the highway or not, the tanker was blocking a good portion of the right lane. Causing more of a bottleneck than there already was, and standing in the middle of the lane to do it? That struck her as the worst sort of dumbassery.

Apparently, that didn't keep the trucker from embracing it, though, because just as she reached the back of the cylindrical tanker trailer, he popped out of the driver's side and climbed down onto the running board, looking back at her, face in shadow. "What seems to be the problem, officer?" he called.

"You mind getting back in your vehicle?" Erin called back. She stayed right where she was, partially shielded by the edge of his trailer, and not out in the lane. Still, not a great place to be if someone came up from behind and plowed into her car—or worse, her. "I'll come up on the passenger side, and we'll talk."

"What's this all about?" He sounded gruff, and not terribly cooperative.

Time to drop politeness and go to assertive commands. "Get back in your vehicle, sir. I'll be around the passenger side in a moment."

"I want to know what this is about." No budge. Not a great start to a traffic stop.

Erin wasn't much for budging, either, especially when a dipshit started things out by refusing a police officer's order. "Get back in your truck, or I'm going to have to arrest you for resisting. You are failing to follow lawful commands given to you by a police officer. Kindly get back in the truck."

"All right, Jesus, fine," he said, and the door squeaked as he opened it. "Bitch," he muttered under his breath.

"Hey, what's this about?" someone called from the truck ahead of this one.

"Get back in your vehicle," Erin called. "I'm conducting a traffic stop." *On this one fucking truck*, she didn't bother to add, *so why don't you and your friends fuck off?* "This does not concern you." *Yet.*

"The hell it don't," that driver called back. "We're a convoy."

She could call out the brake light thing, but it was bullshit. She was tempted to just reach over and crack it right now. With the driver back in his cab, he probably wouldn't hear it. But it wasn't worth it, really. She was just in need of a pretext to answer her curiosity, she didn't want to start any shit, even if this driver seemed to be leaning in favor of it.

Erin walked slowly up the passenger side of the trailer. She couldn't see the driver, of course, even in the big mirrors. The cab was dark. Couldn't see shit even when she got close. She'd have to step on the running board to be able to talk to him, but by the dim moonlight and the nearby light, street she could see that the driver had lowered the window. Good. It'd be embarrassing to have to knock on the window and wait for him to bring it down to talk.

She stepped up onto the dual running board. She made the first step, and started to get up on the next, popping her head over the window and looking inside—

Something exploded with a flash from within, slammed her in the chest, and she bucked, losing her balance—

*

"SHOTS FIRED! SHOTS FIRED!" Casey Meacham's voice screamed over the radio clipped to Arch's belt. "Old Jackson Highway, just up from the station toward town, OFFICER NEEDS ASSISTANCE!"

Arch practically ripped the thing off his belt. "What's happening, Casey?"

"SHOTS FIRED, SHOTS FIRED!" Casey shouted again. "Erin's in trouble! Convoy of tanker trucks heading into Midian on Old Jackson Highway, she made a traffic stop and—I could see the shooting out her window, SHOTS FIRED, officer needs assistance! ALL HANDS, GET YOUR ASSES OVER HERE NOW! Come on!"

A thump, and Casey was gone.

There was a quick exchange of looks between Arch, Barney Jones, Tarley and Chauncey. "Let's go," Arch said and bolted for his car.

*

"That reservoir thing was a surprise," Mary Wrightson said, as they stood under the water tower in Midian, an old white structure that had been aged by rust and rain, time and pollution. It had streaks all down it, lacked for a good coat of paint, and had probably been standing here since the middle of the last century. Maybe earlier, for all Gary knew.

"Yeah," Paul said. He'd caught up to them at the reservoir, which was really just a lake made by the TVA's Little Tallakeet Dam project. "Who'da thunk that the damned Caledonia River was going dry?"

And dry it was, though Gary had been more than a little surprised by it. The drought had been in progress for months, and he'd seen the Caledonia waters recede *some*, but shit—you'd think someone would have noticed a big fucking reservoir above the dam sinking down to the point where the intake valves were half-showing. The lake bottom wasn't even damp; he'd rolled his wheelchair over a decent space of it, and it was so dry he never once got stuck.

But that had just prompted another question—why hadn't anyone noticed?

And another, which had Gary on the current path—if that was the status of the water supply out of town, where it was sourced, what did it look like closer in?

To that end, he was steering the van toward the big water tower on the north end of Midian. This ... he was not looking forward to.

"Listen up, limpdicks," he said, "and Marina and Momma," he added quickly. "I need someone to climb the water tower and open it up."

"What's the matter?" Larry did a little sneer. "You can't do it yours—"

WHACK! "Don't be an ableist prick," Mary said, but Gary could tell by the smack that she'd held back on him.

"What the hell?" Terry asked. "You don't go that easy on the rest of us." He musta heard it, too.

"He's the baby, leave him alone," Mary said.

"He's twenty-nine!"

"He's a millennial," Mary said. "I'm just lucky he didn't live in my basement like the rest of his kind, he'da got crushed when those goddamned demons tore everything to pieces."

"It was a dirty old root cellar anyway," Terry said. "Probably a little too lowbrow for Mr. Craft Beer tastes, Bud Light budget."

"I like what I like," Larry said, still vaguely rubbing his head where Momma had smacked him. "Don't hate me for knowing quality."

"Fuckers, I need someone to climb that water tower," Gary said.

"Don't wet yourself," Paul said. "I'm sure someone'll volunteer." He seemed to realize he'd spoken out of turn a moment later. "Shit. It's gonna be me, isn't it?"

"I'm just as proud as I can be of you today, Paul," Mary said. "First to go to talk to the neighbors—"

"And get left behind," Paul said.

"—now this," Mary said.

"You're so brave, Paul," Terry said, barely concealing a smirk.

"And I know you're going to be right there to help him, Terry," Mary said without missing a beat.

Terry's big cheeks burned. "Fuck." Paul just snorted. Now they were in it together.

Gary steered the van to the side of the road. The tower, once white but scarred over time with the flakes of orange and red oxidation, looked like hell. There'd been talk of pulling it down, but some historical society or another had filed an injunction, and now it looked like it might fall before that settled so they could tear it down.

Pulling it up to the fence that surrounded the tower, Gary threw the van into park and climbed back into his chair, unhitching it as he went and deploying the ramp out the side. It took a little hustle to make it all happen expediently. "Terry, grab those bolt cutters as you get out," he said as he rolled, pointing to the ones he kept on one of the shelving units, strapped into a bin.

He hit the ground rolling, heading over to the locked gate. He stuck out his hand and waited a good ten seconds for Terry to show up. "Get your thumb out of your ass and bring me those bolt cutters, Terry," he said, and as if by magic, the bolt cutters finally appeared. He looked up; it was Marina handing them to him. "Thank you," he said. Plus five percent efficiency. By God, was she getting better during this crisis? Well, the hardest steel was forged by the hottest fires.

He clipped the chain and kicked the gate open as thunder rumbled in the distance. No, not thunder. "What the hell?" he muttered.

"Gunfire," Paul said, brushing past him to the tall, rusted ladder that led up the tower. "What the hell is that, you reckon?"

It started small, but built as it went, like a full-on battle was going on back toward the interstate. "Hell if I know," Gary said, blinking, as though he could see over the horizon to where it was taking place. "Hurry up and let's get this done and we can go find out."

"Man, I don't want to go running into some gangster gunfight," Larry said. He was picking his nose and examining what came out before flicking the results into the dry grass and browned earth.

"You think it is demons?" Marina asked.

Gary wasn't so sure about that. "Maybe. Momma said they use guns a little to fight 'em, but mostly holy weapons cuz guns aren't ... well, hell, I don't know why they don't use guns and just bless the bullets."

"Maybe they're all libtard pussies afraid the guns will jump out of their hands and murder all their loved ones after raping them with their huge scary black barrels," Paul said.

"I know I wouldn't want to be raped by a double-barrel shotgun," Terry said. "Even if it was unloaded."

"You're more a single barrel type, working your way up to the big guns, right?" Larry asked, snorting halfway through the delivery.

"Go fuck yourself," Terry said, then looked at Paul. "Let's get going before I regain my senses and realize I'm climbing the goddamned water tower at night because my big brother wants to put together a demon patrol. And that neither of those ideas makes a lick of sense independently, let alone when you join them together."

"Hm," Paul said. "You got a good point there."

"Debate it as you climb, fuckers," Gary said. "Now move your asses." He waved the bolt cutters at them.

"How long you reckon we're going to let him boss us around?" Paul asked as he started his climb.

"Well, it's been all our lives so far," Terry said, following after, "and I don't see things changing. Maybe after Momma dies?"

"Fuck you, you goddamned vultures," Mary called after them, now a third of the way up the structure. "If I had anything left to my name other than an empty piece of land in the middle of the goddamned real estate crash that is Midian, I'd disinherit your asses. As it is, I might just give the property to you in hopes you get *et* by a demon." She actually said et, but then again, she said et a lot.

They were halfway up, then three quarters. That thunder rumble of gunfire in the distance bothered Gary, and it kept going on, too, even when they reached the top and the tank up there.

"How the hell am I supposed to get in here?" Paul asked.

"You got your demon-fighting weapons?" Gary asked, seeing the glint from something in Paul's waistband.

"Yes," Paul called back.

"No," Terry shouted. "I'm unarmed and alone and defenseless and on my way to grandma's house. Please don't eat me, big bad demon wolf." He slipped a hand into his waistband and came up with those brass knuckles Gary had gotten that preacher to bless. "Fuck y'all for making me do this."

"You know, for idiots, they're at least not that stupid about their own safety," Mary said.

"Remember that time they got on the ATV with Roman candles in their hands and tried to hit a ramp while shooting off the fireworks?" Gary asked.

"That was peak 'Merica," Larry said.

"That's not what I mean," Mary said. "I mean—at least they weren't dumb enough to go unarmed up the side of that tower."

"Yeah, that's way smarter than trying to light off Roman candles while you're doing a dumbass stunt jump worthy of Evel Knievel," Gary said.

The voices of Terry and Paul reached them from above, a little muffled as they circled around the tower. "You remember that Joe Diffie song where the guy paints the water tower …?" Paul asked.

"Yeah," Terry said. "But he doesn't have red paint, so he uses—"

"'John Deere Green.' That's the name of the song," Paul said. "Heh. I always thought it was pretty funny. But I also always thought anyone who climbed a water tower in the middle of the night was pretty stupid, especially if they were looking to pick up a vandalism rap at the same time. Seems like it'd be a lot easier to vandalize something on the ground. At least you could run if you got caught. You ain't running if you get caught up here, 'less you got a wingsuit handy."

"We found the entry," Terry called. "It ain't even locked. Someone could climb up here and poison us all."

"Dumbass, none of us lives in town except Gary," Paul said.

"Someone could climb right up here and poison Gary, then."

"Hey," Paul said, "that'd fix him bossing our asses around."

"I'd come back as a ghost and tell you shitflower brick-heads what to do," Gary called up to them.

"I think we might just have to leave town if we want to get clear of him," Paul said. "All right, we're opening it up!" he called down. "Looks like—well, fuck. You didn't bring a flashlight, didja, Terry?"

"Your phones have a flashlight feature, dumbasses!" Mary called. When she caught Gary looking at her, she said, "Well, hell, even I know that. Come on."

"Oh, right," Paul said. "Okay. This sucks you gotta unlock it to access the flashlight button."

"Mine doesn't," Terry said. "You should switch to an iPhone."

"Hmph. Why would I want to go and do something like that?"

"Because you're an unsophisticated consumer," Terry said, "and most of the features of the iPhone are designed to make your life easier with minimal complication. Whereas this Android shit? It's all fancy and for people who really know what they're doing—which you don't. So why not make your life easier?"

"Fuck you, I know what I'm doing."

"Dumbass, you can't even figure out how to turn on the flashlight on your Galaxy phone without unlocking it. How do you 'know what you're doing'?" A pause, then Terry spoke again. "Hey, do you see— *Jesus!*"

"What the hell was that?" Gary called, but a noise like a horrible screaming filled his ears, coming from around the tower where his brothers were, high and pitched and screeching ...

Otherworldly.

Demons.

*

Erin took the shot right in the chest, a mule kick that thumped her ribs pretty good. She just saw the flash and felt the hit. If she hadn't been off balance switching footholds she might have been able to weather it.

As it was, though, she took a dive, landing on the grass off the shoulder and rolling into the ditch. All the air rushed out of her, and she ended up face up, staring into the starry night, a billion points of light above her and a searing pain radiating out from the right side of her ribcage.

Her hands flew two places; the right found the grip of her Glock pistol, and she pulled it out of the holster with an ease born of long practice, and aimed up, covering the direction she'd just come from. The left, though, probed, looking for the spot with the pain, seeking wetness, blood—she pressed her fingers into a curious hole just below her right breast—

Hardness. There was something—like a brass button there, slightly warm, and she pushed it. Pain pressed out from where it lay against her—

Vest. She was wearing her bulletproof vest. Old habit.

"Die hard," she muttered as the door to the tractor-trailer opened above her and a man emerged, silhouetted under the starry sky and by the running lights of his truck.

"I got her," he called. "She's down here, looks—" He had a pistol in his hand, pointed away from her. She couldn't see his face, but she could see the outline of his body and head—

Erin raised the Glock and fired before he could raise his own gun, before he could realize she was still alive, still kicking. He had the high ground and she was flat on her back. Instinct and training kicked in, and she lit him up, popping him twice in the chest without thinking about whether a 9mm would do anything to a demon—

Crimson splashed along the white painted side of the truck, and the driver tumbled, hitting the ground and rolling down next to her. Shouts in the distance, off to her right, from the rest of the convoy. She could see the sides of their vehicles from where she lay in the ditch, all stretching off down Old Jackson Highway forever into town.

The driver rolled to a stop just a few feet from her. His mouth was smeared with dark liquid, and he was gasping.

Blood. He was bleeding.

He was dying.

He expired right before her eyes, before she got much more than a dim look of surprise from him. He died staring into her eyes, trying to say something she couldn't understand, a dull trickle of crimson working its way slowly down his chin.

Not a demon. Human.

He'd shot her.

And there were a lot more coming.

Erin scrambled, crawling away from the guy, grabbing up his gun as she did so. The shouts from the other drivers were indistinct, but she could hear the chatter of someone else firing now. A bullet broke a rock and shattered the pieces all around her, stinging her legs with gravel. Erin hauled ass up the abbreviated slope as those fuckers let loose, peppering the tractor-trailer in front of her with rounds from whatever they were carrying. It could have been two guns or twenty, it felt like a war zone to her as she ducked behind the—

Tractor-trailer.

Tanker.

Filled with ...

"Oh, shit," Erin said, as she realized she was being shot at through a tanker that might be filled to the brimming with oil ... kerosene ... gasoline ... propane ...

Any one of which, with just a spark, would reduce her, and everything within hundreds of feet of her, to ash.

*

Arch's Crown Vic slid on the corner, tires trying to grab for traction and succeeding, but only barely. He'd freely admit he usually drove like a grandma on the way to church.

Not now.

The Crown Vic leaned hard into another corner. Arch had treated the SHOTS FIRED call like any other OFFICER NEEDS ASSISTANCE. They'd been pretty rare back in the days of regular policing. They were getting pretty common in these days of demons and hellspawn and all else crawling their way up into Midian.

His fingers tightened around the leather. Trees without leaves flashed by at high speed, past the front windshield and by on both sides. The road curved, straightened, curved again, under a sky with stars like holes poked through the blanket of navy, separating him from a divine light that shone.

That was how Arch saw it. Light above, darkness below. But light needed a source, and he knew the source in his mind.

"Five minutes," he whispered. Jones and Tarley were right behind him, Chauncey Watson a little further back in his own vehicle. Five minutes to town, to the stretch of Old Jackson Highway where the sheriff's station lay.

Five minutes was a long time, though. A lot could happen in five minutes.

"Lord, be with Erin, and whoever else comes riding in," Arch whispered. His thoughts were going to be on them for the next five minutes, that and keeping himself from wrecking. Trying not to imagine whatever horrible scenarios could be playing out ... and trying to get there before the worst of them could.

*

Dark, shadowed shapes swooped down on Gary, down on him and the rest, and he waved his machete wildly in the air, thinking that even if these were just a nest of pissed-off bats, that'd sort 'em out and get them the fuck away from his head and his hair and his person.

"Fuck off, you winged demon-ass motherfuckers!" He thrust the machete into the air, heard the popping, smelled the sulfur.

Not bats, then. Unless they were demon bats ...

One of them flew right at him and he got a look. Bigger than a bat by a lot. Looked like the size of a small dog, but bigger in the body. Like—

"It's a goddamned demon winged sloth!" his mother shouted. "Fire sloths! Flying sloths! What is the demon animal kingdom's obsession with fucking sloths!"

"Well, it is one of the deadly sins," Larry said, batting at one of them and turning it to a pop of stink.

"Terry! Paul!" Gary called up. "You all right up there?" A fucking flight of the sloths came at him for opening his damned yap, that'd by God teach him to speak up. He damned near flipped over as two of them got turned to sulfur and the third winged him, hard, in the head. Brained his ass.

"I'm getting fucking overflown by fucking demon sloths, bro!" Terry called back.

"Yeah, this ain't our best day ever!" Paul called, strain in his voice as he batted at the demons. "You know what was, though? That night at the Summer Lights Festival when we all took turns on Maggie Andrews."

"The fuck!" Mary shouted to the heavens, swiping her weapon so hard it annihilated eight flying sloths in a row. "I told you boys to stay the hell away from that nasty gutter slut!"

"We didn't listen," Larry said, whacking a demon.

"I want the record to reflect that I never took a turn with Maggie Andrews!" Gary shouted, feeling his cheeks burn and catching a look from Marina, who swung the Stratocaster into a pair of tangled flying sloths and turned them to a conjoined black cloud. "That was all you fellas, and if I'd known about it, I'd have stopped you myself for fear your peckers would all turn to liquid bile and melt off."

"I always wondered why I ended up with a bunch of bills for the goddamned clap all at once!" Mary shouted. "I shoulda known! 'If she smokes, she pokes,' and the girl took a pack a day at sixteen. Probably took a six-pack of cocks a day, too."

"It wasn't like that, Momma, she was real sweet," Larry said.

"Jesus Christ, was she your first time?" Mary asked, looking daggers at him and swinging hell at the sloths. "Because your first time is supposed to be special, not at the damned town festival getting sloppy seconds after your brothers!"

"Aww, come on, Ma," Paul shouted from above. "We let him go first!"

"Your family is very interesting!" Marina said, swinging the guitar and vanquishing another round of sloths in a puff of sulfur.

"Yeah, they're a real barrel of laughs, ain't they?" Gary asked, trying to keep from burying his head in his hands as he fended off the sloths and wanted to die of shame. He felt a little consolation knowing that he was probably out of the house—and thus free of responsibility—by the time the Maggie Andrews incident happened. "Can we just focus on the winged fucking monkeys flying right now, and maybe worry about Larry dipping his tallywhacker into a cesspool later?"

"She wasn't that bad, dammit," Larry said. "I've been with her a few times since and it's been fine since now I know to wear a rubber. Maggie's good people."

"Maggie's a dirty whore," Mary said. "I hope you don't kiss her, because I know where that mouth has been, and it's not anywhere good. She probably just finishes sucking off one guy and goes right to kissing you. The live sperm count in her mouth could start a whole new civilization."

"Fucking flying sloths, Momma!" Gary said. "Concentrate." They were thick down here, but not as bad as they were up top. He kept a wary eye as they swarmed, hoping Paul and Terry were going to be okay up there.

And dimly—just dimly, because he could feel the threat for his life—Gary still wondered about what they'd find if they actually got into the water tower.

*

"Erin!" Casey Meacham's shout reached her just as a rifle roared. She could see his thin frame as he recoiled from the long weapon held in his hands, some hunting rifle or another, maybe one liberated from the sheriff's gun cabinet. The taxidermist was running toward her now, stopping to fire, then running again, skinny ass standing in the middle of Jackson Highway without an inch of cover every time he stopped to fire.

"What the fuck is this, the Revolutionary War? Get your ass to cover, Casey!" she shouted as he paused to shoot again. Maybe that wasn't much better, given that the truck could be loaded with explosive liquid content. Still, it seemed foolish for him to fire exposed like that.

Casey dashed up to her, breathing heavily. "I called for help," he said between breaths. "All hands. They'll be coming in hot in the next few minutes. Cherry, Darlington, Drumlin, Arch and his bunch … they're all on the way." He looked up at her, all serious. "What are we dealing with here?"

"Humans, I think," Erin said, as a bullet spanged off the tank behind her. "Jesus," she muttered. "I can't believe they're shooting at a fucking flammable tank."

"People do stupid things all the time," Casey said. "Did I ever tell you about when I got my dick stuck in a shampoo bottle?"

"No. And if you try and tell me, I'm going to shoot you."

Casey shrugged. "I just thought maybe it'd be illustrative of the point—"

"No."

"—appropriate to the situation at hand—"

"It's never going to be appropriate to the situation at hand for you to describe how you got your junk stuck in a shampoo bottle, Casey. Unless you're literally standing next to someone who has their penis trapped in a shampoo bottle." Erin moved slightly, feeling the pain radiate out from her ribs. "Fuck." She clutched the Glock tighter in her hand. "Got a radio on you?"

"Yep," Casey said, then leaned out and fired his rifle. When she stared at him with demand for explanation, he said, "If you just lay back and let them keep coming, they start to build momentum. You gotta fire back at these attackers, otherwise they'll get enough confidence to just roll right over you."

"What?" Erin leaned out and fired. "I wasn't asking about—never mind, just gimme your radio." She held out a hand, keeping one eye out down her side of the tractor-trailer. "And yeah, keep firing if you see any of these fucks come running up. I don't want to be overrun."

"Okey-dokey," he said and slapped his radio into her hand.

Erin threaded the mike and earpiece up to her collar, clipping it on and slipping the earpiece into her ear. It was stupid to have run out the door without her own, even for something that seemed as trivial as a traffic stop. "Anyone close? I've got north of ten truckers shooting at me right now on Old Jackson Highway, and I could use some reinforcements. Over."

"This is Arch, two minutes out," came that somber, deep voice. "Did you say truckers? Like, demon truckers?"

"No," Erin said. "Truckers of the armed and human variety. They shot me."

A pause. "You all right?"

"Dinged the ribs, but my vest saved me," Erin said. "We're about to get overrun here."

Casey fired behind her. "Got one!"

"Turning onto Old Jackson Highway now," Arch said. "Straight shot, I'll be coming through town. Jones and Tarley are behind me, along with Watson. Not sure anyone else has got a gun, though."

"I'm armed, Arch," Chauncey Watson broke in. "Got my old .38 under the seat."

"I've got a nice new Smith and Wesson M&P, Arch," Barney Jones broke in.

"Reverend?" Watson asked. "You go heeled?"

Jones chuckled over the radio channel. "Y'all are too young to remember, most of you, but I still remember the days when crosses got burned in my daddy's yard. I've never been far from a gun since then. And with these head cases nowadays bringing violence even into churches, well ... the shepherd needs to be able to protect the flock, you see—a sheep can't do that."

"I have a lovely Ruger in my glove box," Ms. Cherry broke into the channel. "And the doctor and I are a minute away, coming from the interstate."

"You keep a gun in your car?" Dr. Darlington's voice echoed into the channel.

Where the hell had the two of them been? Erin wondered, just for a second. Another bullet hit next to her head, though, and she dismissed that thought, leaning out and firing a round blind. The slide locked back, and she withdrew the weapon, ejected the mag, slammed a fresh one home and hit the release. It slammed a bullet home into the chamber, reloading the weapon with a satisfying clunk.

There was no time for idle questions now. Erin leaned out, just enough to see someone charging up the side of the tractor-trailer at, and she let them have it, firing right into their shadowed chest. The trucker dropped, sliding sideways down to join his brethren in the ditch, and a hail of gunfire forced her back behind the trailer as she waited, wondering which would come first—her reinforcements? Or a shot that would hit somewhere other than her vest?

*

"This is some dark and seriously beyond apocalyptic shit here," Gary said, now ducked into the shadow of his van. The fucking flying sloths had damned near overwhelmed them, even after they'd thinned their numbers. Sure, they'd been aggravating when they'd been thick enough to cover the damned sky, like a pestilence, but they were arguably worse now that they were down to ten or twenty of 'em—tough to count, they were moving so fast at this point. Now that they had room to maneuver, they were zipping out of the sky and attacking and then swooping back out before you could get a holy weapon around to pop them.

"Hey, y'all gonna get us down anytime soon?" Paul called from the water tower. He was still around the other side, hidden from view.

"We're working on it," Gary called back. They really weren't, at least not in the literal sense. Every time they tried to break cover, a fucking sloth would come swooping at them, and Gary had gotten bit in the arm hard enough to realize that these things weren't fucking playing around. He was still bleeding pretty good from that wound, blood pumping down his arm and soaking him to the wrist. "I think those things either have some kind of paralytic in their saliva or else they got a nerve, because I can't feel my right arm that well."

"You gonna cry about it?" Mary asked, eyes alive with hate. "You need me to get you a big-boy diaper and pacifier so you can curl up with your blankie and soil your pussy-ass self?"

"I ain't complaining about the pain," Gary said. "Just warning you. You get bit, your efficiency's going to go down a notch. Why, I estimate losing this arm has pulled me down almost 5%."

"What do you reckon you were at before?" Larry asked, covering in the shadow of the van. "You know, given your legs don't work and you gotta wheel everywhere."

"I'd estimate 200% prior to this injury," Gary said. "Even without my legs, I'm still twice the man most people are. I get shit done, son, nothing stops me." He lifted his machete in his left hand. "Now this may slow me down slightly—arguably not enough that a lazy man, like you, standing still all your life, would notice—but I'll notice. Still kick ten times more ass than you, but by God I'll notice the drop in efficiency. To you, I'll still look like a superhuman, in much the same way as a lazy fatass father who can only lift ten pounds would still look like a superhero to a child who can only lift five. For a couple years anyhow."

"I think losing the use of your legs has made you even more of a douchebag, Gary," Larry said. "You didn't used to have this chip on your shoulder before. You were a bossy asshole, but you weren't like this."

"See, you're just responding to my immense superiority in every arena of life except being a toe-sucking lazy-ass," Gary said. "I'm happy to cede the high ground to you in that area, though—you worthless sack of fuck."

"You two stop fucking arguing while we're being attacked by goddamned demons, will you?" Mary slapped Gary in the back of the head with the flat end of her blade. "I broke up all your idiot fights when you were younger, I hoped your sorry asses would grow out of it. It's just a phase, I told myself. But it wasn't a phase, and you dickweeds are still arguing all these years later, ornery as ever—"

"Yeah, who'd we get that from?" Larry asked with the smirk of someone who hadn't just been whacked by their mother.

"Turn your angry, pissy natures against the demon enemy, will you?" Mary asked. "I'm telling you boys, you are claymore mines, instruments of immense destruction. But you better heed the warning placed on the side of those suckers: FRONT TOWARD ENEMY, you hear me? Stop turning on each other!"

"Aw, we ain't serious about ragging at each other, Momma," Larry said. "We're just fucking around."

"Stop fucking around with each other and start fucking these demon bitches," Mary said, rearing up and whacking a sloth as it overflew them. Her aim was uncanny, her timing perfect, and that thing let out half a screech before it dissolved into a black cloud and vanished in less than a second. "Like they were Maggie Andrews, you hear me? Drop your drawers and give it to 'em, you little fuckers! Make your momma proud!" And she leapt out from behind the van.

"Yes, give dicks to these demons!" Marina shouted, leaping out her own self. "Make them feel swollen penis in asshole, like my whore brother! DICKS IN ASSHOLES!" She charged.

"Well, hell," Gary said, laying his machete across his lap. "Them ladies just got all charged up about killing shit and left us behind."

"I ... don't really want to go out there, Gary," Larry said, shuffling from leg to leg behind the van.

"Don't be a pussy, Larry," Gary said, and put his only working arm down on his lap to drop his weapon so he could start wheeling his wheelchair. "Shit."

"What?" Larry asked.

"... If I try and wheel out there with only one working arm, I ain't going to be able to move very fast," Gary said, finally voicing a thought that had been bothering him for a little while. "And I can't swing a weapon while I'm wheeling ..."

Larry just stared at him. "So ..." He cracked a grin. "... What's your efficiency at now, y'think? Revised down?"

"Push me, you cowardly piece of shit," Gary said. "Hide behind me, and I'll take care of what comes our way. That way, your craven ass will have cover behind my wheelchair, and so long as you don't do anything stupid, like steer us into a giant pothole, I'll protect your sorry, microscopic dick and balls from demon harm. And maybe your mother won't notice what a steaming pile of cowardly shit you are. She'll think you're a hero for wheeling your crippled brother around until this paralytic wears off." And Jesus, he hoped it would wear off, by God. And soon.

"You want me to push you around?" Larry cracked a grin. "For real? Mr. Independent needs a hand from his little brother?"

"Just this once, limpdick."

"Well, all right," Larry said, and took up the handles of the wheelchair, spinning Gary around in front of him. Gary took up his machete, bracing himself. "Let's do this, bro."

"Fuck yeah," Gary said, and they went.

*

Arch slammed his car into a hard stop, tires screeching against the pavement as he came roaring up to the first tractor-trailer in a long, silvery line, parked along the side of Old Jackson Highway. He could see flashes further up the line of tankers, gunfire from truckers moving up the line, pouring their attack at people in the back of the mess.

"Hey, should we—" Chauncey Watson asked over the radio.

"We should," Arch said, stepping on the gas again, and letting the tires grip and rip. Stopping at the head of this thing wasn't going to solve any problems.

He raced the Crown Vic along the length of the trucks, getting up to forty miles an hour in seconds, silvery tankers blurring past, the report of gunshots louder than the racing engine. He saw a shadow of a figure ahead, flashes as they fired their gun toward Erin at the back of the line.

Arch slammed into the man and him flipped up over the top of the Crown Vic, a spider web of cracks spreading out when it hit and bounced off his car. He did not stop.

The next trucker must have heard either the scream or the thump of the first person he'd hit, because they looked back and dove, Arch's headlights illuminating a white face and wide eyes for a second before they disappeared behind a bumper. There was a mild thump as the Crown Vic clipped a foot or leg that didn't quite make it to cover as the car raced past. Arch didn't hear a scream or anything, but then he was going pretty fast by that point.

His headlights were off. He hadn't even realized he'd clicked them off, but he must have—probably about a minute before he'd rolled up on the convoy, that was right. He'd thought about surprise, getting that element and pushing it for all it was worth.

Now he had it, and as he ran up on another surprised face and watched it disappear beneath his car, the thump of a body running under his tires and the discharge of a weapon beneath it as he ran that son of a gun over ...

Well, surprise was a powerful thing.

Three more tractor-trailers until he reached the end of the line, and Arch roared up on a whole bunch of crowded-up attackers, their shadows visible under the streetlights overhead. He didn't slow, just burst on them in time to see more faces, shocked at seeing a car come roaring out of the darkness while they were busy shooting, gunshots probably drowning the sound of the engine as it raced up on them.

He hit one of the three with his grill; the man made loud contact and went flying. Another got sucked under the car, which rattled as the tires bounced over the unexpected speed bump.

The third, though, hit the bumper, flew up ... and crashed into the windshield, shattering it and landing the sonofagun in the front seat.

Arch's cruiser skidded to a stop, dinging against the double tires of a semi-trailer as he slammed the brakes, hard. A couple boots had hit him in the right arm, stinging his shoulder and his biceps, but not impeding him. He lashed out at the body suddenly occupying the seat next to him, a human form, struggling, bleeding, pebbles of shattered windshield glass covering them both.

"Huh uh," Arch said, punching the figure with a hard backhand and getting him right in the jaw. The man writhed and kicked at him, and

Arch saw a pistol flash, a shot going out the open windshield—

Arch drew his own gun and fired, the muzzle flash blinding and the sound deafening in a confined space. It felt like his heart fluttered with the sudden thunder, and the flash of light showed him everything, like a photographer blinding an instant of the photograph into his memory.

The man's face dissolved in a blast of blood and lightning, as though a finger of destruction reached out and caressed the human figure in the passenger seat. Blood splashed warm over Arch's uniform like summer rain, and the top portion of the head was gone, just gone, disappearing above the forehead.

Arch had never killed a man before. He damned sure had now, though.

The body stilled, legs jerking once, painlessly, against his side. No attempt to kick here, just a spasm to signal the end. Then death, the head lolling back.

The head ...

It was nowhere near as destroyed as the body he'd seen earlier tonight, but it was wrecked. No ability left to think or feel, it was just dead and done, splayed out across his front seat and seeping against the passenger side door, brain and blood and life.

"Holy fuck, Arch," Braeden Tarley said, appearing at his door. Gunshots were still firing out there. "That's a guy, not a demon."

"I did notice that," Arch said, staring into the dead eyes of the man in the seat beside him.

"Come on, come on," Tarley said, yanking at his arm. Arch didn't even know that this window had broken, but it had. His hood was all curled up, too, against the rear tires of the tractor-trailer. How hard had he hit?

Arch stumbled to his feet and out of the car, still holding tight to his Glock. Flashes of light were coming from the other side of the wall of tractor-trailers between them, and a car raced by on the highway next to them, not slowing, speeding, just getting the heck out of here.

"What is going on here?" Arch asked. Demons, he'd wrapped his head around. But he'd just left a dead man in that car.

No answer presented itself immediately, just more gunshots in the night. So Arch followed Braeden Tarley toward the gap between trucks, hugging close to the trailers, trying to figure out what to do next.

*

"Die, you demon-spawned, hell-born, devil-tit-sucking motherfuckers!" Gary shouted, whipping his machete at a sloth as it swerved at the last second. Larry was doubled over behind him, running him forward. They were charging over the empty ground between the van and the water tower, make all manner of noise to draw these things in. "Get ready to choke to death on my giant American dick!"

"I ain't seen your pecker since I was like six, but I do remember it being quite commanding in girth," Larry said. "I was swearing to kids in the locker room in high school that my big brother had a dick twice the size of a grizzly bear's. You reckon that was an optical illusion cuz I was just a kid the last time I saw it?"

"No, it's that huge," Gary said. "Barges give way for it."

"Shit," Larry said, letting out a low whistle. "I was wondering if it just looked big cuz I was so small at the time, y'know?"

"Why the hell are you worrying about the size of my dick right now?" Gary asked, swinging the machete. "Is this what you do with your days instead of achieving greatness? Worry about your brother's cock?"

"That's probably like … 2% of an average day's thoughts," Larry said.

"You should be more admiring of the girth of my plumbing business and its huge reach," Gary said. "If you focused more on that, you wouldn't be sharing a fucking futon in your friend's trailer. You gotta build a business of your own." He swung again, fucking got the bastard that time. "That's something you can control. Unlike your pitiful little penis." He caught the pained look. "Well, I didn't know for sure, since I haven't seen yours since you were a little kid, either but—I assumed, based on how small it was then, you were heading toward being unable to please Maggie Andrews."

"I pleased her just fine," Larry said, taking a knee and parking Gary right in place. "I think."

"It's sad that you don't know for sure," Gary said.

"Like you know anything about pleasing a woman."

"Like I said … focus on a business, bro," Gary said. He could see two more sloths fluttering around. Marina and his mother were at the base of the tower, calling up to Paul and Terry to get down. There might have been more over there harrying them for all he knew. "Pleasing a woman, at least in the short term way you're talking about, don't give much long-term reward. You could at least balance things out a little bit, y'know? Work during the day at creating a substantial, service-oriented business of top quality. Then go hedgerowing at night or whatever you call it, hoe-bagging your way through the bar scene."

"It bothers me that not only might you have a point there, but that you haven't bothered to share this wisdom up to now," Larry said.

"Stand your ass up and roll us over there," Gary said, waving his machete at the water tower. "What are you hiding from? Ain't a damned sloth even close to us here. Paul! Throw your weapon at that one hanging out, orbiting around you. He's just asking for it."

A pipe wrench went flying off the tower and sure as shit, scored a hit against one of the last two sloths flapping up there. "What do I do now?" Paul asked.

"I'd hang close to your brother if I were you," Gary shouted back. "Since he's got the only weapon up there to defend you against that last one." He snickered, low enough not to be heard up the tower. "Dumbass. Threw away his weapon. Can't believe he did that."

"Well, he trusted you, apparently," Mary said as they rolled up close by the ladder. Gary couldn't see Paul or Terry up there. "I don't quite know what he was thinking, but ... there it is. Hope he doesn't get fucked over in the end, but I probably won't hold you responsible because he ought to know better than to throw away his only weapon other than his femmy little bitchfists, which we all know hit with all the force of a velvet-covered child's hand slapping you."

"Hey, Terry!" Larry called up, "now you throw your weapon at the other one!"

Gary turned, but Mary managed to slap him first. "Ow, Christ!" Larry said.

"Don't you listen to him," Mary said. "You hang on to that last weapon in case—"

But the sloth swept in just then, and Paul let out a girlish scream. "Get him! Get him!"

The popping sound was like a balloon, but juicier, and Terry must have hit it good. Gary smelled the sulfur from down at the base of the tower. "Was that it?" he called up. "Did you get it?" He was pretty sure they did.

"Yeah," Terry said. "I guess I should have closed the door to the water tower sooner, maybe. Then we could have dealt with these things a few at a time instead of ... all at once, you know."

"I like to deal with all my problems head-on, all at once," Gary said. He shook the paralyzed arm. The feeling was coming back, a little. "Don't let little fuckers hide in the shadows to strike later. You done good, Terry. You too, Paul."

"Even if you did throw your weapon away like a Grade A dickfeather," Mary said.

"What about me?" Larry asked. He seemed to be beaming in the darkness.

"You successfully pushed me all the way over here without tripping over your own insignificant cock and feet. Congratulations on your coordination," Gary said. "The fact that I didn't end up dumped out of the wheelchair is no small victory, especially when we take into account that your shoes ain't properly tied. Well done, fuckstick. I'm so proud of you for not cocking up the minor thing I asked you to do. I'd say good job, but … I don't want to be too effusive with my praise of you, because you have a long fucking road ahead to basic competence, Larry."

"That almost brought a tear to my eye," Mary said, clapping Gary on the back. "You're a real leader of men, son."

"I do what I can," he said, nodding. "Now boys … look in that goddamned water tower and tell me what you find," he shouted up. He had a feeling he already knew the answer that was going to come back.

*

Erin watched the flashes along the side of the tanker, heard the hard pops of the gunfire. They were still coming up the side, the last couple of them. What did you call it when you had your enemies surrounded? A kill box? Something like that. She'd heard Hendricks mention it during pillow talk.

God, her life had taken a weird fucking turn in the last few months.

Erin looked out. The volume of fire coming at her was way, way down. To almost nothing. One round hit the tanker. No explosion. She was acutely aware, though, that it would only take one stray round to end this.

Leaning out, she fired at the shadow hanging out on the corner of the truck ahead, hedging. Looked like he was caught between someone coming at him from the front of the vehicle and Erin back here. He'd gone the wrong direction; must have thought if he shot at her, she'd duck away and he could hide here for a second, deal with the incoming fire from the other side.

Whoops.

Erin plugged him, two shots, trying for three, but the Glock's slide locked back. She was empty and hadn't even realized it. And this was her last mag.

"All clear!" a voice shouted from over the man Erin had just shot. She could see the silhouette in the darkness.

Arch.

"Clear on this side!" Casey shouted, breaking cover on the left side of the tractor-trailer beside Erin. "You get 'em all up the way behind you, Arch?"

"We cleared out the remainder up here," Barney Jones's voice came, echoing off trucks. "There were only a couple. Angry sons of guns." The preacher appeared down the way, from behind a tractor-trailer three up. Ms. Cherry and Braeden Tarley were a few steps behind him. Every single one of them was carrying a pistol. Keith Drumlin emerged a little further up, holding a hunting rifle.

Arch stood over the downed man, staring at him. It was hard to tell what was going on in the big man's head, but Erin had a guess.

The guy hadn't vanished like the demons they'd been used to. He was just lying there, bleeding quietly, already dead.

What the hell had they done?

*

"Well, what do you see?" Gary called, voice echoing up the water tower. He listened carefully. In the distance, the sound of gunshots had long since stopped. Maybe sometime during their fight with the winged sloths.

"It's fucking dark!" Terry shouted, voice doing some echoing of its own. "And …"

Gary waited. Tapped his fingers on the machete's plastic handle. "And?" Another long pause. "Fucking and?"

"Looks pretty low in here, brother," Terry shouted, finally popping his head out of the water tower. "Maybe a foot or two down at the bottom, that's it." He was all the way up on top of the damned thing, service hatch open. "Damned near empty—just like the reservoir."

"What does this mean?" Marina asked, that accent biting into him like a piece of barbed wire caught on his skin. "That the town water supply is this low?"

"Nothing good," Gary said, staring into the distance, trying to get to the full ramifications of that one for himself and failing. "Not a goddamned good thing at all."

8.

"What in the blue fuck happened here?" Agent Ross asked, a few minutes after his fancy black SUV squealed to a stop in the middle of Old Jackson Highway, blue lights flashing from the new, miniaturized gumball machines in his front window.

"Traffic stop gone really wrong," Erin said, holding an ice pack on her ribs. She'd stripped out of her uniform top and vest and was now wearing a coat over her tank top, the ice held in place by her arm, held tight against her body.

"These aren't demons," Ross said, pointing at the row of bodies covered over by white sheets. Blood had seeped through a few places. Erin wasn't sure whether to be proud that her people had done such a bang-up job of landing kill shots that not a single one of the truckers had survived, or be annoyed because there was no one left to question. She leaned toward the former, seeing as how this had all kicked off with one of the bastards trying to cap her.

"I noticed that when they bled and died, yeah," Erin said, trying not to move. Casey had run back to the sheriff's station and gotten the ice pack for her. The bruises were already forming on her ribs. Doctor Darlington had looked her over before starting to deal with the dead bodies. Said she might need an x-ray for the ribs, but probably just some bandaging and rest.

"Maybe you can tell us what happened here," Martinson said, sticking her thick face into this in front of Ross, like she could get him to back his angry ass off. That was fine with Erin; she seemed calmer.

"Simple enough story," Erin said, "I pulled over that trucker there," she pointed to the last in line. "He was uncooperative, but I finally got him to get back in his vehicle, and I approached from the passenger side. When I got up to the window, he opened fire on me."

She lifted up her vest with her free hand. It had a hollow point 9 mm slug ballooned out where it had impacted the vest.

If that sucker hadn't been stopped by the vest ... Erin would have a hole out her back the size of a silver dollar.

Martinson took in the slug with absolute lack of reaction. "He shot at you?"

"And furthermore," Erin said, grimacing as she pushed to her feet, off the back lip of the Explorer's rear hatchback, which was sitting open and working just fine as a rest for her, "his entire convoy decided to get into the killing act after following his lead. They all came after me, guns a blazing."

"It looks from here like a few guns blazed back in their direction," Ross said. Guy was barely keeping himself from leaping off the handle.

"Yeah, that happened," Erin said. "Funny how we might take it personally when someone opens up on our local law enforcement. Troops get rallied, that sort of thing."

"And you ... killed them all?" Martinson asked. She was clearly the cooler head here. It remained to be seen whether she'd prevail.

"I didn't control the aim of my people, okay?" Those ribs were not going to feel better if she kept moving, but Erin couldn't not move, not right now. She was plenty heated. "They're proficient shots." She looked at one of the bodies that Arch had run over. "And good with a bumper, I guess. Look, we didn't ask for this—"

"Yeah, you said the same thing about the demons," Ross said. "But here we find you have a similar response to a bunch of human truckers."

"Who opened fire on us, yes," Erin said. On *me*, she didn't bother to correct. They'd fired at Casey, too, at least. Probably Arch as well. "What did you expect us to do? Sit back and take it?"

"You have to admit," Martinson said, and here her chubby face took on the look of a lecturer, "not a single survivor? This doesn't look good for you. Not a single substantiating witness who isn't already part of your, uh ... well, your militia."

"My ... 'militia'?" Erin just stared at her.

"Let's tick through the evidence boxes, shall we?" Ross took over. "You're a bunch of heavily armed rural folk. You haven't consulted with the government about the threat that's purportedly been afflicting you—"

"'Purportedly'? After I saw your ass hiding out on a car hood with the rest of us as demon snakes came slithering through? And I damned sure would have consulted with the government—if anyone had ever returned any of our calls!"

"It doesn't look great for you," Martinson said. "You have to admit."

"I admit nothing," Erin said, "except that I was an officer in need of assistance cuz I got bushwhacked. Now it seems to me that your response is, 'Hey, she was asking to get shot.' Or something. It's not real clear."

Martinson held up a hand to stay her partner. "I think Ross is just trying to explain to you that what's going on out here? It isn't just about reality. Like we said—people aren't going to swallow the giant, bitter pill that is the existence of demons. Which means when we run across places like Midian that are going down the tubes, part of our job is to solve the demon issue. The other part is making sure that what's happening is explainable."

"I didn't realize the Federal Bureau of Investigations was in the PR business," Erin said. "Does keeping the demons under wraps distract from your actual jobs?"

"We're capable enough to walk and chew gum at the same time," Martinson said with a smile. "But when we see a situation like this, in the middle of a demon incident ... it looks bad. It becomes more difficult to explain. I mean, this is Wild West gunfight stuff."

"Yeah, it's not exactly a normal thing for us, either," Erin said.

"So you haven't had any other incidents like this?" Martinson asked, staring her down.

Erin thought back, and wondered if the flash of panic she felt was visible in her eyes. What was Duchess Kitty Elizabeth's butler's name? He'd been human, and she'd shot him down in the street like a dog. She hadn't known it at the time, though. "Everything else going on around here has been demon related," Erin said. Ignore Jason Pike, too.

Shit.

Martinson smiled tightly. "Well ... we'll take a look into things a little deeper. Wouldn't want anything to ... slip through the cracks." She nodded at the bodies, which Darlington and Arch were still working to pull out and line up, with the help of Keith Drumlin, Braeden Tarley, and Barney Jones. "We can get rid of those for you, too. Send 'em off to our forensic lab."

Erin ignored the irrational spike of panic that told her not to let them take the bodies, even though she didn't think they'd find anything incriminating. It was the unknown, the uncertain, and the fact that the spotlight of the FBI was looking like it was pointing her way—none of that sat well with her. "Sure," was all she said, though.

"We're going to go take a look around," Martinson said. "Why don't you just … wait here?" It carried the force of a command, and Erin sat back down, heavily, on the back of the Explorer.

It was the voice a cop used when telling a suspect to wait right here … while they gathered the evidence to put the poor bastard behind bars.

*

"Goddamn this thing," Gary said as the wheelchair lift started to lower him. He was parked just down the highway from the sheriff's station, where the big brouhaha had gone down right on the fucking street. He didn't really mean to damn his wheelchair lift, because it made movement possible in a way that he might not otherwise have been able to accomplish—damn it for being slow. That was what he was trying to say.

"Son, you look like you're fixing to bust a gut," Mary said, standing out on the highway already. A blustery-ass wind came roaring through, and Gary was suddenly real sorry he hadn't worn more of a coat. Hell if he'd whinge about it now, though.

"I'm fine, Momma," Gary said. His head was still spinning about this shit. Low water in the reservoir, low water in the tower. People running out at the city limits. Months of drought.

And no one knew this?

"Erin," Gary said, catching sight of her and rolling off the ramp a couple inches before it touched the ground. She was sitting on the back of her cop Explorer, and he rolled toward her at high speed. Damned near shot off the limited shoulder in his haste, too.

"Oh, God," Erin muttered as she saw him rolling up. "What now?"

"We got a problem," Gary said, not wasting a lick of time. "I've been running around all day trying to get to the bottom of shit."

"Yeah?" She just stared at him.

"Yeah," he said, feeling the accumulating knot of people behind him. "The house we were at this morning? With the snakes? No water there. Same with the next door house."

"Yeah, I remember you saying something about that," she said. "Right before you took my fucking head off about some other bullshit and stormed off."

"Never mind that right now," Gary said, waving it away. He didn't have time for trivialities.

Erin raised an eyebrow at that. "So … a couple houses in the country ran out of well water. So what?"

"The reservoir at Little Tallakeet is down to the bare minimum," Gary said. "It's damned near empty." He waited, expectant.

"We're in a drought," Erin said, just staring back at him. "Have been since September."

"And the water tower is almost out of water," Gary said. He just stopped at that point, thought unfinished.

"Because of the drought, I assume?" Erin just stared.

"Maybe," Gary said. "We've had droughts before, though—and I don't remember the reservoir getting that low, or any of this other shit happening. No one's even made a peep about that reservoir thing. Which is funny, cuz it provides water to the entire damned Caledonia Valley region here, you know? If it's running low, you'd think somebody might make mention of that—"

"Likely the people who'd have done it are dead," Erin said, fiddling with a police vest sitting next to her. She was all wrapped tight in a coat and seemed to be clutching her right elbow close to her chest. "We have lost an awful lot of people lately, in case you missed it."

"I ain't fucking missed that a decent portion of my customer base has gotten their asses killed, no," Gary said.

"That really what it comes back to you for you?" She stared at him.

"Well, that's my relationship with them," Gary said. "If we were bestest buds, maybe I'd view them through that lens. I don't mean anything bad by it, it's just how I think of them—"

"Pretty fucking cold way to look at the people around here, but okay," Erin said. She glanced past him. "Lucky your family hasn't gotten hit."

"My momma lost her house," Gary said. "She's living with me now. That ain't not getting hit."

Erin squinted, obviously trying to decipher that statement, and Gary just about could have kicked himself for not being clearer. "Well, that's a damned shame about the water thing. I reckon we won't be going through as much now, given how much our asses are getting kicked, and how many people we're losing, and how some folks are bailing town—"

"None of that shit matters," Gary said, shaking his head. "Look, I'm no expert on water consumption, but there is something seriously fucked up about this—"

Erin yawned. "Well ... maybe consult with the experts, then, and get back to me if you figure something out. Because so far, all I'm hearing is we don't have a ton of water, which is hardly surprising to me. But it's also not my first priority."

"I bet it'd be a higher priority if you didn't have enough to fucking drink," Gary shot back at her.

"Is it that low?" Erin asked.

"For some folks, seems like it is," Gary said. "If pumps are running dry ... I dunno. City gets its water from the river ..." He shook his head. "Look, this is a problem."

"Well, I got no one else who can get to the bottom of it," she said, yawning again. "Seems you're the expert. I'm sure you'll figure it out if there's a desperate problem."

"You ain't taking this seriously," Gary said.

That lit a fire in her eyes. "I don't see a problem here that I can take seriously yet. I see a backburner problem. I see a bunch of little tangled, interrelated issues that, if they maybe all come together and form some greater whole—"

"Like a Voltron of a problem," Gary nodded.

"—then maybe, ten steps down the road, I'll have something I have to deal with," Erin said. She pointed over her shoulder. "See these tankers? A bunch of truckers tried to drive into town tonight. These puppies are fully loaded with—hell, I don't even know yet. Kerosene, gasoline, explosive, fertilizer? Who knows. And when I pulled one over to figure out what was going on, they ended up shooting at me."

"Were they sovereign citizens?" This from Terry who was standing back with the rest of Gary's family, amazingly silent up til now.

"How the fuck should I know?" Erin asked.

"Well, usually they'd announce themselves," Terry said. "'I'm a sovereign citizen, not subject to your bullshit authority'—or something like that."

"The only thing the guy said of substance," Erin looked back at him, and made a pistol gesture with her thumb and forefinger, "was 'boom.' After almost refusing every command."

"That sounds a little like a sovereign citizen," Terry said.

"What was the legal basis for your traffic stop?" Paul asked, squinting into the dark.

"Who the fuck cares?" Erin asked. "Whatever it was, it didn't warrant me being shot at."

"That sounds sketchy as hell," Larry said. "You don't even know why you stopped them?"

"There was a fucking tanker convoy rolling through Midian," Erin said, starting to get that creep of exasperation people got after dealing with Gary's brothers for a while. "In the middle of a demon invasion. I was just stopping them to ask a question or two."

"So ... you didn't have a legal basis for the stop? That's what you're saying?" Paul asked.

"What the fuck is wrong with you people?" Erin asked.

"You know, I find myself asking that question a lot," Mary said, almost contemplative. "I keep coming up with the same answer—it's their father."

"Yeah, I'm not so sure about that," Erin said, looking daggers at her. "Gary, whatever the fuck your water problem is, it sounds kinda self-serving—"

"The fuck you talking about?" Gary asked.

"Duh," Erin said. "No water, no working plumbing."

Gary blinked. Well, now that she said it like that, sure, it seemed obvious, but that didn't stop the heat rising from his cheeks. "That's bullshit. I'm not chomping after this because I'm worried about it affecting my business. My business is already in the toilet—"

"Literally," Larry said, bending over to slap his knee with mirth.

"That's a good one," Paul let out a little snicker.

"Because it's true," Terry said. "He works with toilets, and his business is in the toilet—and in the shitter!" He let out a roar of laughter, and the others joined.

"Fuck all of you," Gary said, spinning his chair around to look at them. "I'm not concerned about this because of the effect it has on my business." He paused as he caught a bunch of asshole, knowing looks. "Okay, I'm not *just* worried about it for that—this is serious. Water is life, motherfuckers. You can fight demons all goddamned day, but if you're doing it without any water, you're going to peter out fast."

"Yeah, but we're not out of water," Erin said. "Not even close, in fact. That reservoir is huge. It's low? So what? It's not empty."

"Not like your fucking head, no, but it's just about," Gary fired back at her.

"I got other problems to deal with than this bullshit," Erin said, and it was like a steel curtain descended over her face. Gary had done this a time or two, pissed someone off past their point of rationally being able to consider what he was saying. He felt a pang of regret for that, but he had other worries.

"This is fucking serious, Erin," he said, sticking his finger out in a hard point. "You're going to regret not paying attention to this."

"Come on, bro," Terry said, seizing his wheelchair by the handles and pulling him away. "She ain't listening now. You done pissed hard in her cornflakes, maybe even laid a brown nugget or two in there."

"This is bullshit!" Gary shouted as Terry wheeled him away. He grabbed for his wheels, but the pull was hard, and he only succeeded in slowing for a second.

"Not bullshit, no," Erin said, "just the regular kind of shit you deal with every single day—and are full of, up to the ears. Get the fuck out of my face."

"You need to listen to me!" Gary shouted as Terry wheeled him around.

"Come on," Mary said, patting him on the back, like that was going to solve anything. "This is pointless. It's late. Your momma needs some sleep, and you need a nap, too, son. You are out of control. Let's refresh and figure out our next move in the AM."

"This is serious, momma," Gary said, looking back at her as she kept patting him on the shoulder. The others were following, not saying nothing. "Why ain't anyone listening to me?"

"Because you're a fucking asshole, Gary," Larry said, chipper as all hell. "Nobody likes to listen to assholes."

"You should fucking talk," Gary said. He looked back over his shoulder. There was Erin, not even watching him go. Past her, he saw a couple overdressed motherfuckers in suits—feds all the way, he was sure. He'd seem 'em earlier. They were just watching him get his ass dragged off.

That stuck in his craw, too.

"I *should* fucking talk," Larry said, grinning. "Don't worry, bro—I only know cuz I'm an asshole, too." And that motherfucker patted him on the back.

"I'm the only one who realizes some serious shit is going on here," Gary said, letting them push him away, because … what the hell was the point of staying and arguing himself into the ground? "How does that make me an asshole?" he asked.

"Oh, it's not related," Terry said. "You're an asshole first, it just colors everything else you do. Like that one Greek prophet no one would listen to, y'know? But seriously, this water thing? You are way overblowing it, brother."

Gary bit back a stream of curses as they rode him back to his van, and he let them load him up and get in.

What was the fucking point, after all, if even your blood didn't believe you?

*

Arch stood over a dead body, staring down at the red-stained sheet covering it. "What … did we do here?" he asked, feeling the chill of cold air rushing around him.

"Killed a whole lot of people," Dr. Lauren Darlington replied, apparently checking the vitals of one of the deceased under the sheet. Making sure the job was done, he reckoned, her dark hair falling over her shoulder, partially obscuring her face as she worked. "Congrats. We usually leave that to the demons, but I guess, given how many people are dying in this town, you decided to pick up the pace."

"I didn't choose this," Arch said, feeling the burn of her words. "These men were trying to kill Erin."

"Yeah," Darlington said, letting out a long breath. She sounded as tired as he felt. "I know. But still ..."

"These were people," he said, picking up where she left off. "Not demons."

"I was getting pretty used to dealing with the victims of demons," Darlington said, her blue latex gloves covered in dark blood. The street lamp they were working under cast everything in a soft orange glow. "I'd forgotten what a gunshot wound looked like. How messy they can be. Even compared to—you know, disembowelments, or complete annihilation of a human skull, or—or—gelding—"

That triggered something for Arch. "You ran into one of those?" Arch asked. He'd been meaning to tell her about what he'd seen at the trailer.

"One of what?" the doctor asked, staring up at him while still kneeling. She almost looked like she was ready to pray.

"I came from a trailer house up on Mount Horeb," Arch said. "Female victim looked like someone had mashed off the top of her head above the jaw. We found a dismembered ... uh, member ... in the grass outside. No male victim anywhere around."

She just blinked up at him. "Huh. Yeah, I saw one of those earlier, too. Weird scene, even for a demon attack."

"Because of the, uh ..." Arch wasn't sure what to do with his hands, something to suggest a penis.

"That was the capper, yeah," Dr. Darlington said, standing up and snapping her gloves off one at a time. "A disconnected dick, far from its home." She shook her head. "That's not the sort of shit we've been running across. I mean, even when we found that demon's house a couple weeks ago where he'd been cooking people—the parts were ... well, they weren't like that. He had some basic minimum standards for discards. He didn't try to make sausage out of the sausage—"

"That's what bothered you most about finding the remains of dozens of people all ate up?"

"No," she said, glaring at him. "My point is ... whoever is doing this new thing—I mean, severing genitals? Murdering women? Who knows what's happening to the guys? The sexual component to it is giving me the heebie-jeebies. I can explain most of the shit we've seen lately to my daughter." The blue gloves dangled from her pale hands. "This? I don't know how to explain this."

"Did you explain the hooker that burned up from the inside to her?" Arch asked, actually curious. "Because it feels like that'd provide a framework."

"She knows about it, yeah," Darlington said. "What ... do you think happened to the men? It's not like they're going to just ... leave their penises behind voluntarily. Every man I've ever known would probably rather cut off his hand than lose his dick."

Arch cleared his throat, looking down at one of the bloody sheets covering a body rather than look at the doctor as she said the crass things she was saying. "There was an, uh ... aura to the scene we visited. In the bedroom."

Darlington snorted. She'd never been shy. Arch wondered if that was part of why she'd gotten pregnant at sixteen. "You mean someone had just gotten laid? Yeah, it was like that at our scene, too."

Arch frowned. That was interesting. "Strange thing to have in common."

"Sounds like a horror movie to me. Someone preying on people just after they've gotten laid? The only thing missing is a couple dead teens on lover's lane. And a killer with a hook hand or a hockey mask or something."

Arch's frown deepened. "You have a point there."

"Figures," she said, sighing. "My lifelong love of horror movies finally comes in handy, and it's during the demon apocalypse. Seriously, though—you're doing some kind of victim profiling based on this? Couples have sex, end up dead or with their dicks chopped off ...? Because it strikes me that this data is not going to narrow down the epidemiology much."

Arch stared at her, blankly. "What do you mean?"

The doctor actually blushed. "Lots of people fuck, Arch. It's how our species reproduces."

"We're in a little bit of a crisis here, doctor." Arch looked around. There were silver tankers on either side, flashing lights down the way, no one in the immediate vicinity, listening to them. He still didn't feel comfortable talking at full volume. "That's bound to cut down on ... relations ... some."

She snorted. "I doubt it. Stress may drive the urge out of some people, but others compensate by having more sex, and with different partners."

"That cannot be a normal reaction," he said.

"Why? Because it's not your reaction?"

"Is it yours?" Arch asked it before he realized he might have crossed a line. "I'm sorry, I didn't mean to—"

"No, you got a point there," she said, but her cheeks were even redder now, fair skin orangey in the street light. "No, I'm not out ... whatever. But I'm telling you—people do crazy things in a crisis. There are all sorts of methods of coping, stress management. Liquor stores are sold out in the area. Wines are off the shelf in Rogerson's. It was a good time for Tennessee to allow Sunday sales, cuz people are drinking the town dry. Drug sales are probably up. Prescriptions, too, I'm guessing, based on the number of people who have hit me up trying to get me to write a script for 'em. Sex is the most natural mood elevator of all. I guarantee you some people, apparently not you or me, but some people—they're out there making up for what we're not doing." She cleared her throat and looked around, abashed. "And God, I hope my daughter remains not one of them."

"If she ends up going that route," came a voice from above, and Arch looked up to see Casey Meacham staring down at them, apparently having listened to the whole conversation, "you call me." He held up his hand in a telephone sign to his face.

"Casey," Dr. Darlington said, "she's *sixteen*."

"Hey, in time of demon apocalypse, laws are a little more flexible, that's all I'm saying," Casey said. "Like Lincoln suspending habeas corpus during wartime, I'm thinking age of consent probably moves in a crisis, and she might need comforting—"

"If you come at my daughter," Dr. Darlington said, "I will cut your dick off myself, no demon required."

"And I'll arrest you after she does," Arch said. "Because the law is not suspended, Casey, no matter what you might think." And he pointedly ignored the dozen white-sheeted victims around him that suggested otherwise.

*

Marina pulled off to the side of the road in front of Terry's house, and Terry opened the van door. Gary sat in the passenger seat, waiting, in silence, as he had the entire ride. He was just getting carted around at this point, didn't give a fuck.

"I'm going to stay with Terry tonight," Mary said, leaning into the front seat and clapping him on the shoulder. "Give you the space to sulk and get this self-pity bullshit out of your system." He stared dully at her, and she clapped him on the shoulder again. "When I see you tomorrow morning, I better not hear any of this whiny, loser bullshit spilling out of your lips. Or I will slap the regurgitated taste of your own pussy out of your mouth, you hear me?" She looked over at Marina. "Get him home, all right?"

"I will," Marina said, and his momma slammed the door behind her.

Terry was waiting for her out on the gravel driveway. "You know Frieda's got me sleeping on the couch, right? On account of my snoring?"

"Well, tonight you can do your momma a favor and either sleep with your wife like a real man, or on the goddamned floor, cantcha?" They pulled away before Gary heard Terry's response. It was probably going to be something like, "You should have fucking stayed with Larry," or, "I bet Paul's spare bedroom don't suck as bad as this."

Gary stared at the black of the country road ahead. Hell. He must be as dark as the damned night if his momma would rather sleep on a couch at Terry's than the spare bedroom at his place. "Fuck," he muttered.

"I think you are right," Marina said, breaking the silence as the van's high beams lit the skeletal trees in front of them along the winding country road. "This water thing is bigger than it seems."

"Good to know someone thinks I might not have my head fully up my ass," Gary said, looking into the black beyond the passenger side window.

"Not fully, no." Marina chuckled under her breath, a deep, throaty sound. He looked over at her; dark hair, slightly olive skin. She had that hard-to-define Eastern European thing going on. She didn't show a lot of emotion. Stoic. That was it. While his family was blowing up, she'd just watch with barely an eyebrow cocked at them fussing at each other.

It was hard to read that. He might have been able to deal with it a lot easier if she'd waded in and started doing some swiping of her own.

"You probably think this is all crazy as hell," Gary said. "Demons and all this bullshit. It's interfering with your plumbing career, that's for damned sure."

"Plumbing can wait," Marina said. "Demons seem a more serious threat. But without water ..."

"Nobody seems to think that's a going concern," Gary said. "But it don't make sense to me. Two, three months of drought, and that reservoir is drained? Wells are going dry? I mean, I'm not a waterologist or whatever, but that seems wrong."

"Is unlikely people are draining entire aquifer to water yards now, yes?" Marina asked.

"Exactly," Gary said. "This shit is deeper." He sighed. "I wish I was smarter. Maybe I could figure this out. Or figure out how to say it without pissing everybody off. God didn't give me a lick of diplomacy."

"I have met your mother now," Marina said. "You seem very diplomatic, comparatively."

"Hell, that ain't much of a compliment, but I'll take it," Gary said. "Still and all ... it's like me dealing with that cock-up Ulysses."

She nodded. "He is useless employee."

"Is he?" Gary asked, quiet for the first time today. "I wonder sometimes. I mean, I wouldn't say it aloud, cuz ... he could be working harder. But part of me wonders ... on the black nights like tonight ... maybe if Ulysses had a better boss, one who was less ornery, less aggravating, more ... gracious, I guess ... maybe he wouldn't be such a cockup. Maybe in some alternate universe, where he's got a Gary Wrightson who don't have a massive chip on his shoulder and two useless legs pissing him off, a wicked case of itch up my fucking spine to get things done ... maybe Ulysses is a model employee for that Gary. Maybe he works his way up to 80, 85% efficiency. Maybe he dreams of doing better and doing more ... instead of putting in his hours and revving his car up the second five o'clock hits because he's so damned eager to get the fuck away from me." Gary leaned his head on his hand and looked out the window.

"Your mother was right," Marina said at last. "You really need to get this pity shit out of your system. This is not you."

"That's what I'm saying." Gary turned to look at her. "You know how many times I've read *Think and Grow Rich*? Well, Napoleon Hill says it loud and clear—you should have a mastermind alliance that you can share brainpower with, and there should be no disharmony between you because that gets in the way of your goals. You know how many times I've tried to put together a group like that? Like-minded people trying to just get shit done, move up together? I dunno, a dozen probably. It always ends with my ass wheeled out the goddamned door of the group I've put together. I just ain't got it in me to be harmonious, even though that's what I *need* to be. If someone tells me to catch flies, I don't use vinegar or honey or even shit—I use a goddamned fly swatter and bring 'em all down. Which don't do no good, though I don't know what you'd be using flies for."

"Many dead bodies around here," Marina said. "Flies could aid decomposition, help get rid of smell."

"That's kinda sick, but useful that you know that. I don't know much for sure, Marina, but I know this—I made a super team today of my brothers, and they're—well, they got some problems, no lying. But you and them, well, hell, we showed this town some shit today, man. We kicked some ass. And it wasn't because I was a superior leader. All I did was charge in first and whoop ass like a champ. Y'all made me damned proud, coming in hot like that, your guitar all wild and smashing the demons. But when it came to leading people, like horses, to this water thing? Your leader done dropped the ball. Fuck."

Marina pulled off, nudging the van into the driveway. Gary looked up; he was home.

She turned to look at him, brow furrowed in concentration. "I don't think it is that bad."

"I don't know about that," Gary said. "You think anyone's going to listen to me now? After this ... this ... clusterfuck?"

"What is that thing you say after we fail?" Marina asked. "'We will lick them ... tomorrow.'"

Damned right. No matter how bad they screwed up, Gary was always after it again the next day ... at least in plumbing.

Well, hell. How was demon fighting any different, if everyone was still breathing? Because that was true. Nobody on his crew died, and by God ... "We will fucking lick them tomorrow. And that wasn't me that said that. It was Ulysses S. Grant to William Tecumseh Sherman after the first day of the Battle of Vicksburg, where the good general and future president got his ass fucking handed to him. And he's hanging out under a tree in the pouring-ass rain, and Sherman comes up to him to talk course of action, and that's his answer." Gary slammed a fist against the door. "And we will, by God, lick them tomorrow."

"It sounds ... very inappropriate," Marina said, frowning. "I do not want to lick demons. It sounds like something my brother does to his clients."

"It just means 'kick their ass,'" Gary said. "But in an old-timey way of saying it."

"Ah, makes sense now," Marina said. "If not the awkwardness of it, I thought maybe ... it like licking frogs?"

"That's no good. Hallucinogens? That shit'll fry your brain."

"Is probably true, but ... could not be much worse than what we wake and see every day now, yes?" Marina asked. "You are good leader. And we will lick them tomorrow. In not bad way." She leaned forward and kissed him on the cheek.

"Did you leave your car at the shop?" Gary asked, stirring at the touch of her lips on his cheek. It stunned him for a second that she would do that, and he found himself looking at his lap real intently.

"Yes."

"You can just drop me here, then," he said then looked up. "Oh. That's what you were doing. That's fine. Pick me up tomorrow morning."

"I will."

He dragged himself into the back and into his wheelchair, letting loose the ramp but bailing over the edge carefully before it was done setting up. He hit the button to retract it, and rolled off into the night, waving behind him after shutting the door. He didn't want her to see his face, not right now.

She'd by God kissed him on the cheek. What the hell did that mean?

*

Darla hummed her way around the house. The kids were now in bed, after a long, post-nap period of waging war on her sanity. Little help had come from Marischa, who had locked herself in her room for most of the afternoon. A wealthy Chicago socialite eschewing childcare? Why, how could such a thing be possible, Darla thought, brushing a ton of crumbs into the sink while chuckling madly to herself.

"Are they in bed?" Marischa asked, appearing at the archway to the kitchen. Her eyes looked like she'd put a cold mask on them, white lines outlining them and relaxing some of the wrinkles of her crow's feet that crept in through the Botox. "Finally?"

"Yes," Darla said, humming to herself. "They might even be asleep, though I doubt it." Why wouldn't she be happy? She'd discovered the answer to all her problems this afternoon.

"I'm sorry I wasn't of more use today," Marischa said. "I think something I ate at that pizza place … disagreed with me."

More likely her son's spawn had disagreed with her. Darla could sympathize with that, too. "It's fine, we just watched more *PAW Patrol* this afternoon."

"You shouldn't have them watching TV so much," Marischa huffed. "It's bad for their cognitive development."

"I think it'll all work itself out in the end," Darla said, eyebrows arching in amusement. "And besides—I couldn't quite motivate myself to do anything else today." That wasn't quite true. She'd taken advantage of the time and prepared for the ritual. Which she would carry out tomorrow.

Unlimited power. Itty bitty little sacrifice, compared to what it would deliver. Who could argue with that?

"I was thinking," Marischa said, easing across the kitchen. "We should get out with them tomorrow. Go to the park."

"Sure, that's fine," Darla said. A quick jaunt to the park tomorrow morning would help kill some time. And she'd already done most of the prep, so there was no reason not to.

"We could pack a lunch," Marischa said, and Darla got a feeling she knew who was going to be packing the lunch. "Make a day of it."

"I don't want to be out in this weather all day," Darla said, staring down at the dishes in the sink. They'd gone out for lunch and had PB&J for dinner on paper plates. How was it full again? "It's too cold." That was actually fairly irrelevant.

"I looked at the weather for tomorrow," Marischa said, "the chill is going to break. High around sixty-five. Low at forty. It'll be fine. Best weather you could expect for this late in November."

This was Tennessee. Eight-five was the best you could expect for late November. But Darla didn't feel like arguing. "I'm not going all day. A morning trip is fine."

Marischa's face clouded, more wrinkles emerging at the corners of her eyes. "I can take them myself, then."

Darla snorted. "You? All by yourself? A full day and a picnic?"

"I don't see why I couldn't handle it," Marischa said, back straight, arms crossed over her midsection like she was defending from an impending gut punch. "They like to play on the playgrounds. It seems to me they could easily spend a day doing so."

"Maybe your memory is faulty," Darla said, "but they don't just play on the playground by themselves. They need attention. They come asking for it—'Grandma, come push me on the swing! Follow me over here! Follow me everywhere'! It doesn't stop there, either. You'll have to follow them all day, unless they have an abundance of playmates present to join up with." Which they never did anymore, even on this side of the county. People were spooking and running, the herd creatures.

"I don't see why we can't at least try," Marischa said. God, she was like iron, planting herself in Darla's path.

Darla just stared at her. The ritual ...

"Fine," Darla said, at last. She'd be the one to yield here. Marischa had made up her mind, and if there was one thing Darla had learned from her mother-in-law it was that there was no point in fighting it once the woman had made up her mind. "Fine. We'll do it your way." The acid taste of bile in her throat at yielding seemed to well up as she turned back to the sink filled with its endless, refilling supply of dishes. It tasted like defeat.

*

"Sin," Brackessh said, staring straight ahead. The thought was ever-present on his mind.

Sin. Always. Forever.

Sin.

His followers were gathered around. They swayed, slightly, side to side, in their silence. They had nothing to say, nothing to do. Brackessh was just sitting there. It was the still of the night, and nothing was stirring nearby.

No sin. For once.

It would come again tomorrow. Sin always did. It was rising somewhere right now, surely.

He just couldn't feel it.

Things got ... cloudy sometimes, even for Brackessh. He looked down at his shell. So much essence squeezed into this body. So much knowledge. So much power.

But there ... down there ... *it* stood ... erect.

Sin.

"It is an all-consuming thing," he said to his flock, in their silence. "It will eat you alive if you let it. Better to cut off the offending organ than lose the whole body."

Not a questioning stare among them. They were all his.

He looked to his flock. Some of them were old. Some were young. Some were ... quite fair, he noted, eye running across them. One, in particular ... that first one that he'd met, when he'd arrived in town ...

"You," he said, pointing that one out. "Come here."

The follower stepped forward. Brackessh tended not to notice little things—eye color. Hair color. Skin tone. Most of the time, anyway. They were all mere window dressing of the soul.

But this one ... he was ... muscled. Smooth of skin, tanned by the sun. Blue of eye. Piercing, almost, though the gaze fell well past Brackessh.

Well past Brackessh and his ... swollen ... sinful parts ...

"Look at me," Brackessh said. The follower did. Looked through him, past him.

There was nothing there but a follower. A vessel, purged of sin.

Forever. It would not recur in him.

But ...

Brackessh touched him. Felt him. From collarbone down ... down ... chest. Musculature. Lower. To the scarred, tender flesh where he'd permanently remove the sin from this man. Brackessh's rough hand ran down his follower's thigh, brushing against the thin, black hairs that sprouted from his skin.

"Turn around," Brackessh said, and he did.

His back was broad. Strong. What was it the humans said? He worked out. Brackessh stood, running a hand along his back, and down ... down ... to a firm buttock. Why did Brackessh not notice these normally? Such a strange thing, a subtle curve of flesh, of muscle ... but ... strangely appealing ...

Brackessh let slip his belt, then his pants. His hands found his servant's hips. Not a sound was made as Brackessh entered, not a grunt, not a sigh.

Silence.

Sin.

Brackessh worked his work, eyes open, until he reached his fall and released, his own sin flooding out. The thing done, he placed his jaw on his follower's shoulder, resting, feeling in danger of collapse.

"Sin," he breathed. "It is ... everywhere. Always." He said it for all to hear, not just a whisper in the ear of the follower in whose body he'd just taken comfort. "And it cannot be allowed to ... survive."

He shoved the follower loose; the man staggered, stumbled. The others fell upon him in a second, as they had upon their own lovers, attacking him just as Brackessh had taught them.

"Sin ... must be destroyed wherever we find it," Brackessh whispered, as he watched them kill this vessel of sin. "Purged wherever it lingers ..." He felt the small burn of shame as his own instrument of sin withdrew, flaccid and sated. But it was such a small thing, his own sin. There was so much more in the world.

And he would purge it all.

The blood flowed across the floor.

*

"Erin," Casey's voice came from the distance, causing her to turn. The taxidermist's face was grey, drawn, steely, even. A radical departure for him if ever she'd seen one.

"What?" It felt crushing, this idea that something even worse might have happened. She could tell by the look on his face it wasn't good.

"It's not that bad," Casey said. That did not help. "No, really—it's about the tankers."

Erin stood, rising off the back of the Explorer. In the distance, she could see Darlington talking to Arch, a pile of sheet-covered bodies in the lamplight. Red was seeping through the sheets, and Erin's stomach turned over. "What is it? Was it gas?"

Casey shook his head. "You ain't gonna believe it."

"Propane?" That was explosive. She'd heard of those suckers lighting off and explosions going for miles. If a demon really wanted to do some damage to Midian, kick this fucker toward the apocalypse, that'd be a good way. Get ten of those to go off … hell, there might not be anything left of the town but a smoking crater. "Kerosene?"

He just shook his head. "Like I said, you ain't gonna believe it. We opened up every one of them, and it's all the same." He leaned in, eyes bright. "It's …"

Her mind raced, waiting. What explosive element could they possibly have packed into these tankers? What destructive thing could they have put in them that would have their drivers ready to kill, ready to die for them?

The answer came like a whimper—and then a bang as it slammed home with everything else going on.

"Water. They're all filled with water."

*

Gary had conked out with surprising ease given all that shit that he had on his mind—leading his squad, Marina kissing his cheek, all his failures rallying around him. But he'd worked his ass off today, no doubt, and hell if guilt or worry was going to override his body's natural need for sleep.

He was soundly out, dreaming of something sweet. Of running through a meadow, maybe. Stalking a deer, rifle in hand, like he'd done as a kid before—well, before. He was deep in it when he felt something move in the darkness. Like something was stalking him …

He awoke in his room.

His wheelchair was gone, scooted away from the bed.

And someone … was in here with him.

9.

"Mr. Wrightson," said the black-suited male fed who sat by the side of Gary's bed. Gary came to full consciousness aware of a smell in the room. He took in the serious man looming beside him where his wheelchair had been when he'd crawled into bed.

"What do you want, you pig-fucking federal sumbitch?" Gary asked, sitting up in the nothing-but-boxers he was wearing. Give them fuckers a ticket to the gun show, and the pec show, and, maybe even the snake show. "You got a warrant to be here?"

The fed raised an eyebrow at that. "We're going to have a talk, Mr. Wrightson."

"You can talk to my lawyer, you punk-ass bitch," Gary said, looking around. There was another fed in the corner, and she had his wheelchair, drawn far enough away he couldn't get to it.

"How do you know we're feds?" she asked, a smirk on her face. He looked down; she probably hadn't realized that lump in the chair, under the padded cushion, was his double-barreled shotty.

"If you're not, you're the best-dressed home invaders I've ever seen," Gary said. "And fuck you—I can smell your kind a mile away. I saw you staring at me back on Jackson Highway when I was talking to Erin."

The feds exchanged a look. The male one, the one that was hanging out right by Gary, he spoke. "Funnily enough, that's what we're here to talk to you about, Mr. Wrightson."

"Well, then make an appointment with my lawyer," Gary said. "Her name's Lex Deivrel, she's in the Chattanooga phone book. You'll love her, she's a real ball buster."

"Mr. Wrightson," the man said, leaning in closer. "We have questions. You're going to answer them."

"Or you're going to ... what? Rendition me? Hand me off to Egypt to fuck in the ass?" Gary stared him down. "You going to Patriot Act me? Haul me off to some black site and tickle my balls with electrodes until I talk? Well, I don't give a fuck, I can't feel them anyway." He had his hands still clutching his pillow. He tried to make it look like it was a vestige of him being asleep, but it wasn't.

He was holding a pistol under there. One he'd had that preacher bless down in Chattanooga.

Because he recognized the smell now.

It was sulfur, traces of it in the still bedroom.

Demon feds.

He looked at the woman in the corner. She didn't have a hand near her holster. Dumb move on their parts, thinking … what? He didn't have a gun nearby?

Had these fucking idiots never met a Southerner?

Probably not.

"Mr. Wrightson," the man said, eyes growing darker, "you're coming with us."

"To where?" Gary asked, heaping a little scorn on 'em. "The station?"

The woman snorted. "You're not going to make it to any station. You're going to tell us what we want to know before we even leave this property or those balls you can't even feel? Are going to end up ripped off and in your own mouth—"

"This entire situation is a violation of my Fourth Amendment rights," Gary said, hand closing around the pistol under his pillow. It was a real beauty, a Heckler & Koch Mark 23 he'd bought during high times. A badass .45 pistol that was designed for the Special Forces. They even called it the SOCOM.

"You say that like we should give a damn," the man said after exchanging an amused glance with his counterpart.

"I don't reckon you do," Gary said. "But you see, our founders—smart men, those fuckers—prescribed a remedy for overreach of federal power and violations of our rights. Do you know what it is?"

The man stared at him blankly, and Gary mentally aimed the pistol through the pillow, trying to plot the trajectory.

"Let's fucking skin this cripple alive," the man said, and Gary pulled the trigger.

"It's called the Second Amendment, motherfuckers!" Gary shouted, letting 'er rip.

The bullet passed through the pillow and feathers exploded everywhere. The fed must have been caught by surprise, the dumbass. Even through the blast of white, Gary saw the fed's eyes widen for just a second—

Then he twitched, his mouth opened—

Oh, shit, Gary thought.

And he swirled into blackness, popping like all the rest of those demon zits.

An unearthly roar filled the room as the woman demon leapt through the air and landed on Gary before he could bring the gun around to bear on her. It felt like someone had dropped a Ford Fairlane on him, and damn it hurt, too, everywhere north of the waist anyway. "Fuck you!" he shouted, trying to bring the gun around as she tore into his side with fucking claws, the bitch. He hammered her in the top of the head as she shredded his pants and the side of his shirt, ripping into him good. "You fucking—fucking—fucking—"

He winged her on the top of the head as she looked up at him, eyes fucking black and red. They glinted in the darkness, but when he clipped her with the pistol, she actually rolled off. Didn't explode, unfortunately—he'd been hoping a sharp hit would pop her like the demon zit she was—but she did desist for a second and go over the side of the bed mewling like a demon cat.

Gary knew he didn't have much time. His wrist was aching, and he looked down; the fucking SOCOM pistol was fucked up. The damned barrel was bent. She must have gotten a demon hand on it, and boy, had she done it wrong. "You godless—that gun cost me two grand, you asshat!" That was why he hadn't carried it into battle earlier. It had remained safe under his pillow and served him faithfully this night, until this demon bitch bent it all to shit.

"Fuckety-fuck-fuck!" Gary said, throwing himself off the bed and crawling for the bathroom. It was the nearest thing. Closer than the wheelchair and the shotgun beneath the seat. She was already roaring behind him, and he didn't reckon he'd make it to the wheelchair in anything approaching enough time.

The bathroom, though …

He got himself halfway through the door and fucking rolled, forcing his legs—bleeding like a stuck pig—through and slamming the door just as that demon fed cunt's face came flying at him. Jesus, those eyes, those teeth. He hit the lock and pulled himself upright, barring it with his dead legs.

She slammed against it with her full weight, and he just laughed. "That's some solid ass steel construction, bitch!" As a man in a wheelchair, Gary was acutely aware of his vulnerabilities. Being on the shitter was one of them, and as such, he'd taken steps to make sure that in case the worst happened, at least one room in the house was properly armored against—well, the end of the world. Sure, he had buried a trailer that he used as fallout shelter/TEOTWAKI escape in the backyard, but ... a man needed somewhere close at hand he could run, too.

This was it. He hit the heavy deadbolt lock and slid back down. Safe at last.

The bathroom was small, only five feet by two feet, and Gary looked around. The wiring for a landline phone was sitting up on the wall, lacking an actual phone connected to it. He'd meant to put one in, but hadn't gotten around to it. Mainly because the fucking phone company charged a goddamned arm and leg for them. He'd have happily paid two legs since they were fucking useless and in his way all the time anyway, but nooooo.

"And I don't have a goddamned burner phone in here, either," he muttered. He kept meaning to get one of those, too, to put in a plastic bag in the toilet reserve tank. Business had been good, but his prepping had, by God, suffered for it up till now. There were a couple guns hidden in here, but they weren't blessed and thus were going to be much use against this bitch, who was now slamming her body against the door full force, rattling it. "You might as give up, you ain't getting through that thing, dumbass." And she damned sure wasn't. The hinges were extra durable. All that effort and she'd done no damage to anything yet.

Wait her out. That was going to have to be the play. He looked at the gap beneath the door. It was tiny, a centimeter at most. He had an air vent up top, too, so she couldn't get him out that way, unless she climbed up on the roof and shut it. That'd take hours to suffocate him out, though.

"Looks like we got ourselves a nice little Mexican stand-off here," Gary announced once the pounding stopped. He checked the other guns hidden in the cabinet. 9mm. He couldn't even transfer the blessed bullets in the useless SOCOM pistol to one of the other guns and put an end to this shitshow. "But without any Mexicans. So I guess you could call it a non-Mexican standoff."

She didn't say anything to that. He could hear her moving around out there, though. Doing something. He listened close.

"Tell me what you know about the water," her voice came, startling him. It sounded like it was on the other side of the door.

"How about no, and fuck you?" Gary leaned back. He was watching that gap beneath the door. He didn't think a demon could even get a finger under there, but if she did, he was bringing the bent-up SOCOM pistol down on that finger like a hammer. That'd cure what ailed her—and him. "We are past the point where I'd cooperate even if you got a warrant."

"You're going to regret this—but not for long," she said, and then she shuffled away from the door again.

Something clicked out there. Then again.

Gary listened, trying to figure out—

"Oh, shit." He realized what it was a second before he saw the faint flicker of orange from under the door.

She'd just lit his bed on fire.

She was going to smoke him out.

*

Erin leaned back in the chair in her office and shut her eyes, willing her mind to quit whirling, quit worrying. Neither was happening, so she opened them again for the ten thousandth time tonight. Looked out the window.

Lights were still flashing out on the highway. Casey was taking the tankers off the road, one at a time. Impounding them behind the sheriff's station, pulling the VIN numbers, handing them off to Benny to run. If Benny could figure out how to run 'em.

Erin sighed. She could do it herself, of course. Probably would in the next little while, if she couldn't defeat this failure to sleep.

She closed her eyes again, an image of Nate McMinn's corpse flashing across her mind. Of course. She hadn't thought about the poor bastard all day, but now—now when she needed to sleep—of course he sprang right to mind.

Fuck if this town wasn't going to take every goddamned thing from her. Sleep. Now that was going. Dignity. She'd lost a lot of that with Hendricks, the fucker. At least he'd moved on. Luck was fickle, but people having demons and hell to focus on had at least kept them from watching her wave her ass at him while he wagged his dick at her.

Hell, that was no blessing for anyone but her, but she counted it anyway. Not that anyone else was stepping up to do shit about this now that Reeve was gone.

Still ... "Fuck, I wish you were here, Sheriff," she muttered into the night.

It'd get easier. She probably wouldn't have Nate McMinn and his mangled, eaten-up, regurgitated corpse bouncing around in front of her eyes all night. She'd gone out to their house and talked with Lisa McMinn. Watched the woman break down into tears while Erin tried not play with her fucking belt loops or twitch her hands in her pockets or somesuch nervous shit. None of that.

She couldn't hold still now, though. Not to fall asleep.

And she couldn't get this shit off her mind. It was like her brain was the Brickyard 400, racing around in circles and hitting the same four turns over and over again—Nate McMinn, Hendricks, responsibility, and those fucking feds.

The last one she was thinking about the least, surprisingly, but when she did turn her thoughts to them ... hoo fucking boy, her stomach rolled like the thunder in that Garth Brooks song.

They were coming, according to Ross and Martinson. They'd surely be taking over this tanker thing. And they'd be settling all this demon hash, maybe.

So perhaps, just perhaps ... she could shed that responsibility after all. No more Nate McMinns on her conscience. No more carrying the weight of the town on her slim shoulders. She was fucking twenty, after all. She'd been drinking and carousing and arousing and doing the shit a twenty-year-old ought to be doing up until all this broke loose. She couldn't even legally fucking drink yet, for chrissakes. Leading a fight against a demon invasion?

Nuts. Fucking nuts.

This was all crazy. Every inch of it, and once again, looking around to apportion some blame, Hendricks popped up. She rolled her eyes. It was a complicated tangle of feelings she'd had for the man, the Marine, the demon hunter, but they'd started to simplify toward the end of his stint here—she'd just about flat-out hated him.

Now, though ... she didn't have much room for hate anymore. She could see the flaws in him, plain as day. Hendricks was wounded deep, like a dog that had been abused for a long time and nipped at your hand every time you went to pet him. He wasn't quite that feisty, but he was damned sure blind about a few things, and there'd been plenty of room for a rift to grow between them after the initial hotness of their fuckery had worn off.

If she saw him now? Yeah. There was still an element of lust there. But those warmer feelings, the ones that could have carried her past a series of nights and afternoons and—hell, they fucked every time of day—those feelings?

They were rusted over like an old pickup in someone's front yard, grass growing up around the engine block and wrapping around the popped tires. Dead, or at least buried. When she thought of him now, she felt only pity, regret for the choices he'd made that were bound to keep his ass isolated.

And of no use to her whatsoever in this endeavor. Which was a real fucking shame because Erin was at the point where, casting about, she was looking for a lifeline.

But Hendricks was an anchor, and he'd do nothing but weigh down anyone who attached to him, at least right now.

Maybe that was the shit the duchess had done to him during his captivity with her, breaking his fucking will into pieces. Maybe it was from earlier, and she hadn't seen it as clearly before she'd taken that dive off Mt. Horeb and spent weeks in the bottle afterward.

She saw it now, though. And like one of those old 3D pictures that jumps out at you if you stare at it long enough, it was all she saw when she thought of him now.

Still … help would be nice. Someone to talk to, even. Who understood. "Fuck," she whispered.

A thump at the door. Knocking.

"What?" she asked, trying to sound sleepy. It didn't take much effort.

Casey popped it open, his eyes all big. "Erin, we ran the first of those tanker registrations."

She rocked in her chair, and it squeaked. "You gonna keep me in suspense all night, Casey?"

He shook his head. "No … but you ain't gonna believe who they're registered to."

She took her feet off the desk, leaned forward. "Try me."

Casey swallowed, visibly enough that his Adam's apple moved in his scrawny neck. "They're registered to the federal government. Department of Transportation."

*

The smoke was creeping up through the crack of the door, and Gary was starting to get a little worried. He'd soaked a towel from the reserve tank and had it ready to put in front of his mouth, but mostly the smoke was heading for the ceiling. So he'd soaked another towel and stuck it across the crack. It wasn't totally stopping things, but being as he was on the floor, it'd be awhile before the smoke would get to suffocating his ass.

The moment was coming, though. The door handle—and the door itself—were both hot to the touch. The fire was having its way with his bedding and all his personal fucking belongings outside the door. "God damn you, devil bitch," Gary muttered as he worked.

He was pretty sure the demon had left. He'd heard her feet moving off, reverberating through the house after she'd set the fire. After all, she'd left a fucking crippled man locked in his bathroom with the bedroom completely on fire. He was pretty sure he'd heard her dragging his wheelchair out, too, adding a little insult to injury. He'd had a vision of waiting for her to leave and crawling out to it, wheeling his ass out of the house and down the ramp at the front door in fucking triumph like he was hitting the finish line at the Paralympics. Fuck yeah. I win, gubmint assholes.

That wasn't going to happen, though, so he'd moved on to plan B. As soon as her footsteps had left the house, he'd gone to fucking work. Shut off the water to the toilet. Start using the SOCOM pistol—big, bulky thing, thankfully—as an impromptu demolition hammer.

It worked surprisingly well.

Porcelain shattered, then shattered some more. He busted up the toilet and threw the big pieces out of his way into the tub. It took some doing, and smoke poured in all the while, clouding its way to the top of the shower rod ... then the support bars in the tub ...

And finally, it reached toilet level, and Gary was running out of time.

He'd poured a pretty decent concrete subfloor in this bathroom himself when he did the remodel. If he'd had a good hammer, this would have gone faster.

"I got an iron goddamned will," Gary said, hammering at the concrete that surrounded the toilet pipe. "Me versus the porcelain, I fucking win. Me versus concrete—same conclusion, bitches."

He was giving it merry hell, too, busting up the slab. He didn't need to bust the whole thing. Shards of tile were everywhere, his legs were bleeding like crazy. Mostly superficial, near as he could tell, but maybe some deeper hits. Mostly from that fed demon. He'd dress the wounds later.

If he could.

"You motherfuckers ain't stopping me," Gary said, busting the slab, bringing the SOCOM pistol down again and again, just a repetitive motion. He was a machine, one of those piston driving things they used to push metal into earth.

Boom.
Boom.
Boom.

"Nobody...puts Baby...in a corner," he muttered, his mouth full of smoke and plaster and concrete dust and other shit that his improvised mask couldn't keep out. His breaths were shallow but fast, and he was running out of steam. His right arm ached so he transferred the pistol to the left and kept going.

Boom. Cracks all around the pipe.

Boom. Pushing bloodied fingers in, pulling out shards of concrete. Making a hole to the wood below, busting the panel out.

Boom. Nice little gap now. Enough for a fucking ferret to squeeze through and that was about it.

Gary coughed. The smoke was intense, heavy. Not much air in this room anymore. He paused, leaned, kicked on the ceiling fan. It actually ran. Fire must not have gotten to the wiring yet. Light was still on, too.

"God's on my side, motherfuckers," he said, steeling himself for when the lights and the fan would go off.

He looked back. The doorknob was glowing like that one in *Home Alone*. Touch it, he'd end up with a mark. The door itself looked like it was leaning, bowing under the heat. Not glowing quite yet. Nice light coming from the crack beneath it, though, underneath the fucking smoke pouring out from the frame.

Yeah, this was not his idea of a restful night.

He still kept at it. "I ain't stopping the hammering, Lawrence O'Donnell, you motherfucker."

Boom. More concrete.

Boom. More wood paneling. Now he had enough room to shove a basketball through. He looked at his hips, looked at the hole.

Nope. That wasn't going to do it.

"Motherfuckers," Gary muttered, and just kept at it.

The walls were burning. His lungs were fucking burning. Fires doubled in size every six minutes, he'd heard.

In six minutes ... the half of the house that wasn't on fire would probably be on fire, and busting into the crawlspace beneath at that point? Would be pointless.

He looked at the hole. Maybe a little larger than a basketball. "Fuck," he whispered. Looked at his hips. Looked at the hole again.

Maybe.

This was probably his last chance. "Fuckety fuck," he muttered, and fucking went for it, because why not?

Gary dove for the hole like it was the last goddamned plane out of fucking Saigon, slipping in with his arms straight out and the super duper expensive SOCOM hammer leading the way, because hell if he was throwing away his only blessed weapon now, when he had nothing else at hand.

His shoulders caught on the hole around him and forced himself through, not giving a shit when he felt skin tearing. "Suck me off, you sumbitches," he said. The splinters and busted tile ripped at his shirt, but who needed a shirt? His chest was pure ripped steel anyway, and no one was fucking watching.

Gary wriggled down, wishing maybe he hadn't focused so hard on making his chest strong. Whatever, it didn't matter. Get past the pecs, he'd be home free, then he'd be glad as he fucking crawled under the house that he had muscle upon muscle. "I'm an unstoppable badass," he said, disappearing into the dark, the lights above him flickering, then failing. He was halfway into the hole and stuck, goddammit. He couldn't even see what the fuck he was stuck on.

"Fucking perfect," Gary said, and hammering at where he thought he was caught, shoulders barely through of the hole, head hanging down under his house.

He could see flames licking out from under the house back in the direction of the bedroom, like embers dying as they started to work their way through the wood under the house. It was a hell of thing, seeing the supports that held everything up start to catch.

"Fucking fucks, man," Gary said, hammering at the hole and himself. Something gave; he dropped down a foot and landed on the side of his neck. "God—fucking bless it!" That had hurt.

Now it was time to move. He righted himself—Wrightson'd himself, as he thought of it, putting his elbows beneath him, clenching the SOCOM pistol in hand, cracking his neck left to right. He was still at an off angle, legs thrust back up into the hole. They'd come when called, though, like a good dog.

And he started to crawl.

Stopped shortly thereafter, though, because the legs ... did not come.

"I knew I should have had you useless fucking drags amputated!" Gary looked back. In the dim, orangey light, he could see nothing but his feet disappearing around mid-calf up into the hole. Shaking himself made one leg move—slightly—and fall, knee down, into the dirt of the crawlspace.

No dice on that right leg, though. It was always a fucking troublemaker.

"By God, you will move!" He turned, putting the SOCOM down and grabbing. Twisted his body, pulled, did a sit-up.

Not a damned thing. It stayed right where it fucking was, damn it.

"You fucking useless—efficiency-less—goddamn you!" He smacked a fist against the kneecap, flailing at his midsection, trying to do sit-ups—fuck, whatever.

He hit it again. "Goddamn you! I fucking hate—I fucking hate—I fucking—fucking useless—betrayed by my own fucking legs—useless—useless—" Wet tears were rolling down his cheeks. No. No. Not tears. The wet washcloth was just dripping, by God. Yeah. That was it.

"I'M NOT FUCKING DYING HERE!" He slammed his fist against his thigh, and something jarred loose. His leg released from whatever it was stuck on back in the bathroom, and his ass went thumping to the ground.

Gary let out a whoop of joy and didn't look back. He seized the SOCOM pistol hammer and by God started crawling his way out.

Embers were glowing to either side of him. The grass was high around the edges of the house, but flames lit the night beyond, glowing against his lawn. Ahead, he could see the grove of trees past his yard's end, a knot of thick pines that he cursed and flipped off every time he went by on his zero-turn radius mower, because they were just too thickly close together for him to ride between them and get those nagging clumps of long grass that hid between them and the shrubberies that were popping up. He'd always meant to tame that section of his property. Chop them fuckers down, put in more beautiful green fescue grass.

Now, he crawled for it like it was salvation itself. He busted out from underneath the house and into the fresh air, leaving the glow of the floorboards as they caught behind him and crawling out into freedom.

"Fuck yeah," he said as he got out into the yard. Looked left, looked right.

No federal demon bitches out here. But he couldn't be too careful. He crawled for the woods.

It got wearying at the end. It had been a long day. A real long day. He reached the safety of the treeline—relative safety, anyway—and kept going. Dead leaves crackled against his chest, against his legs. He looked back. He could see the blood coming; he'd probably caught on the pipe, now that he thought about it, but goddammit ... that wasn't going to stop him.

"Fuck you, demons." He put one elbow in front of the other, belly-crawling over a stick. His house blazed behind him. "Fuck you, useless legs. Fuck anyone who opposes my ass—I will run you over. I'ma get me some wet, hot revenge on that fed bitch, too." He pushed the damp rag out from his face, let it hang like a bandana around his neck. "And it's going to feel good, too." Yep, definitely bleeding from the legs.

Gary pulled up next to a tree and dragged himself over, rolled when necessary, got his back against it. He pulled his legs in front of him so he could look at the damage.

Whewee. By God, that was not good.

The right leg, the one that got stuck? It was bleeding worse than the demon-scratched one. He didn't feel any of it, of course, but it explained the lightheadedness that he might have otherwise attributed to just plain old smoke exposure.

"By God," he muttered, pushing his wet, smoke-laden towel into the right leg just on the wound. He considered tying a tourniquet and just passing out, but ... "I'll keep you," he muttered to his leg. "Ain't got time for an amputation right now. But you should fucking pull your own weight, dipshit. You know who's more useless than Ulysses? You fucking are. That's who."

His voice trailed off, and he raised his eyes from his wound to the house.

It burned. Flames were roaring out of the roof now, coming out the windows. Black smoke rolled up into the heavens.

"I'll rebuild you, by God," Gary said, leaning his head back against the tree. "After I demolish these fucking demons and fuck them in the ass. They don't know I can't feel my dick, but they're gonna know after I tear their assholes up one by one, unstopped by the loss of sensation. It's going to be fucking glorious, let me tell you. They're going to feel my crippled ass breathing down their neck and my big cock in their fucking cornholes. I'ma hump 'em til they fall down, my weight on their back. Hell, maybe I'll have a preacher bless my dick into an instrument of holiness, and just fuck them into sulfur hell death."

He stared at the fire, cheeks still wet—from the rag, by God! And watched his house burn, more pissed than ever at these fucking assholes, and more determined than ever to inflict his fucking rage and vengeance on the cornholes of every last one of them. If they had cornholes. Otherwise, it'd be some other hole, perhaps one even less enjoyable for them.

*

Arch found Erin in her chair, staring. Again. Straight ahead this time, not out the window. Daydreaming? He couldn't say, but probably.

"What's up?" she asked, sounding more tired than maybe ever he'd heard her.

"Got a demon pattern emerging," Arch said, sliding on in, sitting himself down in the chair opposite her. Part of him wanted to stand, but this was grave. You sat for the grave things.

"That the one Dr. Darlington and Ms. Cherry and I hit on earlier today?" she asked. "The one with the, uh ..." She waved a finger around to mimic ... well, something.

"Dismembered, uh ... and women with their heads caved in. Yeah," Arch said. "We got three more calls for similar situations. I checked out two of them." He shook his head. "They look ... well, like I said. Patterned."

"Like a copycat killer?"

"Like someone does the same thing every time," Arch said. "It's always a couple that's post ... you know."

Erin snorted. "Coitus? Sex? You can say it, Arch. Hell I know you've done it more than a time or two, at least according to Duncan—" She froze. There was some remorse. "Sorry."

He waved it off. "You know I didn't like talking about it, even before Alison ... passed."

Now Erin looked at her lap, wouldn't look up. "Sorry for bringing up—"

"You don't have to be any more sorry for bringing her up than I have to be for not wanting to talk about ..." He glanced away. "Saying her name isn't going to break me, Erin. I think her name all the time. I think about *her* ... all the time. She was my wife. Her memory might hit me ... might burn me ... might make me regret ... everything that happened, but ... I loved her. And her memory is not so painful that the mere thought of her is gonna ... make me a puddle of a man like I was in the moments immediately after." He looked right at her. "We got work to do. I ain't got time to go to pieces every time I think about her. I loved her, she loved me, and it'd kill her if she saw me sitting by watching this town go down the tubes when I could be helping."

Erin finally looked at him. "You're a strong man, Arch. Maybe you should be the one sitting in this chair."

Arch just frowned. "I don't know that I'm that strong yet. Carrying my weight's one thing. Carrying the weight of the town ..."

"It is a big weight," she said. Sounded hollow.

"You bowing under it?" he asked.

"Maybe," she said. "This killer demon thing ... I don't know what you want to call him ... Dick the Ripper, maybe?"

Arch blinked a few times. "Probably not that, no. I don't think I can rightly say that."

She chuckled grimly. "He's bad, no doubt. Lots of bodies showing up. And parts of other bodies, which ... inspires a question—where are the men that he's unmanned? You think he's eating them like that demon with the barbecue obsession y'all killed in the tunnels? Casting off the parts he doesn't like?"

"I don't know," Arch said. "But I got a bad feeling since we just saw our first victim today and already we got quite the pile of dead and ... uh ... dis ... membered ..." Erin snorted again, "—accumulating. Whoever he is, he's making a dent. And we're already pretty well dented, people going missing here and there, randomly. To make this much of a splash, this much of a noise, this quickly?"

"You think if it escalates from here ..."

"If it escalates from here, in two weeks we'll all be dead," Arch said. "You know how it goes. If we've gotten five calls, there are ten more we haven't gotten."

"Yeah," she said quietly. "Arch ... this other thing, though ... those feds?"

"Yeah?"

"The tankers were registered to the Department of Transportation," Erin said. "Another federal agency."

Arch gave that a moment's thought. "Doesn't mean it's related to the feds you've been talking to."

"No," Erin said. "But the FBI ones ... they're bringing help, they say. Taking things over. Including the tanker investigation."

Arch chewed that one over. "You think there's some coordination going on here?"

"I don't know," she said. "The thought of handing over our defense—they talked about taking over for the watch. Us ... disbanding or something. Leaving town or letting them handle, I dunno. They didn't get specific. But it was very much about us ... surrendering responsibility."

"That doesn't appeal to me much, either," Arch said.

"How long have we been out here fighting this on our own?" she asked, popping up out of the seat and looking fresher than he would have believed given that she looked like she might slide through the chair from sheer exhaustion a moment ago. "We finally, fucking *finally*—sorry—got everyone together on this. Reeve tried. He died. And people finally started putting their fucking—sorry—money where their mouths were. Now, we're not doing great, by any means, but—dammit, we're fighting. We've been fighting all along. Where the hell have the feds been? And now they're going to waltz in here with—I don't even know what they're going to do. But we're going to... just ... give up? Go home? Sit there and wait while they flood the zone with demon hunting agents, maybe?" She sighed. "The uncertainty fucking—shit, sorry—"

"Either stop saying the words or stop apologizing, I don't care which."

"—okay, I'm not really that sorry," she said. "But dammit, Arch. They weren't here for us when we were in all the rest of this crisis. When we were dealing with Gideon, and that one guy at the festival with the super impregnating powers, and the- the Rog'tausch—and—and the legion—"

"Yes. I get it."

"But they're going to swoop in now and save us? Now? After—how many people have died?" She sat back down, heavily. "We were fucking forsaken, Arch. No one gave a hot shit about us then. Why do I get the feeling ... no one still gives a shit about us?"

"I don't think it's an unusual feeling out here," Arch said. "Especially lately."

"I just don't get it," Erin said. "We always talked about how our 911 response time out in the country is ... ten, twenty, thirty minutes depending on where we get the call and how far out it is. It's understood that if you're that far out, you're kinda on your own until we get there. People know that. They accept that. They plan for that. Hell, some revel in it.

"But this ... the idea that these people that are charged with helping us, protecting us ... the thought that they just ... haven't given a damn to do that job until now? Maybe they *were* overwhelmed. Hendricks and Duncan talked about there being a lot of other hotspots boiling. Maybe they really were just up to their asses in alligators. And maybe they're here now to make good on the social compact that we have in this country, that thing where we all pitch in and help each other out."

"Maybe," Arch said. Something about it still itched him, and not for the first time he was glad he wasn't in charge of the decision making around here. "This one demon, though ... the cutting one ... he might hit again before they show up."

Erin got a funny smile on her face. "What makes you think this demon is a 'him'? It sounds like it could be a really jealous and pissed off 'her' to me. A Bobbitt-type demon."

"I don't rightly care," Arch said. "I just want to stop it. But I'm struggling with how."

Erin's smiled faded. "Well ... I don't know how to solve this whole problem with the feds ... but I might know how to draw your demon into a confrontation." She went back to smirking. "Not sure you're going to like it, though."

"Oh? Why's that?"

"Well, if you're looking for a post-coital killer," Erin said, "you need to create a post-coital situation as bait, right?"

Arch shook his head. "I'm not—"

"*You* don't have to," Erin said. "I know someone else you can use." She looked past Arch, through the door. "Someone with infinite lust and insatiable desire."

Arch turned without even thinking about it, or else he'd have known in advance what she was suggesting before he did so.

Casey Meacham was standing out in the bullpen, phone pinched between shoulder and ear, talking quietly into the mouthpiece.

"Oh," Arch said. "Yeah. I reckon that'd do it."

*

Brackessh could feel the sin in this town, now that his own mind, own body, was purged of it. The vessel he'd used to remove it was destroyed, cast out into the darkness to rot and fester, not to trouble the living any longer.

He could breathe free again. Unharried. Unworried.

"We must expand," Brackessh said. "Today will be our day." He looked around at his followers. "We will double our numbers. Triple them, perhaps. I can feel it, the sin building in this town, seeking release." He brushed the face of one of his followers, blood coating the cheek. "We will swoop in once it is granted ... and they will join us ...

"Forever."

*

"Gary!" the shout echoed over the burning of the house, jarring Gary Wrightson out of a nice, sound slumber. He'd been good and tuckered out after the crawl, and smashing the subfloor with his pistol, and ...

Hell. All of it. He'd fought his fucking way out of a demon ambush in his own bedroom with nothing but his wits and a SOCOM pistol.

Fuck yeah. If confidence was a string of victories one put together over a lifetime, this one was going to be a hell of a boost.

Gary swayed to the side, looking out through the trees. A shadow was running around the back of his house, which was still ablaze, fire shooting up to the heavens like some grand bonfire from the carefree days before the demons came. The silhouette had a bottle in hand, glinting in the firelight, and yelled, "Gary! Jesus!"

"I am risen indeed, motherfucker!" Gary shouted, and the silhouette stopped. It turned, almost directly between him and the house, and he recognized the bastard now. "What are you doing here, Paul?"

"Fuck me, Gary," Paul said, breaking into a run toward him.

"I ain't in the mood," Gary said, "I want to fuck some demon ass ... for burning my goddamned house."

"Jesus, Gary," Paul said, stopping a few steps away from the tree trunk where Gary remained upright at a lean. "What the fuck?"

Gary spied the bottle in Paul's hand. "You bring that for me?"

Paul lifted the bottle. It was a George Dickel No. 12. Tennessee whiskey. Smooth as pretty young girl's ass. "I thought you might want to ... you know ... drink it off after today's setbacks."

"The water, Paul," Gary said, waving him down. "It's all about the damned water. Two fed demons came creeping into my bedroom last night, asking me about the water. I managed to kill one with this—" he lifted the SOCOM pistol, "—and escaped the other one into my panic room—"

"Ain't that your shitter? With all that metal plating in the walls and the reinforced door?"

"Fuck, yeah. Because a man doesn't want to be disturbed when he's dropping a proper deuce. But Paul—them fuckers came after me because of the water. We gotta warn people."

Paul stared down at him, then looked at the whiskey. With a lone thumbnail, he ripped a hole through the seal and pulled out the cork. After he downed a long slug, he offered the bottle to Gary.

"You fucking idiot, I needed you to drive," Gary said.

"I can still drive."

"You're fucking impaired now, you dipshit. Why do none of y'all have any respect for the rule of goddamned law around here? Fuck. Where'd you park?"

"Over there," Paul pointed beyond the burning house. "I damned near ran up on your lawn when I realized it was your house on fire. At first, I just thought your neighbors were burning the trees down again."

"Nope, they were trying to end me—as every competitor does when I enter a market," Gary said, plunging forward on his elbows, ready to belly crawl all the way into town if he had to. Or at least to Paul's car. "Well, I have entered the demon hunting market, bro. And they're right to be scared. Because Gary Wrightson is about to show those motherfucking hellspawn why ours is the most feared name in the

Southeastern Tennessee plumbing market."

Paul followed, slowly, a few steps behind. "And … and also, we're going to fuck 'em up, right?"

"Damned skippy," Gary said. "Because that's what Wrightsons do."

10.

The sun wasn't quite ready to rise into the eastern sky, but Ernie Frietag was out on Lake Brightling, a little jobbie not connected to the TVA network, nor the Caledonia River. Brightling was a lake unto itself, some 600 acres of calm waters, chill and peaceful on this November day.

Ernie sank a lure in, seeking smallmouth bass, largemouth bass—hell, even a crappie. He'd be okay with a good crappie.

He'd actually be okay with nothing. Getting out on the lake was its own reward, especially after a hard week at the mill.

A ripple across the water made Ernie sit up straight in the seat on the front of his bass boat. He adjusted his hat, shivered in his thick coat, and looked at the ripples.

Something was moving out there. Hot dog.

His reel rested lightly in his hand, eyes fiercely focused on the ripple in the water. He leaned forward, licking his lips. Hoo boy. He could already taste that sweet bass.

Another ripple. Closer to the boat. He checked; his net was close by.

"Here, fishy fishy," Ernie said. A little grin of anticipation cracked his face. He wriggled the rod. Would it help? Only if he didn't jerk it, maybe. "I got the stuff you want. I do. Come and get it ..."

The next ripple was even closer to the boat. Something was trawling the surface. Looked pretty big, too. But now it was in past his line.

Did it pass up his lure?

"Shit," Ernie said and started to slowly reel in. Bass tended to be tougher to get this time of year, fewer bites, but you could nail some big ones. And from the ripples, this sure looked like a big one ...

"Come on, come on," Ernie muttered. Waiting for another ripple. He had the line about halfway in. Taking his time. Presenting slowly.

"You can come on in, baby ... I'm waiting for you ... I got you ... you just come right on over to Ernie and we'll—"

Something exploded out of the water in a blast that soaked Ernie, a shadow leaping out of the dark lake and hitting the front of the boat, rocking everything. Ernie just about fell backwards over his seat, instead going sideways and landing flat on his ass.

"What the helllll?" Ernie yelled into the quiet morning. He'd dropped the rod.

Something ... was in the front of his boat, not five feet from him.

Something big.

Something ... with glistening teeth and wet, amphibian skin—no, scales! good Jesus—

Ernie scrambled, reaching past the boat paddle for the filet knife. He failed the first try, and the thing sprang at him just as he got a hand on it ...

Swinging it around, Ernie smashed the filet knife into the dark-skinned creature. It caught it right in the chest, plunging on, fearlessly, driven—that damned thing was going to eat Ernie, going to eat him alive, it was—

Except it stopped, slitted eyes going wide in the dim light. It froze, seized up, then—

Pop.

Like a black hole swallowed it right there, yanking it in on itself in a sudden collapse, it was gone in an instant.

Ernie just sat there, soaked and chilled, wet as could be, the filet knife in his hand. Lucky he'd had Bill Miller, the preacher at the Methodist Church, pray with him over it, offer the Lord's blessings for it—and him. Bill had looked a little strangely upon the request, but ... heck. Ernie had heard about blessed weapons and demons down at the mill, and he wasn't too ashamed to say it—

He believed in Jesus—and the devil. And he wasn't ashamed to have a weapon against the latter that wasn't just a book, either.

Didn't hurt to have a holy implement on his boat, either. Maybe it'd help him catch something. And even if it didn't, what could it hurt?

"Well, shoot," Ernie said, standing back up. He was pretty wet. Cold, too. Danged demon interrupted his fishing.

But that happened sometimes to a real fisherman. Interruptions. And this was his day off. Saturday. Tomorrow he'd need to be in church, clearly, with his wife.

Wringing out his sleeve over the edge of the boat, Ernie wiped off the seat and sat down, picking up his rod again. He made sure he kept the filet knife close, in case any other demons got any bright ideas about eating him or whatever.

And Ernie just went on fishing.

*

They stopped off at Rogerson's, and Paul busted open the front window at Gary's command. The alarms went off, screaming. Gary ignored them. He was here for one purpose.

"Get that one—the red one! The red one!" He pointed out the window of Paul's pickup, where it was parked just off the curb.

"They're all red!" Paul shouted, grabbing the mobility scooter and dragging it over the threshold of the busted window. One of the handlebars got hung, and he jerked it until it got free, then dragged it over to the bed of his pickup. Grunting under the weight, he shoved it in, alarm wailing the whole time.

"Where to now?" Paul asked, throwing her into gear as he got in. They were moving before he even got buckled up.

"Cop shop."

Paul did a double-take at him. "We're gonna ... what? Go turn ourselves in for busting into Rogerson's?"

"I don't think they're gonna give a fuck about a broken window at this juncture," Gary said. "We got bigger shit going on right now, bro."

"That's true."

They rode in silence, the klaxon sound of the store alarm fading behind them. Minutes later they were pulling into the sheriff's station off Old Jackson Highway. Paul pulled in head-first, killed the ignition and jumped out. Gary waited patiently for him—sorta, he fidgeted a lot—until he got the mobility scooter around, then jumped for it.

"Jesus, you can't wait ten seconds for me to bring it fully alongside?" Paul asked as Gary pulled himself up. He'd thumped pretty hard, breaking loose the fresh scabbing on his legs. Blood was running down them again.

Gary pulled himself up with some effort. His arms were screaming. He'd had a hell of a day. Beauty sleep interrupted by fucking pig feds and their no-knock raid bullshit. "Violating my constitutional rights, by God," Gary muttered, getting himself up in the seat and smacking Paul when he tried to help.

"Me helping you into the seat ain't violating constitutional rights, bro."

"Not talking about you, *Perry*," Gary said, giving him daggers. "Come on. Everyone else should be here soon." He squeezed the accelerator on the scooter and it zipped forward, damned near tipping him out. "Fuck! This is why I don't like these fucking things, balance is an issue."

Still, he kept from falling out, working his ass off to keep from unbalancing and going ass over teakettle one way or the other. It lacked the support of his wheelchair, but it did have some get up and go. He wouldn't dare use one for long, though—not propelling himself everywhere with the strength of his own arms? That wasn't life to Gary Wrightson, by God. That was like welfare sponging, lazing and letting a machine do the work. Not in alignment with his fucking goals, nossir.

Paul ran up and grabbed the door, letting Gary into the lobby, but slowly. It was a narrow space; not exactly wheelchair accessible. Or scooter, in this case.

Once he was in, he could see a couple people moving around behind the counter. "How you doing, Benny?"

"Not too bad, Paul," Benny said. "What can I do ye for?"

"I've been done enough tonight, thank you very fucking much," Gary said, steering on around behind the counter. He caught a glimpse of Erin Harris in the office ahead. She grimaced as he crossed her view. "Bunch of demons told me to bite the pillow cuz they were coming in dry."

"Uh, hey, you can't just—" Benny sprang to his feet.

Too slow. "Move it or lose a toe, chump." Gary shot past him, scooter blazing at a sweet three, maybe four miles an hour. Yep. This motorized shit could really make a man lazy.

Gary banged into Erin's office with an accidental sideswipe of the frame. "Apologies," he said, glancing at the frame.

"Honestly," Erin said, "that's the least of the consternation you've caused me."

"Well ... I'm not much on apologies, so ... take what you can get," Gary said, then stopped, taking a deep breath. "No. Wait. Okay, let me level with you—I'm a man with no small amount of pride—"

"You don't fucking say."

"—and I realize now that I've perhaps ... been a giant prick," Gary said, keeping his head down a little. Humble, almost. "I might have a bit of a chip on my shoulder at times—"

"Understatement of the year," Paul said, coming in behind him.

"—and I can probably come on a little strong," Gary said, trying to ignore the criticism. Opinions were like assholes, everyone had one, and they were all full of shit. "So I'm here, in your office, where I'd really rather not be in the middle of the fucking night, reeking of smoke like a goddamned ashtray or a dancer down at Moody's—"

"Yeah, what the hell happened to you?" Erin asked, frowning.

"I'm getting to that," Gary said. "The succinct version is, your federal demon friends tried to cornhole me and murder me after executing a no-knock, no-warrant raid in violation of my constitutional rights. Then they proceeded to trap me in my panic room—no, wait, I don't like that name. I didn't panic. I stayed incredibly calm, actually. Didn't lose my head at all—"

"Bunker room?" Paul asked.

"Implies retreat," Gary said, shaking his head. "How about 'internally fortified fortress room'? Yeah, I like that. That's good. My bastion—"

"Fucking A," Erin said, her shoulders slumping. "You telling me those feds …?"

"The ones from the trucker party earlier tonight, yeah," Gary said. "Don't remember their names. The male one? I killed his ass."

Erin's eyes went wide. "Jesus. You killed a federal agent?"

"Well, I vaporated him," Gary said. "Turns out, he was a demon."

Erin sagged, eyes going wide. "A demon?"

"Yeah, I popped his ass with a blessed pistol I kept under my pillow." He pulled out the now-lumpy SOCOM. "I'll have you know they ruined a beautiful piece of machinery. Look at this barrel. I had to use this to bust through the subfloor of my fortress room and enact an escape while my house burned around my goddamned ears. I'm gonna need a full replacement slide and barrel, new grips at least—I mean, just—Jesus."

"But he was a *demon*?" Erin was standing now. "The fed? Ross?"

"Yeah, and so was his female compatriot," Gary said. "Now I'd never much bought into those conspiracy sites saying that the government was infiltrated and being run by some 'other' party. Seems to me there ain't no monolithic group that's capable of masterminding a conspiracy because there ain't nobody keeps a secret that well, especially one as big as, 'Hey, we control the government.' I mean, really, come on. Let's apply a little logic here—but—anyway, I guess that's another place I was wrong. Because fuck, there *are* demons. In the government."

"Benny," Erin said, still standing. "I need Duncan down here now."

"What about Guthrie?" Benny called back.

Erin thought about it a second. "Her, I could do without. Get me Duncan. If Guthrie comes too … well, fuck."

"I'm on it," Benny said, and Gary could hear the phone dialing.

"So … you believe me about the demons?" Gary asked.

Erin just stared at him. "Yeah, I believe you about the feds being demons. Why wouldn't I?"

Gary shifted in the scooter seat. "I just assumed ... I mean I was claiming your federal friends were demons. I kinda figured you'd ... think I was nuts."

Erin shrugged. "We're all nuts right now. Finding out that the people promising help to us from outside are actually demons ...?" She shook her head again. "That's probably the sanest thing I've heard so far today."

*

"This here is the best assignment I've been given since joining the watch," Casey Meacham said, his bare, skinny, concave chest puffed out proudly. "In terms of skill set, this—this is like a match made in heaven. You found the perfect man for the job, Arch."

Arch just stared at the skinny taxidermist, resting a hand on his sword and wishing he was in the midst of a fray right now, swinging it, rather than sitting here on the eastern edge of Midian, a couple miles past the outskirts in an abandoned trailer. This was the side of town where they'd been seeing most of the gelding and death action. The couple that had lived here had died on the square a month back, and the place looked like it lacked for housekeeping in the interval since.

That was okay, though, Arch reflected as he stood in the middle of the bedroom, trying to figure out just how far he was willing to go to make this happen. "I'm ... pleased you're pleased," was the best he could come up with to reply to Casey.

"Truly, my darling," Ms. Cherry purred from the other side of the bed, where she was wrapped up in a black trench coat, "we should let deputy Stan find his hiding place and begin. Lives are in the balance, after all." She raised her eyebrows at Arch. "Unless you prefer to be in the room?"

Arch eyed the small master closet. There was a second bedroom just down the hall, but ... "I'll be in here," he said and stepped into the closet. "Unless you need me farther away?" He looked right at Casey, then to Mrs. Cherry. "Or if you'd prefer—"

"My darling, I have had many audiences in my time," Ms. Cherry said. "You could be in the bed, caressing me from behind, even joining in—and it would affect me none."

"Same," Casey said. "Unless you were just sitting there, not participating. That'd be a little awkward." He seemed to think about it. "But perhaps a smidge arousing, too ..."

Arch bumped his head on the shelf and slid down before closing the folding closet door. His knees were tight against his chest, and he closed his eyes, trying not to listen.

"Now we can begin," Ms. Cherry said, with an oozing of desire. Fake, he assumed, since Casey always paid her.

"Baby, I been ready for this all day," Casey said. "But I really started to get excited after Arch told I was going to get to put it to you while on the fucking clock!"

"You carve time out to fuck me regularly while on watch, Casey," Ms. Cherry said. "We did it in the sheriff's station restroom just this morning."

Arch groaned and put his fingers in his ears. It didn't help much. He was too close to the action.

"How shall we start?" Ms. Cherry asked, muffled through Arch's fingers in his ear canals. His sword was balanced on his knees; he could grab it in seconds.

"Let's do the usual, baby. You know what fires me up."

"Mmmm."

Slap!

The hard flesh-on-flesh contact was loud, even through the fingers in his ears. Arch turned toward the sound, alarmed. Had the demon shown up already—?

"Spank me! Spank me, baby!" Casey screamed.

"Ohhhh," Arch moaned, closing his eyes in the darkness again.

"He sounds like he's enjoying this as well," Ms. Cherry said. Casey just laughed.

"Oh, my goodness," Arch said.

"You're going to be talking about my goodness by the time this is over, Arch!" Casey said. Another slap followed, and Arch tried to hum a hymn to cover it. "How Great Thou Art," in this case.

It didn't work.

*

Darla opened Marischa's door almost silently and stared into the darkened room. It was just after dawn, and light was cracking its way through the curtains. She'd spent a long time thinking about exactly what had to happen here, how things needed to flow in order to reach her desired outcome.

The smell of Marischa's perfume tinged the air as Darla stepped inside. Marischa lay flat on the pillow, a black sleeping mask covering her eyes, a small snort issuing forth from her lips as she stirred.

It was oddly similar to the sound Jason used to make when he slept. Darla made a little face, then shut the door behind her silently.

She didn't really want to wake Marischa, at least not in a loud way. Darla crept through the cloud of perfume, easing over to the bed. The tingle of cool air explained why Marischa was buried under the extra blankets Darla kept in here for guests. She should have been used to it; this wasn't exactly Chicago, after all. But Marischa liked her comforts. She kept the heat nailed at 72 all winter long in her condo.

"Darla?"

Marischa sat bolt upright in the bed. She fumbled for the sleep mask and pushed it up onto her wrinkle-free forehead, blinking blearily. "What are you doing in here?"

"I was going to wake you up before the kids did," Darla said, easing onto the edge of the bed. She had a coffee cup in hand and extended it to Marischa. "They're up already and were asking about you—oh, I don't know, twenty, thirty times already."

"How adorable," Marischa said, caught somewhere between coldness and warmth. Lukewarm, perhaps? She probably was torn. Darla could understand. On one hand, you get that old, that rich, and you just want things your way. Grandkids, sure—but on your schedule. Early in the morning and late at night? Pfeh. Marischa Pike had done things on her own time for decades now. She was the sort who'd prefer to deal with her grandchildren between the office hours of nine and noon.

"They really love you, you know," Darla said, cradling the coffee cup in her left hand. "Especially given everything that's happened lately ... it makes a difference to them that you're here. A big one."

Marischa's wrinkle-free face shifted, eyes moving around as she took that in. "Well ... I have nothing but admiration for what you do with them. I don't know you handle it, myself. No nanny, no daycare. When you and Jason moved down here so that he could take that job, I thought ... well, it doesn't matter what I thought." She looked down at her hands. "A smart woman like you, an educated woman, an ambitious woman—I know you're far more ambitious than Jason was. I was sure you'd be back north in a few months. I doubted they'd have the sort of intellectual conversations down here that you thrive on, Darla. But here you are, and you? You've managed it. Stayed home with the children. Kept the home front ... Well, it's ... nothing short of astounding, really. I don't know how you do it."

She seemed so ... humble. Very unlike Marischa.

"You know what my secret it?" Darla leaned closer, offering

Marischa the coffee cup. "You're right, I'm far more ambitious than Jason ever was. And just doing this ... this motherhood thing? It'd be stifling. I need to think. Engage with ... people and problems ... and I do. I do. But that's the secret. I never saw myself as just a 'stay at home mom.'"

"Oh?" Marischa raised the coffee cup to her lips, pausing. "Why ... this is empty." She waggled the mug.

"I know," Darla said. "It's just there to catch a little of your blood. For the sacrifice."

Marischa angled her head. The words probably weren't making any sense to her; non sequitur.

Darla brought up her left hand and anchored it to the back of Marischa's neck. Then brought up the right, sharpened knife in hand, and ran it across her throat. It was a deep cut, and she caught her before she had a chance to scream.

The blood gushed out over Darla's hands, spraying her blouse—she'd worn an old one for this, as well as a pair of mom jeans she didn't care for—and pushed her mother-in-law back as she bled out. She made noises out of her open throat that sounded like screaming protests from one of those squeeze toys with the squeaker removed. It was wet and sickening and Darla listened to it, offering only the occasional, "Shhhh. Shhhhhh," as comfort, barely deigning to look her mother-in-law in the eyes as she died.

When it was done, she picked up the coffee mug. Some blood had gone in there. Not much. But she didn't need much.

She left the knife where she'd dropped it. She had other knives, better knives. This one was old and she'd be fine leaving it here until later, when she'd deal with the body. That would require more time than she had presently. The current episode of *PAW Patrol* would be done just about—

Thump. Someone hit the door, rattling the knob.

Darla looked down, into Marischa's dead eyes. "Sorry," Darla said, not really sorry. "You just ... got in the way. As mothers-in-law do."

She stood and shrugged out of her bloody blouse and jeans, tossing them onto the bed with the body. There was somewhere between a zero and none chance that the Calhoun County Sheriff's Department was going to randomly check out her dwelling, not with everything else going on around here right now. She felt safe doing so, knowing that they weren't much in the business of stopping murders at this point.

At least not of the garden, human variety.

Darla flipped the light on as the knob rattled again. She caught a glimpse of herself in the mirror. Little spots of red stood out on her neck, her stretch marks looking like angry, purple lines on her belly. She grimaced more at those than the blood droplets on her face like warpaint. "Fuck," she muttered, tugging that extra belly down so that the skin appeared almost flawless again, the way it had before children, before Jason, before—

Well, before.

"Fuck," she muttered, and unlocked the door, switching off the light as she did so. Little Jay was waiting just outside, and she blocked him with a thigh as she slid out, locking the door from the inside and shutting it behind her.

"Mommy," Jay said, looking up at her as he tried to squeeze past. He failed. She caught him with a spare hand and got the door closed. "Why you not have any clothes on?"

"Mommy's got to go take a shower," Darla said, touching a finger to her face. It came away bloody. At least she hadn't gotten it on her panties or bra. That she'd noticed anyway. This way, she could spare herself having to do more laundry. "You want me to put on another episode of *PAW Patrol*?"

He nodded, then his little eyes flicked at the door she'd just shut. "Where's Grandma?"

"Sleeping, sweetie."

"But I want to play with her." He looked so puppy-dog, big eyes.

"Oh, Grandma's tired," Darla said. "She's leaving later. Going home. And we've got fun things to do today." She knelt in front of him. "Lots of fun things."

"Okay," Jay said.

"Where's your sister?"

He pointed back toward the living room. Maybe she'd fallen asleep on the couch. Maybe she was using a crayon on the walls. At least she was being quiet. "Okay, let's go put on *PAW Patrol* again so Mommy can shower," Darla said. She doubted it would work. The kids always wanted to follow her around whenever she was doing something like makeup or showering. Jay because he wanted to stare at her tits and point at her vagina and ask her why she didn't have a penis. Mera was too young to do anything but marvel at her boobs and ask when she was going to get a pair for herself.

"Okay," Jay said again, and he let her take him by the hand and lead him back to the TV. Maybe it'd keep them occupied, just for a little longer, while she got ready. Then, after that—they'd have her full attention.

*

Erin's head was hammering as she sat across from Gary Wrightson in his motor scooter, shifting back and forth, like he was teetering in the seat. "You going to be all right?" Erin asked, finally losing patience after he did it the umpteenth time.

"This damned thing ain't for me," Gary said, seeming to get the balance right, at least for now.

"Where'd you get it?"

"Had to steal it from Rogerson's," he said, and goddamn, he was bold about it. "Best I could do on short notice."

"I reckon Addie Longholt won't fuss too much about it," Erin said. She didn't have much time to worry about it if Addie did. Human crime was pretty low on her priority list right now. "Can you tell me why the fed demons busted into your house?"

Gary nodded so hard he almost tipped himself over again. "It was about what we talked about last time—the water. They must have overheard me and got pissed I was telling you."

"Wait—what?" Erin stared at him. Everything was hard to swallow right now, but this? This was like one of those pills that was sized like a hubcap, guaranteed to hang in the esophagus. "About ... the water thing?"

"Yep," Gary said.

"Christ," Erin said, slumping back down in her seat, staring at him through barely parted fingers. "They're coming en masse today, these fucks. I thought it was an FBI task force, here to relieve us."

"Well, I think we can safely say that if they're here to relieve us of anything—" Gary started.

"It's our lives," Erin said. "Yeah, I made that jump, too."

"Or of our dignity," Gary said, drawing her attention to the fact that he was wearing nothing but a t-shirt and singed boxer briefs in the pattern of the Gadsden flag. She'd noticed that when he first came in but had ignored it thus far until now.

"Why, did they dress you in those before burning your shit down?" She pointed at the snake, which curled its way down the crotch. It was so full of irony, she thought, and didn't shy away from calling it out.

Gary didn't even blush. "Fuck no. And I showed them bastards they can't tread on this." He pointed at his crotch.

"Oh, God," Erin said, burying her face again. Most people would have backed off a notch when she pointed that out, but she'd forgotten who she was dealing with.

"Gary!" The shout came from the bullpen. Mary Wrightson came barreling in, along with the rest of the clan plus that strange Eastern European woman in the jumpsuit that said MARINA on its breast pocket. Gary's mother rushed over to him, her floral-patterned nightgown flapping behind her, and she hugged her face to her boy, nearly knocking him out of the scooter again.

"Dammit, Momma, my dignity," Gary said, fighting to remain upright.

"You're wearing nothing but your undergarments, bro," Larry Wrightson said, coming in wearing tight, worn-out jeans missing the knees. "Hey, is that a Gadsden flag? I gotta get me some of those. I dig the snake curling right on the dick place, man."

"It speaks to the calling of my soul," Gary said with a nod. "Sticking it to every motherfucker who wants to stomp me down. Like these demons." He looked pointedly at Erin. "I'm telling you—they're after the water somehow."

"I could maybe buy that. You know those tankers we stopped last night? Filled with the stuff." Erin stared him down. "But this raises lots of questions. Like why are they bringing in water from outside town if they're somehow trying to steal ours?"

Gary frowned in concentration. "That doesn't make any sense, you're right."

"I dunno, man, you see how much they sell that spring water shit for in the supermarkets?" This from Terry Wrightson. "They're probably stealing ours, because it's superior, high quality spring water, and bringing in stuff that's just drawn out of a tap in Atlanta or somewhere here. You know, real shitwater. Filled with toxins, and cocaine residue pissed out from addicts. Probably hormones, too, because you know everyone in those big cities in transitioning these days—they're going to make girls out of all of us. They can't handle our rugged masculinity. They even call it toxic."

"I know I have real problems dealing with it sometimes," Erin said. "Like right now."

Gary smacked his brother's arm. "Knock it off with that bullshit conspiracy theory shit. This is serious. It involves demons, not some fictional New World Order crap."

"I liked the New World Order when it first came out," Paul said, "but I thought the NWO Wolfpac was the best."

Mary smacked him across the back of the head. Apparently, no one needed her to explain why because she just glared and everyone got quiet.

"What is the purpose of bringing in water?" Marina asked, threading her way through the Wrightson boys. "We are running out here. Other than ... humanitarian? UN type shit?"

Gary blinked a few times. "She's right. We're running out here ... they're trucking it in. Why do that?"

"Humans ... can't survive without water," Paul said.

"Well, no shit, Sherlock," Mary said, giving him the daggers now. "What's that have to do with—"

"No, wait, I think he's got something there, Momma," Gary said, forcing himself upright again in the scooter, balancing between the armrests. "Think about it—if you're a demon that eats people or preys on people or—just flat out hates people and wants them to suffer—"

"This is very good town for you," Marina mumbled.

"It is, actually," Gary said, pointing at her. "But if we got no water to drink—"

"We can't fight without water," Erin said, straightening up in her chair to match him. "Even if we wanted to. Physically can't."

"No humans, no fun," Mary said, looking like she was about ready to rumble—or grumble. Maybe both. "Them dirty sumbitches."

"No wonder the feds were so up on me after we stopped this convoy," Erin said. It was feeling ... clearer, though not entirely clear yet. "If they're really demons—"

"I don't reckon it pleases them if we all scatter to the four corners," Gary said. "People leave Midian, there's more chance of the word getting out. They're probably sitting on it like crazy right now, trying to keep it quiet."

"They admitted as much to me," Erin said, holding her head. "But it's hard to wrap my brain around it, at least in its entirety. Is it the government? Some demon branch of an agency?"

"Yes," came a quiet voice from out in the bullpen. She looked through the door, past the crowd of Wrightsons, to find—

Duncan.

No Guthrie.

"You're getting it now, aren't you?" Duncan asked. "Yeah, the government sits on things. Yeah, there are demons in agencies and the bureaucracy in order to keep things quiet."

"Every goddamned congresscritter is a fucking demon, I fucking knew it!" Paul shouted.

"Almost none, actually," Duncan said. "Less than are found, as a percentage, in the general population. Demons, as a rule, think politics is too dirty."

"Good God," Gary muttered.

"This is like hooker declining Dirty Sanchez," Marina said.

"I don't think that's a perfect analogy," Mary said, and she looked to be really thinking about it. "She could be a germaphobe, or a scatophobic."

"Well, I think we can all agree that demons declining to enter the field of politics because it appalls them should probably appall us even more," Larry said. "Wow, my youthful illusions are really dissolving today."

"Grow up, man, you're almost thirty," Paul said.

"Everybody, shut the fuck up," Erin said, staring at Duncan, who stood just outside the door. "This ... demon FBI group ... they're sending 'relief.' Today. Are they related to the Office of Occultic Concordance?"

Duncan made a move of discomfort. "Tangentially, maybe. I didn't know them, or know they were demons, if that's what you were asking. They hid it pretty well. I assumed they were humans, in on the cover-up."

Erin stared at him. "And Guthrie?"

Duncan stared back. "Hell if I know anymore."

"How will they come at us?" Erin asked, mind already racing.

"They'll roll into town like a relief convoy," Duncan said.

"Like the tankers last night?" Erin asked. "Humans at the wheel?"

"I don't know about this tanker business, but ... probably not," Duncan said. "There's not so much a demon-human alliance going on in government. More like independent units. Not saying there's not some crossover, but this kind of secret? Isn't widely known, even at the higher levels. It goes no farther than it needs to in order to maintain the cover-up. Hell, some of the people covering up probably don't even know how many of our kind work in DC."

"I told you," Gary said, "conspiracies don't work." He leered at Paul. "You hear that? There is no New World Order outside wrestling. Human beings don't keep secrets. They're too social. Too ... self-righteous and braggardly."

"Yeah, yeah," Paul said. "Fuck you."

"They'll come in a convoy," Duncan said. "They'll assert control. This ... place ... will probably be their first stop. Then other critical systems to the operation of a town. The power grid, the wa—"

"Water, motherfuckers!" Gary said, thumping a hand down.

"And everything else," Duncan said. "If they sense a fight ... they'll have enough force to make a stand. Their goal is not aid. It's quiet. If you get in the way of that ... you move from something they're indifferent about, at best, right into the 'enemy' column. And they will have no compunction about wiping your ass out like roaches. Because you basically are to them. Dissent will not be tolerated."

"Disenfranchising of my God-given rights," Gary said. "Hell no, they won't."

"Cold dead hands, bro," Terry said. Every Wrightson nodded in time, like they were all on the same string.

"These demons, though—they're going to walk like feds and talk like feds," Duncan said. "They'll be geared like them—like the ones you already saw. They'll have guns, but some mags with holy bullets, too. Prepared to deal with human or demon resistance."

"And this is all they want?" Erin asked. "To keep things quiet?"

"Maybe," Duncan said. Cagey. "Hard to be sure. Not my department."

She'd let that lie until later. "So they're coming. Here. And we've got to stop them, but they're going to be armed for us."

"Like a fucking army," Larry Wrightson said. "Humans can't keep secrets, but demons can. They're the New World Order."

"Wolfpac in da houuuuuuuse!" Paul said. He got smacked.

"Well, I got a way of dealing with that bullshit," Gary said, and his face was set. He looked straight at Erin.

"These are demons," she said, feeling the whiff of desperation. "With guns. Rifles, probably."

"I heard him," Gary said, not backing down a whit. "But these colors don't run." He pointed at his crotch. "And we ain't getting tread on."

"You wearing them boxers turned out to be real prescient, there, bro," Paul said, nodding along. "What are the odds you'd be wearing them today, of all days?"

"Real good," Gary said, not looking away, fierce determination burning into Erin. Well, he seemed sure. "Every pair of undies I've got is these."

Erin just closed her eyes. That was more than she needed to know.

*

Brackessh could smell the sin, it was so thick in the trailer house. He wasn't even inside, but it reeked of it, wafting through the windows, the scent, the smell ... it overpowered him, made him wish to gag it all out, to remove himself from its nearness.

It would be purged, soon, though. He could feel it rising within the walls, there in the little trailer hidden back underneath the trees, the boughs swinging overhead in the wind.

So much sin. He wanted to gag.

"Come," Brackessh said, opening his door. His servants came flooding out of this car, and the others in the line with them. So many servants, now. They'd been busy this morning, this night. So much comfort being taken all over town, so much sin expunged, expelled. His only regret was that he couldn't be everywhere at once.

So much sin.

It finished within, the release, the diminishment. The thrill ended, reality crashed back in for the occupants of the trailer. Surely it was a hollow feeling; it always was, at its heart, whenever Brackessh felt it. Empty motions, purgation of what should have been soul deep but was really just filth from the soles of their feet up to their eyeballs.

The trailer squeaked, just slightly, as someone within shifted balance. Brackessh reached out with his mind, ignoring the sin still stinking within the place, radiating out of the windows and vents like flies and pestilence. He latched onto the mind within that was clear, that had been purged, latched on with all he had and pulled the sinner toward him ...

*

There was an unsurprising amount of singing in the car as Darla drove the kids along the wooded Dallasberg Pike. She thought that was funny, that all the roads down here seemed to be named Pike— like her. The kids had asked a time or two, and she'd explained the origins of the word "turnpike" and how people used to have pay, directly, for the road use. Hell, being from Chicago, she knew a thing or two about paying tolls.

Dallasberg Pike was a pretty disused road at this point. There were some pines along it, providing a few shades of green mixed in with the dead brown of winter. It was a bleak spectacle, especially with the sun hiding behind clouds. The road rose and fell with the trees so she didn't see much sky regardless.

A little sigh. That was a shame. Fitting, probably, but a shame. Some sun would have been nice to offset to the bitter chill.

"Mommy Mommy Mommmmmmmyyyyyyyy!" Jay chirped.

"Yes, my dear?" she asked, looking at him in that expanded rearview she'd strapped on. Heh. Strap on. That brought another memory to mind of their father, now departed.

"Are we going somewhere to play?" Jay asked.

Darla pushed a wan smile on her face. "Yes. We are going somewhere to play."

She saw the turn ahead, slowed. Took it easy, because she had precious cargo. This was Luwan Trail, an old road with a few farmsteads along it, most of which had been depopulated during the financial crisis. They remained in foreclosure, oddly enough, apparently not a high priority for banks that still had a boatload of toxic assets on their balance sheets. Farm property in southeast Tennessee just didn't seem to be a moneymaker for them. Well, the taxes were probably low enough that the bank didn't prioritize getting rid of them—if they even could. Land this far out was selling at a serious discount, if it sold at all.

Darla listened to Jay harangue his little sister about how he was in charge of her, and she rolled her eyes without bothering to correct him. So young. So stupid. What was the point?

She found the farm she was looking for. Number 22028 was the address. She took the right turn slowly, easing down a driveway that was thickly overgrown by long grass making its way up through the gravel that had been spread here a lifetime ago—for her kids, two or three lifetimes—by someone who'd once cared for this property.

The grass rustled against the bottom of the car, the soft whoosh making Jay squeal with glee. He thought they were in the water, apparently.

Darla steered down the driveway until they reached the end, a small farmhouse that she'd seen on the mapping app. Everything looked overgrown.

"Mommy, is this is a haunted house?" Jay asked.

"No, sweetie," she said, turning back to him and smiling as she put the car in park. "It's just a little run down, that's all." He did not seem convinced, but before he could ask another question she said, "Okay, hang on here a minute. I'm getting the wagon."

There was a cheer from the kids as she got out. That was to be expected.

The wagon was just a little folding canvas wagon that Darla had bought for family picnics. It was neat; it could be packed up in the back of the car with ease, and then it became a full-sized wagon. Blue, not red, unfortunately. And it lacked the nostalgia factor of a Radio Flyer, but still ... nifty. And the kids loved it.

When she opened up the door to get them out, there was another little cheer at the mere sight of the wagon. She smiled and unfastened the safety latch on Mera's child seat on both sides, then reached up to undo the third latch point in the back window. Once it was done, she hauled her daughter, still buckled into the car seat, into the wagon. Oof. It was about forty pounds of lift, and Darla was glad she had the wagon.

"Mommmmmy, lemmmmee out," Mera said, looking up at her mother with big blue eyes.

"No, sweetie," Darla said, closing the door and rolling her around, stopping off at the passenger side door to get the diaper bag. "Mommy's got to do some things here, so I'm going to need you to stay in your car seat. Your brother, too. Just for a little bit while I take care of some stuff." She winked as she slung the diaper bag over her shoulder, then closed that door and went around to get Jay.

She hauled him out the same way, trying not to get too caught up in answering his breathless inquiries about what they were doing here. She wasn't keen to explain demon pacts to him; she was pretty content to keep them both in the dark about demons and all that as long as possible. Checking to make sure the vial of Marischa's blood was securely packed away, heavily padded, in the diaper bag, Darla pulled the two kids, still strapped into the car seats, in the wagon toward the abandoned house.

*

"It shouldn't surprise any of you that we've got a damned problem," Erin said to the assemblage of the watch. They were all kitted out as she'd requested, wearing heavy coats and vests, and camo in a lot of cases, all spread out in front of the parking lot of the sheriff's station. She hadn't really seen them together since the meeting they'd had a few weeks ago where they'd all raised their hands and said, "Yep, I'm in," with varying levels of regret that it had come to this. They'd done their duty since then, every one of them called up and dispatched by Casey or Benny or whoever was on duty. Working in teams, trying to put out the fires springing up around Calhoun County, and Midian, specifically.

Well ... now she was going to ask a lot more of them.

"We ain't got nothing but problems around here," Tony Kelhauser said, prompting laughs from his little squad. Five guys and Terri Pritchard, a woman in her forties who had never taken a speck of shit off of anybody. She and Mary Wrightson would have gotten along real well, Erin reckoned, if they'd been on the same end of town. Or they might have killed each other. Hard to say.

"Well, add another to the pile," Erin said. She was standing upon the hood of the Explorer so everyone could see her clearly. "But we're gonna solve this one right quick. The FBI came to town yesterday, making promises—"

A couple boos didn't stop her.

"—saying they were going to help us, finally." She tried to keep that jaded edge out of her voice but failed. It was hard not to feel that wearying sense of disappointment, betrayal, whatever ... when a group you'd kind of idolized and kind of feared turned out to be not at all what you were expecting. "They promised relief. Today. Agents by the dozens, coming in to help relieve us from having to ... well, to do this shit anymore."

"That sounds like a good deal," Marie Mulligan said from her little group up front. Cellular structure. That was what the military guys among her group had said to do with this. Make small cohesive units first, then cohere them tighter together as time went on. "We could all be done with this, yeah?"

That prompted a murmur. Some people were clearly relieved at the prospect of being done with demon fighting. She couldn't blame them for that; they'd lost people just since forming up a few weeks ago. Long hours, late nights, early mornings—and a lot of these folks were still working jobs or their own businesses.

Others, though ... she looked at Gary Wrightson, who was still in that mobility scooter next to her, and he shook his head without looking up at her. Others in the crowd were doing the same. She knew that feeling, too. It was a real dual-natured thing for her; on the one, trust authority, because ... well, she was authority. On the other ...

Fuck authority. Authority just gets in your way. Steps on you. Stomps on you, sometimes. She'd heard the arguments at her parents' own dinner table. Her dad would politely and calmly argue that in a civilized society, you delegated force to the proper, lawful authorities. He'd been raised in town, in Asheville, North Carolina, a pretty privileged upbringing that had included an MBA from Vandy.

Her mom didn't truck with that. Her mom was a redneck from east Tennessee who didn't trust the government at all. She'd been hardscrabble her whole life and looked at anyone other than a local cop or sheriff as an outsider, not worthy of her respect, grudging or otherwise, until they proved it. She slept with an old Colt Python her grandaddy had given her at eighteen right by the bed and had whipped the ass off of any of her kids who'd even looked at it sideways—until they were old enough to know how to use it.

Erin's mom didn't hold to delegating force. "I'm not waiting for 911 to come get my corpse if someone kicks down my door in the middle of the night," she'd say, causing Erin's father to shake his head sadly. "I'ma take that sumbitch out. Because last I checked, Sheriff Reeve and his boys will be here in ten minutes, but my .357 magnum? It has a response time of 1,000 feet per second. I win that race every time."

She could almost hear the echoes of all those arguments—mostly good natured—in the cheers versus the boos here. In the people hoping against hope that this'd be over. The lawful authorities would come in and set things right, finally and at last. They could all go back to living their peaceful, modern existence.

It was like popping a balloon. "Turns out ... the FBI agents that offered that help ... are demons," Erin said, looking down at Gary Wrightson as she said it. He met her eyes and nodded once. None of that fierce, pissed-off fire was aimed at her anymore. Instead, there was a kind of placid, almost meek gratitude in its place. Maybe he really had taken a bite of humble pie last night. "And that means the convoy they're bringing in today—"

"We're getting invaded by goddamned demons!" Harold Medford shouted, raising his pump shotgun high and racking it. A shell ejected, and he caught it, surprisingly, then reloaded. "Again!"

"It sure looks that way," Erin said, raising her voice above the hubbub that ensued. "But we're not going to sit back and take that one lying down. That's why I called you all up here today." Silence fell, cutting off all the complaint and worry and backbiting—for a few seconds, at least. No one was gonna shut up about this development, not for long, so she needed to get things across quickly.

"We've been fighting this fight alone for a long time," she said, seeking out the eyes in her audience that ... well, they were hurt, there was no other way to put it. They had that betrayed feeling, too, as though hearing that their government was sending more damned demons could be interpreted as anything other than a betrayal. "And I'm sorry that's the case. It'd be nice ... to just go home and lay down our weapons and just ... let somebody else work things out for us."

"Fuck that, that ain't our way," Billy Hoskins said, piping up, eyes on fire. She saw other people nodding. They were like her mother, then, and it'd stick in their craws to hand off responsibility for their town's well-being to some outsiders—even if they were human and not demons coming to make things worse. "This is our town."

"Damn right!" Gary Wrightson said, pumping his fist in the air.

"I agree," Erin said. "Which is why we're going to hold out. We're not letting those demons in the door to make this shit any worse. We're going to be ready for them when they come rolling in."

Ted Bailey raised his hand. "Erin ... I know you say they're demons, but ... these are federal agents, right?" She nodded, and he looked ... damned meek, honestly. "You're asking us to attack federal agents ... on the assumption they're demons?"

"Oh, I'll prove to you they're demons before I ask you to do anything other than sit on the side of the road in ambush, Ted," Erin said. She already figured on this. "Trust me. You ain't going to be accidentally killing any humans."

"Okay," he said, and some of the fight went out of him. Not that there was much to begin with.

"I know a lot of you are tired. You wish this was over. I wish it was, too," Erin said. "But it's not. And that leaves us with two choices—run or fight. And if you want to run—if this ... this news that our government either doesn't give a shit or is actively working to get us killed—if that breaks you, and you want to run? Hell, I don't blame you. I don't envy you, because wherever you go, you're going to be living for the rest of your life under the same knowledge—that you're under the same authority. And with the full gut feeling that when things got tough ... you ran." She mustered up some moral authority on that one, probably more than a twenty-year-old girl should have, but hell ... she'd seen shit. She had moral authority in spades now.

"But the rest of us ..." She reached down, and Duncan handed her up a rifle. "We're going to fight. We're going to win. We're going to keep going until we kick the last damned demon out of Midian, Tennessee ... we're going to take back our damned home. And no government, no demon, nobody ... is going to stand in our way without getting hell rained down on 'em. You with me?"

The chorus was deafening. Hell yeah. They were with her.

*

Gary listened to the cheers, nodding along. He could see why people followed Erin Harris now. She was a little fireball, riling 'em up this way. Some of the crew was still plainly feeling the pangs of what had happened here—being betrayed by your own fucking government that you paid your taxes to and relied on and believed in and whose flag you fucking saluted, by God—that was a kick in the genitals and the guts all in one. Less the genitals for Gary since he couldn't really feel those anymore, but the insult remained the fucking same.

"Hell yeah," his mother said behind him, slamming a heavy hand on his shoulder. "We're going to fuck these demon feds up for what they done to you, my boy."

"No," Gary said, seeing movement through the crowd and putting his hand on the squeeze accelerator for his scooter. "We're going to fuck 'em up because of what they're planning to do to our town." He saw another flash as people crossed in front of him and gave the accelerator a grab.

The scooter jumped and people made fucking way. "Git!" Gary shouted, "Or I'm gonna run you over!"

They moved. Must have taken him seriously. Which was good, cuz he was serious.

A lady in camo pants practically dove out of his way and gave Gary a clear shot to the person he'd seen through the crowd. He pulled up his scooter right to 'em as they stared down at him, cool as a cucumber, eyebrow lifted.

"Gary," Ulysses said.

"Ulysses," Gary said. "I got something to say to you."

"That so?" Ulysses asked, turning sour. "Is it because I'm not at work this morning?"

"No," Gary said. "It's ... that I'm damned sorry for being such a giant, throbbing prick to you, Ulysses. I've been a shithead to you for as long as you've worked for me. I've been bitching to you about your efficiency levels for as long as we've known each other as employer and employee, and it hasn't done a goddamned thing to make you want to work harder for me. It's probably done the opposite, knowing that no matter how much effort you put, I'll find fault with it. Now I'll be honest: sometimes I get ornery ... and I really do just look for the fault, even when you do an otherwise okay job. That's on me being a prick. An ornery prick. I'm damned sorry, Ulysses. I'm sorry for being a dipshit to you."

Ulysses looked he might be able to be knocked over with a feather. "Well, that's ... a hell of a turnaround. What happened to you?"

"I got locked in my bathroom fortress by demons and had to hammer my way out through the subfloor with the butt of a pistol," Gary said. "That kind of experience leaves a man—even a mighty man like me, who's focused on good choices—questioning himself. Really sound questions like, 'What's the meaning of life?' And 'If everything I've done up to now has led me to be locked in without my wheelchair on a cold bathroom floor as my house burns around me ... is this how the mostly useless other people on the planet feel every day when they wake up?'"

Ulysses blinked. "I don't ... think I've ever felt like that exactly."

"Well, it's a shitty situation, Ulysses," Gary said, "and I didn't really choose to be there. It was another shitty thing that happened in a life where shitty-ass things sometimes happen." He clapped a hand on the handlebars of the scooter. "I've always prided myself on conquering adversities, no matter how impossible, but it occurred to me, as everything burned around me, and the smoke filled my lungs, I'm thinking ... I didn't choose to be here. And maybe I can't even make a choice that's going to get me out. I thought about it ... and I figure that's kinda like what you were doing every day you came to work for me when I was being a huge prick. Not really sure if today was going to be the day to endure the fire or if it was going to be the one where the fire got you. Well, I'm sorry. And if I can, I'll make it up to you once this shit's over with. And maybe before. Because I'm going to keep paying you while we're all out dealing with this demon bullshit. Right out of the Reno fund, because having you here, fighting back with the team—it's more important than Reno. Or hookers." And he stuck out his hand, wondering if Ulysses would shake it.

The old duffer seemed to stare at it for a minute, mulling. "I always figured you had a big bug up your ass, Gary. Or a chip on your—"

"Yeah, everyone knows I got a chip on my shoulder," Gary said. "That's a fact."

"Well, you paid me all right," Ulysses said. "That's why I stayed—in spite of everything." He still stared at the proffered hand. "Reckon it wouldn't hurt me to stay longer, see if you maybe ... mean what you just said." And he thrust his own hand out.

"I do mean it, by God," Gary said, shaking Ulysses's hand. "Now let's punch these demons right in the fucking balls—together."

*

"Casey!" Ms. Cherry's shout made it through Arch's improvised ear plugs. He pulled his fingers out of his ear, ignoring the stink of dirty laundry in the dark, and hesitated.

If he elbowed his way out of the closet now, and this was just the normal back and forth between the madam and the taxidermist ...

Well, Arch didn't need to see that.

On the other hand—

"Arch!" Ms. Cherry's cry was abrupt and loud, and Arch slammed out with his elbow, knocking open the closet door, practically ripping it off its hinges.

Ms. Cherry was standing by the bed, buck naked, and Arch looked right at her and up, up—not there, nor there—

She was pointing at the door.

Casey was gone.

"Dang," Arch said, and flew after him. He got around the corner just in time to see—

Casey opening the front door, naked as a jaybird—

It flew open and Casey stepped back out of its path like a robot. He took a step back and five men came in, all lacking in the clothing department—

And, Arch noticed, they lacked in the gonads department.

"Oh my," he said, holding his sword up as they came rushing down the hall toward him.

These were men, not demons, he could tell that much, but their eyes were—well, there was something very wrong with them.

The first was almost to him, screaming, a ululating cry of feral savagery like something out of cavemen days. Arch was frozen in place—

This was a man.

Not a demon—

A gunshot rang out from behind him, and the man rushing at him stumbled, head exploding in a gush of red, brains blowing out the back of his skull, a splatter peppering Arch's shirt.

He threw a look back. Ms. Cherry stood there with a Ruger in hand, still naked as the day she was born, naked as every day she worked, presumably, a hard look on her face. "They are going to kill you—or, worse, depending on how you look at it, do what they did to all the other men." Her eyes blazed like one of the Johnson-less beasts running down the hall at him. "Fight! For your life!"

Arch swallowed. Another was coming.

She was right.

Arch raised his sword high and swung it as the man threw himself forward.

*

Erin felt like a traffic cop or a crossing guard, standing in the middle of Old Jackson Highway. Two of the stolen tankers were parked across the road behind her, and she was standing just in front of them in case she had to beat a hasty retreat behind them in a hell of a hurry.

"Convoy's coming," the radio on her belt crackled. She drew a deep breath of cold air and shivered inside her thick coat. It was a work one, standard issue from the sheriff's department, with the badge and emblem embroidered over the left breast pocket just like the badge she wore on her shirt. Not metal, though. This was stitched on, gold against the coat's brown, and she gave it a passing glance as she drew another breath.

She had the authority here. Hell if she was going to surrender it to some cheesedick fed demons.

This was it.

The road curved ahead, following the rise of the hills on either side of Jackson Highway. She looked up; couldn't see her little waiting army, all disguised and in camo, or hiding and keeping their heads down. Every once in a while she'd catch a hint of glare off a scope, not that those were necessary at this range. Well, a lot of these folks had hunting rifles …

"I sure hope this works," she murmured, looking to her right, where she remembered Barney Jones disappearing with his own rifle …

… after blessing every damned gun and a pile of ammo with what Father Nguyen called "pagan prayer" through gritted teeth.

The first vehicle in the line came around the curve and slowed when they caught sight of Erin and the tankers blocking the road. She couldn't see who it was, but they clearly decided to play it cool after seeing the obstruction. Just as well; they had the approaches on either side of the trucks behind her covered with the department's spike strips, so if someone decided to make a run at either her or the trucks, they were in for a rude awakening and popped tires.

She smiled and waved at the lead car. Another came behind it—and another. The first vehicle was a sedan, every one after it was a damned SUV, and big ones at that. Chevy Suburbans? Ford Expeditions? Whatever they were, they were huge. Probably carrying six to eight people each.

God, she hoped they were demons. If she pulled on one of these fuckers and shot 'em and blood came out …

… Well, the wheels would come off this plan real quick. She couldn't imagine her little militia being sanguine about firing on real, honest-to-God federal agents made of flesh and blood, though she supposed stranger things had happened. No matter what anybody said, firing on a human was a whole different thing from killing demons. Even Gary Wrightson might hesitate before laying down fire on a real FBI agent, no matter what he thought they were coming here to do. She certainly would.

Fortunately, the car slowed, then stopped, the rest of the line slowing up behind it. Erin's radio crackled. "We're a half mile behind 'em." She did not answer. She hadn't planned to, and they knew it. If there was a real emergency, or the plan changed, someone up the embankment would tell them.

"Howdy," Erin said as the feds emptied out of the first car. They were taking no chances, and she wouldn't have, either, if she'd driven into a roadblock, no matter how friendly the local law enforcement face was, smiling at them. And she was smiling, oh, she was smiling. So hard her cheeks hurt from the effort. "We ran into a little bit of a snag while we were waiting for y'all. Had to close this road to outside traffic. For safety reasons."

That maybe relaxed them ten percent. The lead guy was clean-shaven, looked ex-military—textbook how you'd expect a fed to look. Every single one of these agents had their hands hovering really close to their weapons.

Shit. There was no way Erin going to draw on them without having four people shoot her down.

But that was okay. They'd planned for this. Erin sauntered up to the guy in the lead. "Erin Harris. I'm the acting sheriff. Are you the task force Martinson and Ross said were coming? I mean, I assume so." Still smiling, leaving her hand out for the lead guy to take.

He stared at her unflinching hand still parked just above her hip, awkwardly. He kept that hand there, but offered his other, his left, to Erin.

She raised her eyebrows in surprise, shrugged, and clapped her hands together like it didn't matter. Then she stuck her left hand out to shake—

"Glad to see y'all made it," Erin said, hoping against hope this worked. The quick clap she'd done gave her a chance to transfer the safety pin she'd had between her fingers in her right hand to her left—good thing she practiced a lot of magic with one of her brothers when she was a kid—

"Ow—" the agent said as she pricked him. He looked up at her, brow stitched close in surprise. She stared back at him, about ready to spit out an apology when—

His eyes went black, black as night, and darkness swirled from his finger where she'd poked his arm, a burst of sulfur clouding the air and smelling up everything in front of her—

Erin dove for the ground in front of the sedan as the first shots rang out from either side. One of the other agents dissolved into shell-and-hell in front of her, falling before her freaking eyes. The others, she assumed, got taken out as well, as gunfire opened up all around her and the citizens of Midian let loose on these invaders.

*

"Oof." Darla set down Mera in her car seat, finding a spot in the middle of the abandoned house's basement where she was only a few feet from Jay. She put them next to each other like this, almost looking across at each other, not just out of convenience. Though if she'd had to haul either car seat, with kids still strapped in, any further down the stairs they damned well might have broken her.

Lucky, then, that this was a pretty small basement space. She looked back toward the stairs, trying to summon up the urge to move again. "Okay … you two wait here … Mommy has to get her stuff. Then I'll … get you two taken care of with something to do while I get to work."

"Mommmmmmy," Jason said.

Darla sighed, slightly stooped, halfway back to the stairs. "What?"

"I want pizza, Mommy."

Darla sighed again. "Maybe if you're good, we can go to the pizza place for lunch. Okay?"

A little squeal of delight. That'd keep him on his best behavior for all of twelve seconds until he forgot about pizza for lunch. Fortunately, spaced far enough from his sister as to be out of reach, and locked into a car seat, there really wasn't much he could get into. Same with Mera, though she'd been quieter thus far.

Darla came back down a minute later, all her supplies clutched in her hands. The basement was dank, unfinished, concrete walls and only a few egress windows for light. They shed it slowly, casting it across the stone floors. It was kinda creepy, but fortunately, that hadn't set in yet with Jason and Mera. She hoped it wouldn't, either, before she got done.

On the other hand, she was about to summon a demon for a pact. A creepy basement was the least of the things that might scare them in the near future. But she'd picked the locale with care, and there wasn't an inhabited house for miles.

She drew the circle on the ground with powder poured from a jar. It didn't take long, though she did have to answer a couple questions for Jason. Mera had her dolls and was playing quiet-ishly on her own lap, lost in her own imagination and taking no notice of what Mommy was doing.

Once the circle was complete, Darla took the vial of Marischa's blood. Handy she had an easy sacrifice in her house; otherwise, she'd have had to go find some poor soul to murder in order to get this vital component. It couldn't be from a blood bank, either. It had to be the blood of someone murdered by the caster of the spell. Specificity. Darla could get behind that, having read more than a few vague demon tomes and incantations wherein the worshipped party seemed open and flexible with their desires for sacrifice. That was annoying for the time-crunched single mom. Did they want fresh blood from a fresh corpse? Or just blood from someone who'd suffered? "Work with me, demons," she muttered.

This pact, though ... this pact was very specific. She knew exactly what she was doing.

And what she'd get in return.

"Mommmmmy," Jason said, his bright little blue eyes shining in the basement.

"What, sweetie?" Darla asked, pouring out the blood of his grandmother as prescribed.

"What are you doing, Mommy?"

"Fingerpainting," Darla said and stooped to shape the symbol she was aiming for. It was a primal one, of course. All these demons went with primal symbology. Pentagrams for many of them. So tired. So cliché.

That done, she deftly ignored the next question from Jason, and the repeated version of it, five thousand times, approximately. His next, "Mommmmmmmmmy!" intruded on her consciousness and she paused to look up. "What?"

"I want pizza."

"Well, remember what I said about you behaving in order to get pizza?" She opened the page of the book and gave the ritual a cursory reread while she basked in the fifteen seconds of silence after reminding little Jay of his reward, impending only if he did as asked.

"Mommmmy?" he asked, ten seconds after that. She ignored him.

Time to begin.

"Mommmy?" it came again. Mera was still playing.

"Mommy's busy," Darla said, smearing the blood on her hands and setting the book aside. She had this. "I can't talk for the next few minutes. You're going to lose your pizza."

She began the chanting. Demon language was a hell of a thing, so guttural in places and beautiful in others—

"Mommmy?"

—it almost defied human description. It certainly predated English—

"Mommmmmmmmmy?"

—and so many languages that came before—

"MOMMmmmmmmmmmmy?"

—and contained a near-lyrical quality in some of the verses. She hit the second round of chanting, reaching her stride. It was almost like a song, based around a verse, then a chorus, then a verse—

"MOMMMMMMY!"

—and so on. A Nashville songwriter could have spun it out, had they been acquainted with demon language. It certainly would have sounded better than their current hick-hop craze, which to Darla seemed the worst of all possible worlds.

"MOMMMMMMMMMMMY!"

Darla finished, smiling as she did so, and opened her eyes to find little Jay's face scrunched up in tiny rage at being ignored. He was still bound in his car seat, shaking it back and forth as though trying to free himself, though he was much more likely to tip over. "Don't do that, sweetheart," she said mildly, waiting to see if—

Ah.

Yes.

The smell of sulfur was rising, and the circle was glowing around her. There was a crackle of energy in the air, and the blood that formed the circle was igniting, lighting to fire like it was gasoline with a match touched to it. Darla smiled, could feel the warmth of hellfire rising in the room—

Jay screamed as a demon rose out of the ground, black armored flesh like a cross between a gargoyle and a beetle, horns and fangs and compound eyes. It rose two feet above Darla when it was done appearing out of the concrete. It stared down at her as Mera joined the screaming act, dolls cast aside and her focus entirely on wailing and crying in the face of this new threat.

"Ugh," the demon said, looking past her with those reflective eyes, compound and bright, her children showing up a thousand times in the refraction. "I love the screams of children, but I prefer the pained kind. This is just ... loud."

"Yeah, well," Darla said, "that's how kids are."

The demon tore his compound gaze off her children and onto her. "You summoned me, woman. You seek a pact?"

"If you're Beelzahar, yes," Darla said, ignoring her children wailing. She was pretty good at that. It came from long practice.

"MOMMMMMMY!" Jay screamed over Mera's screeching.

"Shhh," Darla said, turning to him. "Mommy's talking with her friend."

That actually settled him down, though not Mera. Jay accepted this strange new input, that her mother was friends with a bizarre beetle creature, apparently confused enough by what he was seeing that he at least stopped crying for the moment.

"Interesting," Beelzahar said. His eyes were like staring in a mirror, his voice scratchy. "What do you propose, human?"

"Do you know who I am?" she asked.

He blinked, the mirrors disappearing beneath armored lids. "You are called ... Darla Pike."

"You know my name," she said, musing. That was not generally a good thing in the demon world. Names had too much power to be able to just casually toss them around. "Or at least ... what it is now. Do you know my contracts?"

Another blink. "I took a cursory look before I came up," he said. "You have quite a few on file with the Office of Occultic Concordance, especially for a human. You're a real dealmaker. And some dark ones, too. Not going to lie, I'm slightly impressed." He raised his head up a little further and looked at the children. Mera was down to sobbing quietly now, and Jay was still silent, watching. "I might become more so depending on what you're offering here ..."

"I brought you the blood of an unsuspecting sacrifice," Darla said, gesturing to the blood around her, which had now burned off into little more than black traces.

"And I've put her soul to good use already," Beelzahar said. "What else ya got?"

"What else do you want?" This was the negotiation. The fun part.

Beelzahar cracked a smile. Fangs. A strangely angular jawline. "I'd take everything you've got, down to your very body and soul, but ... that and your little ones here ... seem to be the only things you haven't ever traded in. I mean, you've traded in so many souls, but ... always at a distance. Always someone you've killed, someone you've taken the power away from. Don't get me wrong, that's interesting. There's a market for that. But ..." He leaned in with the jaw and breathed sulfur breath on her. "When you were younger ... you traded in yourself. Also interesting—to some. Not me. You must have learned your lesson."

"Well, that'll only carry you so far," Darla said, keeping steely-steady.

"Selling to demons ... to the underworld ... most humans don't read the fine print," Beelzahar said, clicking sound coming from deep in his throat. "You, though, you haven't gotten burned, other than that one time. You read the fine print. That's good. I prefer to be in business with smart partners. But you still have to have something to ... bring to the table. What is it ... dear?"

"It could be very dear," Darla said, looking him in those compound eyes. "You know what I want?"

"Everybody knows what you want," Beelzahar said. "A seat at the table. Which is a big ask ... for a human. Or a demon, come to that."

"If you don't ask, you don't get."

"Most people who ask still don't get. Hazard of not being able to pay the price." A click. "What price ... can you pay?"

"The highest," Darla said. "If I can get ... what I want."

Another clicking. It was laughter. "The farther away from you the sacrifice is, the less it means. You've made a web of deals with the blood of those who meant nothing to you. Now ... you've brought your husband's chips over to your side ... a smart move. Clever. But still not a particularly difficult thing to do, inheriting his efforts. To proceed ... to even have a chance at this seat you crave ... the distance will be shrunk. Nothing good comes free, Darla Pike. Are you ... willing?"

Darla stared at him, then lifted her blouse just far enough to reach the knife at her side. She pulled it out and held it in front of her. "I'm willing."

Beelzahar looked past her to where Mera and Jay were sitting in their car seats, just watching now. Silent. "Truly?"

She looked over her shoulder at the children.

All their lives, she'd sheltered them, protected them ... grew them within her body until they could breathe on their own, eat on their own ... but they still required her, constantly, to tend to them, bring them the food, soothe their little injuries ...

They'd depended on her all their lives.

Time to pay up.

"I am," she said, looking right at Beelzahar.

"I want real screams," Beelzahar said. "Real fear. Pain. Betrayal—"

"I know what you want," Darla said, taking a step back, toward the two waiting car seats. "And I'm prepared to give it to you ... if we can reach an agreement." She held the knife lightly in her fingers.

Beelzahar clicked. Another laugh. "If you do this for me ... I take this ... plus all your other accumulated debits ... and I will get you a seat at the table. You will be ... a duchess of the underworld."

Darla just stared at him. This ... was what she'd been working toward all along. She looked at Beelzahar, nodded, once, and then turned back to the kids.

Raised her knife.

It was time.

She took a step toward Jay, first, and this time Mera started screaming again. Leave it to the girl to know when something was terribly wrong.

Jay didn't start screaming until the knife entered his belly for the first time.

*

Gary was firing down hard, because this shit was the shit. Demons were going off like black liquid party poppers, vaporizing as they flooded out the black government SUVs. "Spec Op demon motherfuckers!" Gary shouted, fighting to be heard over the roar of God knew how many rifles firing all in a line.

"There are fuck lots of these fuckers!" Marina's voice cut through the din. She was on the berm next to him, hanging just inside the tree line, and firing a bolt-action rifle that someone had gotten for her. Hell if he knew who. She reminded him, in that moment, of one of those sniper chicks from the battle of Stalingrad. Sure, she was from Poland, but still ... badass.

"We're going to put some hurting on these fucking fake-ass feds, bro!" Paul was beside him on the left, Larry and Terry laid out just past him. His mother was further down, haranguing the shit out of somebody on her other side for ... bad aim, maybe? He couldn't hear. He wished he'd had earplugs to put in, because this was worse than a Def Leppard concert cranked up to max.

Gary blinked as he picked another target. They were putting a hurt on these demons, but only up to a point. There were like ten, fifteen of these big black SUVs, and they were all emptying, but only a half dozen or a so were in the kill box. He could see the big tankers coming up Jackson Highway—Erin had them parked in the lot of that shitbag motel by the freeway, and they came rolling in behind as soon as these fuckers came in off the exit ramp.

They were closing the back door now, pulling off in a blocking V formation as a couple of the rear SUVs tried to back up out of the trap. "Take it in the back door, baby!" Paul shouted as they pulled into place. A couple of cars of the watch pulled in behind and closed the kill box on that side.

But there was a bigass gap on their left, Gary noticed. They'd spread too thin taking the high ground on either side. They hadn't had enough people to cover both embankments fully, that was the problem. So while they were elevated and shooting down on the enemy, the enemy toward the back of their little train was squeezing out, a few demons running up the slope. If they hit the treeline, they could hook around and start ripping into Gary's crew from behind.

"Fuck!" Gary shouted, slapping Paul on the shoulder and pointing. "We got trouble!"

Paul looked and nodded. "I'll get it," he said, and then rolled over Terry and slapped Larry on the arm. "Come on, bro—we got flankers! Start pulling every third person off the line and let's go slam their dicks in the door!"

They moved off, and Gary went back to firing down. There were still an awful lot of demons hiding in those SUVs, though every window was busted out by this point and some of the shooting had tapered off to reflect that. More consideration was being put into firing, now, Gary realized, as he looked over his sights for a target. Well, that made sense. You could only go balls out with your ammo for so long before you ran out, and in the absence of something to shoot, why not wait for a fucking target?

*

Arch didn't like cutting down these men, but there weren't a lot of options, he told himself. Casey was still over there, a few of them between the two of them, standing next to some demon sonofagun, a blank look on his face like he'd had the brains sucked right out of his head.

The blade caught Arch's attacker across the chest, sending the man whirling off. Arch barely recognized him before he made the cut—Arnie Muellenberg, he'd been a bagger down at Rogerson's. Dang. Alison had managed him. Muellenberg hit the wall of the trailer, blinked, looked like he was going to bounce off and come at Arch again, one-handed—

Arnie's head exploded out one side, blood spraying in the direction of the door as another of Ms. Cherry's shots made their mark. "Don't hesitate," she said, sounding a little like she was underwater from the thunderous boom of the gun in the confined space of the trailer.

"That might be difficult," Arch said, readying himself for the next attack.

"I can taste your sin," the demon before him said. Black slicked hair, pale skin—he looked like one of those Goth kids Arch had gone to school with, but greasier. He had dark circles under his eyes, too, and even wore a black trenchcoat. Like a weaselly, greasy version of Hendricks, minus the hat and any semblance of a tan. "It wells up in your soul."

"Not a soul out there that doesn't have any sin to their name," Arch said, catching one of the charging men across the face.

"These men are sinless," the demon said. He waved a knife before him. "I have made it so. They released their sin, and I cut it off at its source."

"He's neutering them," Ms. Cherry said. "Turning them into his personal housecats. Disgusting."

"I can feel the sin in her, too," the demon said. "She reeks of it. She has taken sin in her whole life, in that filthy, hairy gap of hers."

"That's mighty crass," Arch gave the demon a steely eye, whacking the next attacker across the neck with his sword. Blood sluiced out, and he tried to ignore the look on the man's face as he fell at Arch's feet. It was a mercy, he tried to tell himself. Not murder.

"I wax," Ms. Cherry said, bringing a hand down and forcing Arch to turn away. Safer to keep his eye on the threat, anyway, even though there was nobody charging him at the moment. "So I'm not sure what you mean about 'hairy.'"

"You were the originators of temptation," the demon said, his attention on her. "Your sex. Taking the bite of the apple and then handing it off to your man. You drag the corruptible into corruption. You are the wellspring of sin, of corruption ..."

Arch just stared at him, waiting. There was a good twenty-foot gap between them, and he couldn't cover that ground as fast as a demon could, especially if any more minions came in through the door that stood almost equidistant between them.

"You must not get any," Ms. Cherry spat back at him.

"I don't need any of what you've got on offer," the demon said and brought the knife to his lips. "And soon ... neither will he." He looked sideways at Casey.

Casey just stared, standing next to the demon.

The blade glowed as the demon kissed it, setting its edge fiery hot. Arch connected the dots—the demon heated up the blade, and then he'd turn it loose on—

"Casey!" Ms. Cherry screamed and shot at the demon.

She hit him but the demon did not even react. The silvery piece of lead appeared on his biceps as if it had been placed there, then thumped to the floor a second later. Arch scrambled forward—

"Don't let him do it!" Ms. Cherry shouted as Arch charged, trying to close the gap before the flaming knife could reach—

The demon looked Arch in the eye and grinned with teeth, highlighted by black outlines between each, as though he'd bitten into oil and let it cloud his mouth. His hand found Casey Meacham's genitals and he held them there, steadying them, and raised the knife—

*

The blood ran down Darla's face, the screams echoed in her ears.

Jay's screams.

Mera's screams.

They were both at the top of their lungs for a while, until they couldn't anymore. Then they settled down into whimpers as she worked on first one, then the other, in turn. Over her shoulder, Beelzahar breathed and clicked and laughed.

And her children sobbed as she cut them to pieces, one knife stroke at a time.

*

"Shit, yeah!" one of the Wrightsons screamed to Erin's left, over the blazing sound of a distinctly one-sided gunfight. She was peering up over the hood of the big diesel truck she'd retreated behind when the heat had come on the fight. This shit had, indeed, gone off the chain, and now it seemed to be winding down, her people pouring fire into the convoy of federal vehicles, ripping up the black SUVs and the lead sedan with gunfire as they tried to purge every fucking demon from the kill zone.

Her gun slide worked itself back and forward, cycling out a shell as she waited and searched for another target. The hot brass hit the arm of her coat, found a little ridge in the fabric and stayed there, forcing her to take a second and brush it off. She doubted it'd light a fire, but that shit was hot and she didn't need to find out in the middle of a gun battle.

Erin was standing on the truck's drum brake and firing over. There was movement in one of the cars and she drew a bead on it. Someone was hiding behind a seat. Long shot from here, but maybe she could—

Somebody grabbed her by the leg and ripped her off her perch, slamming her down onto Old Jackson Highway so hard it drove the breath out of her lungs. She heard a crack and couldn't tell if it was her teeth slamming together or something breaking. Stars flashed in her eyes. It happened so damned fast it was like she was about to shoot one second and staring at the cloudy sky overhead the next.

"Hey, bitch," said a pudgy face as it thrust itself in front of her. Black suit, dark eyes—

Agent Martinson had found her. And she looked pissed.

*

Arch was swinging forward, trying to land his hit before the demon cut Casey's manhood right off. Arch blanched at that—he might not have been getting much use out of his own right now, but dang if that wasn't a low thing, a hit right to the gut even for Arch, who wasn't exactly an enthusiastic supporter of the ways Casey used that particular organ. But this sort of trauma went gut-deep, and Arch's reaction was primal.

This was a man's route to fatherhood, to leaving a legacy in the world. Somehow all that—deep thoughts for the midst of a sword fight—flashed through Arch's mind, symbol and word, and it drove him all the harder forward, teeth gritted as he went.

Fatherhood. Casey might not have cared about it, but it sure tripped Arch's trigger for some reason—

Oh. Right. That reason.

"Sin must be cleansed," the demon said in that whispery-high voice, and his blade slid down to do the deed. No way was Arch gonna make it in time to—

"AHHHHHHHH!"

Casey's mouth flew wide open, and he recoiled from the blade before it could touch his delicate bits. He stumbled back over a coffee table and glass shattered as he went butt-over-teakettle, exposing his backside and undercarriage to the whole trailer.

The demon just stared after him, frozen in space. "How ... how did you fall back into sin so quickly ...? You should have been mine for hours after ...?"

Arch altered course and planted the sword in the demon's shoulder. His head swung back around, eyes now ablaze. "You—" the demon said, furious—

But he didn't pop into sulfur and blackness, no.

A Greater, then. Dang.

"I will remove the sin from you by force," the demon said, batting away the sword tip, ripping it out of his flesh and throwing the blade aside as he reached out and seized Arch by the front of his shirt. The sword was out of position, there was no hitting the demon with it quickly. "I'll have to cut a bit deeper to excise it all—" the demon's black eyes positively glowed, "but you'll make a worthy servant when it's done—"

"Arch!" Ms. Cherry screamed as the trailer rattled and the door flew open. More of the blank-eyed men were flooding in now, and Arch couldn't do a danged thing about it—

*

"By God!" Gary shouted as he heard a ululating cry rise from below. The firing on the flank suggested that the demons coming up that side were maybe being a little more cagey—or using cover more smartly—than he would have preferred. Either way, they'd pulled off half or so of their firing line to deal with it, and now—

Well, shit.

Now they were getting charged. For fuck's sake.

It had come after some loud scream in the demon language came from behind the tanker trucks where Erin had been firing a minute earlier. But she was gone now, and that cry had been enough to damned near wreck every human eardrum around. Gary felt like he'd parked his head next to a speaker at a Metallica concert. Like the fucking gunfire wasn't enough to ring his damned bell. "I tell you, the laws against suppressors in this country are fucking stupid. They aren't goddamned silencers, they only turn the sound down to the stinking decibel levels of a plane taking off, for fuck's sake. And if we all had them right now, I wouldn't by God be hearing this gunfight like hell breaking out of the earth for the next eight weeks after this—or forever."

And that scream! That fucking scream! The demons were swarming out of the cars—how the hell were there that many of them left? Were they spawning down there? Had they hidden a miniature army, like sea monkeys, in the back of those SUVs? Well, they'd sure as shit seemed to have added water now, by the number of them.

He drew a bead on one and fired. Drew a bead on another and fired. Some of them weren't exploding or imploding or whatever they did when they popped. They were taking the slugs and still coming, bleeding black smoke or something out of their wounds, working their way up the hill and drawing more fire off their buddies. Maybe they hadn't spawned more.

Maybe some of them were just ... invincible to holy bullets.

"Well, fuck," Gary said as the first one crested the rise in front of him.

There couldn't be more than a dozen or so left, but dammit, they were not dying, and that was more than a little vexing. This one came up over the rise and shit, there he was, standing over Gary as he altered his aim to put a round in the fucker. Then another. Then another—

The demon stepped on the barrel of Gary's borrowed AR-15. It bent, and that was the end of Gary trying to put any shots through it, by God. "You motherfucker!" Gary shouted. "How fucking dare you abridge my Second Amendment rights, you goddamned government lackey!"

What the hell else was there to do? He threw himself at the bastard as the demon lifted a foot to step on Gary. An AR-15 would make a better hammer than the SOCOM pistol, anyway, and he was by God not going to go out getting stepped on like a fucking bug. He went for the ankles and by God, he got them, yanking down with all his weight. He and the demon tumbled down the hill as gunfire went off on either side of them, fellow demons charging up the hill and the screams of the townsfolk starting to overwhelm the sound of all the shooting.

*

Erin took a hard hit to the side as Martinson gave her a kick to the ribs. Damn, it stung, fire racing down her flank as her ribs flared in anger at the blow. For her part, Erin let out a little noise, somewhere between a whimper and a gasp, because she'd gotten the wind knocked out of her and it hadn't come back quite yet.

"You just had to stick your nose into this, Miss Small-Town," Martinson said, her eyes dark and feral, the lack of concern for the pain she was inflicting lost somewhere under that howl she'd let loose a minute ago, some kind of signal to the demons to unleash hell. Erin was recovering, but that much she got loud and clear. "You've got delusions of grandeur, don't you? Thought you were hot shit? Well, listen up, Small-Town—you ain't shit." Martinson kicked her again.

Erin's face hit the big semi truck's tire, bouncing off the rubber, the stink of it in her nose along with the taste of blood in her mouth. Had she bit her lip? Was she bleeding internally? Hell if she knew, and an answer wasn't likely to be forthcoming. Erin planted a palm on the highway, the grains and pebbles biting into her skin as she tried to lift up.

"Uh uh," Martinson said and landed a foot on her back, right between the shoulder blades. Erin's face smacked the ground. "You were on your knees when we came here. I think it's only fair you die there. You thought you could ... what? Rise up? Not happening."

Erin's face hit the ground, her lip split and blood oozed out into her mouth. Stars flashed before her eyes again, spots of color in the dark as she tried to pry open her lids.

Martinson grabbed her by the hair and yanked her up, planting a hand on her windpipe. "You really thought you could drive us out, Small-Town?" Erin didn't have the fight in her to struggle, not against this overwhelming strength. Martinson dragged her slightly right, so that she could see between the bumpers of the tractor-trailers. A half dozen demons were swarming up the left embankment, ignoring the volume of fire being poured down on them. "Looks like you took out our Lessers. Well done. But it's not doing you any good because I've still got Greaters."

Martinson shoved her face next to Erin's ear. "This is the thing you fucking little people never got—you can't stand against us. You're the little, we're the big. Did you really think you could fight back? Against us? We may not have the whole damned army or bureaucracy on our side, sweetheart, but we've got more than enough firepower to level your shit town—assuming it doesn't get leveled first by the chaos come to roost here."

The fed put the squeeze on her jaw, a vise of a grip on her chin, yanking her head around so Erin could look into her black eyes. "I should have known, though. See ... most people have reason. They can read the writing on the wall. Not you ignorant hillbillies. Your reading scores are probably in negative territory, and I doubt you learned reason in your backward-ass schools. So let me spell it out for you—you're fucked. We own you. You can struggle all day, but it's going to turn out the same as this little fight between you and me—"

Martinson shoved her over and ran her head against the pavement as she climbed atop Erin and clutched her face. The fed's face was a stone wall lacking emotion. "You lose to overwhelming strength. Kinda poetic. History repeating itself and all that. Too bad you were too stupid to see it coming."

Erin felt her body start to go slack against the weight of the demon on her chest. It was heavy, unstoppably so, and she could barely breathe. Her core muscles jerked and spasmed against the force against them, and she wanted to seize up against the weight. How could she possibly fight against this, she wondered as her hand slapped at Martinson's back, then against her own abdomen, flopping uselessly until it brushed her coat and belt and—

Hey.

There was an old knife still there. It had been present when Barney Jones had done his blessing of them, of everything around them, of all their weapons and their very bodies—

Well ... what did she have to lose?

Erin pulled the knife and brought it up, spiking the damned thing into Martinson's back. The blade hit shell and the demon jumped, black eyes lighting up as she jerked, bringing her hand off Erin's neck and slapping at the pain suddenly inflicted on her back.

"Yeah," Erin said, hoarse, and dragged the knife around under Martinson's arm as she clawed and failed to stop the damned thing. It left a nice slit around her body, and black started to ooze out like a slow fog. "We should probably just give up and let you fuckers run us over." When she reached the midline where the demon's sternum would have been were she human, Erin paused and ripped the knife in a hard circle, coring out an oval around where the heart should have been. Martinson spasmed in pain, arms writhing and jerking, her response completely ineffectual. "We just don't stand a chance against you bastards. Overwhelming numbers and power and all that. We oughta just ... go pray and forget about slapping back at you fuckers who slapped at us first—"

She completed the circle with the knife blade, and Martinson's eyes had gone full black, no sign of pupil now. Shit, that was scary looking. Her mouth was open, and there was no hint of the roof of her mouth, only blackness as dark as the night itself.

"I just don't know why we don't lay down and die," Erin said. The demon tipped over and Erin rolled after her, getting atop Martinson as she hit the pavement. Erin wasn't one to back off a foe, to leave a fight half-finished. Fuck that. She was going to cut the fucking soul or whatever passed for it out of this goddamned thing like gutting a buck. "We should just know when we're beat, I guess. If we were smarter like you, maybe we would." And she drove her hand into the base of the knife, plunging the blade deeper into the demon—

That did it. Something rose from within, a hard drift of black fog freezing as it came out. It was like Martinson was shrouded in fog for a long second, then—

It all rushed out at once and Martinson collapsed in on herself as Erin fell, the fed now gone from beneath her. Erin's knees met the hard pavement, and she just about kissed it, knife clattering out of her hand as she fell.

"Why ... I reckon it's all over but the crying now," Erin said, lips a bare inch above the pavement. "I just don't know why we fucking ignorant hillbillies can't see that." And she smiled, cuz ... hell, that shit was funny. Fuck that demon.

*

"I'll cut it all out of you, deeper than the nub, all the way to the root," Brackessh said, smiling at the man with the dark skin. He could feel the sin, so deep in this one—so very deep. It was so ingrained, strained the whole length of him. How did he live without seeking some release, either from himself or another?

It didn't matter. Sin was sin. If he wouldn't relieve it himself, wouldn't give Brackessh an opening, a scapegoat to clear the sin,

Brackessh would just ... cut deeper. Oh, it would certainly damage him as a servant, make him walk a bit more unsteadily but ... a fellow this big, his upper body would provide so much strength—

Brackessh had a good grip on him. His blade was aflame, and the man's sword was out of position. He had to cut through the pants, certainly, but that wasn't a problem, not with his weapon at such a heated temperature. He brought the blade down, heard it hiss against the man's trousers as it burnt through—

"You ain't cutting nobody's dick off on my watch!" the sinner behind him shouted. Brackessh jerked his head around; he'd seen the little man with the large instrument of sin go tumbling over the table. How could he be on his feet again already?

He wasn't. But he ran the frame of the table into the back of Brackessh's knees, causing Brackessh to go unsteady, just for a moment. The knife slipped, and the big sinner grunted as it hissed into his leg, hot blade eating into the skin—

*

Arch thought his leg was on fire as the blade slipped a few centimeters into his thigh. Dadgum, that hurt! Casey had kicked the table into the demon and unsteadied him—and his hand—enough to do this. Arch wasn't sure whether to be grateful that the demon hadn't hit his original target or be danged upset that he'd just poked his superheated knife into Arch's leg.

Either way, it sure did hurt.

"You neutering son of a bitch!" Casey said, lunging over the table and tackling the demon at the knees. He sunk his teeth into the demon's thigh, causing the demon to jerk slightly, leaving a nice little cut in Arch's leg as he ripped the tip of the knife out of Arch.

Arch just about bent over, sagging, as the pain swelled through him. The demon looked bemused, trying to fight off Casey's assault by whipping the knife behind him as the taxidermist rolled away. He kept his other hand on Arch, locking him in place as Arch regained his wits—and his balance.

Sword in hand, Arch swung it around, pointing the tip at the demon's head.

"You sin consumes you," the demon said, looking around at Arch. "How do you think this will end?"

"As sin always does—with forgiveness," Arch said, the words plucking at his soul. He paused, only a second—

Then drove the blade into the demon.

Brackessh felt the hard sting of a holy blade plunged into his flesh. He loosed a long scream, the pain of it tearing through him. He drew his hand across the sword, trying to rip it out of him. He had never felt this sort of pain, this piercing penetration into his very essence. Certainly, he was a Greater, and it would not kill him, but the agony ...

The blessed edge ripped into his hand as he tried to push it away. Oh, how it hurt! The pain was unfathomably bad, tore into his very essence, tore into ...

Him.

Was this how it felt when he'd loosed his own weapon on these men? He looked at them, flooding in now and trying to attack the woman with the gun. She was a steely-eyed sinner, not flinching as she fired at them, killing them one by one as they entered. She retreated a step at a time, firing as she did so. A click and the sound of metal sliding was followed by another shot seconds later.

But the pain ... the pain stole Brackessh's attention. How could it be so ...?

Agonizing?

The big man stared down at Brackessh as he powered him over, using the holy blade's grip in his very shell to drive him to his knees.

"You don't ... see your sin ..." Brackessh managed to get out. "I know your sin ... have seen it in your soul ... I can ... cleanse it ..."

"You're not who I would look to for that sort of thing," the big man said, looking down at him with blazing eyes. The pain of that holy blade piercing him—it was sheer agony. If he would just remove it, Brackessh could—

"I know who you would go to," Brackessh said desperately. "Forgiveness? It's not as simple a matter as you might—"

"It's that simple," the man said. "Ask, and you're forgiven."

Brackessh tried to string thoughts together. He had to stop this man—stop the pain.

The other one, that naked one, grabbed him from the other side, pushing him to the ground. "Finish it, Arch," he said. Brackessh was unable to resist, the pain was so great. "Quick, before they overrun Ms. Cherry!"

"I am fine!" came the shout from the bedroom, followed by another shot. "I had to come back in here to change magazines, but—I'm fine. They're not even getting close to me." Another shot. "Just fine."

"I forgive you," the big man said, and there was a flicker in his eyes. Sincerity? It was difficult for Brackessh to tell. He was used to the dulled looks of his own servants. To see this—

The blade lifted out of his shell and there was a moment of sweet relief. The agony was gone, that pointed pain and burning.

But only for a moment.

"There isn't forgiveness for all of us," Brackessh said as the man raised the sword.

It fell, finding the center of his chest, the center of his being, and Brackessh felt the pain again—but only for a second.

And as his essence drained away, and fear, long held at bay but still familiar, came back to him as his shell broke, his essence rushed out, returning to its source—not the original one, but the place where he'd been sent after, where he'd spent so much time ...

Where he'd learned fear.

And there was, he knew even before he'd fully left that disintegrating shell, not an ounce of forgiveness to be found there.

*

"Look at this pathetic cripple," the demon fed said, kicking Gary sideways, the AR-15 blow to the ankle not doing a hell of a lot to dissuade this demon from being a prick. Maybe gave him a bruise—if demons bruised.

That kick fucking hurt, but maybe not as much as the hit to Gary's pride at that dead-head motherfucker calling him a cripple. "I'm more able than ten men," Gary said, his roll stopping slightly down the embankment, firm grip still on the AR barrel. Which fucking burned, but hell, he wasn't letting go. He just flipped it around, saying, "Ow, ow, ow," to himself as he took up the grip again.

"But not as able as one of us," the demon said, coming at him again. The demons were all up over the hill now, and the chatter from across the way was the sound of their opposite line on the other side of the highway trying to snipe and help, but probably not doing any better than when they'd shot down on these bastards and failed to kill them. Bullets didn't seem to do the trick with fuckers like this.

The fed was wearing a blazer with "FBI" written across the breast pocket. Gary stared at it, burning hate in his eyes. Fuck if he hadn't supported law enforcement with all his damned heart for most of his life. This was changing his mind, though, making him think that, dammit, the swamp really was after him and his. They weren't even indifferent; they were actively trying to destroy his ass at the moment.

And for what? Daring to stand up say, "Not in my fucking town, you motherfuckers!" By God.

"You're not going to be 'able' for long after I stick this rifle up your ass and bend it more," Gary said, thrusting its barrel out and stabbing. It didn't do shit, hitting like iron against iron when it came up against the demon's leg. "Fuck," he said, staring as the demon looked down at him, its face creasing in a sneer. "Wish the gun grabbers were right and chainsaw bayonets were an actual damned thing—"

The demon's kick was hellacious, caught Gary in the shoulder and chest, and his pectoral muscle on that right side screamed even as his body experienced liftoff. He flew in a good arc, legs trailing uselessly behind him, and Gary cursed all the way down. If fortune had been kind, maybe he could have gotten the legs beneath him to take some of the hit of the landing, but fuck, no, she was a mean-ass bitch, like your angriest ex, and he landed on his face, shoulders and neck, and slid down a full foot to come to rest on the ground.

And fuuuuuck, did it hurt, too. Shit.

Gary spit blood, his lips busted wide. His shoulder felt like someone had taken a long piece of metal and just driven it right into the muscle, then twisted it up into spaghetti. *Dear Jesus, deliver me to death,* that was what he wanted to say.

"But Wrightsons never say die," Gary muttered instead, turning around, head spinning, trying to get his bearings on the demon fucker. "Except when we're talking about others."

"As though I care about your name," the demon said, closing in on him. The steady dying of the gunfire behind him suggested not so good things. Screams and cries came from all around him, but Gary didn't have time to look. He was focused on the trouble that was coming for him.

"And here I thought you were supposed to serve and protect," Gary muttered as the demon reached down for him.

The demon fed smirked. "I do serve and protect—our interests. Not yours."

"Thanks for being honest," Gary said. He hefted the SOCOM pistol he'd kept tucked in his belt, whacking the bastard across the nose with it. It did make him recoil slightly, black cracks in his skin's facade showing through in the bridge of his nose, black goop moving beneath it like oil, somehow contained in the bounds of his head. "I was beginning to think every government servant was a lying sack of shit before you went and hit me with that truth bomb."

"I'm about to hit you with another bomb," the demon said, fingers brushing against the black, swirling mass on his face. "But I guarantee you won't survive this o—"

The demon fed froze, and Gary had his SOCOM clutched tight,

waiting for the bastard to come to finish him. Well, if he was going down, he was by God going down with a fight, doing his level best to cram that bent-up SOCOM pistol up that crotch guppy motherfucker's nose—

The fed squirmed, jerking spasmodically, and distorted, chest expanding like he had a giant worm crawling around inside him. He froze like that for a second, then exploded into nothingness, a black vortex that passed in the blink of an eye.

When he was gone, Ulysses was standing there with a length of pipe that had been sawed off in an oblong way, one edge filed down and sharp.

Gary stared at it. "You steal that from me?"

Ulysses looked at him, then looked at the pipe. "You ask me that after I just saved your life?"

Gary blinked. "Okay. You got a fair point there. Much obliged. We'll talk about the pipe later." Gary hauled himself over on his belly. "We got a battle to win now."

"I think it's won," Ulysses said, and Gary looked around where he was pointing. There were a couple demons still fighting, but they were getting overrun by the people of Midian. Ripped down to the ground and cut up by good old fashioned holy swords and bats and all else.

"Well, shit," Gary said, watching it all happen.

"What?"

Gary looked back at Ulysses. "I don't feel like I pulled my weight in this last fight. Goddamn it."

*

Arch watched the demon disappear into a cloud of his own black bile, and the thing was done.

His servants, however ... were not. They kept flooding in, apparently enslaved long after that thing had died. Arch took no pleasure in running a sword through these men—these wild, crazed, dead-eyed men who'd clearly suffered something he would never want to experience.

The blood ran real slick on his blade, for the first time ever, and the first was ugly, brutal. They were practically throwing themselves on it. And Ms. Cherry was helping, deadly accurate in the face of the pandemonium. Casey held back, still naked as the day he was born, until Ms. Cherry popped the last of them in the head, and the door swung open and stayed there, cold wind blowing into the trailer.

"Damn," Casey said. "That all of them?"

Arch went to the window and peered out. His ears were ringing from the gunfire, sounded like sirens. No movement. He crossed over to the door on carpet that squished with blood.

Nothing and no one was waiting outside the trailer.

He looked back at the bloody carpet, at all the fallen bodies.

Dang.

"Are you all right, Casey?" Ms. Cherry cooed. She'd slipped into a bathrobe while Arch making sure the field was clear, but she still displayed ample bosom at the V of the neck.

"Thought I was going to lose my tallywhacker there for a minute," Casey said, reaching down and … touching himself fondly. Arch looked away. "Can't tell you how glad I am that didn't come to pass. Can't imagine what I'd have done if that'd happened."

"It would have hurt us all," Ms. Cherry agreed.

"I … I think I would have been fine," Arch said, trying to decide whether he was more uncomfortable with the tenor of the conversation in here or the dead bodies piled up all over.

"Hey, man," Casey said, "if one dude loses his Johnson, we are all the less, you know? That ol' Johnny Donne, he had a point."

"Not sure I want to know what you're talking about," Arch said, stepping out of the trailer into the wintery air. "You two might want to get dressed."

"We'll get right on it, after—"

"Not now, Casey," Ms. Cherry said. "We should leave. Check in with the others. Make sure we're not needed elsewhere."

"Aww, I'm sure we're fine. And besides, you know how I defeated that bastard's mind control?" Arch heard him slap something—and he had a suspicion what it was—against his hand. "That's right, baby. I got hard and ready again. My libido is boundless—no demon can contain it. Far as I'm concerned, unquenchable lust is my salvation. I mean, you saw that, right?"

"Lord, deliver me from evil," Arch muttered, slamming the door to the trailer. He made his way down to the car, figuring he'd just sit in there for a little bit until they were done doing—whatever. He knew what, though he didn't want to think about it.

He slammed the door as the trailer squeaked and rocked on its foundations the first time. Turned his head away, tried to think about anything but it.

"I miss you, Alison," he said, looking at his bloody hand, the bloody wound at his thigh. He rummaged for the medical kit and applied a compress, also missing the days when someone else was around to help him with this sort of thing.

*

Erin had gotten back to her feet in time to help put paid to the last of the demons. Straggling members of the Watch were coming out of the woods on the flank now, where they'd stopped that attack before it had run them over. Now a cool wind was whistling through across Old Jackson Highway, and someone was blowing their damned horn from behind the blockade of tankers, near where she'd rumbled with Martinson a few minutes earlier.

But shit ... they'd fucking won.

They beat the feds.

Good God.

"Get out of my way, Ulysses," Gary Wrightson said, buzzing down the hill, holding onto his scooter for dear life. He looked like he was about to be ejected over the handlebars if he stopped too fast, but he managed to get her down somehow, popping on out of the ditch and onto the pavement. She saw the sigh of relief that he tried to hide. "Fuck," he said, as he rolled up beside Erin, "we squeaked those fuckers by the skin of our teeth, didn't we?"

"It was closer than I'd have cared for it to be," Erin said, feeling her bruises. There were a lot of them. Ouch. "But, yeah ..." She looked around at the smoking FBI convoy, riddled with bullets, and the silence of the members of the watch as they started to make their way down the hill to the highway—slower than Gary, but then ... that was just most peoples' way ... "We kicked their asses." And Erin found herself smiling.

*

Darla's hands were covered in blood, blood, nothing but blood. There were pieces ... everywhere. Little pieces, because she'd taken them a little at a time, to prolong the pain. The screams had given way to whimpers, the struggling had given way to twitching when it was exhausted, and all that ...

Had finally given way to silence.

Nothing was moving in the basement save for her.

Her ... and then Beelzahar.

"That ..." the demon's rasping voice said, "... was some of the sickest shit I've ever seen. No, seriously ... wow."

Darla turned her head to find him staring at her, his compound eyes wide, something she'd never seen from a full demon before. "... What?" she asked, through the numbness. Her hands felt so sticky.

"I once made a deal with a crackhead to put their baby in the microwave for a hit," Beelzahar said. "I wanted more, but even a crackhead has their limits. But you—you've got none. Wow." He brought up a hand and sketched out a rough salute. "Kudos. You got some darkness in you. You'll make a fine duchess—if you don't scare the rest of the council away." He looked past her at the mess. "Whew. Glad I don't have to clean this mess up. Yowza."

Darla stared down at her hands. They were covered in—

"Do you want to ... cement the pact?" Darla asked, ignoring the shaking. This wasn't an offer she'd planned to make; the pact was technically sealed by the mere words.

But Darla stared at Beelzahar and offered him a bloody hand. He knew what she was suggesting.

"You know ... I'm going to pass," Beelzahar said, taking a step back. "It's not you ... it's me. I'm just ... not in the mood at the moment." He took another shuffling step back. "Feel like I need to go take a brimstone shower, honestly. Get the smell off, and the ..." He shivered. "Those screams. Yikes. You think you want something, but ... gyah." He shook his head. "Tell you what—raincheck. And when the, uh ... shit goes down ..." he looked behind her again and did a full body shudder of his armored shell, "... you go ahead and gather your power, and I'll be ready to call in that marker for you. Our pact is cemented by force of law."

"So ... that's it?" Darla asked. She dropped the knife.

"Yeah, no, we're good," the demon said, tearing his gaze off the scene behind her. "I mean ... I'm not ... I wouldn't consider myself 'good' exactly ... I'm generally evil ... though apparently, I have found my limits today ... but yeah ... no ... you're all set. Unlimited power, coming to you. Way to go. I'd stay and congratulate you, but ... feeling a little queasy. Peace out."

He snapped his fingers and he was gone.

Darla stood there in the quiet, not daring to turn around.

The deal was done.

She had everything she ever wanted.

She stood there for a long moment, not daring to turn around, before she finally managed to put one foot in front of the other, climbed the stairs, and left the basement ... alone.

11.

"Can I just ... can I get y'all over here for a second?" Gary asked, waving over his brothers, and Marina, and Momma—and hell, even Ulysses, because he was hanging around Gary for some reason after it had all settled out, and hell if Gary was going to drive him off after the old bastard had saved his life.

They all kind of sauntered over at their own paces. Marina came quickest, of course, because she was most efficient. Larry, that lazy-ass slacker millennial, came last, dragging himself over with his AR slung half-ass behind him, barrel pointing not in a safe direction. That made Gary's eyebrow twitch, and judging from the looks Larry caught from Paul, Terry and his momma—who forced him to adjust it so it pointed up—he wasn't the only one bothered by the breaking of fundamental firearms safety rules.

"What do you want, brother?" Paul asked once they were all gathered around. They looked a little beat-up in some ways—Terry looked like he'd caught a fist to the face, nose bleeding and a couple tissues shoved up there from his momma's purse. "We won the fight."

"I know, I know," Gary said, raising a hand to speak with, like a goddamned Italian, and almost falling out of his fucking scooter, that piece of shit. He caught himself in time, but damnation it was a burden to hold himself up in this fucking thing. Who shaped the seat on this? Who made it so that the stupid armrests would eat into his goddamned sides? Fuck's sake.

But that was all shit for another time. He'd get another wheelchair, and soon. Surely some poor son of a bitch had died that had a good one and now no longer needed it. But one thing at a time.

"I wanted to thank you all," Gary said, looking at each of them in turn. "When I started putting this together, it was for two reasons—

because Momma was up my ass about demons wrecking her house, and because I was watching my Reno hooker trip fund dissolving before my very eyes as business sagged with the demon rise." He nodded. "I know, pressing problems, both of them. And y'all came into this fight for your own reasons, and I ain't going to sit here and pretend like we all learned something, and that we love each other like one of those sensitive soyboy little bitch families on TV—I would slap every single one of you right in the sack if you pissed me off—"

"Yeah, we'd slap you back but you wouldn't feel it," Larry shot at him. He almost caught a swat from Mary, but she held off, thinking it through, and must have decided to let it pass.

"—but that ain't what this is about, either," Gary said. "The point is ... y'all came through. We kicked the balls of these fucking fed demons and showed them some shit they haven't felt since ... I don't know the last time humans picked a fight with demons and won, honestly. But I will say that what we did here was an epic level of hillbillies with guns sticking it to the powers that be in a way that this state ain't seen since 1946 with the Battle of Athens."

"Fuck yeah!" Terry whooped. "They showed those fuckers that day!"

"Damned skippy," Gary said, "but we kicked the federals right in the shitbox. And maybe they'll come back with more demons and maybe they won't, but by God, I bet they notice we took out a fucking convoy of them at some point. We kicked the teeth right out of their mouths and if they want to press the issue, they're going to be blowing us with nothing but their gums to massage—" He froze, catching Marina looking at him with an upraised eyebrow. "I mean, uh ..."

"Yes," Marina said, "they will be licking us, the toothless bitches."

"Fuck yeah!" Mary said, causing Gary to cringe. She high-fived Marina. "You go, girl. Way to make these boys squirm."

"The point I'm trying to come to is ... y'all did well," Gary said. "Came through like the champs you are here. And I ... I could have done better for you." He waited. Nobody said anything. "Don't all argue with the point at once—ah, fuck it. Tell you what—I'll try not to be as big a dick as I have been in the past. That fair? And y'all just keep kicking ass."

"I was going to keep kicking ass anyway," Terry said with a grin.

"Fuuuck, yeah," Paul said. "Kick ass, drink whiskey. Rinse and repeat."

"'Til the demon soy-bitch-boys suck us with no teeth, no bite," Marina said, causing Gary to cringe again. His momma just chuckled.

"Yeah," Gary said, trying to keep the discomfort out of his voice. "What she said ... I guess." He leaned forward in his chair, and this time he caught himself on the scooter's armrests. Maybe he was getting the hang of this piece of shit after all. "Let's bring this town back from the brink."

*

Arch steered the Crown Vic around the barricade composed of two tractor-trailer tankers pushed nose to nose. It looked impromptu but effective, and he wondered exactly when they'd planned ... whatever had happened here.

"Wow," Casey said. He was back in his torn-up jeans and t-shirt, leaning against the cage that separated the back seat from the front. Arch preferred him back there, really. "Looks like shit went offff the chaaaain here!"

"Shh, sweetie, people could have gotten hurt," Ms. Cherry said as Arch brought the car to a stop. He stepped out into the chill, catching sight of Erin standing back from a group of people, supervising a shot-up line of black government SUVs being moved. Drivers were hopping in and heading off, taking the shot-up vehicles around the blockade and back toward town, one at a time.

"Looks like you had a little bit of an incident here," Arch said, breaking off from Casey and Ms. Cherry, who paused to look at the goings-on. Arch caught a glimpse of Gary Wrightson haranguing his little group from the back of a scooter that looked familiar.

"Feds were demons," Erin said as he stepped up next to her, joining her in leaning against the Explorer, which was just sitting in the middle of the highway for some reason. "We managed to intercept them on the way into town." She moved, pain creasing her forehead as she touched her rib. "It got ... hectic."

Arch nodded. "We managed to bag the ... uh ... neuterer." She raised an eyebrow at him. "And figured out what happened to the men who had been disconnected from their, uhm ..." She just waited, staring at him. "... Well, their ... their stuff."

Erin cracked a smile. "How painful was it for you to find a non-Hendricks way to express that? It looked painful. Not on the level of my ribs, but ... painful."

"What happened to your ribs?"

"Martinson asserted her federal authority over them with a boot," Erin said, turning back to watching the removal operation. They were down to the last few now. People were making it happen. "Hurt like a motherfucker, too."

"How'd you figure out they were demons?" Arch asked. He imagined someone doing what Alison had once done to County Administrator Pike and putting a knife to their hand. Gently, for sure. Nah. No way. Not with this crowd.

"Gary Wrightson got attacked by them after our little confrontation last night," Erin said. "Something to do with this water business. They tried to kill him."

"That's ... ambitious," Arch said, looking over at Wrightson in his scooter, talking to the crowd. "He ever figure out why they were trying to bring in water while we were running out?"

"Best guess?" Erin asked. "They were trying to cover it up so people wouldn't leave at a faster rate than they were already fleeing. You know, from the demons."

"I guess that makes sense," Arch said, chewing his lower lip. "We're their dinner and a show, after all."

"We're a lot more than that to them, I think," Erin said. "And if it kept us in place for them to do ... whatever with, I guess it was worth tankering in water. And however many federal demons to keep us quiet. Though I have a hard time figuring out how exactly they planned to maintain full order with just eighty or so demons."

"Doesn't seem like that'd do the trick for too long," Arch said. "Same with the water, right? How long would that amount keep us?"

Erin shrugged. "I really don't know."

"Neither do I. And that bothers me."

She just stood there for a second. "So ... what was happening with the guys who got their dicks cut off?"

Arch felt a pained look creep on his face. "The demon was turning them into his own personal army."

Now it was her turn to make a pained face. "For what reason?"

"Said he wanted to purge sin," Arch said. This caused a little prickle inside him. "But I don't think he was interested in purging sin exactly—at least not as I would understand it. Seemed to me he was mostly interested in purging, uh ... libido. From men. And once that was done, he, uh, made sure it didn't rise again." Arch cleared his throat.

Erin snorted. "You walked right into that pun without realizing it until it was out, didn't you?"

Arch did not meet her eyes. "Yeah."

"So why'd they kill the women?" Erin asked, arms still folded. "What was the point of that?"

Arch just shook his head. "Some kind of scapegoat ritual, I guess.

The men purged themselves of their 'sin'—"

"Don't be talking like you didn't think fucking outside marriage was anything other than a sin, Arch."

He ignored her. "—and then they were ready to join his army with a little—I don't know, mind control. I watched him do it to Casey, but Casey managed to break free—"

"As much of a lust machine as he is? I bet he did, in seconds." She was quiet for a moment. "So what happened to the guys he imprisoned and chopped off? They get their brains back after he died?"

Arch just shook his head. "No. They fought to the last."

Erin stared at him. "Jesus. They were human beings, Arch."

"Like those tanker truck drivers, yeah?" Arch retorted.

Her face got hard, then softened a notch after she had a second to think it over. "I guess so." Another moment of silence. "Just between you and me … seems like we've had to kill our fair share of humans since we handed Hendricks his ass a couple weeks ago over that very thing."

"We're hypocrites, I guess," Arch said. There really wasn't much more to say than that. "The best we can say for ourselves—and it ain't much—is that we didn't seek it out. But … we did it, nonetheless. Shame on us." He watched her shake her head, but he didn't have anything else to say as she submerged into her own thoughts.

Arch's thoughts on the matter were somewhat clearer, he suspected—he'd always been a sinner, and though the crime of murder—or killing, maybe, in this case—was not a favorable one, he knew what he'd done and why. "Oh, Lord, forgive me for my sins," he said under his breath, so softly that Erin did not hear him. Or if she did, she ignored it.

*

Darla stepped into the quiet of her house and listened.

Nothing.

Not the sound of *PAW Patrol* playing, endlessly, in the living room.

Nothing.

She forced a smile—her problems were over. Most of them, anyway. A smell hit her nose, making it wrinkle—

Marischa. She'd forgotten about the body in her haste, but …

Opening the door, it was … still there, obviously. Blood had soaked through the mattress, dripping onto the floor beneath. She got down on all fours just to check, and … ugh.

"I think this might be a total write-off," Darla muttered, thinking of the mattress. Disposing of all this was going to be a hell of a chore.

She stepped back out into the hall and nearly tripped over a toy, a little plushie—

She froze, the thing squeaking beneath her foot.

Darla kicked it out of the way and headed for the kitchen, the walls blurring around her.

Standing over the sink, water running, she patted her forehead with a wet paper towel.

The silence.

The fucking silence.

It made her want to chew her fingernails, to smash something, to knock over a bowl of cereal just to hear the damned milk drip. Like blood—

Ugh. This place. The silence infested it like rats. She started to turn on the TV, but *Blaze and the Monster Machines* came on, and she immediately turned it off rather than wait for the box to sync up so she could change the damned channel.

"Oh, my God," she whispered.

There were dishes in the sink that she didn't want to do. Two cereal bowls that had curdled while she was out, the Lucky Charms turned soft and the milk sour—or so she perceived. They couldn't have spoiled that quickly, she was just edgy …

How long did she have to wait? How long before she'd have the chance to call in all these accumulated debts? How long—

How long before this town went down for good, and hell came rising up to take its place?

However long it was, she realized, looking around—dishes in the sink, body in the spare room, empty … other rooms …

She didn't want to spend that time here.

"Fuck," she whispered, letting her gaze flit over her collection of demon volumes. She had … what? Ten? Fifteen of them? Heavy things, too …

But not as heavy as Marischa.

How many vacant houses were there in Midian? Around the county?

Nodding, she made the decision in a snap. There was at least one fancy party house that she knew of—one that was regularly rented out for weddings, overnight retreats—all that jazz. Jason had shown her—it was luxurious. Surely no one was keeping an eye on that now, and even if they were …

She smiled, thinking of Marischa's credit cards. No one would notice anything out of the ordinary if she made extravagant charges. And no one would find her here because ... well, the Calhoun County Sheriff's Department had other things on its plate. She'd rot away here until long after the damned apocalypse had rolled through.

"Fuck it," Darla said. She was done here. She wasn't a mom anymore, wasn't a wife anymore, and she didn't have to live this shit life anymore. This was a sanctuary, and it wasn't even a particularly good one. There were other places she could be, better ones ...

And she'd find one and wait there ... for things to begin the final turn.

*

"What a day, huh?" Dr. Lauren Darlington said as she strolled up, popping into the spot against the Ford Explorer that Arch had abandoned a few minutes earlier. "I decide to spend a little time with my daughter, and it feels like I missed out on everything these last couple days."

"Yeah," Erin said, holding her ribs, and she nodded at the doc, that pain surging through her side. "Except for weiner-whacking demon. You were there for that, right?"

"I did see that," Lauren said. "And the snakes that ate Nate McMinn." A little flash of guilt ran over her face as she stepped closer to Erin. "Raise your arm."

Erin did, cringing as she did so. "Broken ribs this time?" Because being shot in the vest had already been so fun, she'd needed another dose of pain in that area.

"Probably just bruised," Darlington said, giving her a gentle poke. "How bad does that hurt, scale of 1–10, 10 being childbirth—oh, wait, you never had a kid."

"Yet," Erin said, putting her arm back down. "It's not that bad. A three or so. Feels better than it did when the fucking demon kicked me. Duller now."

"Keep an eye on them," Darlington said. "You'll probably look like a banana some aggressive store employee mishandled tomorrow, but let me know if it gets worse. If we had an x-ray, I'd consider putting you through it, but the nearest is a ways off, so ..."

"I ain't got time for that shit anyway," Erin said. "Demon feds rolling into town, some kind of water crisis in progress—"

"Plus, the gate of hell somewhere in town here," Darlington said dryly, "if you believe crazy people."

Erin just smiled. "Not sure I believe the crazy guy, no. Especially since he hasn't talked coherently since he spit that little nugget at us."

"Yeah," Darlington said, smiling, "nothing but demon trouble here, surely. That and the occasional surly redneck—" She froze, and her brow stitched tight with concern. "You feel that?"

"Feel wha—" Erin didn't even get it out before the question was answered.

The ground shook, rumbles echoing over the hills. Her legs just about went out from under her, and a car alarm went off nearby, honking all hell.

"Holy fuck!" Casey shouted, probably capturing perfectly what most everyone—except Arch—was thinking.

It was a damned earthquake. A fucking earthquake.

Erin hit the ground, banging against her knee as she landed, unable to stay upright in the face of the earth shaking with all its fury. It rattled her bones down to every joint, the Explorer's suspension squeaking. Erin tasted blood, felt the pain in her palms—figures she'd probably sprain her damned wrist trying to keep from tumbling over.

"Erin!" Benny's voice sprang to life out of her radio. The ground was still shaking, like someone had ripped a layer of the earth from beneath their feet, or they were standing on a suspension bridge being rocked by the wind.

It settled, slowly, and Erin bit back the pain in her palms and knees—just another to add to the fucking heap—and swiped her radio off her belt. It was the sheriff's department one. "This is Erin. Go ahead." Fuck radio discipline. It was Benny. And the damned earth had just shook. "But this better not be about the earthquake, because—yes, I fucking felt it."

"What? No—I mean, yeah, we had one, but no—I—I just got word from the spotter team out by the highway, over by the Sinbad," Benny said. "The freeway overpass went down. I-75 just got shut there and—" He stopped for a second. "Jesus ... Erin, I just got a report ... the other one went down, too, further up 75 ..."

"That's ... the main way people get to and from Midian," Dr. Darlington said, pushing up to her feet and offering Erin a hand. "If the bridges are down ..."

"TNDOT's gonna close this stretch of I-75," Erin said. "They'll route people north, up State Road 58."

"Far away from us," Darlington agreed. "That'll add some transit time if anyone wants to visit."

Erin did the thinking quickly—it came quickly, rather, because she knew the lay of the Caledonia River valley from the map outside

Reeve's office. "There's only a half-dozen or so back roads that can bring you into Midian. Two of them ... were over that freeway. Two ... run around Mount Horeb ... and I'm guessing they didn't take the earthquake very well ..."

"Oh, shit," Darlington said. "We're ... we're not totally cut off, though—"

"But we're getting pretty close," Erin said, blinking, thinking. "And we just had an earthquake. Here." She looked the doctor in the face. "You ever heard of that before?"

Darlington just shook her head.

"Erin? Erin, you there?" Benny asked, crackling through the radio.

"I'm here," Erin said, trying to make herself sound stronger than she felt.

The main roads to Midian had just been cut off.

"We really are alone," she muttered, thankful that only Dr. Darlington was there to hear her.

Epilogue

Franklin, Tennessee

It was a sunny Saturday morning, and Gunnery Sergeant Micah Winthrop (Ret.) was enjoying the weather. Blue skies, only a little chill—it was nice for November. Sure beat the hell out of winter up north.

He took a long, slow breath of the crisp air. Micah Winthrop had retired here, just outside Nashville, out of the Marine Corps after putting in his twenty. He'd been in Iraq and Afghanistan and all points between, and he'd seen about as much as he cared to.

Besides, he'd seen enough loss here on the home front to make it clear to him ... war wasn't the only place where you felt that pinch.

Franklin was a nice change; small-town America feel with a short drive to big-city Nashville. And the VA was in Murfreesboro, which was close at hand, too. Not that he ever wanted to go there if he could avoid it.

"Frieda?" Winthrop called, looking through the open screen door. He couldn't see his wife inside, but he knew she was in there somewhere. Probably fixing lunch. They'd hit up the farmer's market outside the Factory this morning, and she sure did get excited about picking up stuff to cook with.

He didn't get too fussed when she didn't answer. A pot clanged, and she swore—she was definitely a Marine gunnery sergeant's wife—and he decided staying on the porch would be a real good idea. Watch the street. Where nothing was happening. Keep an eye on the blue skies, and the still-green grasses. Wave at the neighbors as they passed and watch his big American flag flap in the breeze.

He picked up his coffee cup, stared at the black contents within. His skin was almost as dark as the black-ass coffee within, which was how he liked it. No sugar, no cream, and definitely none of this Millennial pussy frou frou garbage drink stuff for him. He whipped that attitude out of the little bitches in the Corps.

A car turned onto his street, and Winthrop turned his head to look. It was one of those metrosexual-looking SUVs, the kind that looked like the Jeeps of yesteryear had lost their balls and then decided to procreate with a Tesla. How that happened, he didn't know, but ...

"Dickless," Winthrop opined as the SUV came rolling down the street.

It stopped at the curb, and Winthrop put his coffee cup down. "What is this fuckery?" he asked. He damned sure wasn't expecting anyone, but they pulled right up in front of his house and—

"Motherfucker." Winthrop got to his feet, coffee forgotten.

It was the hat that sold it. Of course it was the fucking hat; this may have been close to Nashville, but other than the country stars, you didn't see cowboy hats out and about. This wasn't Texas. Winthrop just shook his head, watching as the cowboy got out of the SUV and came around the front of the car.

White as a piece of bread, his face was a little more ragged and ghostly than usual, even for him. Black hat, big boots, and that coat that sprouted out at the shoulders and ran all the way to his feet ... If it had been anyone else, his immediate response to the mere sight of this sumbitch would have been, "You look like a fucking dumbass dressed you, boy."

But Micah Winthrop didn't say that to the cowboy.

Because he knew exactly who had dressed this white boy, and he wouldn't speak ill of the dead.

Especially not her.

"Lafayette Jackson Hendricks," Gunnery Sergeant Winthrop said, sounding to him like his voice just might—maybe—be showing a sign of cracking.

"Gunny," Hendricks said. He didn't sound any better. Maybe worse. Dark circles under the eyes. The boy looked fucked up.

Big surprise, there.

Winthrop didn't know how to take that. Instead, he opened the screen door and shouted inside. "Frieda! Frieda!" He waited.

"What? What is it?" Frieda called back. She stuck her head out around the arch from the kitchen so she could look out the front door. "What is up your butt, Micah?"

"We got company," Micah Winthrop called, without turning his head.

"Well, who is it? Tell 'em to go away. Supper's almost ready," Frieda called back.

Micah just shook his head—but of course she couldn't see it. "Can't do it," he called back.

"Why? Who is it, Micah?" Frieda asked. She might as well be telling the whole neighborhood—heck, the whole town.

"You ain't going to believe it," Winthrop called back, not looking away from the cowboy—dressed like a damned fool, but … he wouldn't insult the one who'd dressed him like that, no chance, "It's our wayward, shitheel son-in-law." He settled his eyes on Hendricks. He looked like something that had been scraped off the bottom of one of them boots he wore. "What have you been up to, boy?"

The Watch Will Return In

HALLOWED
Southern Watch
Book 8

Coming in 2019!

Author's Note

Okay, that one was hell. Or close to hell, anyway. I suppose we're literally drawing closer to hell with every book, so we can't technically be there yet.

You may have noticed this one was shorter than book 6. Also, cheaper, I might point out. Epically long books are epically hard to write, few people want to pay epic prices for them, and these were getting ridiculous in length, so...voila. Shorter, more compact, but with all the depravity you have come to expect from Southern Watch. And less than a year after the last came out! Everybody wins. Except Darla's kids.

I can't promise as quick an interval between releases for book 8, though. This one pained me, physically and mentally, to write. (You can find an explanation for why here: https://www.youtube.com/watch?v=wCyLPIRK3Fc) So it's going to be a while before I tackle HALLOWED, the next in the series. Expect it in 2019.

If you want to know immediately when future books become available, take sixty seconds and sign up for my NEW RELEASE EMAIL ALERTS by visiting my website. I don't sell your information and I only send out emails when I have a new book out. The reason you should sign up for this is because I don't always set release dates, and even if you're following me on Facebook (robertJcrane (Author)) or Twitter (@robertJcrane), it's easy to miss my book announcements because...well, because social media is an imprecise thing.

Come join the discussion on my website:
http://www.robertjcrane.com!

Cheers,
Robert J. Crane

ACKNOWLEDGMENTS

Editing was handled expertly by Sarah Barbour as per usual, with Jeff Bryan and Jo Evans batting cleanup. Many thanks to all of them.

Special thanks to my friend, author C.G. Cooper, without whom this book would probably have been abandoned. He helped with fleshing out the ideas of the story at a point where I was really questioning how I could even get it written. I think we all owe him one for that.

Once again, the illustrious illustrator Karri Klawiter produced the cover. artbykarri.com is where you can find her amazing works.

Nick Bowman of nickbowman-editing.com provided the formatting that turned this into an actual book and ebook.

And thanks as always to my family – wife, parents, in-laws and occasionally my kids, for keeping a lid on the craziness so I can do this job.

Other Works by Robert J. Crane

The Girl in the Box *and* Out of the Box
Contemporary Urban Fantasy

Alone: The Girl in the Box, Book 1
Untouched: The Girl in the Box, Book 2
Soulless: The Girl in the Box, Book 3
Family: The Girl in the Box, Book 4
Omega: The Girl in the Box, Book 5
Broken: The Girl in the Box, Book 6
Enemies: The Girl in the Box, Book 7
Legacy: The Girl in the Box, Book 8
Destiny: The Girl in the Box, Book 9
Power: The Girl in the Box, Book 10

Limitless: Out of the Box, Book 1
In the Wind: Out of the Box, Book 2
Ruthless: Out of the Box, Book 3
Grounded: Out of the Box, Book 4
Tormented: Out of the Box, Book 5
Vengeful: Out of the Box, Book 6
Sea Change: Out of the Box, Book 7
Painkiller: Out of the Box, Book 8
Masks: Out of the Box, Book 9
Prisoners: Out of the Box, Book 10
Unyielding: Out of the Box, Book 11
Hollow: Out of the Box, Book 12
Toxicity: Out of the Box, Book 13
Small Things: Out of the Box, Book 14
Hunters: Out of the Box, Book 15
Badder: Out of the Box, Book 16
Apex: Out of the Box, Book 18
Time: Out of the Box, Book 19
Driven: Out of the Box, Book 20
Remember: Out of the Box, Book 21
Hero: Out of the Box, Book 22* *(Coming September 4, 2018!)*
Flashback: Out of the Box, Book 23* *(Coming November 2018!)*
Walk Through Fire: Out of the Box, Book 24* *(Coming in 2019!)*

World of Sanctuary
Epic Fantasy

Defender: The Sanctuary Series, Volume One
Avenger: The Sanctuary Series, Volume Two
Champion: The Sanctuary Series, Volume Three
Crusader: The Sanctuary Series, Volume Four
Sanctuary Tales, Volume One - A Short Story Collection
Thy Father's Shadow: The Sanctuary Series, Volume 4.5
Master: The Sanctuary Series, Volume Five
Fated in Darkness: The Sanctuary Series, Volume 5.5
Warlord: The Sanctuary Series, Volume Six
Heretic: The Sanctuary Series, Volume Seven
Legend: The Sanctuary Series, Volume Eight
Ghosts of Sanctuary: The Sanctuary Series, Volume Nine
Call of the Hero: The Sanctuary Series, Volume Ten* *(Coming Late 2018!)*

A Haven in Ash: Ashes of Luukessia, Volume One *(with Michael Winstone)*
A Respite From Storms: Ashes of Luukessia, Volume Two *(with Michael Winstone)*
A Home in the Hills: Ashes of Luukessia, Volume Three* *(with Michael Winstone—Coming Mid to Late 2018!)*

Southern Watch
Contemporary Urban Fantasy

Called: Southern Watch, Book 1
Depths: Southern Watch, Book 2
Corrupted: Southern Watch, Book 3
Unearthed: Southern Watch, Book 4
Legion: Southern Watch, Book 5
Starling: Southern Watch, Book 6
Forsaken: Southern Watch, Book 7
Hallowed: Southern Watch, Book 8* *(Coming in 2019!)*

The Shattered Dome Series
(with Nicholas J. Ambrose)
Sci-Fi

Voiceless: The Shattered Dome, Book 1
Unspeakable: The Shattered Dome, Book 2* *(Coming 2018!)*

The Mira Brand Adventures
Contemporary Urban Fantasy

The World Beneath: The Mira Brand Adventures, Book 1
The Tide of Ages: The Mira Brand Adventures, Book 2
The City of Lies: The Mira Brand Adventures, Book 3
The King of the Skies: The Mira Brand Adventures, Book 4
The Best of Us: The Mira Brand Adventures, Book 5
We Aimless Few: The Mira Brand Adventures, Book 6* *(Coming 2018!)*

Liars and Vampires
(with Lauren Harper)
Contemporary Urban Fantasy

No One Will Believe You: Liars and Vampires, Book 1
Someone Should Save Her: Liars and Vampires, Book 2
You Can't Go Home Again: Liars and Vampires, Book 3
In The Dark: Liars and Vampires, Book 4* *(Coming August 7, 2018!)*
Her Lying Days Are Done: Liars and Vampires, Book 5* *(Coming August 2018!)*
Heir of the Dog: Liars and Vampires, Book 6* *(Coming September 2018!)*
Hit You Where You Live: Liars and Vampires, Book 7* *(Coming October 2018!)*

* Forthcoming, Subject to Change

Printed in Great Britain
by Amazon

85844291R00159